OLD WINE

by the same author

★

Private Worlds
Murder in the Bud
The Mortal Storm
Alfred Adler
Masks and Faces
Formidable to Tyrants
The Heart of a Child
London Pride
Within the Cup

OLD WINE

by

PHYLLIS BOTTOME

FABER AND FABER LTD
24 Russell Square
London

First published in this new edition Mcmxliv
by Faber and Faber Limited
24 Russell Square, London, W.C.1
Second impression September Mcmxliv
Third impression June Mcmxlv
Fourth impression June Mcmxlviii
Printed in Great Britain by
Purnell and Sons, Ltd.
Paulton, Somerset, and London

To

OSKAR VON GATTERER

MY UNDEFEATED FRIEND

This book is produced
in complete conformity
with the authorized economy standards

I

The vast old room was like a field at dusk. Firelight flickered faintly at a great distance, making a pool of light on the intricate parquet floor. In this pool of light sat Otto Wolkenheimb, silent and motionless. At one of the five windows another silent and motionless figure stood gazing down on the grass-grown square.

It was the Autumn of 1918, and to these two men of a crumbling Empire it was the end of the world. Their feelings were not those of men who are to be executed to-morrow; they were those of men who have been executed yesterday. Their world was gone.

Otto Wolkenheimb leaned forward and turned on a small reading lamp. The light shone on his high domed forehead, slanting eyebrows, and round brown eyes, set high above his salient cheek-bones. There was no expression in his eyes. They were like a toy of beautifully polished Chinese boxes: each box contains a smaller one, until the last is reached—and that is empty. His lips were thin; it was not possible to say yet, for he was two years short of forty, whether the lines beside them might not, if fortune went against him, become lines of ruthlessness and self-pity. Otto's weakest feature was his mouth; women liked it, but the characteristics which formed it were unfavourable to women. Both men were in suspense; but in Otto suspense was merely the prolongation of an inevitable incident; in the younger man it was an anguish of stubborn hope.

Franz Salvator turned away from the window and walked the long length of the room towards his cousin. His handsome features were worn with exposure; his crisp, fair brown hair was touched, young as he was, with silver. His eyes were large, wide apart and very blue. His finely curved, close shut lips had the strength of long patience; and the short cleft chin under them expressed a steady will. It was a beautiful young face, hammered by hard experience; too resolute for laughter, but breaking into charming tenderness when Franz Salvator smiled. He was slim and tall; he moved with the easy motion of one who has mastered

5

every form of activity. His strength was too unconscious to look formidable; it had been tried to the uttermost, but it had not reached its limit. 'You are sure,' he said, when he stood on the verge of the little pool of firelight, 'that there will be no fighting?' 'I have given you my word of honour,' said Otto, without lifting his head. 'You might be mistaken?' Franz Salvator insisted. 'My wits,' said Otto with a dry smile, 'are at least as trustworthy as my word.' 'Everything has gone mad!' Franz Salvator exclaimed. 'We are blown about like leaves, or trampled into mud!' 'You have become poetical,' said Otto more dryly still. 'But you are right as to the mud—nothing else is left now.' 'Otto!' Franz Salvator said in a low voice, looking about him uneasily at the shadowy furniture as if he feared to be overheard even by such friendly and inanimate witnesses, 'something horrible happened to me in the streets on my way here—I can hardly speak of it. The crowd would have torn off my medals! A woman spat on my uniform! Are the people of our Country turned into wild beasts?' 'All people are beasts,' said Otto indifferently, 'only as a rule they are tame. The whip tames them; and now you see we have mislaid the whip!' 'I told them,' Franz said earnestly, ' "Men! I have only done my duty; is it for this you attack me? Go and do yours!" —and I knocked two of them down. But though they were afraid of me and I have my medals safe, the feeling of madness remains! I cannot understand it—are there no duties left?' 'Ah!' said Otto looking up quickly into the young man's eyes, 'even you question that? It is the point that we have got to face. I hear Eugen.' The door was flung open, and a man burst into the room with bent head as if he were reeling from a blow. 'My dear fellow!' Otto said, rising quickly to meet him, 'so this is the end?' Franz Salvator stood speechless, his hand fingering his sword; his dark blue eyes shone hard upon the newcomer; both his hopes and his fears were gone now; only a fatal certainty and his own strength remained. 'I have come from the Palace,' gasped Eugen Erdödy, 'it is finished. They go!' He sank down in a heap in one of Otto's deep arm-chairs, his eyeglass swaying helplessly before him, and his round cropped head bent over like an old man's. Eugen Erdödy had as a rule the faultless rigidity of a mechanical doll; to see him crumpled up shapelessly, without order or dignity, was as shocking as to see the doll with a broken spring cast helpless on the ground. Otto looked at him with a slightly irritated sympathy. There was

6

everything to feel of course, but it was a pity to feel, even everything, so much. There was a lack of spiritual economy, Otto felt, in abandoning yourself to emotion. Eugen did not see as Otto saw, that there is no more use making a stir about the end of a dynasty, than about the end of a rat hunt—the important point in all abrupt closes is not to be the rat.

The loss of the Hapsburgs was an overwhelming public catastrophe, but it was a public catastrophe; and Otto kept his strongest emotions for purely personal disasters. 'It was bound to come,' he said considerately, after a pause. 'Take some cognac, my dear fellow! The Kaiser had the wrong temperament for a king. I said to him a week ago that it might be necessary to break a few heads, and what do you suppose he replied? "Bloodshed for my Country I have had to bear, but I will never bear it for myself." Emperors who cannot bear bloodshed have to abdicate.' Eugen poured the cognac with a shaking hand, and drank it hurriedly without appreciation. He did not even glance at the exquisite Venetian glass out of which he drank, though his heart was fixed upon such treasures. 'It was better to go as you did,' he muttered, 'than to see the end come. I was with my Archduke. I had wound up all his affairs. He will return to the country and live on his estate. I did not wish to be a burden to him, so I refused his offers, and said farewell. Then the Socialists were announced. He said, "Stay a little, Eugen." Half a dozen canaille entered. I could have accounted for at least three of them. Socialists are always flabby. But it was against orders. I said, "Gentlemen, what do you want?" They said, "We wish to see the Kaiser." The Archduke made a face, and turned his back on them—I am personally attached to my Archduke, but I must admit he is without dignity. The door opened and out came the Kaiser into the Hall of Audience, as if those creatures were his masters. I saw in a flash that they would have been satisfied with a few concessions; they did not expect abdication. He gave them everything. No one could stop him. I seemed to hear the centuries crash behind him. At the end he held out his hand to the dogs and said, "None of my people are my enemies." ' 'I dislike ends,' said Otto, shrugging his shoulders, 'particularly sentimental ones. Last week I gave the Kaiser my final advice. He refused it; and I begged leave to resign. I was not trained to be a philanthropist, nor do I find that I have the natural aptitude. Like all idealists, the Kaiser acted for the good of his enemies and left his friends to suffer for it. The class who have supported him is to be destroyed because he feared to kill half a dozen worthless persons. It would be laughable if what deeply affects one personally were ever laughable!' 'Yes, our life is gone,' agreed Eugen gloomily. 'There is the Danube on one side and a little old cognac left on the other. To which do you propose to devote yourself, Otto?' 'Do not let us speak of ourselves!' interrupted Franz Salvator. 'The Kaiser has gone. I do not judge him, he sees perhaps further than we, but he is not the last Hapsburg, the line is not dead! If he cannot return to us—and I, for one, will never despair of his return!—there is his son. We can prepare for him—fight for him, when he is ready for us! Eugen, you spoke to the Kaiser, you know his mind? Will he not return?' 'Ah!' said Eugen, staring heavily at the shining floor, 'men who go—make a mistake! To return is not so easy when to stay has not seemed possible. You ask what is in his mind? But what is in men's minds does not count; only a man's acts make history.' Eugen sank back into silence. His sympathy with Franz Salvator was deeper than words, deeper than tears. He wanted to get drunk and forget it. Blindness! that was what Eugen hungered for. Everywhere there were new evils to see, fresh hearts broken by them, more intensive ruin. Only in the cognac beside him was safety, because only there would unconsciousness blot out the evils he could not help. Otto could speak! He would explain to Franz Salvator all that could be explained. Otto cared for Franz less than Eugen cared for him. He could bear to see hope turn cold in his young cousin's eyes.

Otto put his hand on Franz Salvator's shoulder. 'My dear boy,' he said slowly and impressively, 'the Kaiser will not come back. We are in the hands of the rabble who attacked you in the street just now. Be careful not to displease them, for they are our masters!' 'Never! never! I will shoot myself first,' cried Franz Salvator. 'Why are we sitting here doing nothing? Can we not gather some of the Army together and try to make order?' Otto shook his head. 'An army once disbanded,' he said dispassionately, 'is a mob. Ask yourself what our soldiers have got by fighting their enemies these four harsh years? Wounds, starvation, death, defeat! And you would ask them to fight again—not against their enemies this time, but against their friends? Be reasonable! We do nothing, my dear child, because there is precisely nothing to be done. There is no Treasury, no Army, no Court, no law! There are a great many good people in the streets who think they have —instead of these things—freedom! To-morrow they will find that they have freedom—to starve. We shall share it with them.' Eugen moved a shaking hand toward the liqueur bottle. 'We are *kaput!*' he whispered, and the shadows of the vast room echoed the hopeless word, '*kaput!*' Franz Salvator was silent. The sense of defeat had been for months like something acid in his blood; but he was young and very brave. He could not envisage what defeat meant. He had told himself, and he had told his men, that there was no disgrace in being conquered. One of two fighters must always lose; and no loss that is without shame is final. But he was no longer on the field of battle where suffering is simple, and the heart meets it simply. He was caught in the treacherous obscure trap of the civilized world. Slowly he coloured to the roots of his hair, and looked with puzzled eyes from one of his two friends to the other. Eugen was broken; his eyelids were red and swollen, his hands shook. Something disintegrating and final had taken place in him. His spirit had retreated. Otto was not visibly changed. There was a scarcely perceptible line in his forehead between his oblique eyebrows, but his good-humoured calm was the same as if they were all safely back in one of their serene and brilliant yesterdays. He met Franz Salvator's puzzled eyes, and leaned slightly forward, placing the tips of his beautifully manicured fingers together. 'I want you to understand,' he said in a low resonant voice, 'that there is no such thing as Austria! No such race as our old race! Our class is finished—as finished as a last year's drink! As nobles we exist no longer; but we are still men!' 'You are right! You are always right, Otto!' cried Franz, with grave enthusiasm. 'We are men, and we can still die like men!' Otto's curious eyebrows flickered above his bright expressionless eyes. 'We can still live,' he said quietly, 'and it is life, not death, that demands of us wit and courage. I do not know whether life is worth living or not. It is a formidable question; but the answer is easy. For so long as life is worth living—live it!' 'But where? But how?' exclaimed Eugen. 'I foresaw the downfall. I placed my little fortune in security; but all I have will only keep us in bread—you—Otto—Eugénie—Franz and myself; and when have any of us evinced the slightest interest in bread?' 'You are perfectly right,' agreed Otto; 'if I had nothing better to suggest than an undignified scramble for crusts, I would embrace your alternative. But before I tell you what I have to suggest, I will ask you to repeat seriously what you see before you. Eugen, you are the eldest; is it your considered opinion and intention to drink yourself to death?' 'It is,' said Eugen, without a moment's hesitation, 'unless I find the process too long. If I tire, I shall seek the Danube. I have always disliked water; but a great deal of it at a time is at least conclusive.' 'And you, Franz?' Otto asked. 'You will end matters by a bullet?' 'If I cannot earn enough to keep Eugénie and myself in decency,' said Franz Salvator. 'But I am willing, if Eugénie is, to try working first. Personally I prefer death to the present conditions, but I shall not of course desert Eugénie.' 'Ah,' said Otto with a faint smile, 'Eugénie will, I have no doubt, encourage the idea of work, and by work you mean what is usually alluded to—I have never quite understood why—as "honest toil"?' Franz Salvator flung back his head impatiently. 'What else is there for me to do?' he asked. 'I have strong arms.' 'A life of honest toil,' said Otto, 'is not, I fear, particularly remunerative, and I doubt if it will keep you and Eugénie very much above the level of mere bread-winning. Now I will propose my alternative. I may as well say before I go any further that I have no scruples left. Scruples were for the old régime. I shall give up immediately all the virtues that we cultivated in the days which were fit for them. It will be a bore of course, and no doubt we shall have lapses. But the privileges which invented our old virtues will be absent; and we shall learn to match ourselves to our opportunities. We have been fast friends, Eugen and I, for twenty years, and you, my dear Franz, entered our fellowship ten years ago and became in every way one of us. I am the Head of your House, and you accepted me as your leader. It has been an honour, and I hope you both feel that I have not abused it?' 'Never!' cried Eugen and Franz Salvator simultaneously. For the first time during the afternoon Otto was moved, the readiness of his words deserted him; he hesitated and started again at a tangent. 'Looking back on my life,' he said, moistening his lips, 'I can say that our friendship has been the best thing in it. I do not undervalue women; but one does not think of them singly. I have had two friends; you, Eugen! and you, Franz Salvator! I shall have no others. If I have been your leader in the old world, I suggest that you give me your confidence in the new. To you, Franz

Salvator, I shall entrust Trauenstein. You love the country, you have always shown a great aptitude for land. I shall ask you to oversee and work the estate to the best of your ability, and I will send you sufficient money for the purpose. I shall be delighted if your sister will occupy with you part of the Schloss—there are I believe three hundred rooms, so you and my mother should be able to accommodate yourselves together without inconvenience. As for you, Eugen, I shall require your legal knowledge and sound head as much as any Archduke, and I ask of you nothing but to carry out and safeguard my schemes—as I retail them to you. Naturally we shall remain in Wien. All three of us had better marry foreign money. In a very short time now the foreigners will swamp us; but they will be, if we use them aright, a fructifying swamp. I propose to let the flat above us to the English at an extremely favourable rent.' 'That will be a good step,' Eugen asserted, 'but it is not in itself a career. How do you propose to earn money enough to supply Trauenstein, and keep yourself comfortably here in Wien?' Otto glanced rapidly from one to the other. He had a momentary reluctance. He knew what he was going to do, he had known it for a long time and without hesitation; his reluctance was for the form his action must take. He disliked explanations; but of the two men before him only one would follow him blindly. Otto was anxious, if it were possible, to convince both. It would therefore be necessary for him to explain part at least of his intentions. 'I have made rather a study of history,' he observed at last, 'and in history there are many parallel occasions. Moments of chaos like this, for instance. We have spoken of the world as dead; but worlds don't die, they change their fashions of life. One sign of vitality still exists, even in this dismembered city. There are a few hundred Jews in Wien who will regulate our new-found freedom and starvation to fill their own pockets. They will survive.' 'What has that to do with us?' asked Franz Salvator impatiently. 'We are Austrians, not Jews!' 'Remember,' said Otto, 'what we have already told you, Franz—both Eugen and I. You were under the impression that you fought for your Kaiser and your Fatherland. But there is no such person now, no such place. There is instead, "The New Jerusalem," a place and a people that have their own laws—their own privileges. Come, my dear Franz! my dear Eugen! don't let us be tragic! We have lost all we possessed—granted! But hadn't we each of us something extra?

Hardly a possession at all, but a quality or two that we can draw on at a pinch? I at least feel that I am a match for Jews! And I have asked one of them here this afternoon to play the first round with me. This gentleman is old Mandelbaum—the grocer. He is to be made minister in my place. I rather fancy that he does not go in for the honour solely for the salary! Mandelbaum is nearly the master of Wien; but not quite. Since we cannot prevent his power —let us at least share it!' 'Why should I dirty my hands because my heart is broken?' demanded Eugen sharply. 'I am a little man; independent, and without ambition. No! no! Otto, we cannot sink as low as that!' It was evident that Eugen understood what Otto meant to do better than Franz Salvator; but it was less certain that he would refuse it. Franz Salvator spoke hesitatingly. 'But of course,' he said, 'I would look after Trauenstein for you! Gladly! gladly! it would be a life work. If I had money enough I think I could make it produce more, but I do not see how you can raise the money? This Jew—Mandelbaum—is it from him you expect to raise a loan? You and Eugen know better than I of course—but I had always understood it was dangerous to borrow money from Jews?' Otto's eyebrows came together, and for a moment he looked extraordinarily like one of his Tartar ancestors when that ancestor felt a check to his usually omnipotent will. 'I do not intend to borrow exactly,' Otto explained with dry patience; 'my methods are not quite so crude, nor do I wish that you should even meet this Jewish gentleman. He will be my affair and Eugen's. For, Eugen, I am certain on reflection you will not leave me to deal single-handed with a power you so much dislike? I ask your assistance and I feel sure that you will not leave me in the lurch.' 'No! no!' agreed Eugen thickly. 'I am here—count on me, do what you will! But remember that I am not conciliatory in my manner to Jews. If you wish to make a good impression upon this one—withdraw me for the present!' 'But,' interrupted Franz Salvator nervously, 'why should Otto wish to make any impression upon Herr Mandelbaum?' There was a moment's pause before Otto said, 'My dear boy, because I propose to use Mandelbaum, and in order to use him it is necessary for me to please him. But my conduct is my own affair; all that I find necessary for you is to understand—before you hear it from outside sources—that I *do* intend to use Mandelbaum. I shall negotiate through him with the present Government, offer them my exper ience, my foreign languages, my facilities of approach to foreign powers; relieve them in fact of their ignorance—and naturally I shall expect to profit a little by the exchange!' Franz Salvator looked his cousin Otto straight between the eyes. 'But you cannot,' he said resolutely, 'you cannot mean to do such a thing, Otto? I am stupid! I do not understand you. You would associate with Socialists? The very men who have pulled down our Kaiser! Make bargains with Jews? Earn money out of our ruin? I am mad! Because what you say is impossible! But I know that it is impossible! You are not in earnest? I am too thick-witted to see the joke?' 'You see how it seems to him, Otto?' Eugen murmured, sinking lower and lower in his chair. 'It seems to him you have made a joke—as bad a joke as God made when He invented man!' 'I am making no jokes,' said Otto severely. 'Try to be reasonable, Franz. What can you do to make money? You would make an admirable circus rider; but unfortunately there are no circuses at present. Eugen is by training and by inclination a Court official; and there are no more courts. As for me I have what I have always had—my own intellectual resources, and I propose to use them as I think right. I do not ask you to accept any responsibility for my actions; you will merely profit by them.' 'But that I find impossible!' said Franz Salvator slowly and with evident pain. 'Then you and Eugénie will starve,' replied Otto angrily. 'I cannot understand a conscience that exposes a woman to starvation!' 'Eugénie would prefer starvation, Otto,' said Franz steadily. 'It may be necessary both for men and women to accept death; it can never be necessary for them to accept dishonour. Eugen! why do you not speak? You do not approve of Otto's intentions?' 'I? I approve of nothing except cognac,' said Eugen heavily. 'People say more comfortable keep sober! Damn lie! More comfortable keep drunk! Moderate drunkenness, that's what a man wants! Sober men think; thinking devilish unremunerative at present! Kaiser gone! Country gone! Mandelbaum dirty Jew—but rich! Must have money! Money and blood—only things men are never ashamed of!' 'Eugen speaks sense even when he's drunk,' said Otto approvingly, 'and you, my dear Franz, talk nonsense even when you're sober!' 'Eugen!' Franz leaned over the huddled figure, 'you won't let Otto make money out of politics? At any rate you won't share his infamy?' Eugen raised his head and fumblingly replaced his eyeglass; it took him a long time to get it fixed; at last he was satisfied and looked from one to the other of his cousins as if he were trying to sum up their differences. 'Sympathy,' he said at last, 'entirely with you, Franz, but reason with Otto. Decent ideas no damned good, like country—*kaput!*' 'Oh, but this is horrible!' Franz exclaimed. 'It's worse than anything that's happened in all these beastly years! I wish the war had never ended!' 'But it has not ended, Franz,' Otto said quietly. 'That is where you make your mistake. We have entered into another phase of it, that is all. A phase you don't understand. We have no country left, therefore we have no duties towards it. We have only a world full of enemies, and we are at liberty to use the weapons of our enemies.' Franz Salvator looked at him sternly across Eugen's bowed head. 'A man never gets rid of his duties towards himself,' he answered. 'If you associate for profit with Jews and swindlers, that is what you will become—a Jew and a swindler! and we can have no further dealings with you.' 'No! no!' cried Eugen hoarsely. 'We've been friends all our lives. Can't let that go! Can't let that go, Otto!' He lurched forward with his head on the table and burst into sobs. Franz Salvator hesitated and looked once more at Otto; but the Head of His House merely leaned forward and removed the priceless liqueur glasses into a place of safety.

II

The Countess Rosalie Zalfy sat in the corner of Otto Wolkenheimb's sofa and wondered what was the matter with him. She had often sat in that particular corner before; for three years in fact she had sat there more often and with more pleasure than anywhere else; but she had never before had to wonder what was the matter with Otto.

Life was very simple for Rosalie; she loved horses, smart men and chocolates, and she had always had them. She was a beautiful horsewoman and as pretty as if she were paid for it. She came from an excellent family, and looked barely respectable. Her husband had an easy nature, and tastes that he was very glad she had no wish to share. They gave each other a great deal of margin and used all of it up.

Rosalie was as fond of Otto Wolkenheimb as she had ever been of any one. He gave her good horses to ride, Russian furs, occasionally jewels, and constantly large boxes of Gerbaud chocolates—the best in the world. He never asked anything of Rosalie except that she should be good-humoured and well-dressed. Otto disliked large-hearted sympathetic women, and if it were a question of wit, he had enough for two. To have had an intimacy with an intelligent woman would have bored him very much. What he liked was to find out other people's foibles while he himself remained hidden behind an attractive mask; he had no wish to correct any of the weaknesses he discovered, but he had every intention of profiting by them. It cannot be said that Otto was deeply in love with Rosalie; but until now she had been exactly what he wanted. Now she was too expensive. Eugen had gone into all his affairs most carefully and had told him briefly but firmly that Rosalie must go. She must go unless she would stay without horses; and it was going to be a little difficult to put this condition to Rosalie, who had never in her life done without anything that she wanted.

Rosalie felt already the chill of sacrifice in the air. She nestled deeper into the cushions, smoked a little nervously and wondered if her new hat, which was composed of two humming birds and a piece of cerise velvet, was all that she had supposed when she bought it. 'You are very silent, dear Otto,' she said at last, 'and you go up and down, up and down in front of me as if you were waiting for a train. Since I have been here for at least five minutes, it would be prettier of you to behave as if the train had arrived!' Otto laughed a little impatiently. 'Everything, my treasure,' he observed, 'comes when you come. If I am a little restless it is natural enough; because, with equal certainty, everything goes when you go!' 'But I am not going to go until to-morrow morning.' Rosalie reminded him. 'Heinrich is in the country, and I am supposed to be consulting a doctor at Baden. I would take off my hat, but it is so pretty on, or at least I had supposed so before I came here! Outdoors it is snowing and dark, and, oh, how one envies all those wicked Allies who have their own limousines—the brutes —and need not take dirty street trams and spoil their shoes in puddles! Look at my feet.' Rosalie had beautiful little feet, and Conrad, on her arrival, had made her shoes cleaner than her own servant had made them before she started out. They were hardly feet to look at dispassionately, quite apart from the melon-coloured silk stockings which rose for some distance above them; and yet Otto insulted her by looking at them dispassionately. 'When will you be able to buy a car?' Rosalie went on after this unsuccessful pause. 'Talk to me about it first, dear Otto. I have so many ideas! Are you going to get some horses over from England next Spring? I suppose that now everything will be a little easier, a little more amusing, unless these wretched Socialists spoil all our fun? It was a pity, wasn't it, about the Kaiser abdicating? I shouldn't have thought you would have let him, Otto darling. It gave me quite a shock! But it won't stop the racing, will it?' As a rule Otto thoroughly enjoyed Rosalie's heartlessness. It seemed to him ideal to possess a woman who, in addition to looking like a doll, had exactly as little feeling. Perhaps he would have enjoyed it to-day if he had not had to appear before her in a less attractive light than usual. When he answered her it was with a very slight edge to his voice, natural in a husband but regrettable in a lover. 'I suppose,' he said, 'that since we last met there have been one or two slight changes, and I am afraid you will find their results tiresome. Money, for instance—that very coarse object about which we never speak—any more, I suppose, than roses talk about manure?—is going to be what business men call "tight." I don't see any prospects of discussing cars with you, or even fresh horses. In fact I fear what we shall have to discuss is getting rid of the horses I already possess!' Rosalie laid down her cigarette. 'My dear Otto,' she exclaimed, 'not the horses!' She sat up straight, uncrossed her melon-coloured legs and looked perfectly serious. 'Socialists,' Otto continued, 'a body of people you so inappropriately describe as wretched—don't like horses except for purposes of traction; and as we are to live under a Socialist régime it will be unpopular not to appear at least to sympathize with their absence of taste.' 'But, Otto darling,' cried Rosalie, in horror, 'why should we sympathize at all with anything we don't like? Sympathy is such a bore! Besides I really don't think it would be quite right to please Socialists. Heinrich says the only way to stand Democracy is to go into the country and keep quiet with what you've got. But I thought we would manage to keep half our flat going in town too, and do a little racing while Heinrich stays in the country and sends us up butter and birds. Don't you think that would be an excellent plan? Perhaps you have heard there is to be a Reparations Commission sent over here by the Allies—quite nice people some of them—and what I thought was, they can give dances and dinners and all that sort of thing, and we can—well—we can go to them, can't we? We really ought to forgive our enemies, oughtn't we—when there's no point in not doing so? You know English people so well too, you could easily get me some for the other half of our flat—fortunately we have two kitchens—and probably I could dress on what we made out of them. That would be an immense economy! It's disgusting having foreigners here of course, but since they are bound to come we may as well make use of them, mayn't we?' 'The prospect of their usefulness has not escaped me,' replied Otto a little dryly. 'But, Rosalie, hitherto I have had a career. I haven't troubled you with it since there has been no reason at all why I should. My career lay in my hand, as it were, and gave me plenty of leisure to spend in your delightful company. Now I am without anything, so that I must start a fresh career for myself, and it will take practically all the time I have to arrive anywhere.' Rosalie took up her cigarette with a trembling hand. 'To arrive?' she asked. 'To arrive? I don't understand. What need has a Wolkenheimb to arrive?' 'None, if the world belonged, as it did once, to ourselves,' said Otto a little wearily, 'and every need if it belongs, as it does, alas! at the present moment, to the "wretched Socialists" and the intelligent Jews.' Otto spoke indifferently, and he had never spoken indifferently to Rosalie before. He usually kissed her often, looked at her continuously, and told her in a great variety of ways that she was adorable. When they wanted to be serious, which happened very seldom, they spoke about the two most serious things in the world—clothes and horses. Otto knew practically everything about those two subjects, and what he knew about other less serious subjects he kept to himself.

Rosalie realized that he was a very distinguished and brilliant person; that was what made him so nice to go about with. People looked at his dome-like brow, his high cheek-bones and remarkably luminous brown eyes; and everybody looked again. Otto wasn't handsome, but he was impressive; so impressive, and so well did he carry what height he had that every one thought of him before they thought of any one else in the room. It was not until they said, 'Graf Wolkenheimb was there,' that they went on to say who else was; and now he had begun to talk about not

17

having leisure and making a career. Had he begun to tire of her? Rosalie glanced across at one of Otto's old Venetian mirrors. She saw with satisfaction her fluffy hair and the perfect angle of the humming-bird hat, her large blue eyes, made up, imperceptible she was sure, at the corners, her cheeks perfectly pink, perfectly smooth, and neither too full nor too spare. Her mouth was her strongest point—it was exquisite. Later on it would probably go down at the corners, but it would be safe for another ten years; and her teeth were the finest in Wien. The mirror showed her a reassuring sight, and if Otto had tired of her it was entirely his own fault. 'But what shall we do without horses?' she gasped. 'Otto, my dear, we simply can't live without horses!' The door opened and Conrad appeared, very flurried and unhappy, ushering in another woman. They were both astounded. In all the three years of their intimacy nothing like it had ever happened before. It was so astounding that Rosalie leaped to the conclusion that Otto had intended it. What made it worse, what made it a million times worse, was that she knew the other woman. The Princess Eugénie Felsör was Otto's cousin. She had a perfect right to come to Otto's rooms at five o'clock in the afternoon; and her reputation was so unblemished that if she had any particular intention in doing so, it was almost certain to be innocent. If there was one quality that Countess Zalfy disliked in other women more than another, it was innocence; and innocence allied to good looks she positively loathed.

Five years ago Eugénie had been the most beautiful woman at Court. She had lost the bloom and roundness of youth and health, but the lines of her head and face retained their haunting charm. She looked now like a work by an old Master in which the colour has faded but the grace remains. All her life was in her deep velvety eyes. They were dark hazel in colour and made a golden light between the shadow of her long lashes. But as she came into the firelit room out of the cold air, she looked as if there hadn't been any War to fade and blanch her beauty. Her eyes were brilliant with anxiety, her white wan cheeks flushed with colour. Otto darted forward and kissed her hands one after the other. He made her sit down at the other end of the sofa. 'You know,' he said, turning to Rosalie, 'the Countess Zalfy of course? Her husband has left her here for an hour to cheer me up while he did a little business.' 'Of course we know each other,' said Rosalie coldly, 'though one never sees the Princess now that she has so devoted herself to good works.' Rosalie nearly sniffed, and snapped her little pearl-like teeth together after she had spoken. She would have to stay now till Eugénie left, so that Heinrich's non-existence could be left securely in the clouds; and she had just made up her mind that unless Otto relented she wouldn't stay. She didn't want to stay, she hated Eugénie, and while Eugénie was there she couldn't take any satisfactory means of finding out if Otto would relent or not. 'It is years since I have seen you, Eugénie, years,' said Otto, with a feeling in his voice he was unable for a moment to disguise. It was entirely his own fault that he had not seen Eugénie for so long, but it was nicer for both of them that it should seem hers. 'And yet,' said Eugénie, smiling, 'I have remained always in the same place.' She was not going to have any niceness beyond what she couldn't help; what she couldn't help was the exquisite niceness of her presence. Otto was the least embarrassed of the three. Eugénie had come in very appropriately, and though Conrad was going to receive the sharpest rebuke of his career after the two ladies had gone, no harm had been done by his inadvertence. It was a delightful situation to watch two such beautiful women hating each other on the same sofa. One, the woman Otto had always loved, but in the depths of his heart feared—feared too much ever to marry—and the other, so successfully married to some one else and ministering to his lighter tastes with the whole of her very small, very neatly arranged heart. Rosalie had been on the point of melting into tears—they had now frozen. Eugénie had been on the point of making a difficult emotional appeal—she couldn't make it at present. And Otto was profoundly glad that she couldn't make it. He had not had to raise a finger to prevent these disagreeable manifestations from taking place. By their mutual presence, these ladies were preventing each other from causing Otto anything but intense entertainment. As if to make everything perfect, Conrad had the sense to bring up Eugen. If Eugen was surprised at the company before him, he did not show it; imperturbably he kissed the hands of Eugénie whom he adored, and of Rosalie whom he disliked; of the two he was slightly more cordial in the greeting to Rosalie; that was because no-one in the world was ever to guess what he felt for Eugénie. Nor indeed had any one guessed it, not even Eugénie herself; though she had an instinct which told her that whatever she said or did would please Eugen, even things which in any one else would have displeased him. Tea came in and little cakes, more magnificent than any Eugénie had seen for years. She dared not eat them, but she drank, with a strange sensation of delight, the unaccustomed tea. She was glad that Otto wandered away with Rosalie to the other side of the room. 'Eugen,' she said quickly, 'you are not surprised to see me here, after what Franz told me? I asked for leave from the hospital— I had to come.' 'I am not surprised certainly,' said Eugen, systematically beginning on *Schinken-Brötchen*; 'nothing at my age surprises me, but I am perhaps a little sorry since I guess your errand to be useless, and fear therefore that it will be painful.' 'Oh, I hope it will not be useless,' said Eugénie nervously; 'only I cannot speak to Otto before the Countess. I hope her husband will soon be here to pick her up, he has left her with Otto for an hour while he had business to see to.' 'So,' murmured Eugen, continuing with a *Sardinen Butter-Brot*. He knew that Rosalie's husband was at that moment in Styria. 'Since you wish it I will take her to him immediately. I know where he is likely to be found.' 'Dear Eugen, you know everything,' murmured Eugénie gratefully, 'only of course I am very angry with you; you must realize that I am too angry to bear it! What Franz told me of you yesterday is both unbearable and unbelievable—that you should intrigue with a Jew Politician! I cannot, I will not believe it!' Eugen chose a *marron glacé* dispassionately before he replied, then he said, 'Eugénie, do not believe what is unbelievable and do not bear what is unbearable. How very sensible of you to wear that ermine wrap! Sensible, I mean for your purpose here; and how extremely dangerous to wear it in the streets! Do you not know that it is likely to be torn off your back by one of our delightful new citizens who object to fur unless it is displayed upon their own persons?' Eugénie blushed. 'I had nothing else,' she explained, 'except my hospital uniform, and I am glad I did not wear that!' 'So am I, so is Otto, and without doubt if the question were put to her, so would be the Countess Zalfy,' Eugen gravely assured her. 'But nevertheless please wait here until I have deposited the Countess with her husband. You will quarrel with Otto and refuse his escort home, but you will not quarrel with me, and I shall therefore have that pleasure.' 'But why should I not quarrel with you?' Eugénie asked earnestly, 'seeing that I consider your conduct far, far worse than Otto's? Otto has the excuse that he is ambitious! You have none!' 'Because you cannot quarrel with a person whose devotion to you is as complete as his self-control,' replied Eugen calmly, 'and if you will think for a moment you will remember that I am now an old man, forty years old, very humble in spirit, and never lifting my eyes higher than my head. All these years, however, I have had two marked qualities: I have served my friends and I have punished, when it was within my means, my enemies. These two characteristics you will not expect me at my advanced age to change. Therefore you will not quarrel with me. You will say, "Eugen, your conduct is outrageous. When will you come to spend the evening with us?"' 'Franz has quarrelled with you,' Eugénie observed uncertainly. 'Franz has quarrelled with himself,' Eugen corrected her. 'A malady incidental to the young. Otto and I have already overlooked it. Countess Zalfy,' he added, slightly raising his voice, 'I am desolated to deprive Otto of your society, but your husband, whom I ran across just now at the Club, promised me the privilege of escorting you to him at six o'clock. I told him I was coming here, and he suggested the pleasure of your company as a reward.' Rosalie tossed her head. She knew that Eugen knew as well as she did where her husband was; her little face had sharpened and her blue eyes had a hard sparkle in them. As she approached Eugénie this sparkle became menacing. 'I will not then wait any longer for my husband,' she said. 'The Princess, having no occasion to wait for hers, will no doubt have a longer and perhaps more entertaining visit than my own. I must confess I do not find Graf Wolkenheimb quite as amusing as usual!' Eugénie met the angry eyes looking down at her, with calm disdain, and looked away again in silence. She was seated, and Rosalie was standing, and yet it did not seem to the two men watching them as if Rosalie were looking down. 'The fault is of course mine,' said Otto coldly. 'I apologize profoundly for my straying wits, Countess; such a state of things, let us hope, will not occur again!' Rosalie looked back at him while Eugen held the door open for her. 'The opportunity for them to stray is not likely to occur again,' she said in a clear hard voice. This was the end. Otto gave a sigh of relief, as the door (by some arrangement of Eugen's, which may have consisted in pulling the Countess through it) closed after her. Otto had escaped a scene, but he disliked excessively even scraping the edge of one in the presence of Eugénie. 'I am sorry,' he said gravely, 'that the Countess Zalfy was so impertinent to you. I fancy she was put out about something, and she has rather less self-control than a spoiled child.' 'It does not matter,' said Eugénie indifferently. 'I don't care in the least what people do or say—when they are not dear to me; but, Otto, when they are dear to me—I care very deeply.' 'We are extraordinarily unlike then,' said her cousin, approaching the sofa, 'in that as in other ways; I, for instance, care extremely what the world in general thinks of me, and I do not yield at all readily to the opinions of those one or two people to whom I am personally attached.' 'Yet you used to care for my opinion?' said Eugénie, fixing him with her deep velvety eyes, eyes in which a man could plunge beyond his depth. Otto plunged, and found it difficult to come up again afterwards. 'If I had ever held your good opinion,' he said at length, 'I might be afraid of losing it.' 'You held more than my good opinion,' said Eugénie in a low voice, 'you held my heart. No! no! stay where you are, Otto! The time of which I speak is over; but I have my memories. They are very dear to me. I am here to-day to fight for my memories!' Otto had sprung towards her, but at her words he turned away and walked to the window which looked across at the Votiv Kirche. The Square was wet and full of dim shrouded lights moving swiftly to and fro. Otto stood with his back to Eugénie. It was so easy to make light love to a woman you didn't care for, so utterly impossible to make it to the woman you loved. Her memories! What about his own? Eugénie had been his, at a word, when she was seventeen. She was the most beautiful creature in all their circle of beautiful women and gallant men; so lovely that it was impossible to forget the delicate glow and texture of her youth; and he had been idiotic enough to let her go to a man twice her age. He hadn't wanted at twenty-five to settle down and have a home, to hold himself in, and put down his racing stable; and he had thought Eugénie would have seen afterwards that, since he had always loved her, it was perfectly within their power to make the best of things. Eugénie had, however, been inaccessible; though Otto had explained to her that her marriage was just the way in which inaccessibility could most easily be dispensed with. He had made passionate love to her; and Eugénie had ordered him out of the house. These were his memories.

Since her husband's death they had met again, but Eugénie wore unbecoming clothes, and was immersed in a children's hospital. Otto disliked diseases, and people who had anything to do with them made him nervous. She was free now, free and inflexible. The tones of her voice made his heart beat as if he were a boy again; and he dared not look at her lips. 'I don't know what you mean by love,' he said, without turning round, 'it's charming of you, of course, to say I had your heart, but I don't think at the time when I asked for it, you made this fact very obvious to me!' 'Oh, Otto,' said Eugénie, 'but you knew!' Otto had to turn round, he had to come back to her with a sigh of angry despair, and sit where the torture of her eyes could play on him. He thought it distinctly unfair that Eugénie should have had, in addition to her beauty, a voice that pierced his heart. 'You must excuse me, Eugénie,' he said as coldly as he could; 'if I had known then, it would only have annoyed me a little more intensely than it annoys me now to be told of it. Women's hearts have never been of the slightest consequence to me, when they withheld the favours that should accompany their hearts. I don't want to be a brute, but you are trying a man who *is* a brute very hard.' 'Dearest Otto', Eugénie murmured with the dangerous humility of a proud woman, 'no harder than all these cruel years I've been tried myself: I am not silly. I am not a prude. I gave you all I could, all I dared! When you tried to make me break my word to Rudolph I had to send you away; but with you went all the joy of my life: and all the joy of my life is with you still!' 'Please, Eugénie, please,' Otto said brokenly; 'how singularly little joy you must have had, and how singularly base you make me feel!' 'But you aren't base,' she murmured, laying her thin hand on his; 'oh, Otto, it is because I know you aren't base that I came here to-day. I—I am rather a proud woman generally, but I don't care about my pride now. I only care to keep what I have in my heart. It isn't, dearest, that I want you to love me again. I know you can't, that's all over now—I am an old woman who has lost a child and who lives on, I don't know how—until she can rejoin him. It is only if you do this thing, if you lower your name and betray our honour—why, then I shall have lost all the romance I ever had—and you know, Otto, it can hurt more to lose a little, if that is all you have to lose, than to lose a great deal.' Otto said without looking at her, 'Take your hand away, Eugénie!' She obeyed him when, if she had disobeyed him, she might have won him. Otto felt free to speak now; but he kept his eyes away from her face. 'Of what do you accuse me?' he asked lightly. 'You are an incarnate reproach, but so far you have failed to mention what you are reproaching me for.' Eugénie was silent for a moment; she knew Otto too well not to realize that he would outwit her in any argument; her only chance was to move him into sincerity. 'I do not know anything about business,' she said at last, 'but I know what a man's honour is. Can you keep yours safe if you mix in commercial affairs with a bad Jew?' 'You refer to my good friend Mandelbaum perhaps?' Otto asked her. 'We are all obliged to associate with Jews now. If I am not mistaken your Doctor Jeiteles, of whom you hold so high an opinion and for whom you work in your hospital, is a Jew?' 'He is a good man,' said Eugénie simply. 'I work very gladly under him. Can you work gladly and honourably under this Mandelbaum?' 'I do not work under him,' replied Otto, biting his lips with annoyance, 'I work with him, or at least I propose to work with him. There is a distinction, and I think that I am the best judge of my honour.' 'That is why I came to you,' agreed Eugénie; 'I knew you to be the best judge of your honour, and you are content? There is nothing in this association that sticks in your throat?' 'The old world is finished,' said Otto impatiently; 'our old standards must crumble with it. I have decided to let mine crumble. If you ask me, am I doing to-day what I should have done yesterday—no! I am not! If I did I should lose Trauenstein and become a beggar. Is that what you wish?' 'It is not very terrible to be poor, Otto,' Eugénie said humbly. 'One works hard every day. One finds—it is curious!—one finds as much happiness as there is. I had not thought it possible; one thinks too much of money when one has it—now that I do not have it any more, I find that one ceases to trouble about many things. Of course to have nothing at all would be terrible; but you are so clever, so much cleverer than we are, that I think you would not find you had nothing even if you had to give up Trauenstein and work as we do. Perhaps you might work on the estate—and save it? Franz believes there is money to be found in working it?' 'Trauenstein is heavily mortgaged,' said Otto dryly; 'I must pay the interest on it out of what I make, and that is why it is necessary for me to make what I can. One does not develop an estate without capital.' Eugénie said nothing.

She sat there patiently looking at him with eyes full of love and trust. She believed that stripped of all he possessed Otto would be a great man; she did not know that Otto *was* what he possessed. His passion, his pride, his life itself, had passed into his possessions; he was no more able to conceive of life without them than Franz could have conceived of life without honour, or Eugénie life without love. 'What you ask is impossible,' he said after a pause. 'I must live as best I can, Eugénie. I know what I am doing; Eugen also knows it and has accepted it. I do not say it is fine or noble, but it is necessary. If you and Franz dislike it too much you can always refuse to know me. A man can only act by his own eyes. I think that mine see further than yours. But it is natural for you to take your brother's view of my actions.' 'I do not take Franz's view,' replied Eugénie; 'that is why I came here. I wanted to find out your own. That is what one judges people by, is it not—when one loves them? What hurts me is that I feel you know that you are doing wrong and that you would be happier if you did not do it.' 'What makes you suppose that?' asked Otto with a quick glance at her. 'Do rags strike you as the kind of thing I should be happy in?' 'We should all be together,' said Eugénie under her breath—'whatever happened we should be together. Long ago, Otto, just such a chance came to you—forgive me—you know how you chose! We broke our hearts over it when it was too late. I was too proud to plead with you then—now I have forgotten my pride. I would not let it stand in my way to-day. I said, "I cannot let him be unhappy again".' Otto covered his eyes with his hand to shut out her face and said, 'Must we continue this discussion? It is profoundly painful to us both, and since as you tell me you no longer desire my love, it seems to lead nowhere. May we not take it for granted that I am infamous, faithless and of course heartless—and then would you mind going away? Eugénie! Eugénie, have pity! I can't stand this any longer! If you go on sitting there—I'm damned if I can stand it! And I'm not going to give in!' Eugénie rose, half frightened, half triumphant, to her feet. It was incredible to her that Otto still cared, and yet if he did not care, why was he so moved? Why did he cover his eyes with his hands so that he could not see her face? Why did she herself feel the old enchanting cruel excitement catch at her heart again? It caught at her heart; but it did not move her inflexible judgement. She loved Otto, loved him as perhaps in her young and innocent life she had not known how to love, but her spirit loved him more than her senses. At a touch he would have been at her feet—and she did not touch him. She murmured instead, 'But, Otto, then —if you care for me, you cannot possibly stoop to this baseness?' 'Why do you talk of such things?' he said between his teeth. 'I only know that I am not going to alter my life for you, and that if you stand there another minute, I shall never let you go.'

Silence settled between them, dangerous with memories. Their wills fought each other while their senses dragged them towards surrender. Eugénie knew her only safety was in flight, and yet to leave Otto was like destroying a part of herself. Otto knew nothing but passion and the fear of Eugénie's eyes if he let himself go. It was the only fear he had ever had; yet he knew that it would not hold him for long. Eugénie spoke at last, 'No—if you will not change, I cannot,' she said in a low breaking voice. 'Then go!' said Otto without looking at her. The door opened and Eugénie saw Eugen standing in the passage. Without a word, as if Otto had been ill, she stepped quietly from his side with her finger on her lips and joined Eugen. Eugen looked past her at the bowed figure of his friend and, drawing her gently into the passage, closed the door. 'What singularly cruel things', he observed dispassionately, 'good women do to men!'

III

Eugénie dressed hurriedly and went out shivering into the deserted streets. Usually she loved her morning walk, it freshened her for the day's toil, and sometimes she carried a vision of beauty into the wards that lingered throughout the day. From the bridge, which crossed the Canal leading to the Prater Strasse, she could see the hills of Kahlenberg and Leopoldsberg round as apples, caught by rosy clouds and shining down upon the City. To-day the fog covered them, the cold was pressing a white clammy sheet over the whole plain. The houses stood up in the sickly light, like dark shadows of old sins. Eugénie hastened; she felt a bitter revolt against ugliness, and against the futility of struggling with it. What had she gained by keeping alive a few hundred miserable babies, while Rosalie was charming Otto with her humming-bird hats? She came to a bleak and wind-swept yard, enclosing the abandoned grey barracks, now used as a children's hospital.

Eugénie stood still for a long moment before she entered the door of her ward; she waited until her face changed; her lips softened, her eyes became full of laughter. She went into the ward at last as if she had been wafted in by music. There were sixty beds in the long narrow room, and each one held a child. The name of a Saint was written over the door. This was the ward of St. Agnes, and these were St. Agnes' lambs; but no kindly-hearted butcher was there to put them out of pain. They were all under the shadow of tuberculosis: abscesses, defective limbs, defective organs, or simply the persistent dwindling of vitality. Some of them were terrible to look at, mere scraps of bone and skin. Some had the remains of beauty, like menaced flowers blown first this way and then that by the harsh wind of their disease. Yet when they saw Eugénie each of them smiled. She went from one bed to the other, with her eyes full of love. The bitterness in her heart had gone deep; and was hidden deep; none of it escaped her. The night sister gave Eugénie her notes and said a few words, lingering—although night nurses seldom linger—to take her part in the festival of Eugénie's presence. It was a festival in spite of the long weary night; the sour fetid smell of the ward, so seldom aired on account of the scarcity of fuel; in spite of the pain in the little wizened faces. Washing, dressing, bed-making, breakfast; one by one these regular processes took place, and each child was so loved, so encouraged by its sense of unique importance, that every process, however painful to the little injured body, became a pleasure to the child's responsive mind. The two young nurses who worked under Eugénie, ignorant rough girls whom she had trained, were full of the same spirit of tenderness. Everyone who worked in the hospital learned it as an inviolable rule. No voice was ever to be raised, no child to be disheartened by a frown. As to punishment, how could anyone punish those whom life had so condemned?

At breakfast Eugénie received a fresh shock. There was no more cocoa. With their black bread the children would have to have a dreadful drink made of acorns and hot water. There was no sugar to sweeten it with. The nurses looked at her and then looked

27

away again. Nobody said anything. At ten o'clock came the Doctor. This was the hour for the dressings; it should have been the most painful hour in the day, but just because it might have been, it was turned into their highest pinnacle of joy. The door opened; every face turned towards it as if by clock-work, and Dr. Carl Jeiteles entered. He stood there for a moment with his eyes twinkling, his hands in the pockets of his white linen suit, his whole being concentrated upon the little world of pain in front of him, and from it came a moan not of pain but of joy. 'The Herr Doktor! The Herr Doktor!' Each day they greeted him with fresh rapture, as if they were greeting the sudden presence of God. All who could stand, fell upon him in a struggling mass; but those who could not move knew that he would stay with them longest. He disentangled one by one the clustering figures climbing over him, and Eugénie, standing by his side, laid her hand on each head in turn, lifting each face tenderly to his, and gave him the child's history since he had last seen it; and in turn he took each child in his arms, kissed it, dismissed it with its own joke, its own encouragement, for the day; and then the next, and the next, without haste, without intermission, until he stood free again and went to the beds for the dressings. Piteous little faces scowling with pain opened like flowers as he bent over them. His touch, infinitely gentle, quick and sure, gave pain, but something in him promised a sure relief from pain. He was going to make them better; they lay still in his hands, moaned a little, cried a little, and when it was over he stayed by each bed long precious minutes, remaking the shattered confidence, turning the little frightened mind back to security. No matter what else he had to do or how long the day's work stretched before him, Dr. Carl Jeiteles never hurried these morning visits. 'We must', he would say to Eugénie, 'put the heart as well as the little body right for the day.' He and Eugénie bent together over one baby in silence. She was a year old, and only the size of a tiny doll. She was dying of pneumonia and starvation, only she wouldn't die. She lifted blue eyes heavy with fever up to theirs, questioningly, as if they could tell her why she was so painfully there, and closed them again as if she saw they could not answer her. The little body, shaken by its cruel breathing, refused to let the spirit go. 'See how she means to live,' Dr. Jeiteles said with a sigh, 'this poor little one! It would be better *not*—all this fight—for at the end it will be the same as if she had not fought!' He lifted the little body in his hands, raising it higher to ease the difficult breathing. 'We have nothing to give her; even the cocoa has stopped,' said Eugénie harshly. 'I know—I know, Sister,' Carl Jeiteles said apologetically; 'it seems that if we had the money there is none to be got.' Eugénie bowed her head. She had given more than half her fortune to the hospital; if she gave the whole of it, she could not live. She had sometimes thought of giving it all, in spite of the fact that she was a good Catholic and knew that suicide was a sin. However, she had not been allowed to do so because Carl Jeiteles refused to accept any more money from her. He lifted his eyes from the baby, and met hers. His quick searching spirit pierced her outward serenity and felt the trouble at her heart. 'Sister,' he said, 'at 10.30 I will have Joachim for his hip operation, at eleven little Mitzi for the ear, and at half-past twelve I will ask you to come to me for a moment while I am in the dispensary. This little one dies to-day, I think, in spite of her great will. Do not trouble her with any more of our bad food. A little morphia if she struggles—and then it is over!' 'Yes, Doctor,' said Eugénie. She wished he would stay; while he was there a curious confidence persisted in making itself felt; but he had other wards to visit, and operations to perform. He was escorted to the door by his swarm of babies, and at the door he stopped and waved his hand to the cot babies; and all the cot babies waved back, except the dying baby and one tall little girl who stood at the foot of her cot and talked all day long to herself, and never saw anybody because her mind had gone.

Eugénie settled back once more into her struggle for the children's happiness; she brought out their toys from a big cupboard. Then she got Joachim and Mitzi ready for the theatre. Joachim took a stuffed rabbit with him on the stretcher, and Mitzi a headless doll. After the two children had been taken to the theatre, she went back to the dying baby and sat by her for an hour.

Eugénie thought how much better it would be to go through the hospital with a morphia injection and give each child enough for an eternal sleep. Then she would send them all in hundreds of little coffins to the Allies with the cattle they were proposing to exact under the Peace Treaty. She wanted the cry of the children out of her ears; the pain out of her heart; the sight out of her eyes.

She put all the comfort she had into the children who came back from the operating room, and at last she found she had none

29

left. She waited impatiently for the baby to begin its struggle so that she could give her the morphia and know it was all over. But the baby would not make ready for death; her incomprehensibly strong heart beat steadily on. Eugénie had often wanted to see a child escape before, but she had wanted it with exquisite gentleness, with her prayers following the little spirit up into the Virgin's arms. But to-day it was with a deep impatience that she waited for the child to die and without any faith that its spirit would go from a mother on earth to the Mother of all mothers in Heaven. She looked at the clock, sent one of the nurses for the dinners, and went out of doors into the icy air without her cloak. She crossed the courtyard to one of the smaller sheds which was Carl Jeiteles' dispensary, but she no longer wished to see him; she was angry even with Carl Jeiteles. What was the use of pretending happiness when there was no happiness? Of loving, when there was no place for love?

'I am glad you have come,' said Carl Jeiteles gently; 'we have had very good news, Princess. I wanted to tell you myself. Professor Wenckebach has come back from England and has brought us stores of disinfectants and drugs. I was afraid to tell you last week—we were very near the end of the chloroform.' Eugénie said nothing. 'Princess, you are glad?' Dr. Jeiteles asked pleadingly, looking round from his dispensary table. 'Certainly I am glad of chloroform,' said Eugénie icily. 'As there is now nothing the children can eat, it would be kindest to put them all under chloroform and keep them there. This morning I gave them black bread, and hot water with acorns in it, and half of them refused to touch it. For dinner they are to have carrots, and at night they will again be offered black bread and acorn juice. Yes, I am glad the English have sent us chloroform. I hope they have been sufficiently thanked for it. Is that all you have to say to me?' 'No,' said Dr. Jeiteles, 'it is not all. Sister, you believe in God, I think?' 'I did,' said Eugénie harshly; 'one lives and learns, Herr Doktor. I should not myself care to be responsible for having made this world.' 'I do not believe in God,' said Dr. Jeiteles still more gently. 'You are a great lady and no doubt you have read much and filled your mind with noble ideas. I do not myself find that these things are a help to one. But if there is no God, there is certainly a greater responsibility laid on man. You feel that to serve these children is a waste; but one thing I see, whether it has an end or not, that out of these struggles some live, and that all those who fail to live, if they are served with tenderness and understanding, suffer less. They actually suffer less, Princess; this is a fact. My way of looking at it then is this. If you believe in God, help God. If you do not believe in God—help man. That is what I had on my mind to say to you.' 'I am ashamed,' said Eugénie in a low voice, 'I will go back into my ward, and I will try not to fail our children again.' 'You have not failed them yet, Princess,' said Jeiteles, smiling at her, 'and I had not for a moment supposed that you would. I only thought perhaps you were a little disheartened. An affair like the coming to an end of the cocoa this morning is disheartening. I find it so myself. Remember, you do more than I; you keep the light burning in sixty little hearts all day long. There is one thing that would be worse than anything we have yet seen, and that is if you let the light in those little hearts go out.' Eugénie held out her hand to him. 'I will not let the light go out,' she said steadily. The shabby Jewish doctor bent over her hand and kissed it reverently.

At five o'clock the children had their supper, and to make up for their having had no cocoa, Eugénie stood in the middle of the ward and sang to them. She had a beautiful voice. She stood by the cot of the dying baby where she could look down at it every now and then; her hand rested lightly on its tiny hands. She sang the *Lieder* that the children knew and loved. The doors were all thrown open so that the other wards could hear as well. First she sang:

> '*Schlaf, Herzens Söhnchen,*
> *Mein Liebling bist Du!*'

And then she sang:

> '*Ich weiss nicht, was soll es bedeuten,*
> *Dass ich so traurig bin.*'

As the last notes rang out through the heavy fetid air, Eugénie glanced across the ward and saw a little group of people who had entered silently: Dr. Jeiteles and two strange women. Eugénie knew in a flash (even if she had not seen the expression of Carl Jeiteles' face) that this was the first Relief Mission; and she knew what its coming meant. Only the little baby lying under the touch of her hands must die—all the rest of them—that silent, suffering, helpless little band—were going to live; and some of them were going to get well.

IV

She came flying out of the hospital as if she had been a missile from a catapult, and plunged against Franz Salvator with a velocity that nearly knocked him off his feet. He caught a glimpse of her under the nearest lamp post: a short thick mass of maize-coloured hair; a pair of grey eyes under level brows nearly meeting; a tip-tilted nose and pointed chin, with a wide, sweet, generous mouth set now in lines of fierce pain. She was no more aware of Franz Salvator than if he had been a letter box; she steadied herself by his arm without glancing at him and prepared to dash forward again into the wet windy darkness. 'Is anything the matter?' Franz Salvator asked her in English. He felt convinced that she must belong to the least ceremonious of the nations. 'Ah! you're English?' Carol Hunter said, pausing in her flight. 'Then for God's sake take me somewhere out of this infernal place—I can't stand any more of it. It's pretty near done me in!' 'You had better come into this shed,' Franz Salvator answered. 'It's Dr. Jeiteles' consulting-room and always open. You must, I think, be one of the ladies from the Relief Mission? I was told they were to be here this afternoon. We can wait here till the others join you.' Carol followed him up the rickety wooden steps into the dispensary. There was nothing in it but locked cupboards, a kitchen table with a green-shaded electric light, and two deal chairs. Franz Salvator pushed one towards her, but Carol Hunter did not sit down. She was not upset as Franz Salvator was accustomed to see young girls upset; she showed no inclination towards tears nor any need for support. She strode up and down the room with her hands in her pockets, kicking her feet out in front of her like a schoolboy in a passion; and to Franz Salvator's intense astonishment for several minutes she cursed without a pause. She took no notice of his presence, so that he was free to observe her thoroughly. She was small and beautifully made, her feet and ankles, her wrists and hands, the set of her head on her slender throat, were as fine as the points of the Medicean Venus. What, however, was strikingly unlike any Venus was the complete absence in her of any softness. There was no ounce of superfluous

32

flesh on her slender, compact little body. She was all velocity, suppleness and energy. She had an air, that was strange to Franz Salvator in young girls, of perfect independence of her surroundings. She might often have been annoyed in the course of her short life, but it seemed to Franz Salvator that she had never been embarrassed, nor was it likely that she ever would be. When she stopped cursing, she flung round and looked at him. 'Well,' she said savagely, 'I don't know what you feel, seeing those hundreds of children all minced up and useless, as if they'd been put through a mangle—by our beautiful war for freedom!—but I tell you, I feel pretty cheap! All soldiers' children, that doctor says—neglect, starvation, bad blood—and they tell me these are the lucky ones! There are hundreds more on the waiting list, babies like little broken dolls hidden away under some rubbish in ice-cold rooms to starve! God, it's a pretty world! Are you an Englishman?' 'No,' said Franz Salvator; 'I have the honour—a sad one, but I still hold it an honour—of being an Austrian.' 'How you must hate us!' said Carol Hunter. She stood still now on the opposite side of the table, and looked straight into Franz Salvator's eyes. 'I have used up my hate,' said Franz Salvator slowly, 'in the four years I spent fighting. The top of a mountain and no diet to speak of—reduces hate.' 'I'd hate being beaten,' said Carol fiercely, 'and I'd hate what beat me—as long as I lived, I'd hate it!' 'You would if you felt beaten, no doubt,' agreed Franz Salvator, showing his shining teeth in an amused smile, 'but you see the trench I happened to be in was an Italian trench which we took early in 1916, and as the enemy never did anything to induce us to leave it, although we disliked very much giving it up at the orders of our General when the Armistice was signed, we did not feel particularly beaten. We felt perhaps cheated; but it is better in the long run to be cheated than to cheat. I have learned that there is no middle way.' 'I don't see how you can be so calm,' exclaimed Carol. 'Don't you mind seeing your children all spoiled, like so many broken egg-shells? They won't get better! I don't know whether the lady in there who looks like the ghost of a Madonna thinks they will—she's so pleased at having our milk and cocoa to give them that she's forgotten what the rest of their lives will be like. Her gratitude cut like a knife, that's why I ran out. She behaved as if we were bringing Paradise straight into those children's lives, and it was only little tins of food.' She sat down suddenly, and put her head in her hands. 'I'd like to be sick!' she said, 'sick to my stomach! That's all there is to it.' 'Don't be too upset,' Franz Salvator said gently; 'you have seen the worst all at once and all together. Try to remember that each child has only its own tragedy, and that for the rest of us it is not so bad. We have gone down little by little, our sufferings and our needs increased slowly, and the shock of them wears off. I am not clever—and how do you say it in your English?—but one becomes less and less startled by pain as one's own vitality decreases. These children do not know how sad their lives are. My sister—for I think it must be my sister whom you describe as the ghost of a Madonna—can nurse them all day long without being at all startled. What might startle us would be if you showed us a room full of healthy children with beautiful colour in their round cheeks; then we should feel the contrast; but in our minds now there are no great contrasts, only a sliding scale of pain.' Carol Hunter looked at him with eyes that seemed to eat into his face. 'I've got to get this known,' she said half to herself and half to him. 'People have got to know about the state of things. It won't do just to sit down under it. People have got to know, and then they've got to act. Don't you want to do something yourself? But maybe you are doing it?' Franz Salvator sat down on the other side of the table. He was puzzled by the young girl opposite him; she seemed to speak as if she held the reins of the world. 'When I can stop thinking about bread,' he said quietly, 'and how to get it, perhaps I shall be able to be of some use to my country. At present I work eight hours a day, teaching English at a Berlitz school, in order to provide myself with food. It is an occupation like any other, and I am glad of it, but it leaves remarkably little margin for altruism.' 'What are you here for then?' she asked abruptly. 'It is a dark night, and I came to take my sister home,' explained Franz Salvator. 'I am happy that I came, for this is the first time—since it was my duty to kill them—that I have spoken to one of our late enemies. We are very international here in Wien, and I have missed very much being cut off from those foreigners with whom we have always had most in common.' 'I'm American,' said Carol Hunter; 'I came over with our ambulances, and drove one for our Army in France. I'm used to soldiers, and I've seen wounds and death—but till I came to this country I didn't know life was so mean. I knew it was terrible—it's fine though to be able to stand up against terror and

34

get the better of it! but there are things you can't stand up against——' Franz Salvator nodded. He pitied her intensely, but as he looked into the brave eyes fixed on his, he would not have her cheated of the truth. Truth is cruel, it is sometimes so cruel that people cannot bear it; but if it knocks the life out of one, at least it does not poison; and those who can stand it are the stronger for it all their lives. 'I'm twenty-one,' she went on after a pause. 'Of course I pretended to be older to get out, and my father helped me. My·father was all I'd got—I don't count a step-mother, and a lot of half kin—a whining set. My father was a sport. He raised Hell to get me to Europe though he couldn't come with me, and six months after I got here, he died of angina pectoris. I tell you, that hit me! I'm not one of your soft-hearted girly-girlies that wash down on their troubles, but when I do care for a person I care hard. I came out here to succeed, and I'll do it too—but it's a queer feeling to find that the person you wanted to make good for is out of it. Like getting to the point of a joke and finding it hasn't got one. Did I tell you I'm on a paper? No? Well, I am, it's the New York *Meteor*, and has the fourth largest circula-tion in the world. When I got that cable about my father I was in Paris; and I'd got Clemenceau and was fishing for Foch, and then I ran into Dr. J. Simmons just coming out here. I went for an interview, with the cable in my pocket, and I got all balled up. She just took hold of me by the collar—like you might a stray dog—and ran me out here. She said if I kept my eyes peeled I'd find good and plenty going on in Wien—and she was right. I shall stay in this country quite a while. Have you anything to hand over about yourself?' Franz Salvator hesitated. He was a reserved man, and incapable of quick intimacy; there was probably no form of research from which he shrank so definitely as that of looking into his own mind. What he liked was doing things with people who knew all about him, or with those who knew nothing about him and had no reason to find out. But he did not want this frank-eyed girl to belong to the latter category. Her confidence had touched him, and he wished to make her a response. He pulled out his card and pushed it across the table towards her. She looked at it without recognition. It was apparent that his name—which was three-quarters of his life, meant nothing to her. 'I am twenty-six,' he said slowly; 'I've lost all I had; and my job as a soldier has gone too. I thought a good deal of being a soldier. I could ride once; but I shall not be able to afford a horse again. Most of my friends have been killed. It is not a long history; and there are so many like it that it is not even interesting.' 'It interests me all right,' said Carol quickly. Franz Salvator hesitated and looked down. 'I have a friend,' he said in a low voice, 'that I cared for more than those who died. He sold his honour for comfort; and to-morrow perhaps you will find me doing the same thing. All I can safely tell you is that I won't do it to-day!' She stretched her hand suddenly towards him. 'You're a dear!' she said with conviction. 'I guess your honour is pretty safe—I'd stand for it any time.' Franz Salvator bent his head over her hand and kissed it. 'Thank you,' he said, 'I shall remember that.' Carol stared at him in some surprise at his emotion. She had no idea of how very near this impassive young man had stood to the point of despair. Before she had rushed against him in the dark, he had felt himself slipping away from his own control, his nature itself had not seemed worth while. In giving up his faith in Otto, he had seemed to be giving up everything. Now in a moment he knew, with the resiliency of youth, that there was after all something else. A new turn of the road—a fresh view of life. This young creature before him with her vigour and her incredible optimism had fired his blood afresh. The door behind Carol opened Dr. Jeiteles, Eugénie, in her white nursing-dress, and Dr. Simmons came in together. Carol turned to face them. 'Oh, there you are,' she said. 'Well, I stood all I could swallow, Dr. Jeiteles. I'm sorry I couldn't manage that last ward, but I saw enough. I'll try to start a real prairie fire about your hospital that'll bring in money. People in America can feel all right, and when they feel they pay, but I've got to get your story hot and running, before it can catch up with them. Will you give me a few facts?'

Franz Salvator stood waiting for Carol to explain his presence, but she gave no explanation of it; that she should have picked up a strange young man and be found alone with him in the Doctor's dispensary had not seemed to her a cause for comment. It was Eugénie who introduced him to Dr. Simmons, the head of the English Relief Mission. Dr. Jane Simmons was a tall, spare woman dressed in a long khaki overcoat with a cowboy's felt hat on her head. She looked neither like a man nor a woman, but like some strange sexless hybrid, born to carry out functions which had nothing to do with either emotion or charm. The sights she had just been seeing had not in the least discomposed her—she was used to pain—it was the material upon which she worked. She gave Franz Salvator a perfunctory hand, and looked at him with eyes which were unresponsive to anything but human damage. After this automatic recognition she returned instantly to Eugénie who, flushed and brilliant with renewed hope, poured out to her in a kind of passion the needs and history of the hospital.

Franz Salvator stood stiffly outside the little group of four; he felt troubled and as if perhaps he had given himself away without cause. He had dragged his confidence out of his heart with the utmost difficulty to offer it to this young girl who had so spontaneously given him her own, but she was talking to Dr. Jeiteles with the same intensity and friendliness with which she had talked to Franz. Franz Salvator was not a snob, but he knew there was a good deal of difference between a Jew doctor and a Hohenberg—and that the difference was not in favour of the Jew doctor. But Carol Hunter did not so much as glance in his direction until Dr. Simmons touched her on the arm and told her they must go; and even then it was Dr. Simmons who proposed to drive them home. Eugénie laughed with pleasure. 'I have not been in a car', she said, 'for years; it will be like flying!' 'Will you drive or shall I?' Carol asked Franz as they stood in front of the Mission car. 'I will drive,' said Franz Salvator, 'if you will allow me. I am fond of driving.' 'I thought you would be,' said Carol; 'you've got the hands of a man who likes to do things.' She had thought about him then, although her dismissal of him had been so casual? She swung herself into the seat beside him and lit a cigarette, protecting the match from the wind carefully in the hollow of her hands. Franz Salvator was used to women upon whom he waited hand and foot. It amused but rather shocked him to see a girl so physically competent. Carol leaned forward, so that the light caught her face. She had the quietness of another man. Franz Salvator felt himself vaguely disturbed by her, not because she was a girl, but because she used her privilege so little. Like most handsome men he was aware of his attraction for women. He was not vain of it, he sometimes disliked it; but he knew he had it. But, upon this girl beside him, he had no influence at all. He had aroused interest in her, not because he was a man and handsome, but because he told her things which she wanted to know. Dr. Jeiteles had interested her quite as much; Eugénie had interested her a good deal more. He had seen the girl's eyes soften suddenly as they rested on Eugénie's face. Her interest was as lively as a flame, but it had the purity of flame: nothing existed in it but the force of its own fire. They reached the door of Eugénie's flat before the silence between them was broken. 'Shall I see you again?' Franz Salvator asked hurriedly. She glanced at him speculatively. 'Yes,' she said at last. 'There are several things I'd like to have from you. What's your number? I'll ring you up some time.' '1708,' said Franz Salvator, 'but I would hardly have suggested a telephone. This is where my sister and I live, but if you will allow me I will drive you to the Mission and walk back.' Carol leaned across him without answering, and held out her hand to Eugénie. 'I want to see you again,' she said impulsively. 'May I come and see you?' Eugénie smiled uncertainly. 'It would be the greatest pleasure,' she said with gentle cordiality, 'to see you. Perhaps I may come some Sunday afternoon when I am free and call upon you and Dr. Simmons?' 'Why did she say that?' demanded Carol as Eugénie vanished through the dark gateway. 'Doesn't she want me to come to her house? Not that I mind. I want to see her anyway. I'd sit on the steps of a railway station if I couldn't see her any other way. She's like something carried in a procession. You just want to watch her pass by with lights and music. Aren't you proud of her?' Franz Salvator was prouder of his sister Eugénie than of anything on earth, but he was far too proud to say so. He murmured that he was glad she was appreciated. 'She is a good woman,' he added simply. 'Well, there are good women all over the place,' said Carol indifferently—'quite a drug on the market, good women are—that isn't what grips you about the Princess. She's so beautiful, she makes you hold your breath. You kind of know she's that way inside as well as out—she's so beautiful, she's safe, you couldn't break her. I tell you there aren't many women, or men either, that you couldn't break. All the same I don't know why I'm not to go and see her. Is she too grand for visitors?' 'On the contrary,' said Franz Salvator, 'Eugénie is so humble that she has never been known to get on a tram unless I dragged her on one. She thinks everyone has more right to a convenience than herself. No doubt she wishes to save you time and trouble by coming to see you!' 'Well, she can come,' said Carol briefly; 'this is where we hop off.' Franz Salvator guessed by her gesture rather than her words that they had arrived at the Mission, and pulled up the car. Carol jumped off before he could help her. It was Dr. Simmons who thanked him formally for bringing them home.

Franz Salvator found himself strolling back into the Stephansplatz with the feeling that his interests had been tremendously aroused and his personality entirely overlooked. It was a strange but not unpleasant sensation.

V

They were immaculate in person; no one in the smartest London club ever had fairer or more highly glazed linen, cloth of finer texture or a surer cut. Their boots had the lustre of black pearls; their studs gleamed with austere brilliance, and their fur-lined coats were magnificent and orthodox. Their hearts were full of bitterness; and they sat side by side in a tram. It was a tram that had long ago seen its better days slip into worse ones, and its worse ones lose the last of their blighted security. How it kept going at all on its worn uneven lines was a wonder. Insufficient currents of electricity sent it forward in a series of jerks and whines. The interior of the tram was stuffy, cold and dirty; and it was over-filled with people who shared these disadvantages, and accentuated them. They had long ago ceased to care how they looked; their clothes were all survivals from the days before the War; their faces were lined and drawn with hardships that had sunk into habit, and habits which had lapsed beneath hope. Nevertheless neither Otto nor Eugen felt the slightest sympathy for them. The common misfortune of defeat does not bind people together, it disintegrates them, for misery is more individual than joy. If they felt anything at all for the emaciated, lack-lustre beings who hung on straps above them or pressed their dingy persons closer together on the hard wooden seats, it was rage against them for having, as they would have put it, 'driven away their Emperor'. Their pity was for themselves; that they should have to sit in a tram surrounded by a half-starved populace was the sharpest of tragedies. They were both miserable, but Eugen was far more under the spell of his misery than Otto. Otto had his schemes before him; they fluttered beyond the screeching trams and rested in luxurious limousines. 'Enough!' Eugen ejaculated harshly, and staggered, in and out of a line of scarecrows, to the door. 'But we are not there yet,' objected Otto, who had followed him in astonishment. 'It is true,' agreed Eugen, letting himself down heavily on to the broken pavement, 'but I have sat in this Chariot of Demos long enough. There was a time when the imagination of Tiberius and Caligula seemed to me a little extreme. I confess now I find these remarkable men to have been misjudged.' 'We shall arrive late,' said Otto indifferently; 'however, on the way I can explain to you a little about our fellow guests, which is perhaps an advantage. Our talk after dinner with Mandelbaum will be a simple affair; he will try to get us into his hands, and he will find, I think, perhaps with some surprise, that he has not. I ask nothing of you but to watch me play my hand and when I signal to you, you will reinforce me with whatever card you see that I want. But the earlier part of the evening should be amusing. Have you ever heard of Elisabeth Bleileben? She is a very clever woman, and, as you know, I do not use this expression lightly. She is at the head of half the Charities in Vienna, and at the throat of the other half. Her virtue is so far above suspicion, but I believe she did very well out of her charities. I have met her once or twice; she has great energy and a brutal wit. She is so vivacious that I have not yet been able to discover if she is good-looking or not. Her general appearance is that of a slightly excited leopard!' 'I know whom you mean,' assented Eugen; 'they made her husband a Minister because he could speak English. Before the Downfall, he might have been a shoemaker—never, I think, a good one. I hear he is getting over his surprise at being a Minister, but with other people the astonishment is permanent. No doubt his wife bluffed him into the appointment. Be careful of her, Otto. Women who make stupid men a success, may be dangerous to clever ones. What part do you suggest her playing in our concerns?' 'It is impossible she should still be in love with her husband,' replied Otto, 'and if she is not, she might assist me in making use of his position. I should like to have at least two Ministers under our influence so as to play one off against the other. This is always a good arrangement. Do you not agree with me?' 'Possibly,' said Eugen cautiously. 'You say that she has been known to do very well out of her charities. Is this merely a pious rumour on the part of the other charities less ably run than her own, or can it be proved? I do not ask if the rumours are true since that is a minor matter; but successful concealment is a major one.' 'Have I not told you that she is intelligent?' said Otto brusquely; 'nothing can be proved against her—except her husband!' 'Then if she is discreet,' said Eugen indifferently, 'it becomes merely a matter of taste. It is superfluous to ask to what race she belongs since she is a philanthropist who has not suffered pecuniarily from her exertions.' 'Of course she is a Jewess,' said Otto moodily. 'But would Rosalie be capable of lifting a finger to help me? I shall have to teach Elisabeth how to dress, and how to sit still. Her feet are as solid as tomb-stones. She walks like a duck approaching a worm. One knows that she will not fail to get the worm, but one resents her not making the approach a trifle more seductive. Still a clever woman learns fast, and when she wants to attract she learns even faster. I think I may say that she already wishes to attract me. This evening I propose to make her take a decision about it.' Eugen shrugged his shoulders. 'It is your affair,' he muttered; 'I, as you know, prefer the gutter where it is, to seeing it transferred to the drawing-room.' 'We are not all so fortunate as you,' replied Otto suavely, 'able to unite in the person of a cook both our affections and our conveniences!' There was a short silence. Then Otto laid his hand lightly on his friend's arm. 'Now, my dear Eugen,' he said persuasively, 'we come to a business in which I shall need your help. There is to be an American heiress at Mandelbaum's to-night who is attached to the Relief Mission. She owns a newspaper. I have arranged with Mandelbaum that you are to take her in to dinner. Find out for me if she will be at all possible as a wife. I have come to the conclusion that I must marry foreign money.' 'What will your mother say to an American?' demanded Eugen, standing still. 'The Gräfin as you know is not international. I fancy that if she thinks of America at all she supposes it to be inhabited by Italian organ-grinders and Red Indians!' 'My mother', said Otto, 'will have to become reconciled to any wife who will enable me to keep Trauenstein, and you will find that when she has set her mind at rest on this subject her manner to my future wife will be beyond reproach.' 'Here', said Eugen, feeling under a brilliant lamp for a bell draped in ivy, 'is the goal of your ambitions. Go a little slowly with the Elisabeth if you wish to impress the American favourably. I understand their strong point is the Puritan instinct.'

41

Frau Mandelbaum was waiting for her guests with that slight thrill which, even after twenty years of solid entertaining, still played upon her lethargic senses. She liked to put on her best clothes, to sit at the head of a well-furnished table, and watch Julius take people in. Frau Mandelbaum did not call it taking people in, she called it entertaining them, but she knew very well that Julius never entertained people whom he did not propose sooner or later to take in. Frau Mandelbaum played a very inno- cent part on these occasions. She provided excellent food and paid great attention to the points Julius told her to make. To-night he had explained to her that the head of the English Mission was her principal guest. She would have to talk English to him, but she wouldn't have to talk very much. She must say that Austria would perish without an English credit, but she needn't try to ex- plain why, she should just mention that Julius himself knew all the reasons better than anyone else. Frau Mandelbaum had a very fine white neck on which Julius had hung a string of medium- sized pearls. Her mouth always went down at the corners when she thought of these pearls, because they might have been much larger if Julius had not given pearls to other ladies on whose necks they had no legal right to hang. All her guests except Graf Wol- kenheimb and his cousin arrived punctually. They sat about the brilliantly lighted, freshly upholstered room as if they had met by chance at a railway station and had begun to be a little uneasy at the lateness of their trains. Julius took them in turns through his three reception rooms and showed them several square yards of newly bought impressionist pictures. Frau Mandelbaum bought the carpets; they were rather like the pictures. She had never met Otto or Eugen before, nor except for the Downfall would it have been possible for her to meet them; but Julius had told her that everything was altered, Otto Wolkenheimb would be glad to get a good dinner, and she needn't go out of her way to be polite to him. Still when he did arrive, distinguished and bland, about twenty minutes late, she felt obliged to go a little out of her way.

Frau Mandelbaum was thankful that Dr. Simmons sat on her husband's left hand, as far off from her as possible. She was frankly terrified by the head of the Relief Mission. This lady wore what is known as a 'djibbah', a formless garment which fell from her shoulders to her feet in one straight line. A good deal of coffee- coloured lace was wound rather cheerlessly about her throat. She was even more alarming than she looked. She had already revealed to her hostess that she did not care for food and that she was uninterested in the servant problem, except to think that servants ought to have more freedom and higher wages. She had no children and—in spite of being called a doctor—no husband. When she said she hadn't got a husband, she looked as if she didn't want one. Even Julius was not quite at his ease with her. When he paid her a long and flowery tribute upon her generosity as a Relief worker, she looked at her plate as if she didn't like what was on it, and said in the driest of tones that she was interested in the results of malnutrition. It was a great relief for Frau Mandelbaum to have Sir Roger Colet to talk to, and to observe that he gave his unswerving attention to her rather than to the shocking child on his other side, who had sat on the sofa before dinner (that shrine sacred to the persons of married *Excellenzen*) showing an expanse of French silk stockings (quite unsuitable in a Relief worker) beneath her sheath-like skirt. Carol saw only Sir Roger's rather high shoulder and round red neck, and her notice, insufficiently claimed by these features, rested instead on the sallow sardonic Austrian who had taken her in. He had very thick black eyebrows and was much interested in his soup. Carol was not sure how to begin a conversation with him, so she gave a fleeting glance across the table at poor Dr. Jane Simmons who was trying to discover, without committing herself, if there was the slightest sincerity in the disinterested offers of help her host persisted in thrusting upon her. Jane didn't want to be insular and suspicious, but she had lived long enough in a world, whose corners had struck her as sharp, to distrust at sight any lavish offer of assistance. Rich people of course often did want to help poor ones, sometimes they even (though this was a rarer manifestation of their generosity) knew how to do it, but they seldom proclaimed their intentions with so much insistence the first time you met them. Eugen raised his head abruptly from the mushroom soup. 'That English lady is your friend?' he asked Carol. 'She appears to be in trouble, and I find it wise that she should take that view. It is always well to be a little alarmed when business men take to philanthropy.' 'Yes, she's my friend,' agreed Carol; 'at least I hope she'd say so, but one never knows with the English. They're so kind, half the time you can't tell whether they like you or not.' 'And the other half of the time?' Eugen inquired politely. 'Well—the other half they're just as cold and stand-offish as fish,' said Carol, with decision. 'She says I mustn't call her Jane because I've only known her a month —don't you call that freezing?' 'It seems to me', said Eugen, after a searching glance across the table, 'even stranger that you should wish to call her "Jane". It is a liberty that I should not have ventured upon had our parents vowed us to each other from our cradles.' 'I like to get to know people,' said Carol firmly; 'it's no use trying to be distinguished with me; either I'm all in or I'm all out. With Jane I'd like to be all in. With the Mandelbaums I'm not so sure—by the by, are you any relation to either of them?' Eugen gave a low prolonged chuckle. 'That privilege', he said, 'has been denied me. I have been a fortunate man in many ways. I am as great a stranger in this house as you are yourself, but as I am a good Viennese, and therefore fond of gossip, I could easily tell you the life history of our hosts and their fellow guests.' 'I wish you would,' said Carol eagerly. 'I think life histories are the nicest kind of conversation, don't you? Who wants to know what people think! Do begin with the man opposite, the one who looks like an English Prime Minister—with the high up eyes and the dinky side whiskers?' 'Ah! I see whom you mean,' said Eugen, lifting his glass and screwing it carefully into the socket of his eye and looking fixedly at Otto. 'I know everything about him, so you will excuse me if I tell you very little. Especially as he doubtless hopes to be more communicative himself. He is the cleverest man in Austria. His family have always played a distinguished part in our history. Graf Wolkenheimb himself has been the trusted councillor of Emperors. At the present moment he is explaining to our hostess how to make marmalade which tastes like oranges without using oranges. The rest of his life will probably consist of variations upon this experiment; but I think he will not always be so generous as to explain how he does it! Frau Mandelbaum, whom he is addressing, is a lady who has substantial compensations for one great disadvantage. That disadvantage, as perhaps I need hardly point out to you, sits at the bottom of the table. The lady upon Graf Wolkenheimb's other side is very remarkable. As a young girl she married beneath her; that in itself was an achievement, for her family was already so insignificant that one would not have supposed a mésalliance to be possible. Her husband is one of those men whom nobody notices unless their hats blow off. She has made him a Minister. I understand that she now possesses all that she

44

wants to possess, and that she has never had to pay for it. She is an admirable organizer of Charity; and her generosity in giving to others what she has no further need of herself has made her universally respected. Do you not think that so much orange velvet is a little fatiguing to the eyes?' Carol laughed: it was a clear springing laugh which made Otto glance across the table with appreciation. 'I should think you must have the most unpleasant tongue in Wien,' she said, 'but do go on; you're the only ill-natured Austrian I've met and I'd hate to waste you.' 'You shall not waste me,' said Eugen, with unswerving gravity. 'Beyond the Jewish lady, of whom we have been speaking, is the richest banker in Wien. He has also this to attract your attention: he is, let us hope, the ugliest man in existence. I see you shudder as you look at him. He resembles, does he not, those animals we blush to look on as our relations? Animals who sit in trees and who look pleasanter with a good deal of foliage distributed about their person. His father was a great rascal and made an enormous fortune. The present Baron is a very little rascal; only sufficiently so to retain the fortune left him by his father. Your friend Dr. Simmons is sitting on his other side. It is impossible to tell what any lady so distinguished and intellectual thinks, but we may at least imagine that any passion aroused in her by our worthy host, she will manage to control. We come then to our host himself. I am a deeply religious man, and I prefer not to criticize the works of my Creator. Still one must admit, there has been a little inadvertence somewhere. Perhaps he mistook his rôle and should have appeared on one of the earlier days of creation? One sees him as a wolf, for instance, without that slight effort which is required to accept him in evening clothes. Now we must lower our voices to touch upon my lovely neighbour, although fortunately I have ascertained that she does not talk English. She is just observing that she likes her oysters large and fat, and I think that the subject interests her so deeply that she will not suspect us of talking about her. She is easily the most beautiful of the lower classes of Wien. Her mother married her at sixteen to the banker opposite, whose appearance so greatly attracted you. It was thought that at that age it would not be so startling. All the great bankers of Wien have good-looking wives. This is a mystery which you as a woman can doubtless explain better than a poor little bachelor like myself. The Baronin, however, loves her husband; many interested people have ascertained, and regretted,

45

this extraordinary fact. In Wien beautiful wives are not, thank God, rare; but beautiful wives who love their husbands (the cause for gratitude is even greater) are practically non-existent. We do not encourage such an economy. On the other side of you sits the head of the English Mission. We like him. When we might have suffered even more than we have suffered by the revolution which upset our dynasty, Sir Roger Colet kept us safe by insisting on a general amnesty. It is owing to his efforts that the head which is now at your disposal is not reposing somewhere near Beethoven, in the cemetery which you must visit, even before it is necessary to lay a commemorative offering upon my grave. I could tell you many things rumoured about this Englishman, but I will content myself by saying that he likes good wine, treats women as well as they deserve, and prefers sport to any other religion.' 'And now you may tell me about yourself,' said Carol, meeting his eyes fully. 'Do you say unkind things because you are unhappy, or because you have an unkind heart?' Eugen paused for a moment; the directness of her speech evidently struck him favourably, for he smiled for the first time before he answered her. 'Does not America have to be called in to explain all the little problems of Europe?' he asked her. 'It is enough for me to tell you that I am a nobody, who was once attached to a somebody, and who is now entirely at your service. At the same time I am going to be unselfish enough to suggest that you address a few words to your other neighbour; he is in need of compensation, poor fellow; I see he has just tasted our host's manufactured burgundy. The grapes that went into these bottles appeared in an earlier life as gooseberries.' As Carol obeyed him she again observed Otto's eyes resting on her with approval. 'You seem to admire that girl's dress,' Elisabeth remarked to Otto a little tartly, 'or is it that you like a woman to be shaved like a poodle? This is the third time you have looked across the table at her.' 'It enchants me,' said Otto, 'that you should have taken the trouble to notice my discretion. I do my best, you see, to hide the distraction caused me by your company.' Frau Bleileben shot a glance of suspicion at him out of her tawny eyes. She would have given a great deal—and hers was a nature careful in its generosities—to discover how much meaning lay behind the screen of Otto's philandering. 'When a man always knows what to say, is one not right in supposing that his feelings hardly exist?' she said in a low voice. 'On the contrary,' said

Otto, 'words cover feelings, they do not destroy them. Sometimes they even reveal them. Where is your husband to-night?' 'In Paris,' said Elisabeth dryly, 'pleading the cause of Austria.' 'We shall look for an improvement in our condition then,' said Otto smoothly. 'Your husband's career must be a source of great interest to you?' 'There are women', said Elisabeth, 'who even in this benighted country, might prefer to have a career of their own!' 'That you already have,' replied Otto, 'but it would interest me very much to know if charity implies a private life equally devoted to the cause of morality? One looks at the good English lady over there who appears to unite the virtues of an angel with the garments of some obscure period in history—and one has no doubts. But I find myself as my eyes come back to you—wondering if you are satisfied simply to represent civic virtue?' 'One makes the best of one's convictions,' said Elisabeth. 'I have never pretended to any great love of my kind. I dislike disorder, disease and waste; and I have tried to remedy them. In my private life I do the same.' 'You speak as if no such thing as pleasure existed,' observed Otto thoughtfully. 'Is making the best of one's convictions incompatible with the lighter side of life?' 'To tell you the truth,' said Elisabeth, 'I have my little jokes, but I have very few pleasures. Perhaps I am not easily satisfied, or perhaps my circumstances don't provide me with what I should look upon as pleasures.' 'One can supplement one's circumstances,' said Otto gently. 'Not if one is a woman,' said Elisabeth; 'one's circumstances are bounded by one's married life.' 'But—a—surely', murmured Otto, 'one can supplement one's married life?' Elisabeth shot a keen mocking glance at him. 'Is your suggestion purely benevolent?' she demanded. Otto's eyes lingered on hers for a brief significant moment. 'The purest type of benevolence,' he observed, 'in fact, the only one I am inclined to trust, is the expression of a mutual interest. You are a woman in a million. What could I not have done if I had only had the happiness of meeting you at some freer period of your life!' Elisabeth hesitated. 'If you had met me before my marriage,' she answered, 'you would have tried to do what you are trying to do now. You would have tried to turn my head —and who knows, perhaps you would have succeeded?' 'My heart would have been at your feet,' said Otto softly. 'At how many feet has your heart been already, and at each foot how long has it remained?' Elisabeth demanded. Otto smiled imperturbably. 'As long', he said, 'as the temporary owner had the brains to keep it. You can measure therefore how long in your case my heart would remain. Life is a short period in comparison.' 'You are serious?' asked Elisabeth incredulously. 'I was never more serious,' replied Otto calmly. 'You are the one woman in the world for me. *J'y suis, j'y reste.*' Elisabeth laughed again a little uncertainly, and returned to her dinner. For years she had been the faithful wife of her uninteresting husband. She had made up her mind to make the best of him, and she had made it. It was not a very good best, but she had thought at least all there was of him was her own, and lately she had found that he was hers no longer. His Excellenz Bleileben, infatuated by his sudden promotion, had decided that he was attractive. It was not true, but at that time in Vienna all men who had any fortune were attractive enough. Elisabeth, who flew into rages at the slightest opposition to her domestic sway, was hushed before this tremendous burst of insubordination. She hid her knowledge of it until she had decided upon what course to take. She had been sick of her husband for a long time; she was thirty-eight and there would not be many years left in which being sick of her husband would leave her with any agreeable alternative. Then she met Otto—Elisabeth knew her values. Otto was a real 'piece', belonging to the best period. As a gentleman and an aristocrat he was flawless. It had always been Elisabeth's secret dream to have an aristocratic lover, but only if the advantages were mutual. She did not intend to run any danger of finding herself the weaker party. Her eyes flickered, and her vivid face, with its thick nostrils, slanting eyebrows and lips, became more than ever like that of a slightly excited leopard. 'How does one know what answer to make to such an observation?' she murmured. 'If you do not mean what you say, it is an insult, and if you do mean it—is it any the less an insult?' 'Such an offer on the part of a man of the world to a woman of your capacity', said Otto, 'is a serious compliment. You are a charming and delightful woman. I shall learn much from you, but you will also learn something from me. You see I am quite frank with you. I admit that you have something to learn. A woman without a lover is as incomplete as a sail without a breeze.' 'It is true,' said Elisabeth with sudden humility, 'I have a great deal to learn. I am surprised by your suggestion, but I am not shocked nor am I displeased.' 'I hope I know better', said Otto gently, 'than to make such a suggestion to any woman

whom it would displease. I am neither a Prussian nor a Turk!'
'No,' said Elisabeth, 'but that is what puzzles me. You are an
Austrian noble, and I am a Jewess. I am also a woman of virtue.
My life has not been spent in attracting men, it has been spent in
doing business with them.' 'You shall do business with me too,'
said Otto, smiling, 'but you won't do your business any less well
because I find you attractive.' Elisabeth without answering turned
away for a time to her other neighbour. She talked to the Baron
for ten minutes without her accustomed verve, and as she turned
away Otto observed with satisfaction that Eugen was managing
to entertain the little American very successfully. She had a
charming smile and her hands were dainty and well manicured.
Elisabeth's were overdone; they were not the hands to sustain the
attention they provoked. 'One is rather reversing the order of
things,' Otto said to himself. 'I should have kept the little one, who
is delightful, for my mistress, and Elisabeth who will be very useful, for a wife. Still it would tire me to have too useful a wife.' He
was not impatient for his answer. If it had been unfavourable, he
knew that it would have come earlier—it would, in fact, have
come before his offer had been made. He went on entertaining
his hostess until he was aware that he had kept Elisabeth waiting.
The dessert was on the table; in a moment Julius's sharp green
eyes would be used like missiles in the direction of his wife.
Thirty seconds before this silent signal took place, Otto turned
again to Elisabeth. 'I do not know,' she said in a low voice, 'even
how such affairs take place.' 'But nothing in the world is easier
than to find out,' said Otto, 'and for such a discovery, I put myself entirely at your disposal.' 'Very well then,' said Elisabeth
slowly, 'I consent.'

Frau Mandelbaum sighed luxuriously. She had eaten an excellent dinner, and she sighed partly because she had eaten it and
partly because, since it had been excellent, there would be no
reproaches from Julius. 'I wish,' she said to Otto, as she rose a
little ungracefully from her chair, 'that I had met you before,
Graf Wolkenheimb. It is really wonderful what you told me about
that orange marmalade. It tastes as if it were made of oranges,
and there is no orange in it—nothing but a little lemon peel and
very careful cooking! Wonderful! But I have always said that with
careful management of materials one can do anything.'

VI

The point of the entertainment had arrived. Julius had given the signal to his wife to leave him with Otto and Eugen. The other guests had gone comfortably off in their own motors without infringing upon the sacred petrol which Mandelbaum loathed to put at the disposal of his friends. Six different kinds of inferior liqueur, planted on a rose-painted glass-covered table, and surrounding a gilded box of much advertised cigars, gave to Julius an impression of festive generosity. This was the moment he had longed for; he had fed these two men before him, fed them well, for a particular purpose; now he was going to dictate to them. He stretched his legs out before him and licked his lips with satisfaction. In front of him, with his back to the light, was Otto Wolkenheimb. He had chosen a comfortable chair; his legs were luxuriously crossed; the finger tips of his expressive hands were lightly pressed together; his eyes rested speculatively, but without hope, upon the labels of the liqueur bottles. Eugen seated himself in front of a flaming scarlet sunset, in which a flock of sheep were implicated. He felt, even though his eyes no longer suffered from the glare, as if he had a fire at his back. He smoked one of his own cigars, and looked as remote as St. Simon on his pillar. 'What,' asked Mandelbaum, with a genial grin, 'do you think of the English, Graf? They conquered us on the field—or they paid the French to do it—whichever you like, we shall never know the truth; but what do you think they are up to with this vaunted peace of theirs? I saw you talking for some time with our respected friend, the English Commissioner—about birds, was it not? How his eyes lit up when you mentioned them! Well, how would it be, if under the cover of those very birds we managed to pluck the sportsman himself for our own table?' 'The English,' said Otto, bringing his bright brown eyes back from the liqueur bottles to his host's face, 'are a simple, steady people; not insignificant. Their strength, I fancy, lies in their simplicity. We sharper Europeans can seldom bring ourselves to believe that what stands behind their blunt spoken word is really only a lucky ignorance.

We think their statecraft subtle because it has often in the long run proved successful where ours has failed, but a long study of their character has led me to believe that their policy is merely a series of astonishing blunders, retrieved at the last moment by a supreme common sense. Our theories, on the other hand, are really subtle; we have in them both skill and logic nicely adjusted to meet the dangers we foresee. Our theories will stand anything except practice. When it comes to carrying our policies through, they break down under the stupidity of life. The inadvertence of experience is too much for us. The English imitate the stupidity of life, as certain animals are found unconsciously to take on the protective colouring of their surroundings. We call this imitation hypocrisy, but I do not think it is anything so intellectual as hypocrisy; it is the clock-work instinct of a very strong animal in the moment of danger.' Mandelbaum stirred uneasily. He did not want to listen to abstract reasoning. For one thing he distrusted it intensely, and for another it could be carried on by people like Otto Wolkenheimb as if they were still what they no longer were —at an advantage. Julius wanted to use the man before him because he knew that Otto had his uses. For instance, that very evening how differently Sir Roger Colet had spoken to Otto, without any of that rather formidable politeness with which he addressed Julius! Julius had climbed high, but there were still people whom it was enormously important for him to please, and with whom he wouldn't be able to make his own terms unless they were pleased. But it was one thing for Julius to admit to himself his social inexperience and quite another for Otto to take advantage of it. Otto had got to learn that he couldn't. He was poor, without influence, and naturally unpopular with the Socialists. The pan-Germans hated him; the Christian Socialists—Conservatives though they were—distrusted him, although they feared him even more than they distrusted him. If Julius consented to lighten Otto's poverty and to allow him to take his place in the new order of things, it would only be if Otto consented to leave his top-dog ways behind him. There must be no mistake as to who was master and who was man.

Julius knew that he had just given Otto a dinner that Otto, without straining his resources to the uttermost, couldn't have given him. It was therefore absurd of Otto to sit there looking as if he owned everything in the room and Julius was a man sent for to tune the piano. Julius poured himself out a third liqueur with a steady hand and an ominous brow. Both his guests had tried the liqueur, sipped it and left it. This was an economy; but at the same time it was an insult. Julius knew what his liqueurs were made of, but they were quite good enough for the impoverished aristocrats before him.

'All we want of the English,' he said roughly, 'is for them to sit here, keep order and spend their money; and all that I find necessary to know about them is how to make them do it. The other Allies don't count. France, because she thinks of nothing but how to destroy what is left of Germany, and the Italians, because they can't do us much harm without making the Serbs and Czechs too important for their own interests. They may even do us good, because they wish to expand and may bring capital into the country. They'll ruin the Tyrol of course and destroy Trieste to benefit Venice, but they'll help Wien. To go back to the English. I daresay you wondered why I had those Relief ladies here to-night—the plain one, I mean—the pretty one of course any man would like to have in his house; and keep there! Well, I had my reasons. I'm interested in Relief as much as anybody. It keeps starving people quiet. The state of the child life in Wien is appalling. If something isn't done about it pretty soon the future is going to be handicapped, and we may see a plague that would wipe out half the city. I want Relief brought in. These ladies have solid money behind them. They're worth keeping in with. I've subscribed heavily to their Mission, and I propose to lend them a warehouse for their stores. What puzzled me to-night was that that Dr. Simmons, as she called herself, didn't jump at it. Three times I shoved it into her hands, and she got vaguer and vaguer each time, as if the damned loose-witted hen was thinking of something else! Why the devil didn't she take a perfectly good warehouse offered her for nothing and be thankful?' 'Incredibly generous of you, my dear fellow, to offer it to her for nothing,' said Otto, hiding a yawn; 'I can only suppose a lady so formidable as the one we are discussing has received so few offers in the course of her life, that her first instinct is to refuse. You must return to the charge.' 'The point is,' said Julius bluntly, 'they're going to get a large supply of condensed milk through from Switzerland for the babies, free of all duty. The Swiss are letting them have the milk cheap for the Mission. My idea is to get them to order a larger supply than they need—say twice as much—and hand the surplus over to me at cost price.

What do you say to that for a scheme? Babies aren't hit by it, Mission people score over it, and town people benefit as well— see?' 'Admirable, my dear Mandelbaum,' replied Otto, 'but in your place I should not have offered Dr. Simmons the warehouse quite so insistently.' 'Why not?' asked Mandelbaum, with some heat. 'That lady,' replied Otto thoughtfully, 'whom we might describe as a "female lady of the opposite sex," struck me as having a remarkably hard head. Her manner was no doubt vague, but I should be surprised if her thoughts were anything but clear. I have an idea that she was asking herself whether she wasn't expected to present just such an equivalent in return for your magnificent offer of the warehouse!' 'Well, why not?' Mandelbaum again repeated. 'I tell you the babies don't suffer for it, nor does the Mission. As far as they are concerned it is an absolutely straight deal.' 'Yes, but it is a deal,' said Otto thoughtfully, 'and Anglo-Saxon heads of Relief Missions do not indulge in deals. You see, if the Swiss found out, they would curtail the milk supply.' 'They aren't going to find out,' said Julius impatiently; 'I tell you I know how to do these things! What I don't know how to do is how to handle the Englishwoman. I'm not used to ladies in business, and I'm not sure, as you say, that she'll take my idea in the right way. If one of you fellows would undertake to bring her round to my scheme, I'll see that you don't lose by the transaction.' 'I shall not,' said Eugen, without moving his eyes from the tips of his shoes, on which they had been steadily concentrated, 'connive at playing a trick upon a lady.' 'Even,' asked Otto with his flickering smile, 'if she has the bad taste to resemble a gentleman? It's an entertaining idea of yours, my dear Mandelbaum, very ingenious indeed! Nor am I as particular as my friend. Since we are doing the lady no harm and ourselves positive good, and since we all know that it must be beneficial spiritually to the Swiss to be made a little more charitable sometimes than they intend, I am quite willing to join in your attempt. You are sure, I suppose, that you can avoid all undesirable publicity?' 'Perfectly sure,' said Julius scornfully. 'How do you suppose I have made my fortune—legitimately? People with legitimate fortunes don't keep four motor cars—not in times like these at any rate!' 'I am sure,' said Otto cautiously, 'that you must have used great skill and consummate social tact.' 'Skill—yes,' growled Mandelbaum, 'that kind of thing takes skill. Well, Graf, that's my first offer to you. If that goes through I shall have plenty of little jobs of the same sort in which I can pay you to be useful to me. I don't quite see where your friend comes in if he's so particular, but that's your business, not mine. We never put anything in writing of course, and we keep our mouths shut.' 'My friend,' said Otto, 'is also my legal adviser. The law is so incomprehensible to the lay mind just at present that I hardly care to undertake any project without a legal opinion. I frequently find myself reversing the words of the Apostle to the Gentiles, and saying, "All things are expedient for me but all things are not lawful." A little expert pressure, a little adaptation here and there, and one finds that the law—expands.' Julius nodded; he wasn't quite sure from Otto's manner if he yet grasped his subsidiary position, and he knew he must not put too much emphasis on it at the start. Fine gentlemen had weak stomachs. They couldn't take money unless it came to them out of silk purses; and though they would have to toe his mark, it would be perhaps wiser to let them take the preliminary steps as if they were toeing their own. 'I reckon,' he said contemplatively, 'on making a good deal of money over this milk deal if it comes off, and under the circumstances, if you bring the lady round to giving the double order to the Swiss, I am willing to let you have twenty per cent of the profits.' Julius' sharp eye slewed round upon Otto as he stated his minimum, and he was gratified, although surprised, at Otto's not making any attempt to put up the percentage. It was obvious to him that Otto knew less about business than he had supposed possible. 'Very generous, I am sure,' said Otto pleasantly. 'I can see no reason whatever for my refusing your offer.' Eugen looked up from his boots with a surprise as great as Julius' own. 'With access to your books of course,' Eugen said grimly. Julius gave him a prolonged uneasy stare. 'I'll satisfy you of course,' he said after a pause, 'in the usual manner.' 'I am not easily satisfied,' replied Eugen coldly. 'I choose also my own manner.' 'I am sure,' intervened Otto suavely, 'that when it comes to business you two will understand each other perfectly. I had a little proposition of my own to make, but perhaps it is rather late?' 'For me,' said Julius, 'business is never either too early or too late.' 'Then,' said Otto, waving his hand gracefully towards Mandelbaum, 'I will lay before you the history of my little project. While I was still in power, the owner of an important Armament firm—in which several international financiers of an expert race were also interested—approached me upon one of several possibilities threatened by our military débâcle. It had occurred to this far-seeing gentleman as early as 1916 that it would be as well to draw up plans by which he could avoid the patriotic pleasure of sharing in the results of this débâcle. He therefore first assured himself of the discretion and influence of certain people in Czecho-Slovakia, America and Switzerland. In the event of defeat and the consequent dismemberment of our Empire, the frontier of Austria would naturally pass to the north of his factory area, enclosing it in the relics of our broken country. But if neither the local authorities nor the Austrian Government brought pressure to bear there was no reason why Czechland—which has a not inconsiderable acquisitive instinct—and the high financial experts already mentioned, at work in Allied and neutral countries, should not evade comment and slip the frontier to the south of his works instead of the north. Geography has been known to yield to common sense. The usual historical and sentimental reasons would be forthcoming. The really important point in the negotiations was the passivity of Austria. So important was this point that the gentleman who approached me suggested placing a sum of Swiss francs in a bank in Zurich, in two names, one in the name of a nominee appointed by myself, and the other in that of a reliable acquaintance of his own. The ostensible object of this sum would be to found a branch of his firm for making sporting rifles for the Swiss; and it would pass automatically into the hands of my nominee when the Peace Treaty was signed and the works found themselves secure in Czech territory. I was, however, when this offer was put before me, a servant of the Kaiser, and at that time—a few little qualities—like honour, integrity and patriotism —which one would hardly care to boast of now!—prevented such transactions from taking place. They did not, however, prevent me from looking into the matter. If it should ever be necessary— either as a threat or as a reassurance—I hold the proofs of the offer. Therefore I can at any time produce them to bring about a similar position or—to prevent it. You and I, my dear Mandelbaum, are no longer the trustees of a great Empire, but little birds feathering their not inexpensive nests. May I ask if you have any moral objection to controlling the passivity of Austria?' Mandelbaum grunted. 'What is your offer?' he demanded. 'That's the point.' 'We can, I think,' said Otto, 'very fairly make the same

55

conditions as you have generously offered to me in the Swiss affair. On the success of the undertaking you will receive twenty per cent of the profits, the remainder of which will be my own.' Julius raised his heavy head like an animal under a sudden blow. 'Twenty per cent!' he growled; 'but that is not enough for me! I have the political pull; you cannot hold Austria passive without me! But I can carry the job through without you as soon as I have the names and the details. I should be prepared to give you something for them of course—not a percentage of profits but an agreed sum down. Half a minute will give me time enough to find out the firm! You must remember I shall have to keep the whole Cabinet quiet, and in the House the Pan-Germans will be full of objections. I may have to make concessions of my own—and all you have to do is to give me a few details!'

'I think you underestimate the value of silence,' said Otto indifferently. 'I hold the whip hand of all those who were or will be connected with this offer since should any one act upon it without my participation, I have it in my power to disclose the whole proceeding. I think, upon reflection, you will see that my suggestion of mutual profits is as fair a one as your own. You will soon, I am sure, accustom yourself to handling your fellow ministers. You have nothing else to do; the local authorities have already been successfully approached. The whole affair is a very simple one.' Julius clenched his heavy fist on the table. After all his precautions he had blundered. He had shown his hand first. Why hadn't he waited, and got hold of Otto's project before stating his own? If he took the deal in Otto's teeth, as it were, would Otto dare to break him? That was the worst of men like Otto, they weren't insignificant enough for tools. People listened to them. The English, for instance; they simply must not know that Mandelbaum as a Minister took—well—not exactly bribes, call them 'recognitions.' If only he knew what Otto would dare if he braved him. Or what he could use on his side as a make-weight against Otto. If only he could read that indifferent ironic face, if only he could force that delicate manicured hand to lay its cards upon the table. Otto smiled pleasantly. 'But really,' he said, rising to his feet, 'we are staying unconscionably late! Wasting your valuable time, my dear Mandelbaum! Pray excuse us for prolonging so delightful an evening! And assure your wife once more for us that we are more than grateful for her charming entertainment. Ah!

you are more fortunate than I, all your powers are reinforced by the pleasures of domesticity!' Julius gave a grin that might have passed for a smile. 'I can spare time,' he said a little awkwardly, 'for your project. Perhaps we might raise the milk business to thirty per cent profits, if what you suggest is practicable and worth half profits to me to carry out.' 'You are too generous,' said Otto, without sitting down again. 'But I prefer to keep to your original offer, and to make it the basis of my own. For the future we might lay our hands upon the table and make half profits our working policy. We should then know exactly how we stood, and our interests would be identical. But since the first of these projects is undeniably your own, and the second mine, it would be unfair for me to ask an advance upon your original offer; nor do I feel anxious to enlarge my own.' Julius cleared his throat. 'I also,' he said, 'believe in going slowly. Of what do the profits in this Armament deal consist?' 'My dear Mandelbaum,' murmured Otto gently, 'do you not think that the indulgence of curiosity should be a mutual pleasure? Am I to understand that you intend to enlighten us upon what you expect to gain from the Swiss project? Of course, if you are—? No? I see by your open countenance that you are not! I entirely agree with you! When we are acting on half profits we will make our revelations as mutual as our interests; but in these two little affairs—in which we only provide helping hands—we will remember the scriptural injunction, and keep those selfless members each from knowing what the other one does!' Julius Mandelbaum's eyes became flat in his head, and all expression faded out of them. 'Good, gentlemen!' he said after a long pause. 'I agree; but why the devil doesn't this firm of yours come to *me* now I am in power?' 'A question of habit,' Otto murmured, 'no doubt. A question of looking for authority where authority no longer exists. It will pass, as all our errors pass, into the purifying ocean of democracy!' Julius looked up sharply; he felt that Otto was laughing at him, but Otto was looking particularly grave. 'We are your debtors,' he said, meeting Julius' suspicious eyes, 'for a truly interesting occasion.' Eugen bowed with his heels together, the deep perfunctory dip of military training, and Julius took them to the front door himself. He afterwards remembered that it would have been more dignified to ring for a servant, but he would in that case have missed the satisfaction of watching his two guests descend into his rain-soaked garden. They had no car, and it was an inclement night.

Before they reached the twisted iron gates at the bottom of the short drive, Eugen spat fiercely on the ground. 'All that,' he said bitterly, 'leaves a very bad taste in the mouth, Otto!' But Otto paid no attention to his companion's feelings. A smile hovered around the corners of his mobile lips. 'That was a damned good phrase of mine, you know, Eugen,' he murmured, 'about the purifying ocean of democracy.'

VII

When Elisabeth returned from her dinner at the Mandelbaums' the look of the things in her room irritated her; she felt as if each piece of furniture was an attack upon her nerves. The furniture stood there, because it couldn't stand anywhere else; there would be no room for it. Her rooms were like Elisabeth Bleileben's life; she had chosen her life for herself, but it had stifled and cornered her. At eighteen, passion had caught her in a flood there was no resisting; it had thrown her violently (against the wishes of her relations) into the arms of a tall, handsome Jew with soft coffee-brown eyes, great fluidity of expression, and a belief in himself which had impressed Elisabeth, before she realized that self-confidence is a gift without integrity. It was twenty years since she had this fit of passion, and she had been so horrified by the want of judgement which had plunged her into so shallow a stream that she had resisted every subsequent attack upon her emotions. She felt that she knew love for what it was: a fierce and uneasy impulse that came upon her in gusts of feeling for three or four years after her marriage, and then, appalling and quite final, satiety. She did not want anything more to do with Wilhelm Bleileben. She skipped him daily, as if he were a leading article in a newspaper. Even if something unusual had happened to him, she wouldn't have had the patience to wade through it word by word. The only emotion which had remained to Elisabeth was an occasional desire to slap the two small flaxen-haired girls, dreadfully colourless and good, with whom Providence had blessed her.

She was brought up to believe that a woman's sphere is the home, and for several stormy years Elisabeth limited herself to this form of activity. Both she and Wilhelm liked rich, well-cooked food and rooms filled with hard bright furniture. Elisabeth saw that, within the means provided for her, the food was richer, the rooms more violently shining, her own clothes and the children's more brilliantly dedicated to checks and stripes, than any of her circle could afford. From morning to night Elisabeth's brilliant eyes, her harsh voice and her pouncing wits harried her servant and transfigured the house. Wilhelm was deeply satisfied with her domesticity; and in time the monumental quality of his self-complacence aggrieved and finally disillusioned Elisabeth. She no longer wanted a model home; besides, when she had thoroughly outstripped all her contemporaries, she began to long for new fields of competition. Wilhelm made no more money than he had made when they were first married; and Elisabeth saw that nothing fresh could be done without money.

It was then that she chanced upon a real brain. Max Cohen, a consumptive cousin of her mother's, came from Poland to Vienna to start a wholesale business in furs. Elisabeth took trouble over Max Cohen. She found out what he was really like—how much his brain was worth and how far his constitution would be likely to carry him. After several months' impassioned wrangling she drove her husband into partnership with him. Elisabeth was thirty, and she still believed that a woman's sphere is the home. But she kept an absorbed eye upon Max and the wholesale furs. The two men talked business with her every evening. They fed on her organizing and enlightening brain, and if her ideas seemed to be produced from the small tartan frocks that she was making for her daughters, they nevertheless inspired transactions between Archangel and New York. Max swiftly acknowledged her powers and revelled in them. Wilhelm took personal credit for all her designs and acknowledged nothing but the tartan frocks.

It was her horror of his pride in her for being an ideal wife and mother that drove Elisabeth into the business world. She learned secretly from Max all the practical handling of their business, bookkeeping, and the laws and evasions of trade. She fitted herself for a business career without Wilhelm's discovering that she no longer had time to make home-made jam; and when she had done this she half consciously let Max Cohen die. Over and over again she could have saved him. All he needed at first was a winter at Davos; even a reprieve from the harsh winds and dusts of Vienna would have extended his short career. He was sanguine, and Elisabeth played on his hope. He was consumingly ambitious, and she never for a moment failed to keep his ambitions ablaze. They were making more and more money, and she encouraged Max to believe that he was indispensable to the golden flood. She helped him to ignore all his warning symptoms until he suddenly found himself face to face with death. Nothing he could do was any good then, but Elisabeth herself, carefully chaperoned by an old aunt, took him up into the mountains to the best sanatorium in Austria. There he had all the things which could have saved him earlier: well-cooked wholesome food; the scent of pines; the clean air of the snows; Elisabeth's untiring and quite magnificent nursing. Max Cohen was a brilliantly clever man, but he died believing Elisabeth Bleileben was the best woman in the world and leaving her his share of the fur business. Elisabeth felt the loss of his intellectual companionship deeply; but she now had money of her own.

After a year's careful investigation, she forced her husband to sell the business at a staggering profit, and made him (with the capital at their disposal) the director of a bank. The war broke out, and Elisabeth launched herself into war charities; her organizing talents gave her immediate influence, and won for her at least an outward association with the most exclusive aristocracy in the world. Whatever she touched succeeded, and ran, if not smoothly (for Elisabeth had a passionate temper and used it with dismaying frequency), swiftly and with pecuniary advantage. She often made social blunders, she often antagonized when she should have pleased, and her fellow workers abhorred and feared her; but she never made any business mistakes. Her accounts were impeccable. When the era of starvation set in, inexplicably (but without a stain on her character) she continued to feed Wilhelm, the little girls and herself upon rich and totally unprocurable food. Perhaps Mandelbaum knew how she managed it; she supplied all her war charities from Mandelbaum's firm, and after the Breakdown Mandelbaum's influence secured her husband his startling promotion to the Ministry.

Wilhelm Bleileben, hardly believing in his own good fortune, was tiresomely certain that he deserved it. Elisabeth, whose father had been a pawnbroker (she spoke of him as having been a collector of antiques), was now addressed as 'Excellenz' and sat always on the sofa.

She had succeeded beyond her wildest dreams; everything had helped her, from the delicacy of Max Cohen's constitution to the calamity of the European war; and yet Elisabeth was not satisfied. Something which she could not define eluded her. She had yearnings which the small choked flat at the corner of the Ring did nothing to appease. Something was vaguely wrong with the flat. It smelled too much of food; the collected treasures of a lifetime turned up too often. The two good little girls were as good as ever, but they had become menacingly larger. They took up too much room; so did Wilhelm Bleileben. They were rich enough to afford a larger flat, but wouldn't a larger flat be simply more of the same thing? Was it so much size she wanted as a difference in the quality of life? At thirty-eight one begins to ask whether what one has got is really what one wants. One asks oneself this question with an uneasiness more urgent than in earlier periods of doubt. Elisabeth had not a contemplative mind, but she was accessible to fact; she seldom deceived herself. She saw that what she had not done she had very little time to do—and that what she was not, with all her magnificent energy and ruthless will, it was improbable that she would become. She had touched the end of her personal resources.

It was in this time of intellectual instability that her husband became unfaithful to her and that Elisabeth first met Otto Wolkenheimb. The first of these two incidents, although it came too late to reawaken her interest in her husband, gave her a queer mental shock. It showed her that she had less power than she thought she had. Elisabeth had been an extraordinarily useful and faithful wife to Wilhelm and, she had supposed, genuinely attractive; and yet it hadn't been enough for him. Ten years earlier she had been Max Cohen's friend, never anything more than his friend, but it had been enough for Max Cohen; it had riveted him to his bachelorhood. He said to her once, 'Elisabeth, I am not in love with you, but you entirely prevent my falling in love with anyone else. After you, I should find any other woman dull.' Hitherto Elisabeth had not had her virtue greatly tempted. She was too busy to be tempted, and perhaps, she told herself harshly, not attractive enough. She challenged men's minds before she invaded their senses, and nothing keeps a man's senses so silent as the attack of an intelligent woman upon his wits.

Elisabeth had known that money was the first thing to procure, and she had procured it; but money did not in itself satisfy Elisabeth; even the power which she obtained by it did not satisfy her. What she wanted (she saw it plainly the night of the Mandelbaums' dinner) was beauty; a beauty not wholly material, but which she could use materially in her daily life. She wanted before she died to be surrounded by something finer than she had—more delicate and with more taste. She had recognized the charm of Otto Wolkenheimb with a bitter humility. His ease, his intricate lightness, were qualities she hadn't got. Perhaps Elisabeth might have been content—if it hadn't been for the war—with a simpler outlook in which virtues were essential and manners were not. But her charities had thrown her with the aristocracy, and she had found in them something which she couldn't buy. She knew far more about business than they did, but they knew something which wasn't business and yet which gave them a kind of power. Couldn't she acquire this secret knowledge? She asked herself the question breathlessly as she sat in her small florid bedroom rejoicing for the moment in its being silent and unshared.

Elisabeth had no continuous privacy. She was forced by want of space and her husband's traditional horror at marital separation to share a room with him. Out of this led that of the two little girls. She could hear them getting up in the morning and their nightmares if they had any at night. They could hear—with the dreadful superiority of childhood—the bitter altercations which took place with unstudied frequency between their father and mother.

She got up impatiently, and went into the room of Paula and Marie. There they were as usual, round rosy cheeks on white pillows, neatly plaited colourless hair tied with thick white ribbons. She turned up the shaded light on the little night tables and regarded each in turn dispassionately. 'Ugh! why did I ever have them!' she exclaimed disgustedly before she clicked off the light and returned to her own room. Elisabeth had been a good mother to Paula and Marie; even now, if they had suffered from anything, she would have swooped to their assistance. In all their childish illnesses she had been an indefatigable nurse; but they gave her no feeling of intimacy. They belonged altogether to their father's side of the family. Elisabeth had never once surprised wildness in their mild blue eyes nor any desire for adventure in their blameless careers. Their occasional naughtiness took the form of feeble greed or feeble laziness, never of rebellion. But as a rule they were not naughty, they were dreadfully, dismally good and as self-complacent as only good little girls can be. They reminded Elisabeth of her husband, only they were worse because after all Wilhelm was a man. He sometimes swore and once he had boxed his wife's ears. For half an hour it had nearly reawakened Elisabeth's affection for him; then he returned with his tail between his legs and apologized. Elisabeth never forgave him his apology.

She sat down on the edge of her bed and swept her husband out of her mind with as much ease as she had disposed of the little girls. Nobody in life held her back from what she meant to do. Nor did she have any conviction of sin. Elisabeth went to church three or four times a year, but she believed in nothing. There was only one real obstacle to her escape from morality; she had been respectable for thirty-eight years. She undressed slowly, looking with a new distaste at the monograms in the centre of the pillowslips, the buttoned sheets and thick red silk eiderdowns. It was difficult to get away from these domestic symbols; they did not seem to go with a life of sin. Elisabeth was not afraid of discovery; two clever people, neither of them impulsive or young, can easily outwit a fool. Everything would go on the same outwardly; no intimacy existed to challenge this new supremacy. There would still be the crowded little flat with its solid silver picture frames and bright maple wardrobes; washstands that made washing a necessity and not an art; and a looking-glass that seemed to accentuate the dinginess of duty on winter mornings; but her mind would no longer be there—it would be safely afloat in large mysterious rooms—rooms in which everything had a history as well as a use, and nothing was definitely bright; soft, silent rooms, through which her own voice—distorted and nerve-racked—had never set its harshness. That was what she wanted, not to be harsh any more, not to be violent or vulgar, but to find a place in her own heart where she could be at peace. She was so often turned out of her imagination by the crass materialism of her daily life. But if this was what she longed for it was also what she feared. Would she, when she entered into this region of delicacy and beauty, be fit for it? Wouldn't her own ruthlessness and brutality spoil for her the very experience for which she longed? Wasn't she too old to change? It would be so wonderful not to shout any more, never to tear through intercourse as if it were a crowded street with a flying 'bus to be caught at the other end. Would she be able *not* to chivy and bustle her companion, and above all not to sour her own feelings with suspicion and distrust? She wanted so passionately to be happy, happy not only in her circumstances but in her strong and wayward heart. She had been everything else. She had enjoyed grim moments of triumph over the wills of others, she had felt the agitated relief of giving way to paroxysms of anger, but neither her strength nor her achievements had brought her peace. To have a lover—now, when she was conscious of this inner trembling of the heart, this fear of the finish of things! To start afresh upon the path of youth with all the sanity of experience and with the intimacy of a man who could give her what no-one else had ever given her: considerate understanding and delicious friendliness! Was not such an adventure worth any risk? It would take the taste out of these stagnant nineteen years of Wilhelm, his shaving, his teeth-brushing, his dreadful little habits and arrangements, and the possibility of a conversation which often ended in a row, simply because Elisabeth could not get away until she had done her hair. Her married life unrolled itself before her like a limp and ravelled elastic; there was no longer any grip in it. She must let it go—and with it that iron lump of respectability to which she had been for so long pointlessly attached. Let her be young and gay and free as she had never been—and then let Nemesis come in any form it liked! She would not mind Nemesis once she had had her fling! But she could not help asking herself why did Otto want her? Perhaps because the world was new—and its newness belonged to her class and her type? Otto was a survival; he had as much to learn from her as she had to learn from him, and after all it might be the truth when he said that he had never met any woman like her before. The aristocracy were mortally dull. Elisabeth had not seen much of them, but she had seen enough to know that, if they had not belonged to the most exclusive society in the world, no-one would have wanted their company. Their style was perfect, but few of them had anything beyond their style. Elisabeth swore to herself that she would give Otto a good time—if he gave her one!

She would throw under his feet the pick of her brain and all the fruits of her experience. Suddenly, inexplicably, Elisabeth buried her head in her fat little second pillow and wept a few very small, very astounding tears. She wept because she was not young, because she wanted beauty, and because she wondered if after all she was not too stiff and too tough to be moulded, as she wished to be moulded, by those delicate fingers which had hitherto known only the most delicate and precious of human substances.

VIII

As Otto Wolkenheimb strolled to and fro in his library, he was intensely conscious of the effect of his background. He was not easily impressed by backgrounds; but he was vividly conscious of the impressions they made upon others. He knew that, to anyone who lived in a dingy little room, the lofty ceiling with its beautifully moulded cornices would give a bewildering sense of space; and he was glad that the splendid crystal candelabra shone like some trophy from a palace. The room was free of little things, and the few pictures (dull, Otto personally considered) had good names attached to them and were satisfactorily darkened by the tone of time. Seen through the large north windows, the towers of the Votiv Kirche occupied the vacant space between the bookshelves and his old English writing desk as if they were part of his furniture. Otto leaned out of the open window and looked down upon the broad glistening avenue of the Universitätsstrasse, across the gardens to the pink crenellated barracks and over countless irregular roofs to the distant blue hills. The air came fresh from the Wiener Wald, and carried with it a breath of pines. It stirred in Otto memories of his home at Trauenstein. Otto loved his home, but he loved it with a certain impatience. It had been spoiled for him, like everything else he valued, by the changes of the Breakdown. His peasants no longer revered and admired him. They claimed as rights what he had given them as privileges or what he would have given them as privileges if he had been rich enough to afford his own instincts of generosity. What Otto disliked most about the new order of things was the way in which it upset his sense of his own virtues. He knew that he was a generous and considerate landlord; but when he was suddenly pinched and driven by the loss of more than half his fortune, was it the moment for his peasants to rise up and chivy him into allowing them the same indulgence which (in the goodness of his heart) he had conceded to them in the days of his prosperity? Yet his peasants entirely ignored the goodness of his heart—they said they were ruined too, and they demanded higher wages and lower rents. In many cases Otto had had to give way or lose their labour altogether, but the struggle had cost him his amiability and left him with no desire to revisit Trauenstein unless he should once more become its master. He strolled back from the window and looked with sardonic eyes at the Oriental vases full of expensive flowers which he had ordered to welcome the first visit of Elisabeth Bleileben. He knew that she would like expensive flowers: mauve orchids and strong-smelling lilies. Otto had studied women all his life with an untiring pertinacity. He understood their differences of time and type.

Elisabeth had the disadvantage of her years; but she had also the acquiescences. She would take things for granted, and be grateful for what she got. In his relations with women Otto was seldom dominated by passion; not at least by a passion for the women themselves. The passion which ruled him was a much deeper affair, and women were merely its priestesses. The master passion of Otto's life was his deep personal vanity. Each new woman, over whom he acquired the influence of possession, showed him himself afresh. They were like a series of mirrors in a magic gallery; from each one he flashed back upon himself at a different angle. He was at his best when he came fresh to a love affair. As time went on repetition dulled the brightness of his image. It was an effort to appear always charming and never to take the ease of a moment's selfishness. Generally Otto became quickly disillusioned with the uninspired Priestess who allowed the reproduction of himself to fade. There was no woman with whom he could always be so interesting as in the first half-hour of their intimacy. Sooner or later her attention waned or she advanced some awkward claim of her own and spoiled the delicacy of his romance. It had been Otto's experience that women were less disinterested than men. Their very sympathies had tentacles with which to grasp more effectually what they wanted. It was a pity, Otto often felt, that he was forced by his fastidious nature into taking a sentimental view of love. It would have been far simpler if, like most men, he had been purely sensual. The attitude of the gourmand is always much less expensive than that of the gourmet and on the whole more satisfactory. Material gratifications are not exhilarating, but they frankly cure simple wants by simple remedies. The trouble with Otto was that he had not got any simple wants. This business of Elisabeth Bleileben, for instance, stuck in his throat. He knew what he could give her; and he knew that besides the substantial gain to his fortune he would get a certain amount of interest, even a certain amount of pleasure, from the effect he was going to produce upon Elisabeth. She was going to be very useful to him, and as a reward he was going to transform her life. He felt no scruples at all in persuading her to give up her respectability; on the contrary the thought of her discarded virtue, preserved for thirty-eight years, exceedingly amused him; but the fact that he was about to make love to a woman who scarcely attracted him struck him with acute shame. 'Interest! Interest!' he muttered disconsolately to himself as he looked down at the curved sinister leaves of the mauve orchids. 'Isn't that after all a little too base? To place one's kisses like fortunate investments? No! Eugen is right. There is something very ugly in this new life after all! But we must live—we must live, and if one is to live at all, it must be comfortably!' Otto heard the distant thrill of an electric bell, and a moment later Elisabeth was announced.

In an instant his facile, dramatic mind had changed. He was back in the magic gallery of mirrors again seeking once more, with the old eagerness, the charm of his new presentment.

Elisabeth came forward slowly, a little timidly, into the great room. It was, as she had expected, very quiet and mysterious. The forms and colours of the furniture were too harmonious to catch the eye; they seemed to withdraw themselves from any intrusion upon the inhabitants and melt into a common background. Only the heavily scented flowers with their strange tortured outlines impressed themselves vividly upon her senses. The room seemed full of old silences, broken long ago by voices different from her own. The distance between her and Otto Wolkenheimb felt insurmountable. In another moment he was beside her laughing down into her eyes. Elisabeth was grateful that he attempted no embrace. He kissed her hand gallantly and lightly, and led her to the corner of the sofa which Rosalie had for so long adorned. He did not do this purposely to introduce a comparison, but because it was the most becoming seat in the room for a woman who had reached an age when she looked her best with her profile merged into the background of cushions. But when Otto saw Elisabeth there he thought of Rosalie, and the thought pricked him suddenly and made it difficult to keep the light of admiration in his eyes. Fortunately this was a woman of intelligence, and Otto could appeal first to her brain. He made her laugh, and he made her say something to make him laugh. Slowly the immensity of the distance between them grew less. Otto gave her tea, beautifully scented Russian tea, and her nerves sank into quiet. Then bit by bit Otto built up her confidence in herself. He made her forget that her clothes were not what he was used to; that she was just a funny little Jewess, and that no funny little Jewess had ever penetrated into this room before; and as her sense of value increased in her own eyes, the importance of her respectability waned. Otto's laughing face seemed to say to her through the screen of his careful speech, 'My dear child, it's such a little thing, isn't it? Less, I assure you, than the difference between having a cup of tea or doing without.' Whether he talked to Elisabeth of the awful conditions of Vienna or of the amusing domestic complications of the Mandelbaums did not matter; it was what, under the veil of words, he was doing for her that mattered, and—even more—that Elisabeth understood triumphantly what this was and let herself go to meet it. She was not too old or too stiff, after all, for that delicate manipulation. He was making her what he wanted, and she was going on with it to the end. If she had any ruthlessness left (and it really seemed to Elisabeth as if it had all melted away like the last patch of snow on the mountains under an insidious sun) it lay in the fact that nothing—nothing on earth—should prevent her from going on with this experience to the end. Her eyes met his brilliantly, provocatively. Suddenly they stopped talking. The room filled once more with silences that were not their own. But Elisabeth's intensity broke through the alien silences; it seized upon Otto with a force that brought him to his feet. He stood in front of her biting his lips and smiling; then very gently he laid his hands on her shoulders. Elisabeth stood up to face him. She was not swept off her feet, she was drawn very slowly off them, but the force of her own feeling made her unaware of how anything took place. She only knew that her consent was there. Far, far deeper than Otto's demand was Elisabeth's consent. The passion that met Otto was so fierce that for a moment it lighted his own. There was no mistaking the image in this particular mirror; it shone upon him as if he were a god. He held his breath at the sudden exposure of his beauty; and then, like Narcissus, he plunged into the fateful waters to clasp his own image to his heart.

IX

They were no longer strangers going carefully towards each other over a long and difficult road; they might have known each other all their lives.

Elisabeth explored his rooms with an intense and joyous curiosity; only a few of them were inhabited; their size made them too expensive to keep warm. The shining domed salon was empty, but beyond it Otto's bedroom and bathroom were like a scene in a fairy tale. For the first time Elisabeth saw what luxury was like. Not the luxury which can be procured for large sums in first-class hotels, but a luxury evoked from centuries of cultivated habits. 'I see now why you're so good-tempered,' laughed Elisabeth. 'You can move about in peace without tripping over somebody else's boots and shoes! *Mein Gott!* Marriage!' 'You don't appear to approve of that ancient and venerable institution?' Otto asked with amusement. Elisabeth shrugged her shoulders. 'For the very young, the very simple, or the very good,' she said, 'perhaps— the alternatives are so excessively poor or so romantically risky— but for a woman of my age and my intelligence, I ask you! Why, it is like living in a thimble with a hippopotamus!' 'But if one possesses rather a large thimble,' suggested Otto, 'and is slim— as hippopotami go—what then?' 'Even then it would be the same!' replied Elisabeth frankly. 'I have had nineteen years of one man. Is it asked of me to have nineteen years of pork chop? Oh, I know all about the beauty of constancy—especially in wives! I have practised it. There is something sacred, is there not, in always sitting in one chair, always kissing one cheek, always darning the same socks and watching the same kind of tempers arise over the same kind of irritations? Or in knowing how one is expected to please and in forcing oneself to do so? There are some kinds of women who are meant for wives; to feel sure that nothing is going to happen to-morrow which has not happened to-day satisfies them. I was unfortunate; I chose my career too soon. This is the first time I have breathed—literally breathed—for all these wasted years; and, *mein Gott!* I mean to go on breathing!' A cold sensation crept down Otto's spine. Elisabeth's voice had sunk into a guttural dangerous sound. Her eyes were fixed on him like the eyes of a wild creature sure of its prey. Was she not perhaps too sure? Otto had never been anyone's prey before, and no woman had ever been sure of him with impunity; but if they had had in the end to show how they could get on without him, they had had the tact not to make him suffer for it—beyond the passing inconvenience caused him by his naturally sympathetic nature. There was something in Elisabeth's deep voice and in her sly keen eyes which made Otto uncomfortably aware that if she had to suffer it would not be alone. She would show no graceful feminine decency in her retirement. If she had to retire at all she would drag with her, not without noise and fury, as much of the broken situation as she could carry; and there would be no decency left. Fortunately the end of the situation was a long way off. The beginning had gone very well; but without too much hurry Otto wanted to deflect their tête-à-tête to business. The continued absence of Excellenz Bleileben in Paris was a convenience for the moment though Otto foresaw that his return might perhaps become an even greater convenience.

They settled once more in the library. The last light of the dying day lingered clear and chill above the rounded hills of Leopold and Kahlenberg. Once more Otto drew in a breath of the fragrant frosty air which seemed to come from pine forests of long ago. 'It blows cold,' said Elisabeth; 'these great empty rooms at dusk are full of shadows. Have you a ghost here?' 'Yes,' said Otto, closing the window. 'I have a ghost; but she will not disturb us.' A bitter smile played round the corners of his lips. His ghost had haunted him for many years, but she was discreet. No-one had ever seen her but himself. He muttered half under his breath as he turned to bring cigarettes to Elisabeth, a line of the strange little English poem 'I have been faithful to thee, Cynara, in my

70

fashion——' 'What do you say?' asked Elisabeth. 'What cigarettes you possess, you bachelors! These must be made of gold.
I am sure that you said something in English, a language I
do not very readily understand.' 'Only a little tribute to my
ghost,' said Otto, smiling. 'The only perfectly quiet woman I
have ever known! These are my friend Eugen's cigarettes—in
his dislike of Jews he allies himself with the most select of Turks—
and these cigarettes are the result.' There was a moment's silence.
'I am a Jew,' said Elisabeth in a low voice, 'not by religion—for
I have none—but by race. You think of us, I suppose, as your
cousin the Baron does—as dirt—dirt beneath your feet!' 'My dear
Elisabeth,' said Otto quickly (he was sincerely distressed at his
own tactlessness), 'I think so little on such a subject that, as you
see, I can afford to share with you the poorest of jokes about it!
Yesterday perhaps questions of race counted for something in
Austria—to-day, believe me, they weigh less—less than the ash
from this cigarette! Do not distress me by giving way to such re-
actionary ideas. What does it matter to me what your family is?
We are both independent and modern—we belong to ourselves.'
'Say rather to each other,' said Elisabeth in a moved voice, 'for I
feel since I came into this room as if I were born afresh and belonged wholly to you.' Otto bent forward and raised her hand to
his lips. It was necessary to their partnership that Elisabeth should
have this feeling, but he hoped that she would not express it too often.

Then he introduced carefully and very lightly the subject of
business. It surprised him to find how instantly Elisabeth responded to his signal. The light of passion still shone in her dark
narrowed eyes, but her softness fell away from her. She became as
sharp and pointed as a rapier. Her wits, he assured himself, were
really magnificent, and she showed him at once that they were
completely at his service. It was not necessary to hoodwink her,
but if it had been necessary, would it have been easy? Elisabeth
had loved him for barely an hour; but she had done business all
her life. She told him how she had invested her own fortune. A
part of it had gone to win her husband his position as director in
one of the foremost Viennese banks. The rest of it she had placed
in Mandelbaum's business. It was a private transaction between
Mandelbaum and herself; not even her husband knew of it. Their
connection paid them both; and to it her husband owed his position as a Minister. 'People talk such nonsense about honesty,'

71

Elisabeth explained. 'Of course one must be honest! How else can one be trusted, and without confidence how can one exploit the public? Honesty is as necessary as fat! One cannot cook without fat, but one may be paid for butter and use fat instead, which is a considerably cheaper commodity, and indulge oneself with the difference between the two prices. Every penny of what has been given me for charity I have used for charity, but I have used it in a business way, and made here and there substantial profits for myself. Necessarily you will do the same. With Mandelbaum's assistance I have guided my husband into several profitable transactions, but Mandelbaum is a Jew. I neither like nor trust him— oh, yes, there is something to be said for your prejudices when it comes to the Mandelbaums of our race! And my husband is a fool! I am therefore always on the *qui vive* to save ourselves from being robbed. I suggest, therefore, without Mandelbaum's knowing what we are doing, that you take his place with my husband. What he can do as a Minister you know better than I do and as well as Mandelbaum; you will help him to do it, and naturally share in the profits! Do not drop Mandelbaum, however; he is not a safe person to drop. I shall excuse the withdrawal of my husband from his influence by using Wilhelm's vanity against Mandelbaum. Mandelbaum has no tact; he can easily be made to offend my husband and not so easily to excuse himself. It will seem to him that the estrangement is entirely my husband's doing, and as long as I continue to be his friend he will suspect nothing. This is my affair; I know how to manage such things. Now, about the milk deal. How do you propose to work it?' Otto leaned back in his chair and smoked reflectively. In the subtly diffused light Elisabeth looked remarkably well. Otto could just see her vivid eyes; her strongly marked features were attractively vague, and her conversation was really much more interesting than he ever remembered Rosalie's to have been. Nevertheless Otto rather disliked the assured tone—almost the tone of authority—with which Elisabeth handled business questions. 'Do we not go too fast?' he murmured. 'You are the first woman I ever made love to—who talked business. I must get used to the sensation!' 'Do you dislike it?' Elisabeth asked quickly. She hoped with anguish that he did not dislike it—for it was all she had to offer him that was different from the offerings of other women more fortunately endowed. 'Not at all,' said Otto soothingly; 'I find it very agreeable. The resemblance between making love and making money never appeared to me before to be so close or so desirable. Usually we take elaborate precautions to keep the two pursuits apart. It is very restful to take no precautions at all and watch them rush together as naturally as two raindrops on a pane. A charming American poetess once wrote, ''Love, when we met, 'twas like two planets meeting!'' Noisy, I thought, for the affections alone, but delicious if it is meant to describe the amalgamation of fortunes and affinities.' There was nothing in what Otto said to act as a reproof to Elisabeth, but she was faintly conscious that in describing to him her business methods she had felt herself the more practical of the two; and it occurred to her now that when they next talked business it would be as well not to appear quite so efficient. 'As to the milk affair,' Otto continued lightly, 'I suppose it to be a simple question of tact. I can't myself undertake to handle the English lady at the head of the Relief Mission. She doesn't want to be made love to. She doesn't like being admired. It is out of my power to intimidate her even if I had the desire to do so—which God forbid! Nor can I at this moment offer her anything for her Mission more satisfactory than my very good wishes. You are in a position to do better. Can you not suggest that she should buy a double quantity of this Swiss milk and hand over half to you for your charities, receiving instead, if she wishes to receive anything instead, some facility which you in turn can offer her? You can then hand over the milk to our friend Julius and receive its equivalent for your good works? It will be a delightful interview, and I regret that I cannot be present. You both have such strong heads—but as she has only one idea and you have several, I hope that the final laurels will rest upon your brow. If they do not—I must try my hand on the young American. She runs in and out of all the Relief Committees in turn, and her enthusiasm, backed by American dollars, might prove useful to us.' 'Would it not be best,' asked Elisabeth after a perceptible pause, 'to apply first to this young girl—myself?' Otto took another cigarette, wandered towards the door and turned on a delicately shaded lamp. 'I can see you better now,' he said approvingly. 'Have you tried how delightful you would look in black, a diamond or two, and a little white chiffon? Few women are striking enough in themselves to stand black and white. You must come with me to-morrow to a little place I know of where we can pick up an effect or two. You are difficult to dress, and I fancy you haven't given enough time to it, but it would be worth it, my dear Elisabeth, I assure you, it would be worth it!' 'I will come wherever you like, and you shall choose for me,' said Elisabeth humbly. 'But about the little American girl, shall I not go to her myself?' Otto shook his head. 'I think not,' he said reflectively; 'you see we must if possible have the head of the English Mission working with us. It is only in the last resort that I shall approach Miss Hunter. I fancy a young girl is more impressed by the appeal of a man of my age than by the appeal of another woman cleverer and more attractive than herself. And now, my dear Elisabeth, let us talk no more about business! It is a subject one can easily have too much of. Let us talk about yourself!' Otto was standing behind her, and as he spoke he flung down his cigarette, took her head in both his hands and drew it back until his lips reached hers. He did not much enjoy kissing Elisabeth upon this occasion; but, for the moment, it settled satisfactorily the question of the little American girl.

X

There were fifty men and women collected in the big Mission rooms, having tea at large kitchen tables after a long day's work, and Elisabeth came in among them like a tropical bird disturbing a colony of rooks. She regarded her fellow-workers with impatience: was it coming out to Austria for Relief work that affected the way their hair grew on their heads? It was sensible of the women to wear serge skirts and sports jackets, but need they wear such serge skirts and such sports jackets? Must their noses always shine? Did kind hearts always go with unbecoming flushes, and altruism find itself at home only with the forgotten waists of women and the bottle necks of men? Elisabeth was pleasantly aware that she did not look in the least like a Relief worker. Never had she seen so many middle-aged women so little conscious of any necessity to please and yet so perversely ready to be pleasant. They had given up their homes; come many hundreds of miles; diminished their incomes; they were living uncomfortably in holes and corners on tinned foods and all in order to benefit mankind. Elisabeth, sitting in a corner waiting for Dr. Simmons to receive her, hated and despised them. She longed to tear away from them all those illusions and proprieties which made their lives significant. She wanted to send crashing through their sympathy and kindliness some monstrous brutality of fact. Above all she hated their having pretensions to wits. Elisabeth knew her own limitations, she had not had time to read, she knew nothing about Art; but whatever depths of ignorance lay beneath the sharpness of her wit, she had wits. If you turned those women loose on the world without what was in their pockets, where would they be? Flopping at street corners with empty stomachs; but if you took away from Elisabeth tomorrow all that she possessed, she knew that on the day after she would have provided herself somehow or other with her usual number of meals. Elisabeth had none of the loose moral luggage of philanthropy; scruples, for instance, or inane and self-complacent pities were unknown to her. These people denied themselves in order to do good; and Elisabeth was both exasperated at the folly of their self-denial, and vaguely puzzled by a benevolence that shut itself up in a *cul-de-sac*. She did not for a moment suppose that these Mission ladies did nearly as much good as she did herself; but they put themselves out more; and why should you put yourself out more when you were bringing nothing in? Although Elisabeth never pretended for a moment that she would suffer herself in order to relieve the sufferings of others, still she was willing and anxious to get suffering relieved. It grieved her to see her city dirty and ill-kept and its people slow and sodden with starvation and hopelessness. She felt sorry for the wreckage of war and the still greater wreckage of the peace. She was perfectly ready, after she had set her own house in order, to work upon the houses of others, but she did not pretend she loved other people; and she frankly disliked those that it was necessary to help. These Mission people were soft, that is why she despised them; but she hated them for quite a different reason. She bit her lips with sheer rage when she thought of the enormous opportunities ignored by these soft and simple people. It was true that Dr. Simmons had definitely checked the mortality in the child life of Vienna. But how much else she might have done with all that solid English gold! What far-reaching impulses might not have been set to work; what amalgamations and dazzling personal triumphs might she not have achieved! As Elisabeth thought what she and Otto Wolkenheimb together might have made of this fund, so inhibited and misplaced by empty scruples, her fiery hazel eyes grew hot and her lips twitched. So deeply was her imagination aroused that she failed to realize a fresh subject of annoyance approaching her till Carol Hunter, with a cigarette between her lips, her hands in the pockets of an emerald silk jersey, stood straight in front of her. 'Dr. Simmons is free now,' she said, with a pleasant little lift of her thick eyebrows. 'Won't you come along and see her?' Elisabeth's eyes riveted themselves upon the slim boyish figure and the bush of straight gold hair. Did Otto like her? Why did Otto like her? How rich was she? That look, at once of ease and freshness, was it expensive or merely characteristic? The silk jersey was heavy silk, the shoes and stockings were French, the cut of the short skirt as simple as Art. No doubt, Elisabeth assured herself, the girl had to pay for such simplicities. 'I am delighted to see you again,' Elisabeth cried with a delayed pounce of enthusiasm. 'We met at the Mandelbaums'! Do you not remember me, Miss Hunter?' 'Oh, yes, of course,' said Carol, narrowing her keen grey eyes, 'I remember you perfectly now.' She recalled in a flash the violent orange dress and Eugen's little sketch of Frau Bleileben's history. Only what had become of the violence? To-day Elisabeth's clothes seemed to have slipped imperceptibly into a style so discreet that they had become positively distinguished. She was in black and white, with a hat that shaded her belligerent dark eyes until they shone with deceptive softness. But it was not only Elisabeth's dress that had changed; her bearing had imperceptibly altered. She moved less aggressively; even her voice had a softer cadence. It was as if she had been plunged into some rectifying chemical which had completely transformed the rough ingredients of her personality. 'Dr. Simmons was so sorry to keep you waiting,' Carol explained as they threaded their way through the room. 'She had a committee meeting which only committed itself to sitting. They had first one good idea, and then another good idea, and then all sorts of good ideas which chawed each other up! Dr. J. handles 'em wonderfully, I must say, for her. Once in a while she sticks in a point that festers; but most of the time she looks into the middle distance and knits.' 'She has a gift for silence, I have noticed,' agreed Elisabeth, with her eyes fixed on the neck of the girl in front of her. It certainly was attractive, the line of gold cut so clean and straight against the smooth white skin; a wonderful neck, Elisabeth mused idly, to slip under a guillotine.

Dr. Simmons was in a small room only divided from the living-room beyond by a wooden partition. The dreadful simplicity of it annoyed Elisabeth. There was nothing to be seen except Dr. Simmons sitting at a desk; a small table, with a tea-tray insufficiently supplied with a dry cake; and a good deal of cigarette smoke. Dr. Simmons had a very bad headache; a slight flush rested on her hollow cheeks; she was looking quite peculiarly thin and vague. She would have given all she possessed for half an hour's quiet and a cup of tea by herself; but she had not had those luxuries for two years. 'Don't go,' pleaded Elisabeth to Carol, 'unless you have some particular engagement. It is delightful to see you both together; I have thought of you so often since our meeting. We cheer ourselves, in working out our difficult problems, with the example of our foreign helpers! I have come to ask a favour,' added Elisabeth, turning towards Dr. Simmons rather reluctantly. 'But first do tell me—why do you always knit?' Dr. Simmons flushed at this attack upon her personal habits. 'I find,' she explained, 'that it helps to keep my mind clear in conversation and—that it prevents me from speaking too precipitately perhaps.' 'It looks,' said Elisabeth dryly, 'as if you thought conversation was not enough. Perhaps you are right. I am not one myself for many words so I will come directly to the point. You know in my way—simple and practical—for I am a woman of business, nothing more!—I work for Austria. You have had the kindness to interest yourself in investigating some of my little charities, so I think that you must know of my methods?' 'I admire very much,' said Dr. Simmons cordially, 'some of their results.' 'You are too kind,' said Elisabeth, 'but I don't deny that what I put my hand to turns out well. You see I do not put my hand to problems that are hopeless. I leave that for sentimentalists of whom in our poor country there are still far too many. I have been interested lately in a fresh and urgent problem. The factories in the districts outside Wien are in a very grave state—some, as you know, have had to close, others are working half time, and the children of the employees are in a shocking condition. I should like to start a scheme for their relief, and you could greatly assist such a scheme if you would order for me—on the same terms as the Swiss

Government has arranged to let you have it—say, half as much condensed milk as you need yourself at present here in Wien.' Dr. Simmons raised her eyes; they rested for an imperceptible moment upon Elisabeth, and then relapsed onto her knitting. 'But the Swiss Government,' she said after a short pause, 'would they not grant you the same terms for your charity?' 'It is not so simple as it sounds,' explained Elisabeth. 'In the first place behind you is a great deal of money—Allied money—and if I may say so Allied influence. Your work is well known all over the world. My work is not known outside my own district, and the Swiss Government would probably take the line that what is insignificant can very well be left to run itself.' 'Your husband is a Minister,' objected Dr. Simmons; 'you have therefore an official position to back anything you demand?' 'An Austrian Minister, yes,' agreed Elisabeth, shrugging her shoulders, 'in a Government that may last—half an hour! But, dear Dr. Simmons, I know your co-operative spirit. Surely your assistance—a mere matter of form as it is for you, but, I assure you, a serious help to my little charitable efforts—will not be refused to me? I felt so confident of your willingness to make the matter easy.' Dr. Simmons laid down her knitting. 'But as I see it,' she said reflectively, 'it is already easy. There should be a point of mutual advantage, should there not, in any co-operation? And I fail to see such a point in what you suggest.' Elisabeth's hands shook, she dropped her eyes for a moment to hide the fierceness of her glance. She longed to tear Dr. Simmons' knitting away from her. What a woman she was, colourless, faded, a worm for slowness, and yet capable of obstructing a creature whose flights were as unerring as a hawk's! 'The need of the factory people is very urgent,' Elisabeth said, moistening her lips. 'I do not wish to waste time over a correspondence likely to be protracted and not at all certain to be favourable. If you could help me I could act immediately.' 'I am afraid the only suggestion I can make to you,' said Dr. Simmons cautiously, 'is for you to go direct to Berne. The journey is short, and you, with your natural quickness, could probably arrange the matter in a few hours.' 'The Swiss Government will not do for two Societies what they will do for one,' said Elisabeth, with laboured politeness, 'and my time, though not of course as valuable as your own, is very fully occupied.' Dr. Simmons said nothing. Elisabeth played with a black suède bag

78

fastened by a tiny diamond flower. Flashes of fierce temper came and went in her eyes and showed in the lines about her nose and mouth, but her will held them vehemently down. Dr. Simmons looked more tired than before; her flush had faded into paleness; her usual vagueness had become so marked that she seemed barely present in the room. The only part of her in which consciousness remained was in the long thin fingers which moved to and fro to the faint clicking of steel needles. 'I feel,' said Elisabeth, breaking the silence which was creeping around her like defeat, 'that to keep the factories going is one of the most vital of our needs in Austria. It is bad enough to be a foodless land—but to be a work-less land——' 'I quite agree with you,' said Dr. Simmons gently; 'as far as we can we are working on those lines—we make grants of raw materials to many of the factories so that they may continue to keep open.' 'Then,' said Elisabeth triumphantly, 'since you do that—why should you not—with less expense—accommodate us with part of your grant of milk? The only difference I can see is that in the one case you pay for raw material for the factories, and in the other—I pay you for the milk for the children!' 'Certainly we would not refuse to widen our field in the direction you suggest if our own Stores or our policy justified us in doing so,' said Dr. Simmons, 'but I am rejoiced to think that you are in a position to finance this charity yourself.' 'And yet you will not help me to do it,' murmured Elisabeth, stretching her lips in a smile. 'You are not very logical!' 'I will certainly lay your suggestion before our Committee,' said Dr. Simmons, 'but I think it is only fair to warn you that we usually avoid responsibility for what we cannot control.' 'In other words,' said Elisabeth, rising to her feet, 'you hardly trust me sufficiently for co-operation! I understand!' Not even for Otto's sake could she do more. The Swiss Government itself would be easier to handle than this intolerable woman with her false air of being meek, and the temperament of a balking mule behind it. 'I am sure you do not understand,' replied Dr. Simmons pleasantly, 'if you can entertain such an idea! But I think, like you, that all charitable concerns should be run upon strictly business lines. We have made some mistakes in the past by attempting amalgamations which were beyond our power to control, and which, therefore, made us sometimes accountable for things we should not ourselves have done. I do not think our Society intends to take any further risks

79

in the same direction.' 'I do not see in this instance where the risk comes in,' said Elisabeth impatiently. 'I should be delighted to pay in advance for my half of the supplies, and I can hardly suppose you doubt my distribution of them?' Carol held her breath. Was this what J. doubted? How still she sat—and how flat and tired her eyes looked—and how curious it was that she did not mind more, making herself so disagreeable! 'That is true. I would not put it like that,' said Dr. Simmons reflectively, 'and yet it is also true that for a Society like ours, it is, I fear, indispensable for us to keep our arrangements separate from those of other people.' 'Then you refuse quite definitely,' said Elisabeth, 'to help me in this matter? I must say I am even more surprised than I am disappointed.' 'I am afraid we must seem very stupid,' Dr. Simmons murmured, 'but I assure you we are grateful that you gave us the opportunity of co-operating with you; and I am distressed that in this particular instance it is unlikely that we can take advantage of it.' An irresistible desire to slap the woman who was so cleverly circumventing her took Elisabeth quickly to the door. She must go home then, having failed—failed with this old woman (Dr. Simmons was as a matter of fact two years younger than Elisabeth) and leave Otto to deal with this little gold-haired, white-necked child! She looked quickly at the girl who stood waiting by the opened door. 'Cannot you come with me?' she said under her breath. 'I wish to speak to you alone!' Carol followed her obediently. She felt a vague sympathy for Elisabeth, dressed up so smartly, with such a baffled power in her eyes. It seemed to her that people did not often say no, or say it with impunity, to Elisabeth Bleileben, and as Carol was conscious of the very same masterfulness (it was a pity to call it tyranny) in herself, she could not help being sorry for the bitterness of this outraged lady's defeat. She took Elisabeth into a little room off the entrance, full of dust and typewriters. Elisabeth threw open the window and took in a deep breath of air. 'Oh,' she hissed, 'what a comfort to be with an American after these cursed English! Everywhere! Everywhere they are the same! They have the best beef in the world and they cook it to leather—their pockets are full of money, and they use them to sit on. You can't get them to move, and when you run away from them, it is to find them somewhere else! The Germans told us zeppelins would blow their little island into the mid-Atlantic, but I knew it was more likely that they would blow away the Atlantic, and leave the English high and dry on their island, going to church on Sunday—without so much as a glance over their smug little cliffs to see by what they were surrounded!' 'I guess you feel better now,' remarked Carol, with even greater sympathy. 'We all feel that way about the English sometimes, whether we fight with them or against them. As for J. she can thin out the weeds better than any patent lawn-mower I've ever seen.' 'Are you definitely leaving her?' demanded Elisabeth. 'I do not wonder!' 'Well—I leave her, yes,' agreed Carol slowly, 'but I don't exactly want to—I'll admit I have a queer out-and-out pash for J. She keeps me guessing. What I want to know is—is she really inside her clothes or not—but I never shall!' Elisabeth shook her head impatiently. 'You show your good sense,' she said coldly, 'in leaving her, at any rate. Now this matter I speak of is important. Would it be possible for you on your own, to arrange with one of the other Relief Societies what I have suggested to Dr. Simmons? Certainly I could go to them myself—but I should prefer not to risk again a frost like to-day's. I fancy most of their stores come direct from America? That would suit me as well as Switzerland, and I can pay the usual Relief prices.' Carol hesitated; she was not afraid of Elisabeth. She had never been afraid of anyone in her life, but as she met those small piercing eyes she felt a singular reluctance to disappoint them. After all an appeal would cost her nothing. Relief Societies could look after themselves, and Elisabeth Bleileben was the wife of a Minister and noted for the faultless way in which she handled her accounts. 'I don't see why not,' she murmured; 'I do know most of them.' 'Let us come at once then!' cried Elisabeth with swift triumph. 'You shall speak for me, it will arrange itself! Ah, the American dispatch! What a mercy it is to deal with it!' Carol seized a beret off a hook in the hall and crammed it on her head. They shot down the stairs together, and out into the narrow street. 'What made you come over here?' Elisabeth asked as they hurried into the Stephansplatz and plunged into the nearest taxi. 'That I cannot understand! You are too young to be so amiable for nothing!' 'Ah! I'm a canny little vulture all right, all right!' said Carol lightly. She had no desire to share her sympathies with Frau Bleileben. Elisabeth nodded grimly. 'You are wise,' she said. 'Those who pretend, like that Englishwoman, to have no fish of their own to fry, make very poor cooks for themselves or others! But what

is it you want to pick up?' 'Well, how about princes for dollars?'
laughed Carol. 'Or do you think I oughtn't to fly much higher
than a Graf?' 'Ah,' said Elisabeth, 'but let me tell you that
princes in this country are of less weight than postage stamps. It
would be wiser for you to go to England; you could marry there
one of their great noblemen; that would be worth your while. Go
to England, yes, that is the right place for you, and go soon. Do
not waste your time here!' 'Now I wonder why she gave me that
advice,' Carol asked herself coolly, as they entered the offices of
one of the South American Relief Missions. 'I shouldn't have
thought Excellenz Bleileben was so disinterested about unattached
young girls! But she wants me to go all right. She wants me to go
so much that she'd like to push me all the way across without
letting go of her grip! If she was a gimlet I wouldn't like to be
the thing at the end of the hole she was making. She'd get there.'
It was hardly necessary for Carol to do more than introduce
Elisabeth. Everything went like cream; the atmosphere was one
of celerity and dispatch. In five minutes they were once more outside on the doorstep congratulating each other. 'It is almost a
pity,' said Elisabeth regretfully, 'that you go so soon to England—
but you are wise to go immediately; after a war men marry
quickly—I fancy you are one of the few women of whom I could
make a friend!'

XI

Eugen Erdödy had lived in the Josephplatz for ten years.
When he had first taken his flat there it was a fashionable
quarter. Now it was no longer fashionable, but since to
Eugen's mind fashion had ceased to exist he was untroubled by the mere shifting of democratic fancy. The Josephplatz still contained more dust in summer, less sun in winter, and
at all times more noise than any other street in Vienna. Eugen's
flat was on the second floor; it consisted of three medium-sized
reception rooms, his bedroom, a kitchen and a servant's room.
No one in Vienna was allowed by law to possess more than two
rooms: nevertheless Eugen retained his flat exactly as it stood,
and it was probable that he would continue to retain it. The

Wohnungsamt visited it in due course, but in some mysterious way their visits passed over Eugen's flat like a brake that will not act. Many people take pains to keep what they possess, but Eugen differed from most people in that he knew precisely what pains to take. His schemes developed very slowly like the carefully selected wines in his cellar, and when the moment arrived to put them into practice they had acquired the bloom of maturity. He saved himself a great deal of time because he never attempted what he could not do.

Eugen would have asserted that he lived entirely alone, and in a sense it was true; his intellectual processes were solitary; but Lisa was in the kitchen. Eugen Erdödy was famous for his possessions; he had a singular gift for finding treasures, and appropriating them, at a cost astonishing to better-known connoisseurs. Of all his collection Lisa was perhaps the most skilfully obtained, and the most personally remunerative, of his finds. He was sent for one day to consult with an old friend upon a domestic catastrophe. The problem was that of a dishonest servant. It was a distressing case, for the girl had been much prized; she came from a good peasant family, the chief people of a mountain village; she was intelligent and adored by the children of her employer. The sound of their adoration could be heard breaking mournfully through the house as Eugen entered it.

Frau Hofrat Eiselsberg overwhelmed Eugen with her righteous indignation and her desire, fast growing into an intention, of sending for the police. The proof was damning, silver had been missed, and after a careful search discovered in the girl's locked trunk.

'I will first see the girl,' said Eugen patiently extricating himself from a cloud of fierce irrelevancies, 'and then I will give you my opinion.'

The girl, isolated from her screaming charges, sat in a locked pantry, shivering and weeping. She denied nothing, she confessed nothing, she looked at Eugen, once or twice, out of drowned blue eyes—without hope. At the bottom of those eyes Eugen discovered her honesty shining like a flower, and after half an hour of patient ingenuity, he gave his opinion. 'Dismiss her certainly,' he said to the Frau Hofrat; 'you no longer trust her, therefore she will be of no further use to you. But do not send for the police. She is young, you are merciful, and such cases are always expensive. It is my invariable advice never to take a person poorer than yourself into a court of law.' The Frau Hofrat was not merciful; she disliked youth except in her own children; but she was a careful housewife. 'I will dismiss her', she agreed at length, 'without a character indeed, I will tell everyone that she is a convicted thief.' 'A thief', murmured Eugen gently, 'is enough. A convicted thief she cannot be unless she has been through the Courts.' Privately he gave the girl his address and told her that he thought he knew of a situation where she would be kindly treated. Lisa came to see him the next day; and she had remained with him for ten years. 'Do you know why I take you,' he asked her on the morning of her arrival, 'in spite of all that the Frau Hofrat has to say against you?' 'Because you are kind?' whispered Lisa. 'Certainly not,' said Eugen firmly; 'I am very far from being kind, but I know a thief when I see one, and you are not a thief.'

He took her over his flat and told her the approximate value of his treasures. 'These are my fortune,' he explained to her; 'should you repeat to anyone the sums I mention or even describe at all accurately any of my possessions you would endanger them; but you will talk to no-one about them; and I will teach you to take the same care of them that I take myself.'

Lisa blinked and said nothing; she had always thought before that fine furniture was big furniture, but something told her that the shining *Biedermeier*, the polished chestnut surface—which looked as if the inside were as rich as the out, the delicate shapes of the chairs and table legs, the fine lines of Eugen's small desk by the window, were perhaps richer than anything she had ever seen. 'This is my little *Biedermeier* room,' Eugen explained. 'Dust is not known here. I will show you the cloths I keep to make the polish look like sunshine. You will observe that there are only three pictures. Over the mantelpiece is a Brueghel. Many people prefer it to Dürer, but I do not. Dürer is too expensive for me. He has gone up on the wave of fortune, I do not say too high, he was always among the highest, but I got this Brueghel before people knew what Brueghels were worth. You will observe the serenity of the colours, although the drawing is naturally beyond you. I found this Carlo Dolci Cupid in Naples; it belonged to an excellent young Marquis who knew nothing about pictures, and believed that he knew all about cards. This belief was a misfortune for him and a windfall for me. There is a law that works of art cannot be taken out of Italy—but you see it looks very well upon this wall, does it not? The warm golden brown of the skies and the roseate flush on the wing have a great charm. That Cranach was given me by my Archduke for a little service I was able to perform for him. Those slender scarlet figures, against a background as brilliant as a jewel, are a speciality of Cranach's whether he does a hunting scene or a Nativity. There is only one other clock in the world like this—perhaps you have seen it in the Maria Theresa room in the Hofburg? It is *pietro duro*, and those are the signs of the zodiac as well as the hours and days—all marked as you see, as plain as an alphabet. On this table you may study the Battle of Lepanto—it is of ivory. You are surprised that the figures are all so minute and yet so perfect—that the background, those trees and the little castle are the size of my thumb? I admit it is an achievement to make the whole of a battle come before one in six inches of ivory. Such things took a lifetime to make—and they were worth a lifetime.

'This room is my office—you will always show people in here and you will never leave anyone alone in it—except the three people who are to be treated as myself, the Herr Graf Wolkenheimb, my cousin, the Princess Felsör and her brother, Herr Von Hohenberg. In fact these three people are to be treated better than myself, since they are worth more to me. The next room you will have to learn very carefully—it is not probable that you have yet learned how to treat a Gobelin? This is a sixteenth-century silk tapestry, Brussels, of course. I have a special, very light brush for it and you must use it as if you were blowing dust off the Madonna. Never step on the rugs, they are Persian; that says nothing to you of course, but they are the right Persian. I travelled for many years before I acquired them; and I took time to understand the secrets of texture. That is why, if you touch those little carpets, they seem to melt away under your fingers. Colour of course I already understood—stand a little to the left to get the light on the rose-coloured rug. Does it not resemble the shades of the sky after a brilliant sunset has passed and left in its wake memorable flakes of cloud? This purple one is, however, perhaps the best; the sharpness of violet has been burned out of it, but the bloom remains. These are carpets which invite the proximity of China. Those two blue vases and the green jade bowls belong to the happiest moment of a dead civilization. It would be worse to break those vases than to destroy a life—since men are reproduced easily but dreams never. I keep my glass here too—you will hear people talk of Venetian glass—they make it still, but not like this. This is what people's minds were like before they made ingenious things that smell and hoot and hurry! This charming modern world, electrically rushing towards the devil and marconiing the news of it across space, does not make treasures. People were very ignorant in the fifteenth century, they only understood form. You see this glass—and this colour. They had no bathrooms or telephones when they made this; they had only selection as fine as gossamer and as hard as any monster made of steel! You will handle these things as if you held the Sacram nt between your fingers! Do not think me profane—no-one who loves beauty is profane. You are a good Catholic, are you not?' Lisa looked surprised; it had not occurred to her that any Catholic could fail to be a good one. In her village in the mountains most f the peasants went to Mass daily, and nothing ever happened without the Church; she had not been long enough in Vienna to know that there was a world which was not connected with the Saints. 'I am a Catholic,' she said shyly, 'and I know how to handle holy things.' 'That is well,' said Eugen approvingly; 'you will remember then that everything in this room is holy.

'Now my third sitting-room you will see at a glance is different. There is only one object of essential value here. You see that marble hand upon my desk? You would think, would you not, to look at it, that it was warm? Some young girl has opened her hand to take hold of life—or perhaps to give all that she has towards it! Nevertheless that hand has been cold for more than two thousand years.

'I live in this room—it is therefore made for comfort as well as spiritual satisfaction. No-one who has sat in that chair has ever wanted to get up again. My friend Graf Wolkenheimb spent thirty English pounds on a similar chair—but after a few hours he discovered that the angle of the neck was less assured. I spent several hours in that chair before buying it, therefore no-one will ever discover in it any failure of comfort. It is the same with that sofa—each cushion is as soft as the kiss of a mother; it is also a great deal less tiresome as it demands no response. Now we will come into the kitchen; every day for one hour I will teach you how to cook. Never hurry—never economize and let everything

86

taste clear—that is the theory of good cooking, the application must be taught.'

Lisa knew very little when she came to Eugen Erdödy; but she had obedience and steady wits, and upon this foundation he made her one of the best cooks in Vienna. The relation between them gradually became more elastic; finally, and without pressure, it grew intimate. Eugen treated her with scrupulous fairness. 'I never intend to marry,' he told her, 'and I am permanently in love with a lady who has other ties. All that I can offer you, therefore, is my constant protection, and I shall offer you that in any case. Nevertheless I believe that the arrangement of nature for a man and woman to live together is more intelligent. If you do not live with me you will probably wish to marry some one in your own class of life. The work would be more arduous, and although I am a modest man I think the entertainment provided by such a person would be distinctly less than I could offer you; but I want you to understand clearly that my offer is not obligatory. Should you agree to it you will lose nothing in the eyes of the world, because people always make the assumption that no relation between a man and a woman can be innocent if it has any opportunity to be otherwise. In the eyes of God—which I know nothing about—it cannot, I feel sure, be any more absurd than our little legal arrangements. Think it well over.' Lisa seldom understood Eugen's words, but she always understood what he meant. She went into the kitchen and made an *Apfel Strudel*, an even better one than usual, and then she returned to Eugen. 'Let it be as you wish,' she said solemnly. 'All that I have learned since I have been here, has been good for me. Why should I stop learning?'

Eugen told her nothing about his friends or his work, but she knew all his tastes and habits, and the kind of sore throats he was liable to catch in the winter. Lisa's religion was divided between the festivals of her church and Eugen's wishes. If her two authorities had conflicted she would have suffered severely; but fortunately the church and Eugen ran on parallel lines. Eugen made a substantial provision for her in his will, but he did not tell her that he had done so, nor did it ever occur to Lisa to wonder if he had. Her attitude to Eugen was that of a thoroughly intelligent and well-treated dog. She knew that Eugen would look after her—how he did so was his affair. She did not know how God proposed to look after her in Paradise, but when she died, God (prompted by the Blessed Virgin) would no doubt make suitable arrangements for her; and Eugen would do the same on earth. She would have liked to have children, but Eugen told her it could not be managed. She could see for herself how difficult it would be, living in a house which contained such frail and priceless things. But if Lisa had been in the place either of God or Eugen she would have stretched a point so as to include a nursery. She felt sometimes as if some of the children she met in the streets or in the gardens looked at her a little reproachfully for not being a mother; but she had a docile nature and learned typewriting instead, which was perhaps a greater help to Eugen, with his law papers.

XII

It was the happiest hour of Lisa's day. Eugen sat opposite her in the kitchen, where they always shared their midday meal. He had finished with approval a kidney omelette, a *Natur Schnitzel* and a slice of very fine *Dobosch Torte*. He now sipped slowly and appreciatively, his fourth glass of every-day but inimitable Barsac. Kings might have envied Eugen his cellar, but they could have hardly rivalled his palate. Lisa gave him systematically the news of the day. She informed him of all that their neighbours had done; she told him how many people there were at early Mass, and exactly what she had paid in the market for her purchases; she repeated to him a few tart and well-chosen words with which she had been inspired to address the hall porter's wife on the subject of washing down the stairs. Eugen listened sympathetically, but of what he himself had effected in the course of the morning he said nothing. There was, however, a blandness and serenity in the manner in which he sipped his Barsac which spoke to Lisa of a good conscience. An affair in which Eugen was deeply interested was going very well. He had had an inspiration. It had come to him in a flash that the little American girl Otto proposed to marry would do even better for Franz Salvator. Otto's schemes were Eugen's business; but Franz Salvator's interests lay dangerously near his heart. The scheme itself was not so very difficult—its execution had gone like cream; but one point had required a skill that Eugen had no need to feel ashamed of. Nobody had guessed for a single instant the hand that had poured the cream. It was fortunate that Carol Hunter had conceived a romantic passion for Eugénie—and Eugénie an equally romantic gratitude to the entire Relief Mission. Very little manipulation had been needed to complete the initial stages of Eugen's plan. Dr. Jeiteles had played into his hand. The good Jewish doctor was genuinely alarmed about Eugénie's health. Nothing had been easier than to persuade him to insist on her leaving the hospital for a few months' rest. Should she succeed in finding foreign tenants, the rent would enable Eugénie, at last, to buy for herself a few of the comforts of which she stood in need. Dr. Jeiteles had therefore bethought himself of the only two foreigners he knew—the sympathetic ladies of the Relief Mission. Would they care to take it? Dr. Simmons could not move, but Miss Hunter without a moment's hesitation had fallen in with the idea. Franz Salvator arrived breathlessly to consult with Eugen. Could they get the Hungarians legally out of their flat without hurting their feelings? Eugénie insisted that whatever happened their feelings must not be hurt. Franz Salvator was a little embarrassed by his own eagerness, which, he explained to Eugen, was simply a repetition of Eugénie's; he was also a little amused at having a young girl resident under their roof, and perhaps a very little alarmed as to the possible consequences. In fact he was in exactly the state of mind into which Eugen had proposed to plunge him. Franz Salvator had not fallen in love with Carol at first sight, but his first sight had roused in him every intention of subsequent ones. As to the Hungarians, Eugen, who disliked them intensely (they were his own cousins and related to Eugénie's husband), reserved to himself the right of getting them swiftly out of the flat—with unruffled feelings. 'They shall think,' he explained to Franz Salvator, 'that we are doing them a favour in letting them go, in fact I propose that they shall pay to get out. Only say nothing of the American lady—and make Eugénie hold her tongue. You must both appear to desire them frantically to stay.' 'How are you going to get rid of them?' Franz Salvator demanded. 'Did you ask your General that question when he ordered an attack?' replied Eugen composedly. 'Leave the strategy of this affair to me, my dear boy—and execute the little order which I have ventured to suggest to you.' The business was satisfactorily settled at twelve o'clock that morning. The Hungarians, warned gravely by Eugen of their financial liabilities in connection with the central heating (an indefinite liability which might fall upon them from next Quarter Day in respect of a privilege they had not been rich enough to use) agreed eagerly to leave. Otto would be told of her new address by Miss Hunter herself; and Eugen's name, from start to finish, would never once appear. There was only one slight cloud upon the horizon. The Gräfin Wolkenheimb proposed to call upon Eugen; and she would require a good many explanations of an evasive nature before she let things take their course. The relation between mother and son was a happy one; the Gräfin showed tact; Otto's manners with his mother were often affectionate and always polite; but the success of their relation was entirely based upon the Gräfin's never knowing what Otto's actual arrangements were. She would not have liked them nor would Otto have changed them, so that the simplest plan (suggested by Otto and carried out by Eugen) was to keep her in a state of permanent and agreeable ignorance.

'Lisa,' said Eugen, shaking his head sadly as she offered him the Barsac for the fifth time, 'this afternoon four glasses are enough. After the fifth glass I am conscious of an innate pleasantness in things, which I find to be misleading. A deep unclouded pessimism is the right condition in which to receive a visit from the Gräfin. This condition arrives of itself by the time she leaves me; but it sometimes has to be artificially produced before she comes. I am expecting her to arrive at two-thirty. At three o'clock you will bring in black coffee and a slice of this admirable Torte. Unfortunately I shall not be able to digest another slice at that early hour, but the Gräfin will appreciate it. At four you will return and say that a gentleman has come to see me upon most important business. You will then show the Gräfin out.' 'And what shall I do with the gentleman?' Lisa asked with prudent foresight. 'I cannot leave him in the *Biedermeier* room alone?' 'You can leave this particular gentleman alone in any room you like,' replied Eugen, 'as he does not exist. It is possible that the Frau Gräfin will ask you a few questions. She may, for instance, want to know where the Herr Graf is. You will not know. You will not know— even, my dear Lisa, if you are bursting with accurate information —anything that the Frau Gräfin asks you. I only wish it were safe for me to model myself upon the extent of your ignorance.' 'What shall I do if the Herr Graf himself calls while his mother is here?' Lisa asked anxiously. 'You will tell him that he is out of town and that I should advise him to remain out of town for the week-end. Give me my cigarettes, dear child. I will close my eyes for five minutes until she comes.'

The Gräfin was punctual to the minute. She was a small brisk woman between sixty and seventy. She wore a chestnut front a little to one side, and her clothes suggested the idea of shelter from adverse elements. In her ears hung a pair of diamond earrings worth a fortune. She had no eyelashes and no eyebrows, which gave to her eyes a sudden and disconcerting expression like that of a person who enters a room without knocking. The Gräfin had never been beautiful, but she had always been powerful, and though the reins were no longer in her hands the habit of using them remained unbroken. She looked sharply at Eugen for several moments before she consented to sit down in a less luxurious chair than he was anxious to offer her, and when she sat down, her eyes moved unwaveringly over his possessions.

'So far you have sold nothing,' she said after Eugen had kissed her hand a second time with respectful affection. 'That at least is a good sign in this deplorable period. When do you expect the return of the Kaiser?' Eugen shrugged his shoulders hopelessly. 'In five years,' he replied, 'if he has patience. Never, if he is impatient!' 'Do you not know what happens to people who remain away for five years?' demanded the Countess. 'No? Well, no affection survives a five years' absence. If my husband whom I adored returned from the tomb, what should I do with him? Should I eat once more the things which gave me indigestion in order to please him? I think not. Would Otto rejoice that he must give up an estate he has starved to the bone by his extravagance? No! Let the dead rise again in heaven where there are many mansions, and where, so far as we know, relations are not obliged to live together. But if he wants to return to his throne, let the Kaiser be impatient! I have known perhaps three patient people in my life. Did they ever gain anything by it? On the contrary, Providence saw that they were fitted to bear misfortunes and took every advantage of it. Where is Otto?' 'I believe that he is at this moment out of town,' said Eugen regretfully; 'how unfortunate that you did not notify him of your arrival!' 'I wanted to take him by surprise,' said the Countess gloomily, 'but whenever I take him by surprise he is out of town. It is a most peculiar coincidence. I have, however, seen Eugénie and Franz Salvator.' 'I hope that you found Eugénie well,' Eugen murmured politely. 'Not at all,' said the Countess, 'on the contrary I found her very ill. So ill that even that Jew Jeiteles has turned her out of his hospital for a rest. Probably she will die young. Without consulting me they are going to let their flat to a young American girl. It is quite obvious from what they tell me of her that she is an adventuress. She insists upon paying them a rent big enough to swim in. I say insists —because those idiotic children have implored her to give them less! But probably she has no intention whatever of paying it, and will steal Eugénie's few decent things—all of course left in her portion of the flat. They have no reference of any kind beyond that she came out here with Dr. Simmons and now proposes to leave the Mission. As you know I distrust philanthropy, but I even more distrust those who give it up. If you become too dishonest to remain on a relief mission—how dishonest you must be!' 'Dear Gnädigste,' Eugen said, 'people may have other reasons for resigning from Missions. I understand that this young lady for instance, has a great fortune and owns an American newspaper.' 'Ah, you understand all that, do you?' exclaimed the Countess in triumph at having at last drawn a statement from her cautious adversary. 'Well—if she has a fortune she is perhaps respectable, but on the other hand if she has anything to do with a newspaper she is certain to be an adventuress.' 'You must admit, however,' said Eugen softly, 'that there is all the difference between a rich adventuress and a poor one!' 'Yes, I admit it,' agreed the Countess, 'but I don't like celebrities in the air. Proofs should be obtainable. If she is indeed rich, in the present state of Austria, Franz Salvator might do worse than marry her. What do you suppose Eugénie said when I pointed this out to her?' Eugen shook his head. 'She said,' the Gräfin asserted with acidity, 'that the idea had never occurred to her. I do not say that it was Eugénie's fault she lost her husband and child—but you cannot be surprised that she lost a fortune! A woman like Eugénie would lose anything!' 'Except her virtue!' Eugen said under his breath. 'Except her virtue,' repeated the Gräfin contemptuously, 'and no doubt she would hold on to that at a moment when it would be much wiser to let it go! But since Eugénie did nothing to bring the girl under Franz Salvator's nose, will you tell me who did? Such clever arrangements do not happen by chance.' Eugen looked completely nonplussed. 'Perhaps,' he suggested, 'Franz Salvator himself conducted the affair?' 'Franz Salvator!' said the Gräfin, with still greater scorn. 'If a plum fell into his mouth I doubt if he would have the sense to remove the stone! No! the idea is without doubt your own, Eugen Erdödy! Since it is a good one I wonder that you take the trouble to lie to me.' Eugen flung back his head and laughed heartily. 'What an imagination you have, dear Gnädigste!' he said at last, wiping the tears from his eyes. 'Here am I, a poor little bachelor boy living as simply as a chicken, and you suggest my influencing this strong-minded American heiress whom I have for a few moments said a few poor words to— over a dinner plate.' 'Ah, you've talked to her, have you?' asked the Countess. 'Then if you've done that you could do anything!' 'You flatter me more than I deserve,' said Eugen, 'but as a matter of fact all that passed between us was curiosity upon her part as to who Otto was, and my poor little attempts to satisfy it. I must say, dear Gnädigste, that if I had any Machiavellian designs they would naturally take the form of first providing a rich wife for Otto.' 'I daresay that you consider him first,' said the Gräfin, her unsmiling, unshaded eyes resting flatly upon Eugen's face, 'you should—since you are his man of business! But I have always observed in practice you act first for the well-being of Eugénie. Pray do not contradict me. It is a waste of time since I am always right.' 'If you wish to claim supernatural powers,' said Eugen politely, 'I of course withdraw into my restricted little region of fact. I hope that you will find my coffee possible to drink. You remember these cups? The Empress Elisabeth presented them to my mother as a wedding-present.' Lisa had entered the room noiselessly, curtsied to the Gräfin, and laid a round beaten-silver tray with the coffee cups on a table beside her. An aroma like the scents of Paradise entered the room with Lisa and deflected the attention of the Countess. 'Lisa understands coffee,' Eugen said indifferently. 'Each time it is freshly roasted, freshly ground, sufficiently strong and properly made; it should therefore be drinkable.' 'It is drinkable,' said the Gräfin gravely; 'to expect coffee to taste as it smells is an illusion, but in this instance the reality is extraordinarily near it. Lisa, how did you make this *Dobosch Torte—Schleichhandel* of course, since this butter is real?' 'I do not know, Gnädigste,' said Lisa simply; 'the Herr Baron ordered it.' Lisa withdrew. 'Such a scandal!' murmured the Gräfin. 'I often wonder I allow myself to visit you. And now—she does not even wear an apron!' 'Secretaries seldom wear aprons,' said Eugen pleasantly; 'it would go badly with a typewriter.' The Gräfin ignored his explanation. 'A mother makes many sacrifices,' she said, eating the *Dobosch Torte* with infinite relish; 'this is one of them!' Eugen bowed. 'Immorality must exist,' the Gräfin went on, 'but to meet with it in the home! Terrible! Terrible! Terrible!' 'Indeed it would be most terrible,' agreed Eugen pleasantly. 'Fortunately I have not got a home so that these difficult questions do not concern me. Will you not take one more little cup of coffee?' The Gräfin leaned forward suddenly. 'I want you to tell me,' she said sharply, 'on what my son is living? Wait one moment, do not lie to me until I point out to you the directions in which it would be useless. Two months ago Otto wrote to me that he must sell all his horses immediately. He sent for them to Wien; they are here still. They are not sold.' 'Horses cannot be sold as easily as apples,' replied Eugen soothingly. 'Doubtless Otto wished to sell them to advantage. Probably he is discriminating among the foreigners. More arrive every day; and they need discrimination.' 'And while he is discriminating among the foreigners,' said the Gräfin, licking her finger lightly and following the crumbs of the *Torte* around her plate, 'does it help him economize to buy a motor? I hear that one is to arrive next week.' 'Ah,' said Eugen serenely, 'you have heard of that little flutter? He tells me it is advisable as an advertisement.' 'An advertisement of what?' demanded the Gräfin. 'Of ruin? It is ruin, allow me to remind you, that we are suffering from at present. I am having great trouble at Trauenstein. Otto must do something about it. The peasants threaten to strike unless their wages are increased and their hours shortened. They used to work while the sun shone; the sun still shines as many hours as it did, but not apparently for them! I have no money and no more timber must be cut. If we lose our timber we lose the value of our property. I came here to see what I can do. I find Eugénie and Franz Salvator living in the utmost indigence, and I find Otto with his horses unsold, and contemplating a Mercédès limousine. I think some explanation is due to me, and I warn you, my dear Eugen, that I shall not leave Wien until I receive it!' 'I quite agree with you about the timber,' said Eugen reflectively; 'no more must be cut. If the peasants are troublesome Otto must go down and see them again. He quieted them last time. In the meantime I can let you have some money.' 'But what is he doing?' persisted the Gräfin. 'From where does this money come? Do I not know his income? Have I not seen my *Kronen* melt like butter? And why does he neglect his cousins, whom he adores? I asked Eugénie, and her reply was most unsatisfactory. She said she thought Otto disapproved of her nursing. I asked Franz Salvator, and he said that since he teaches eight hours a day in the Berlitz school he gets no time for visits or visitors. You know them well enough to know what such excuses mean. It is not Otto who dis-approves of *them*—of their nonsense we all disapprove—it is *they* who for some reason or other disapprove of Otto! Come, come, my dear Eugen, cease twiddling with that eyeglass ribbon and give me a satisfactory answer if you can! Upon what does my son Otto live? Is it upon women?' 'My dear Gnädigste,' said Eugen, lifting a warning hand, 'you shock me inexpressibly!' 'Stuff and nonsense!' said the Gräfin, pouring herself out a third cup of coffee. 'Your power to be shocked went with your first knicker-bockers if not before! Answer my question!' 'As far as I know,' said Eugen, with a candid air, 'Otto is now living by a series of financial experiments. He is as you know very able; and troubled waters suit expert financiers. I really cannot tell you any more because my simple little legal abilities fail to grasp the intricacies of high finance. I should suggest, my most respected old friend, that you should personally ask Otto to give you an explanation of his resources.' 'Should you!' said the Gräfin dryly. 'I think not —one does not consult an eel upon how it escapes from one's fingers! However, one thing is perfectly plain to me. In the state in which our poor country is at present no financial pro-cesses are likely to be reputable or solid. What you mean is that Otto lives by his wits?' 'Wits that produce motor cars,' observed Eugen, 'are worthy to be called financial operations. The position of things as you suggest is not solid, but hitherto Otto has moved among these mercurial conditions with a lightness that has rival-led their own.' 'And Eugénie and Franz Salvator disapprove of his lightness so much,' said the Gräfin thoughtfully, 'that they would rather starve than profit by it?' The expression on her face troubled Eugen; she looked suddenly older. The Gräfin's intelli-gence was unblunted by the fatigue of age, but her strength to combat what she disapproved had weakened. 'The world has changed, Gnädigste,' said Eugen gently. 'What must one do? Stay as we are and die like fishes taken out of water or accustom ourselves to the sharper processes of air?' 'In other words,' said the Gräfin, with a sigh, 'what must we be, dead fishes or birds of prey? No! no! I dislike what you tell me very much, my dear Eugen, and what you do not tell me even more! I am glad that we still possess at Trauenstein land enough for our graves. It is time, I think, that we took to them, and left juggling with rival currencies to Jews.' 'I suffer for you—and with you,' said Eugen simply. 'But Otto is a fine fighter, and—although I do not say— because I do not believe—that there-is anything left worth fighting for—we must expect him to use his instincts.' The Gräfin closed her eyes and opened them again with the suddenness of a trick. 'Is it a necessary part of the fight,' she inquired, 'to have Jewish mistresses instead of women of our own class and race?' 'I am an unmarried man,' said Eugen cautiously, 'and therefore of course know very little of such matters, but I should suppose that Otto must effect an economy in possessing a Jewish lady of settled means—that is perhaps why—if there is any truth in such a scandal—he has not had to sell his horses.' 'And yet you say he is not living on women!' exclaimed the Gräfin bitterly. 'Pardon me,' Eugen contradicted her gently, 'if I point out to you that there is all the difference in the world between living on women and associating with a woman who does not live on you.' The Gräfin spread out her hands with a hopeless gesture. 'Eugénie is a fool,' she said abruptly. 'She could have saved us from this. I have no patience with over-scrupulous women. She was a widow who had every reason to be relieved when her husband died. If she had expressed her relief normally and kept her fortune Otto would certainly have married her. But she chose to fritter away his feelings and her money on a hospital. Now she looks like a broomstick and hasn't two Heller pieces, and my poor boy is thrown to a pack of Semitic wolves! Let us speak plainly, Eugen, for though I know you always try to deceive me you have my son's interests at heart. A marriage is the only thing left to us in order to save him from swindling and worse. Since a marriage with an Austrian or a Hungarian is practically out of the question, one must accept a mixed one. As things are I should make no objection to an English woman or even a Czech. The woman must be well connected and have money, that is all I ask.' 'On our side, what have we to offer?' asked Eugen despondently. 'It is no longer enough, Gnädigste, to say that Otto is Otto Wolkenheimb of Trauenstein.' The Gräfin was a woman of superior intelligence, but for a moment she looked quite stupid. It sounded to her incredible that it was not enough to know her son was Otto Wolkenheimb. 'But,' she muttered, staring straight before her, 'Otto——? Eugen——? I do not understand.' An intense bitterness invaded Eugen's heart. It was as if he saw all that his class had stood for slipping away from him into an unplumbed sea. He was no King Canute to order back the waves or to believe in any royal interventions. These rising waters would, he knew, cover all the shore and drown those who had not the wit—or, perhaps, the cowardice—to flee from them. The old would go first, and Eugen loved the old; the young (born from ancient races into the new world) would never even have seen the lost Atlantis of their fathers. 'I will do what I can,' he said at last. 'Relieve yourself of any fear of this Jewess— she is married already—Otto is fond of English people; perhaps he will find someone suitable among them. Should you object to the American girl in the event that Franz Salvator fails to connect himself with her?' 'Of course I should not like him to marry any of our late enemies,' said the Gräfin bitterly. 'But this is not the moment for talking of what one likes. It is the moment to nerve oneself to do without it. Bring me any decent woman you can. All I ask is that she should have money and bear children!'

Lisa reappeared. 'There is a gentleman waiting to see the Herr Baron,' she said, 'upon important business. He says that he has an appointment for four o'clock.' 'That is true,' murmured Eugen apologetically. The Gräfin rose and blinked her unsheltered eyes. 'Good-bye, my dear,' she said. 'Do what you can for me! You have told me a pack of lies, but you are a good boy and your heart is with us. I know that I may trust you.' 'Till death, Gnädigste,' said Eugen, bowing low over her hand. He went downstairs with her and out into the street. The Josephplatz was full of noise and dirt and there was no carriage in which to put the little old lady with her diamond earrings and her powerless tradition. Eugen walked with her to the nearest stopping place of the shabby red tram and put her into it as if it had been a coach and four. He did not replace his hat until she was out of sight. If he could do nothing else for her, and the race for which she stood, he could at least show her the ceremony to which she was accustomed. In fact slightly to accentuate his manners was the only outward sign which Eugen Erdödy allowed himself to make in a world where all that led to good manners had ceased to exist.

XIII

Carol could not help feeling as if they were different from anyone else. They sat together, a little apart from the other guests (for they had come in late), looking like originals of Praxiteles strayed into a company of plaster casts. Neither Franz nor Eugénie were merely handsome; and the difference had not anything to do with their clothes. It was a look they had been born with and could not shake off. What was it, Carol asked herself, that made their beautiful courageous heads so distinct? Why did they have that graceful set of the shoulders, so that whenever they walked into a room they suggested a procession? The Relief workers were all refined, the few Austrians they had invited were of picked intelligence; but the eye slid over them, as if they could not be anything else but background, and remained riveted upon the tall brother and sister, as if wherever they chose to sit must be the centre of the room.

Franz Salvator's eyes met Carol's with a smiling intensity. He already knew that he was going to like nothing in the occasion except her presence. He was in a very bad temper, but you could not have told it from his smile; and Eugénie was in a worse one, but it only made her loveliness a little more intense. They had quarrelled for the first time in their lives because Dr. Simmons had invited them to her evening party. Franz Salvator only discovered on their way there that it was to consist of an account of Jew baiting in Budapest and that Jews (among whom Dr. Jeiteles had been invited) were to be present. 'You cannot meet Dr. Jeiteles socially,' Franz had asserted; and Eugénie had said that she considered such a prejudice vulgar. As they came in Eugénie had given Dr. Jeiteles her hand to kiss with marked cordiality, and assured him earnestly how glad she was to see him. Her action confused Dr. Jeiteles, enraged Franz, and surprised

Eugénie herself. It caused the other Jews a mixture of amusement and bewilderment; and the Relief workers, who were all Anglo-Saxon, thought nothing of it at all. They did not know that they had asked a member of one of the oldest Magyar families to hear a criticism of crimes committed by her husband's personal friends; and forced two social elements to meet which centuries of studied isolation had kept apart. 'It's going to be rather an exciting party,' Carol said as she handed Franz a box of cigarettes. 'Light up and be comfortable—the man over there with the red tie—bottle-necked shoulders and Adam's apple—is going to speak. Doesn't J. look a dream in that brick-coloured garment? She's awfully handsome really if she'd ever looked in the glass and taken hold of what she saw there. Where are you going to sit, if I take your chair?' 'I shall stand behind you both', murmured Franz Salvator, 'to keep off the ten tribes. What possessed your friend Dr. Simmons to set them loose upon us?' Carol stared at him. 'What does he mean?' she asked Eugénie. 'The man who is going to speak comes from Birmingham—doesn't he look it?' 'He means nothing,' said Eugénie gently. 'Except that he very naturally wishes to keep your company to himself.' 'That also,' agreed Franz Salvator, 'but that goes without saying. Wherever one was, one would wish your company there—here it preserves one from extinction! When are you coming to us, Miss Hunter? Our Hungarian cousins went last week like melting snow; everything is ready for you—even an old cook from the mountains; and I am more than ready—I am a little impatient!' Carol met his laughing eyes—and there was something behind his laughter which was like a sudden warning. 'Somebody or other will have to keep their head in that flat!' Carol said to herself. 'Let's hope it's going to be me!'

Dr. Simmons leaned forward and briefly introduced the object of their meeting.

'Mr. Bolt', she said in her dry indifferent manner, 'is about to tell us of his experiences in Hungary. We shall be very grateful for your consideration of his story, and for your advice upon the problem which it illustrates.' 'I don't fancy your advice will be much good myself,' observed Roger Bolt with that absence of politeness which he felt constituted sincerity. 'Still I don't mind letting you know what the Hungarians are up to. The whole world ought to know it, and the whole world ought to stop it, but it won't. It's far too busy lying and looting. Any country will keep a blind eye on crimes that don't interfere with its own, and if you Austrians think yourselves any better than the rest of us, it's simply because at present you're too powerless to do any harm.' 'You paint a charming picture of the world,' said Professor Adler, smiling. 'I don't say that it is unjust, but I think that its severity may make us all a little critical of your story.' 'You can be as critical as you like,' replied Roger Bolt, 'but if you're a Jew, as I suppose you are by your name, I should simply advise you to keep out of Hungary. I went to Budapest last week to open a food centre for the babies. All the authorities spread themselves to help me. You'd think they were a lot of cats coming to lick up the cream out of the condensed milk tins! They couldn't do enough or say enough to make things easy. Eighteenth-century manners and third-century morals—that's the Hungarians for you.' The young man shot a baleful glance in the direction of Eugénie. 'Why third-century morals?' murmured Professor Adler to himself. 'I always thought third-century morals rather good. Christianity hadn't had time to wear off, nor the Church sufficient power to cripple it.' Roger Bolt waived the question of Christianity into silence. 'I had an introduction', he went on, 'to a man called Joseph Bauer, a Jew of course, an educated, honest man, any man's equal, most men's superior. He put me on to some of the worst districts and gave me some invaluable Relief tips. He was the only person I met who didn't want anything out of me in return. He also told me a few plain facts—at my request—about the "White Terror". I know my job was babies—as you so carefully pointed out to me, Dr. Simmons, before I left here—but I happen to believe in right and wrong. I didn't propose to act immediately on the notes I took. I meant to bring them back to lay them before the authorities here in the usual way. I kept them carefully locked in my dispatch case. Someone must have opened it in my absence and guessed where I'd got my information from. I was to meet Bauer at a little restaurant on Wednesday, but he wasn't there. He hadn't been seen since the evening before. His wife was in despair. She declared that the police had got hold of him and that she would never see him again. She implored me to try to save him. Of course I thought she was putting up a bit of a fuss, but I went to see some of the Allied Mission people and asked them if it was likely to be true. They gave me my first jolt. One by one they all said the same damned thing. I suppose you can guess what it was, Dr. Simmons, since you've had some experience of Allied Missions? They said, "Leave it alone". Then I went to the head of the police and he said, "No doubt the fellow is off on a spree—that's why his wife's so upset!" and he laughed. I said, "Then he isn't in one of your prisons?" and he said, "Certainly not! Why should he be—if he keeps the laws, I shan't touch him. But don't you bother about Jews, my dear chap; let me advise you to stick to your babies." I guessed he was lying, so I set straight off for the prisons. If you want to know how I got in—I bribed my way in— and if you want to know what with, it was with Mission stores. Perfectly immoral, no doubt, and I shall catch it from the Committee, and if I had to do it over again, I'd do exactly the same thing. Anyhow I got in, and I found Bauer. He was locked up in a stinking cell the size of a rabbit hutch and as cold as ice. He said, "For God's sake get me out"; his teeth were chattering so loud he could scarcely speak and he looked—well—he didn't look the same kind of man he was before. Have you ever seen a bullied dog? Something so scared it has gone wild? He looked like that. Two days before we'd been talking about Freud—but the fear of death scatters most men's philosophy. He told me they'd flogged the man in the cell next door to death—the night before. Not the prison authorities—but some Hungarian officers broke in and did it—to teach Jews what to expect when they asked for a secret ballot! I went back to the Allied Missions. They said, "But what were you doing in the prison? You oughtn't to have been there, you know. You'll get us into trouble!" I said, "But I *was* there—for God's sake get that man out before they do him in". They said they hadn't any authority, but they'd do what they could. They could cut the whole of a Continent up to suit themselves, but they couldn't save one poor little persecuted Jew. I see just how the Crucifixion happened now. That's the kind of Jew people kill—and that's the way they do it. I asked how long it would take to get Bauer out. The young man I'd been allowed to see said, "Oh, in a week or two—I daresay something can be done". I told him what the cell was like and what had happened to the man next door to Bauer, and he said, "Impossible, my dear chap—someone's been pulling your leg", and went out to lunch with his bit of fluff at the Ritz. I went back to the head of the police, and told him where Bauer was. He said, "But what were you doing in one of our prisons? I'm sorry but you'll have to go back to Wien if you don't keep quiet. Bauer is a menace to the State, that's why he's in prison if you want to know; leave him to us". What's the State? And what kind of menace to any decent country is an honest little man like Bauer, who only asks to earn his bread and his right to think in peace? We've got the power, let's down him because he thinks—that's statesmanship!' Roger Bolt's unpleasant blue eyes were hot with anger and his knees trembled. Hermann Breit rolled his heavy head and groaned with sympathy, and Dr. Adler surreptitiously looked at his watch. 'I went to see the Prime Minister,' Roger Bolt went on in his harsh hurrying voice. 'I waited four hours in his house. I just waited. When they saw I was going to sit there till the Day of Judgement they let me see him. First he said my story wasn't true. Then he said I didn't understand the conditions of Hungary. Then he made a joke about Jews. Finally he assured me that nothing serious would happen to Bauer. He would be a humane man I should think—unless it hurt him to be!' 'He *is* a humane man,' said Franz Salvator sharply. 'I do not believe that he would consent to any cruelty.' 'No,' said Roger Bolt with a catch in his voice, 'and yet this cruel thing happened. Before I left he promised to telephone and get the case looked into. I went away feeling a little happier, but somehow or other as the evening came on I couldn't help feeling less happy. You know Budapest? In the evening it gets gay—the restaurants fill—and there's gypsy music in the air—and people walk up and down beside the river. And not so very far off, in a lump of buildings I could see from the Bridge, was Bauer in that cell. I went back to the prison again. By then they'd had their instructions and they wouldn't let me in. I couldn't eat or go to bed—I just stood outside the prison while it got dark. East of Wien all you've got to do is to find a man's price. Finally I got hold of a man who said he'd let me in in the morning for fifty English pounds. I hadn't got half that sum in the world—but I started rushing about raising it—fortunately everyone keeps awake half the night in Pest. I raised it somehow or other; and in the morning they let me in.' Roger Bolt covered his mouth with his hand. Dr. Simmons sat as still as something carved long ago out of stone. Carol leaned forward and let her cigarette go out. The men sat looking at the floor, all except Franz Salvator, who kept his clear blue eyes fixed sternly on the face of the speaker. Eugénie shut her eyes—she did not want to see or hear any more—but she knew that she would go on seeing and hearing long after everything was over. She had been made so that she could not get away from pain unless she could lay her hands on it and heal it. 'I went in,' said Roger Bolt unsteadily. 'I said it was morning, didn't I? They didn't stop me, but some of them looked queer. Somebody said they hadn't expected me so soon. I'd been out by the river pretty early. The hill where their kings are crowned was a black lump, and a fog ran like giant cobwebs over the town. The door of Bauer's cell stood open. My guard pulled me suddenly back behind it. Four men in long cloaks came out of the cell, pushing their swords hastily into their scabbards to get them out of sight. I couldn't see what was on the swords. I waited pressed back against the wall; one of them slipped on something and swore, and the others laughed and made a joke, I suppose about what he'd slipped on. "That's a narrow one!" the guard whispered when they'd gone. "If they'd found I'd let you in, God knows if we shouldn't have joined what's in there, Jew or no Jew. I've earned my fifty pounds!" "Not yet," I said, and I lit a match and went into the cell. I suppose you ladies wouldn't like to hear what I found there. Most of it was blood; and the rest of it was Bauer. God! I didn't know any of us had so much blood! They told me he was dead. I said his name over and over; but nothing answered me. Then the fellow I'd bribed said, "Come, come, get away quickly; you'll be arrested! Here's an officer!" I suppose I didn't get away quickly enough. There was a lot of row, and they took me along to our own people. I saw the young man again, the one that had gone to lunch at the Ritz. He said he'd heard about the "suicide" and I'd made a great deal of trouble and must go back to Wien. When I said what I'd seen, he told me it was too dark to see anything, and I'd probably been a bit excited. In my pocket I had the names of the men who had come in and murdered Bauer —the fellow I bribed had given them to me. He told me that a murder like Bauer's only happened to Jews. Sometimes the officers got fined a few hundred *Kronen* just to show it isn't officially permitted.' The young man's voice broke suddenly. He took out a large red pocket handkerchief and without concealment wiped his eyes with it. Carol felt her animosity die; you cannot dislike a young man who so innocently wipes his eyes on a symbol of revolution. She saw too what she had not noticed before, that they were sleepless eyes. 'You have the names with you?' Franz Salvator asked curtly. Roger Bolt took out a dirty piece of paper; he hesitated a little over pronouncing the difficult Hungarian names. Professor Adler took the paper from him and read them in an even, unmoved voice. They were the names of four men whom Eugénie and Franz personally knew. Dr. Simmons sat with her hands in her lap looking straight in front of her as if the things of sense were not solid enough to hold her clear gaze. She had forgotten her party, forgotten the young man whose story burned in her heart. She had forgotten everything but pity. Carol had sometimes felt as if Dr. Simmons had no feeling, she was so abstracted and so personally austere, but now she knew that Jane had nothing else but feeling; only this feeling that possessed her was without the taint of personality. At last Dr. Simmons stirred out of her deep silence and looked across at Hermann Breit. 'Herr Breit,' she said, 'will you tell us if there is anything you think we can safely do?' 'Very little, I'm afraid,' said the old Socialist sadly; 'it would be perhaps of some use to speak to your Minister here, and you might write to important people in England—a little pressure—discreet pressure here and there from those who have power? I do not know! The Hungarian nobles have always been very cruel, and the people do not yet know their strength. Some day there will be a Green Rising, and then perhaps that little paper you hold in your hand, Herr von Hohenberg, may be useful.' 'To me it is useful now,' said Eugénie, leaning forward and speaking in a resolute low voice, 'for at least I can save myself from ever speaking to any of these men again. They are dogs—wild dogs—they should not be treated as human beings any more!' 'My sister overlooks the fact', said Franz Salvator slowly and emphatically, 'that these men—all of whom are our friends or the friends of our family—were driven wild. It is terrible to be a mad dog—yes! and such an action as this gentleman has witnessed is an action of a mad dog—I admit it—but what of those who have made these dogs mad? I hope that these gentlemen who are present will not take personally what I have to say—but a country that has been overset by a Red Terror—that has seen its families broken up—its homes destroyed—its King driven into exile, and believes, as these Hungarian officers believe—that this tragedy was made by Jews, instigated and embittered by Jews—

and that, although Bela Kun and his myrmidons have been overturned, yet these Jews remain, and will always be a hidden bitterness, a fresh instigation to fresh terrors—are they to be wholly cast off—wholly blamed—if they seek a fierce revenge?' Professor Adler shrugged his shoulders. 'All this bitterness—these Red Terrors—these White Terrors—are beside the point,' he said coldly. 'A country that has a Government should be at least able to safeguard its prisoners, nor should those who have made a Government be the first to break its laws.' Carol Hunter looked up indignantly at the young man standing behind her. 'I am surprised', she said sharply, 'to hear a brave man trying to defend a band of cowardly assassins! And for no better motive than fear. What kind of Red Terror can you get out of a man like Bauer? It's worse than wicked to think such stuff, it's paltry!' Franz Salvator bowed. 'It is interesting to be taught', he said icily, 'by a countrywoman of those who lynch niggers, that race hatred is paltry.' 'In America', said Eugénie, meeting her brother's eyes with a strange hard pride, 'they kill negroes who have committed crimes, or whom they at least suspect of having committed despicable crimes against women—this man had committed no crime at all. Miss Hunter's heart is touched, as mine is—as all our hearts are touched, I hope, by the injustice of this action!' 'For four and a half years', said Franz Salvator passionately, 'I have seen brave men die—die, if you like, unjustly—men of enormous courage, of great value in the world—day after day—night after night. Why should we all be asked to become so indignant at the death of one poor little Jew—even if he was honest and died without cause? The best men of our time and of our country died—and died in vain!' 'Seeing all that ought to have taught you a little sense,' remarked Carol Hunter crushingly; 'anyhow your officer friends died voluntarily, they weren't dragged off in a time of peace to face black murder in the dark. What I think ought to be done is to have it all out—start a stunt through all the newspapers—names, facts, details—just dash it bang in the face of the Public—and see if there isn't red blood enough left in Europe—egged on by America—to stop Hungary sitting in a corner and chewing up her Jews out of spite!' 'Miss Hunter expresses herself delightfully,' said Professor Adler, smiling, 'but she has overlooked one great difficulty—so I think has Mr. Bolt. We have all heard a very moving and touching story—I think we all—even Herr von Hohenberg, whose sympathies are so strikingly against it—believes this story to be true. But if it is to get into the newspapers, where are the proofs? We shall make our statement, and officially we shall be contradicted—our papers will be held up for libel—the public conscience will be soothed—and so soothed that if a fact we *could* prove did come along later, it would be twice as difficult to rouse anyone's belief in it. Miss Hunter, weren't you struck by the creative power of the first official who heard of this crime—it is the only creative power given to officials—the marvellous instinct for cover—with which he immediately exclaimed, "Suicide!" If you make this crime public that is what will be not only said, but satisfactorily proved by all the Government authorities.' 'I wonder if you're right,' said Carol Hunter thoughtfully. 'I hadn't thought of that. But I'll be even with them yet; I'll go down myself and do my own ferreting out!' 'I went there six months ago on the same errand', said Professor Adler in a grave voice, 'at the risk of my life—seeing who I am, to investigate a crime that sounded to me unmistakable and which personally concerned me. It was in fact the murder—under very dreadful circumstances—of my brother-in-law. I think that he was murdered; the body—after infinite difficulty and danger I was able to see the body—was unrecognizable, but we have never heard of my brother-in-law since. Most of the other stories I have investigated or sent people to investigate for me have been false. After one true story a crop of false stories immediately arises. There will be many false ones after these two murders—it is not the moment I should choose to go to Hungary to investigate—later perhaps, when the little trouble we shall be able to make—and I fear it will be very little trouble—is over, they will begin again, and it might be useful then to go down.' 'And, Dr. Jeiteles,' asked Dr. Simmons, 'what is your opinion?' Dr. Jeiteles had not spoken since Roger Bolt began his story—he had sat with his face in the shadow, looking away from Eugénie. 'My thoughts', he said sadly, 'are worth very little—I only beg that you will be personally very careful not to get mixed up in the matter. The Relief Mission must never touch politics—it is of the utmost importance that your branch in Budapest should be reopened. Let nothing interfere with that. I would let a few Jews die rather than many children.' 'I am of your opinion,' said Dr. Simmons; 'what I can do quietly I will do; and I ask of you all great discretion for the sake of the children.' 'Eugénie, are

you ready?' asked Franz Salvator stiffly. Eugénie rose slowly
her feet; her usual air of gentle deference was gone. She looked
stately and very sure of herself. She held out her hand to Dr.
Jeiteles and said so that the whole room heard her, 'Good-bye,
Dr. Jeiteles. I hope that if you can overlook the fact of my Hungarian name—you cannot dislike it more than I do at this
moment—you will come and see me soon.' 'She's got a nerve,'
whispered Carol Hunter delightedly to Dr. Simmons. Dr. Simmons watched the tall brother and sister leave the room together
side by side, their heads erect, their eyes looking straight in front
of them. 'I think she'll need it,' she observed reflectively.
'Perhaps I ought not to have asked them both together, but
it was very satisfactory to get the views of two such different
minds, both formed by old traditions.'

XIV

The City was silent except for the rustle of footsteps, and
dark but for the lights in the café windows. Those
Viennese, who had no money but loved late evenings,
since they could not pay for any other form of entertainment, had gone out to look at the moon.

Franz Salvator and Eugénie walked quickly towards the Rathaus Gardens; neither of them spoke. Franz Salvator was so unused
to being angry with Eugénie that he hardly knew how to form his
reproaches. He felt that she had suddenly done him an injury, and
yet it was his deepest faith that Eugénie was incapable of doing
anything wrong. He was as amazed and shocked by her outbreak
to-night as an ardent Catholic would be at a strange antic taking
the place of the ordered ritual of the Mass. He waited anxiously
for Eugénie to explain or to excuse herself, but Eugénie did
neither. She walked beside him with her head held high as if
she were proud of her inexplicable conduct, almost as if she felt
an injury had been done to her. She paused by the Rathaus
Gardens and said in a determined voice, 'Let us sit here a little
and talk.' Something had to be done about their anger, they could
not go back to their empty rooms with it; but it surprised Franz

Salvator afresh that Eugénie should take the lead in putting their anger to the proof. The moon rode high above the statues on the Parliament House, the garden was a sheet of frosted silver. The fountain in the centre was surrounded by a group of chairs all filled with people. They made very little sound; tired with the day's work and oppressed by the heat, they sat where they could feel the freshness of the lifted column of water and listen to its continuous whispering. Above an ink-black pool of shadow rose a magnolia tree; the great buds lifted themselves firmly upwards on boughs bare of leaves, as solid as if they were made out of stone. The air was full of the scents of flowering bushes, lilac and syringa; and sometimes on a little puff of wind there moved a fragrant breath of the distant Wiener Wald.

'I am very much offended,' said Franz Salvator at last. Eugénie sighed. She knew how deeply she had offended him. At first she had been proud of her attitude, but by now her anger had died down, and her pride had lost its significance. She was so accustomed to share Franz Salvator's feelings, that in the interest of exploring them, her own had ceased to be vital to her. But if her sympathy with Franz had taken the wind out of her sails, she still knew where she intended to go. Something had happened to-night which, however much she cared for Franz Salvator, must not happen again. He had taken for granted that she would accept their old traditions and allow him to act for her; and she could do neither of these things. She knew now that their old traditions—some at least of them—were mistaken, and that when she differed from Franz she must act and speak for herself. Loyalty was the deepest quality in both their natures, and to-night it was their loyalty which had been attacked; but in Franz Salvator it was loyalty to a code, and in Eugénie it was loyalty to a spirit. Naturally enough, Eugénie said to herself, Franz Salvator was offended. He had had to listen to the history of a crime committed by his personal friends, and to hear judgement pronounced upon them by ignorant foreigners and biased Jews. Franz never admitted that his friends were in the wrong except to the friends themselves. When he heard them attacked, his first instinct was to fight on their side, and he thought it secondary to discover if their side was right or wrong. When he did discover it was wrong, it made him angrier and caused him to fight harder. That was one of the reasons why he was so angry now; but there was a deeper reason,

which made Eugénie still sorrier for him and all the more determined to try if possible to reconcile him to a shock against his
very heart. He was angry with Eugénie, not only for forsaking
their friends, but for taking any side at all. He wished to keep her
above the arena of battle. She should have remained a symbol
of what fights were for. She was his saint, his martyr; the human
being most sacrificed and sanctified by the war. Franz Salvator
was too young to feel his cousin Eugen's despair at their changed
world, and too manly to sit at home and sulk over his lost
luxuries, but he did want to keep Eugénie in her niche. Eugénie
was half touched and half exasperated by his attitude. She was
only thirty-two, and she had stopped saying to herself, 'Here I
and sorrow sit'; she wanted to get up and walk about. But it is
improbable that she would have acted—at the cost of upsetting
Franz Salvator's cherished feelings—if she had not to-night suddenly found herself being made part of a system that it horrified
her to accept.

'Yes, I know that you are offended,' she said very gently, 'and I
am very sorry, dear Franz, that I have offended you. I think I
spoke impulsively to-night, and that it would have been better if I
had waited till we were alone to discuss our differences; but it is
difficult—when one feels strongly—not to speak, and I felt very
strongly.' 'I too felt strongly,' said Franz Salvator sternly, digging
his cane into the gravel in front of him, 'but not as you did. I felt
we had been insulted! We should not have been invited to listen to
a story told against our friends, and I am astonished that you do
not agree with me—at least upon this point!' 'But, my dear, remember,' urged Eugénie, 'that the English don't know who are
our friends and who are not! No doubt Dr. Simmons realizes that
we belong to the same class, but I am sure that she did not dream
we knew personally any one of those names read out to-night.'
'Perhaps she did not,' admitted Franz Salvator; 'it is incredible
the mistakes foreigners make! That they do not know is not their
fault, but that they do not try to find out before violating our
most sacred feelings, is—to say the least of it—exasperating! That
was what made it so—so impossible that you should ask Jeiteles
to come to our house! For you to repudiate our friends was bad
enough, but in the face of that repudiation that you should add a
welcome to a Jew shocked me to the heart!' 'But, my dear,'
Eugénie murmured, 'you yourself have always liked Dr. Jeiteles.

Remember he neither introduced nor encouraged the discussion, and he could no more help hearing that story than we could ourselves.' 'You seem to have noticed uncommonly sharply what he said or didn't say!' growled Franz Salvator; 'as to liking him—in his place he is well enough, but his place is not my sister's drawing-room!' 'Certainly I noticed how he behaved,' said Eugénie calmly; 'he is my friend, and I was grateful to him for sparing me the pain of hearing his judgement upon my husband's old companions. I knew that it could only have been as adverse as my own.' 'Eugénie, I cannot bear to hear you speak like this!' said Franz Salvator sharply. 'You disgrace our ancestors! I have honoured and admired your work in this man's hospital for four years: do not make me regret it!' 'That you should regret honouring me,' said Eugénie in a low voice, 'would make me sad, Franz; but that you should honour me for the wrong things would make me sadder still; and if you think that I can work for four years in the mutual service of our country with a good man and not respect and like him—you are doing me an injustice, whether you admire me for it or not!' 'One is not obliged to make friends of people with whom one works,' said Franz stiffly. 'I teach the sons of grocers in the Berlitz schools, and I am on cordial terms with them, but I don't ask you to receive them socially. It is foolish to consider Jeiteles your equal. He is *not* your equal!' 'No,' said Eugénie in a still lower voice, 'I know very well he is not my equal, Franz—he is my superior! Listen a little—don't only be angry. You yourself admit that to-day we are in a new world; its values are new and all its ways. We see, don't we, by this war what is the fruit of race hatreds and pet nationalities? Are any of our countries or those of our enemies the better or the nobler for what we have been through? I think not. Patriotism is not so great a virtue as we all thought; generosity is perhaps a greater, and I believe that generosity of mind is the greatest of all. Dr. Jeiteles trained me as a nurse, he taught me all that I know, he did not treat me as a Princess—why should I treat him as a Jew? Let us be prepared to go a little further still and to admit that there are no races which we can afford to despise, and no titles which in themselves are worthy of respect. I am a Princess only because I married Felsör, but I am a fully qualified nurse because I learned how to nurse, and I assure you I am much prouder of that title!'

Franz Salvator had never before heard Eugénie talk so much, or with so much intensity. It startled him nearly as much as it annoyed him. Eugénie was noted for being a perfect listener, and perfect listeners seldom break out into fluent and antagonistic speech. 'You are talking great nonsense!' Franz Salvator replied roughly. 'It is true that the world has changed, and that we are ruined, but we should be worse than bankrupts—as you yourself agreed about Otto—if we threw away our principles!' 'But is it a good principle to despise Jews?' asked Eugénie eagerly. 'And if a principle is not good, of what use is it to keep it? I do not see that any grave harm can come of treating Jews as equals—but I did hear to-night of a horrible crime that came from despising them! What we blame Otto for is not that he has ceased to despise Jews —but that, while despising them, he is base enough to make use of them! That indeed is perhaps a worse injury than beating them to death!' 'As Eugen puts it, it is a little different,' said Franz Salvator uncomfortably. 'I do not uphold Otto, nor for the matter of that do I uphold Aladar, Sandar and the others; but I see why they did it. It was one of those madnesses that come when everything turns black. Women don't understand such things. They should not know that such moments exist; but for men there are occasions so terrible that a man must be brave indeed to stand above cruelty. The Hungarian temperament is fierce, fierce and excitable! They have the East in their blood. It is deplorable what they do when they are roused. But it lies in the race; they can no more help it—than the most docile of wolfhounds can help flying at the throat of a stranger in the dark. My God! to hear foreigners speak as they did to-night! Very kind, very intelligent even, but, oh! Eugénie, so immune! They are brought up so safe— those English—on that damned little island of theirs! How can they understand what is done where the only frontiers are men's blood and women's tears? Think of those hordes of evil vermin crawling out of Russia, out of Poland, like bugs! Spreading their infected way into Budapest, under-selling, under-buying us, sucking like leeches the value out of our money and the honour out of our public life? Think of these things, you who should know what they mean, and ask yourself if it is so strange that our Aladars and our Sandars should rush at them with sticks as you would at an army of rats!' 'An army—yes,' said Eugénie consideringly, 'but one poor little man—trembling in his cell!' Franz Salvator swore under his breath. They were silent as if the gulf of difference between them could no longer be bridged by words. Eugénie's eyes fixed themselves upon the white whispering water. They were nearly alone in the gardens, the vague shadows on the seats had melted away to their homes. The moon had sunk behind the Rathaus tower; a golden glow still lingered in the sky; half the night was gone, and there was still no darkness. 'Franz,' said Eugénie in a voice that made him turn his head quickly towards her, 'do you remember that it was in May my Rudi died—not this night—but one just like it—towards morning—when the stars had grown small and far away and very cold? I tried to think of him—afterwards—in the stars—but I could not—they did not seem the place for a child. You know—no-one else knows—what it cost me to go on living. For a year always, I saw all day long—and in my dreams at night—nothing but his death. The world went down into his grave, and I could not lift one of my thoughts out of it. What kept me sane was my work in the hospital. When there were so many beds to tend, I could forget the one bed that I was no longer tending—and where so many suffered I could escape sometimes the sufferings of my own little one. You know that I am better now, don't you? So much better that I have stopped thinking of Rudi's death. The child himself has come back to me. Often I feel his hand in mine, and hear his hurrying questions. I can almost—almost pass a toy shop now.' 'Don't, Eugénie dearest, don't!' Franz Salvator whispered, his large strong hand covering hers firmly. 'You must not! I know! I too sometimes cross the street! But why torture yourself to tell me these things to-night—as you say—you are better—really better now!' 'Because I want you to know why I am better,' said Eugénie resolutely. 'Dr. Jeiteles has never spoken to me about my child, but one day he asked me to sing to the ward songs I had only sung to Rudi, and I said, "No—I cannot—those songs are sacred to me," and he said, "Things are not sacred, Sister, unless they are used." Oh, Franz! it was as if all my sorrow rose up in me and cried to be let out! I had not used it, and from that day I have tried to use it, and in using it the child himself has come nearer to me, and the weight of my grief has gone. I am very proud Dr. Jeiteles is my friend, I am proud he is a Jew. Be angry with me if you must, but don't be angry with him, for he will not come and see me. He saw your eyes!' 'If you wish it,' said Franz Salvator slowly and painfully, 'I will go and apologize to him to-morrow, and I will say that I should like him to come and see you!' Eugénie rose and put her hand in Franz Salvator's arm. 'We will wait a little,' she said, 'there is no need to be in a hurry. Now that you have said—this brave thing—I shall not be afraid any more. I know that whatever comes we can share it together; I shall not have to act alone, nor say to myself that Jews are the only good men.'

XV

Eugénie would never have dreamed of refusing to take Carol as a tenant even if she had wished to refuse her. If Carol had asked her for all she possessed, Eugénie would have given it to her and then apologized for not possessing more. She thought that anyone who had come to help their country in distress was entitled to the uttermost friendship and service of which any Austrian was capable. Franz Salvator, although he was usually more measured in his enthusiasms than his sister, agreed with her on the subject of their tenant. Even if Carol no longer helped the Mission, she had helped it. And now that her interest in Austria was not confined to Missions, she was helping it even more by the careful publicity she gave to its problems. It was dreadful to both brother and sister to be forced to take any rent from her, and after they had reluctantly agreed to take it they argued for hours as to how they could best expend part of it, without her knowledge, in making everything more festive to receive her. They consulted every available authority upon the habits of Americans; short of human sacrifice they were prepared to fall in with all their customs, however strange they might seem. Franz Salvator had very soon to put his tolerance to the test. He had expected that when he next met Carol (after their heated controversy on Jew baiting) it would be suitable for one or both of them to apologize. He had prepared a very careful and polite statement which, without damaging his loyalty to his Hungarian friends, might show Carol that she had judged his point of view too hastily and without a thorough grasp of the facts. But a greater tolerance was required of him. Carol ignored the whole occasion. She met him in the highest of spirits, carrying a beaded waste-paper basket in one hand and a rose-crested parrot with grey feathers in a cage in the other. Apologies were no longer in the air, and Franz Salvator hung up the parrot's cage in the sunniest window of Eugénie's old drawing-room and hurried out to hunt for the exact kind of bird seed suitable for 'Annabelle's' extensive but fastidious appetite.

'One must remember that Carol is wonderfully free,' Eugénie warned Franz, 'and not be surprised at her going out alone, even in the evenings.' 'Strange! very strange!' murmured Franz. 'But by then I shall have finished my work and be able to escort her where she wishes to go!' 'She sits in cafés and talks with newspaper men,' Eugénie warned him. 'Dr. Simmons tells me it is part of her profession and need not alarm us.' 'But what a profession for a woman!' exclaimed Franz Salvator in pained astonishment. 'And what dangerous imbecility on the part of her relations to allow a young girl to take such risks. Think to what it exposes her! We must carefully explain to Marie that the Americans are a people who are respectable whatever they do, and no more open to misconstruction than the Saints.' Eugénie looked a little uneasy; she had already explained a good deal to Marie, and Marie had taken her explanation in the same manner that an indulgent mother listens to the first flights of a child's imagination. Marie was forty; she looked as if she was made out of wood—particularly hard-grained wood—and she had round black beady eyes which it was difficult to imagine shut. She had come from her distant mountain home when Eugénie sent for her, without expending half of what Eugénie had given her for her fares. She had walked ten miles from her home to the nearest station, stood for eighteen hours in a freight train, and on reaching the distant outskirts of Vienna she had once more walked five miles to avoid passing the customs, in order to retain without difficulty the contraband articles she had concealed upon her person. Marie listened with an impassive face to Eugénie's suggestion that she was to cook for a foreign lady in the other half of the flat; and while she listened she had carefully unwound a ham, suspended from her waist, and drawn from mysterious corners of concealment two litres of fresh cream, a dozen eggs, and an endless procession of sausages. 'You will be doing us a great kindness, Marie,' Eugénie had finished. 'I shall be doing my gentle-people a kindness, shall I,' Marie repeated, 'by remaining in a part of the flat which is furnished while they are in rooms as bare as a Convent Friday, and by waiting upon a stranger while they wait upon themselves? The kindness to the strange lady I see very well, but I do not see any other kindness.' Franz Salvator explained. 'If you look after the Fräulein, we shall profit by it. She pays American dollars for our rooms, and we shall have food for her dollars.' 'For the first time I perceive some reason,' said Marie, without enthusiasm, 'and later, if the young lady is rich enough, perhaps the Herr Kapitän will marry her?' Franz Salvator grew very red, and murmuring, 'For God's sake, make her understand, Eugénie!' hurried out of the room. 'There is nothing to be ashamed of in a good marriage,' said Marie, looking severely after him. 'Even love, though foolish, is no shame once it has been blessed by a priest.' Eugénie tried to efface Marie's romantic theory, but she soon gave up the effort. Marie's impressions were not easy to efface; they were instinctive and infrequent; and it would have been as easy to uproot a mountain as to change an idea once it had been imbedded in the hard and gritty substance of Marie's intelligence. 'If this young lady, who is a friend of ours, could not be with us,' Eugénie explained, 'we should be forced by the Government to take in strange people who might be a great trouble to us and steal all our things. There are so many thieves now in Wien, Marie.' 'Of course there are thieves,' agreed Marie. 'People who have been honest all their lives look in the glass when they get up and say: "Can I still be honest to-day?" Without a Kaiser there must be thieves! I myself would steal from a stranger without it disturbing my conscience. What business have strangers to be here? If they were good people they would naturally remain at home.' Eugénie expressed her enthusiasm for Relief Missions while Marie methodically disposed of the smuggled stores. 'It is possible,' she said when Eugénie had finished, 'but the gracious Princess always sees jewels where others only see stones. Young high-born ladies if they do good at all should do it under the roofs of their parents, and if they have no parents their nearest relation should arrange a suitable marriage for them or dispose of them in a convent.' 'But, Marie, Americans have different customs from ours!' Eugénie urged. 'That is what I complain of,' replied Marie. 'Why should they have different customs from ours unless they are heathen? And I know well they are heathen, for my uncle's child took service in a family of American people in Salzburg, and they cooked always without butter and never went to Mass. But do not distress yourself, gracious Princess; I am here now and I will prepare a little ham and cocoa for your supper and that of the Herr Kapitän. As for this foreign lady— many things are terrible in times like these; but money in a household is not one of them. I shall accommodate myself to her if she leaves me liberty in the kitchen. Does the gracious lady permit me to ask how the Herr Baron Erdödy and Fräulein Lisa are?' Eugénie with great relief responded freely to this subject. Marie's black beady eyes fixed themselves upon her face. She had asked this question out of politeness, since she had already called at the flat of Baron Erdödy and questioned Lisa minutely upon each member of the family. Lisa was also a Tyrolese peasant, and she withheld successfully one or two facts from Marie's relentless probings; but she was not as old as Marie and therefore less astute, and she suffered from the awkwardness of having lost her respectability; she knew that Marie despised her for having mislaid a virtue which in her own case had never been seriously threatened, and the knowledge that she was despised had shaken her powers of concealment. 'And how, if I may ask,' continued Marie while she skimmed slices off the ham as thin as the edge of a leaf, 'is the Frau Gräfin and the Herr Graf Otto?' Eugénie thought she kept her voice as normal as usual in answer to this last inquiry, but she failed to carry a conviction of normality to Marie. Marie finished with the ham, and folding her hands across her apron observed, 'They say—but naturally I do not know what truth there is in such a saying, that the Herr Graf has suddenly become rich and that he consorts with *Schiebers?*' 'I think he is rich,' answered Eugénie hesitatingly, 'but I do not understand business. In these hard times people are very ready to say unkind things about those who are more fortunate than themselves. Nevertheless we see very little of the Herr Graf—and—and perhaps it is better as it is.' Marie made no comment. She knew everything about her family's affairs; if they had been in her hands she would have managed them a great deal better. She knew that Otto should have been the Princess's husband, and when the Princess became a widow Marie waited for the event to take place, and deeply disapproved of its not having done so. She knew even before she came to Vienna that Otto had made a name for himself in the small financial circle of men who had never been heard of before: men who had their homes outside Vienna and sent their wives and children to the Semmering because they were afraid of being hanged to the nearest lamp-post if they remained too near the city. In Marie's opinion these financial magnates were formed by destiny for lamp-posts. It was well known how these men made money; they speculated in foreign currencies; they sent their own exchange flying up and down, ruining hundreds of their fellow citizens in order to buy and sell their own securities at a fabulous profit. Fortunes drove about their heads and settled upon them like wild birds on unknown islands, while the middle classes of Vienna watched their savings melt like snow in May. Marie, although she was an ignorant peasant, knew the names of these men; knew in some cases the commodities they had cornered and doled out to their pinched compatriots at ruinous prices. To the starved and driven population of Vienna, money was like some magic genius. If you possessed it, you had only to rub your lamp and ask for what you liked. No man refused you. They looked with longing eyes towards the golden stream, some drop of which might fall upon their parched docility. But the peasants were not docile; the land was still productive, and, though they often played into the hands of the *Schiebers* by holding up their stocks till the prices became ruinous, they hated their financial dealings with an activity which would have led to lamp-posts had they—instead of the starving mild-hearted Viennese—been forced to put up with *Schiebers* in their midst. Marie, looking around her beloved family's empty rooms, cursed Otto in her heart. Up till that moment he had been one of the 'Family,' respected, uncriticized, accepted, but he was abolished now with a completeness which left no scrap of his personality exempt from malediction.

'Yes! If one has one cow,' she observed aloud reflectively, 'it is always better not to be too familiar with those who have seven.' 'But he would help us, I think—if we would let him,' Eugénie said gently. 'The Herr Graf was always generous, Marie!' Eugénie sighed. She did not know how to explain, without blaming Otto, why she and Franz Salvator so steadily refused the tentative offers Eugen had made to them to share Otto's benefits. Franz did not even take the trouble to refuse; his eyes met Eugen's upon one of those thankless errands, and when Eugen looked away again he knew that it was no more use expecting to help Franz Salvator through Otto's money than to bring back a Russian Czar through a petition signed by Lenin and Trotsky. Franz Salvator would do nothing against Otto now. He would speak to him if they met; but he would only take Otto's hand if it were empty; and even Eugénie, for all her gentleness, would not have accepted help from Otto to save her life. In the old days they would have shared everything they had—but in the old days nothing that they had had come to them through trickery. Marie with her small beady eyes steadily fixed upon Eugénie's troubled face, knew this as plainly as if it had been shouted in her ear. 'They won't,' she said to herself, 'touch his money, because the Herr Graf has become a rascal, and it has broken my Princess's heart. Still it is better to have a man who has broken your heart out of the house than in it. I made a mistake about that marriage. What the Herr Graf wants is not a wife, but a cup of coffee with a little weed-killer in it.' 'The Frau Gräfin,' Eugénie said after a pause, 'lives now almost entirely at Trauenstein. But she was in Wien the other day, and she asked after you, Marie.' 'My humblest greetings to the Frau Gräfin,' replied Marie, with a prompt curtsy, 'and thanks for the honour.' Eugénie hesitated. 'And the Herr Graf,' she said, turning towards the door, 'he also—never forgets you.' Marie said nothing at all about the honour done to her by the Herr Graf. Eugénie lingered for a moment. She guessed that Marie knew all and would forgive nothing. Then she went out of the room with her head bent, because Eugénie never quite got over the feeling that if Otto had done anything wrong, it was for her to feel ashamed.

XVI

It was six years since Eugénie had been to the races. She wondered if Eugen remembered, as they sat in silence in the shrieking red tram jolting to the edge of the Prater, the last time when he had driven her in the smartest of tandems. It had been just such a day in June, 1914. The chestnuts were out in long lines of white and pink blossom, the leaves flaunted a hundred shades of green; green sheathed in grey; green breaking out of coppery brown; green pale as silver, and green that shone in the hot sunshine like flame. Green lay flat under the trees as if each blade of grass held light within, while overhead the deep blue of the sky was broken into patterns by the flickering emerald leaves.

'It is the same world as then,' said Eugénie softly, as they turned off the dusty road on to a grass path through the trees, 'and yet I feel as if someone had breathed on a glass I was looking through; everything is a little vague, a little dim!' 'The Prater is covered with dust to begin with,' replied Eugen disgustedly, 'utterly overgrown, and filled with your charming friends—"the people." Nature does the best she can, but I have never thought very much of nature by herself. She is like a woman who needs expensive dressing to appear tolerable.' 'And I was thinking just the opposite,' smiled Eugénie. 'I was thinking that since nature is the same, and so beautiful by herself, so generous with her little flowers in the grasses, we ought to be content to let the years take all the rest. Look at those silver birches in a group over there— how young they are—so slender and so pale—they look as if they had been made out of moonlight.' Eugen put his eyeglass into his eye and looked obediently at the silver birches. He had a grudge against silver birches. He was not given to poetic images, but when Eugénie was very young it was to that particular tree he had secretly compared her. He had thought of the silver birch as a fountain sending up jets of green and golden leaves around its white and slender stem; and he had resented having to see it stripped of its cascade of glistening leaves to face the storms of winter. When he looked at the silver birches he did not see the trees; he saw instead Eugénie's face when she was young and happy and secure enough to be as careless as the Spring. 'You have a contented spirit,' he observed dryly; 'when I come to the Prater I come to look at horses, and I am not easily consoled by being asked to look at trees, which if I were in charge of this particular wood should most certainly be thinned. There are, I believe, only thirteen horses running to-day, and with this new outrageous tax we shall be lucky if we retain what we have. We shall certainly get no more horses from Hungary.' 'How excited I was,' said Eugénie, 'last time we came here. Do you remember, Franz Salvator rode, rode and won? The Emperor himself congratulated him. I felt as if I had a hundred hearts all beating in my throat at once! I had not meant to come again. You must, I think, have had some special reason in asking me; what was it,

Eugen?' Eugen paused before he answered her. He required occasionally such moments of silence with Eugénie to separate what he was thinking from what he intended to say, an operation which, in talking with anyone else, he performed automatically. 'It seemed to me,' he replied cautiously, 'since you are no longer working in the hospital, a good moment for going back to play. The weather is fine, Otto and I still have our old box, nothing better suggested itself to me. The one pleasure that is still the same is the pleasure of your company; so it occurred to me to try to induce you to give it to me on this reminiscent occasion.' 'But, Otto,' Eugénie objected, 'may not share your pleasure, Eugen? Did you ask him first?' 'No,' admitted Eugen, 'it did not seem to me necessary to ask him. In the first place, Miss Hunter is to be with him and he will therefore have her society as well as ours; and, in the second place, I take for granted that Otto *will* be pleased to see you. Why should he not be? You have given up trying to make him do what he knows is right; that, I think, was the only grudge he had against you?' 'You forget, I think, that I too have a grudge,' said Eugénie bitterly. 'Do you think it is nothing to me to have my cousin, my friend, the head of my house, called a swindler and profiteer, and not to be able to contradict it? My blood and my thoughts are stained by Otto's dishonour, and your dishonour also, Eugen! For although I know you take no *willing* part in his affairs, nevertheless that you are in them at all is a disgrace! You are my friend; and if I did not know that it is relationship alone that binds you to Otto and his miserable money-making, I should have broken my friendship with you as ruthlessly as I sometimes feel you have helped to break my heart!' 'My dear! my dear!' said Eugen gently. 'If I have given you pain it has not been ruthlessly—the way to your heart lies across my own. Never think that I gave way lightly to Otto or without regrets. Only ask yourself was I wrong to stand by him when if I left him I took away the only check he had upon a path that may lead to misery and must lead to danger? You judge Otto hardly. Forgive me! but to think too well of a man is seldom a great kindness. Otto is an intellect and a great force; without money he loses the only material he can find in the modern world to work on; and if he loses his use of his powers he would sink into bitterness and the lowest kinds of dissipation. I speak plainly because in times like these only plain things count. You have confused your judgement with ideals and standards which existed, but which exist no longer. We are cast back into barbaric conditions. The strong use teeth and claws. They survive. The weak perish. A few people, like yourself, live nobly and use up their strength rowing against a stream that is too fierce for them. When you die there will be no more like you! We shall produce a new type, fitted for the new conditions; born in armour, invulnerable to beauty or to sacrifice. Machines will have done their perfect work. There is still a soul in a few pictures, in a few beautiful shapes and colours; there is no soul left in man!' 'If there is no soul,' Eugénie cried passionately, 'at least let us make our mortal lives worth something! To betray God—to destroy the spirit—is an abstract wrong. There may be pardon for it! But to betray our brother man—to fatten on his ruin—ah, Eugen! you know as well as I do, you feel as I do—it is despicable!' Eugen was silent for a long time. At last he said gravely, 'If you feel like this about Otto it would have been better not to come. As for myself, it is perhaps true that I have sunk too easily into the mire. You must remember that I believe there is nothing else; and I retain my hope that by remaining in the mire myself I may keep Otto from being quite submerged.' 'Ah, but we know,' said Eugénie in a gentler tone, 'why you are acting with him. We deeply regret it, but we respect your motive. I cannot respect anything at all about Otto.

'I had a long struggle before I accepted your invitation, knowing that I might meet him here. In the end I came. I came because I wished to see what was left—you know the feeling—of all those old memories! I wanted to see if I could——' She hesitated again. 'Bear them?' Eugen asked gently. 'Oh, bear them—no!' cried Eugénie. 'I have borne them for many years. No! I wanted to see if I could get rid of them, once for all, as one gets rid of fear, by standing still and looking it in the face!' 'But memory is all we have got now,' objected Eugen; 'to get rid of it would be to get rid of life itself. I come here—week after week—for an exactly opposite reason. I want to cultivate memory. To bring the old days closer, to find again, through some trick of the eyes, something fresh out of the past. The course itself evokes memories. A chance horse reminds me of horses I had forgotten; when I exchange greetings with the trainers, old victories come back to me, or old defeats. I hardly care which, for all of them were better than anything one gets now. I am a modest man, very little satisfies me—

I feed my memories on any old straws that the wind brings me.'
'You are not modest at all!' flashed Eugénie. 'You are too proud!
You won't risk the new world! No future is good enough for you!
I am not like you. I want to make myself over again. That's why
I want to test my courage here to-day; but I should try with a
much lighter heart, Eugen, if you would try with me!' 'Try—with
you?' asked Eugen, raising his thick eyebrows. 'But, my dear—I
can't! When I was quite a young man I wanted the moon and I
understood that what was usually done under those circumstances
was to cry for it. I refrained. Those who cried for the moon in my
experience did not get it; and their tears weakened them. I at
least have profited by retaining my strength; and I discovered also
that there was nothing else to cry for. As I did not care any more
about my personal life except to make it as comfortable as I could
and to escape those things which I felt tiresome, I interested myself deeply in the Court. I did not want, you understand, to make
a career for myself, but I was part of a system, a system I believed
in, and which justified me to myself. I knew what I should be at
forty, at sixty, and after my death I knew exactly what would be
said of me, "That good fellow Erdödy was useful—he knew everybody and everything about everybody. He was discreet and it will
be difficult to replace him." I do not believe in survival after death,
but should there be such a thing, and I should overhear that tribute to myself, I should be extremely gratified. Also I should know
that it was just!' 'Dear Eugen!' said Eugénie, 'but you are only
forty now! Why will you shut yourself into the past or, worse still,
follow Otto into a commerce that you despise? It is my idea to try
and surround myself by the intelligent new world, the world that
hopes to build up Austria and to make out of our very losses and
restrictions a new way to serve her. All the people I shall try to
bring together will be poor people, professors, doctors, writers——'
'Jews?' interrupted Eugen with a swift glance at her lighted, eager
face. 'Yes—Jews!' said Eugénie impatiently. 'The picked brains
of an intelligent race which has become a part of us!' 'I have told
you,' said Eugen slowly, 'that I take for granted what you do is
right. Franz Salvator, I understand, even associates himself with
your plan. He is young and no doubt the war shook his sense of
caste. Mine has not been shaken. The people you mention would
not entertain me. I should consider their manners bad, and their
sense of values would be obscure to me. Frankly I should dislike

them very much. I thank you for trying to include me in your new hospital for intellectuals, dear Eugénie, but the operation would be too radical for me. I should die under the anæsthetic. I must remain what I am, a poor little monarchist and your devoted friend! You will not, I think, refuse all association with those who are not in the lower order of life? No? You relieve me infinitely. Do what you like then with your new world—short of marrying a Jew! That would be, I must confess, the final disappointment.' 'Why do you speak of my marrying?' asked Eugénie, deeply hurt. 'All accidents are possible, I suppose, but this is of all accidents the least likely. I am only trying to find something to fill my life with again—something that will not hurt me!' 'Please forgive me!' said Eugen quickly. 'What I said was atrocious. As to marrying again, I believe the only known safeguard against second marriages is not to have entered upon a first, but I may be mistaken. In any case I had no business to insult you because I dislike the kind of people you intend to receive. They cannot have worse manners than I am guilty of. Before we join Otto and the little American, tell me that you forgive your stupid old Eugen; but tell me also that you forgive Otto the worse sin of competing with Jews? For if it is bad to despise them—it must be worse to imitate them! Or if you cannot forgive him, remember that you are too good for him and that to be too good for a vain man weakens him in his fight against his lower self.'

Eugénie stood quite still and fixed Eugen with indignant eyes. 'You mean that because I would not be his mistress I have helped him to be base?' she demanded. Eugen met her indignation with unchanged gentleness. 'It is nothing which you have done or left undone which has hurt him,' he replied. 'It is what you are. You could not help this. You would be right to be angry with me if I had asked you to try. But will you not remember that Otto also is what he is, and that he has suffered nearly as much from caring for you perhaps as you have suffered from caring for so light a man?' Eugénie hesitated. 'I wish you would not call him light!' she said in a low voice. 'Ah, then you have forgiven him!' said Eugen, smiling a little sadly. 'It is probably only I—who remain unforgiven?' They had reached the grand stand; and Eugénie looked away from him without answering.

XVII

The eyes of the two men met above a mass of papers on Otto's desk and measured each other carefully. Eugen leaned back with a gesture of weariness. Otto shrugged his shoulders impatiently and began to walk restlessly about the room. 'Well,' he exclaimed at last, 'why don't you say something, Eugen, instead of sitting there like a hen on a chalk egg? Surely you have not been through that haystack for nothing?' 'I find,' said Eugen after a brief pause, 'a good deal to say, but I doubt your patience. On one side we have this heap of liabilities, past and to come—there cannot be such another in Wien—and on the other your balance is overdrawn. The overdraft, I understand from the bank, is final. This is the result of more than a year's co-operation with Jews. I see something also which you have neglected to mention to me, but which I very much dislike—there appears to be a second mortgage here upon Trauenstein, a mortgage made in the name of Herr Julius Mandelbaum. A man out of whose hands it would have been well to keep.' 'One must have foreign capital to speculate with!' said Otto impatiently. 'I tried everyone else first, but Mandelbaum is the only man who could lend me a thousand English pounds—and I am not in his hands. He will never foreclose with Elisabeth between us. All their interests are mutual!' 'Ah,' said Eugen. 'So you are in *her* hands. They are not small and they struck me as powerful. Do you like the sensation?' Otto groaned. 'How was I to know,' he said, coming to a standstill before his friend, 'what a liaison with a middle-aged Jewess would be like? I had never had one! Hitherto the ladies who have honoured me with their friendships had other resources. Elisabeth has none. If I had had any idea of what a woman of forty who has always been respectable demands from life! The worst of it is she pays! She is no expense to me, and she brings money in. She is to come, as you know, this afternoon, and she tells me she has at last got hold of an investment that is worth a capital sum. That is what I need—hitherto the money coming in has been altogether on too small a scale. Our little plans have succeeded; that milk scheme, for instance, came through so easily—I thought the future plain sailing! And my arrangement for the Armament factory would have prevented the second mortgage and given me permanent security if those damned lily-livered old maids that call themselves a League of Nations hadn't suddenly blundered in upon it and made everything impossible! No, I've had no luck—unless this idea Elisabeth brings with her this afternoon clears off the rubbish heap before us! But at what a cost! Why should I have to spend my time with a woman I dislike under the added disadvantage of having to be pleasant to her?' 'I am glad that you put this question,' said Eugen after a pause, 'since it is one I was about to put to you. Do you not think that your plan at the time of the Breakdown has proved a mistake? I disliked it then, but I was willing for you to try it, since without a trial one could not have persuaded you of its drawbacks. Now I think you have sufficiently tested them.

'You have enjoyed measuring your wits against Mandelbaum; and at first you got the better of him. You have advantages that he has not; but you have this disadvantage. You have only your wits to use, and he has forty years' commercial experience behind his wits. That deed I came upon just now may be an excessively ugly business, my dear fellow, and I think it should prove to you that the game has gone against you. The game—and the candle for which the game was played. We come now to this Jewish lady. She has done for you all that you imagined she could; she assists you, she even protects you. If you were madly in love with her one would turn away one's head. "Deplorable!" one would say. "But men do these things, and while doing them—whatever the result may be—they enjoy them." But you are enjoying nothing—except the protection of a Jewish lady. My dear boy, this is worse than deplorable! It comes as near as possible to a thing so ugly that I shall not name it. Can we not find a way out of the whole affair and leave these dubious fishermen to fish in their troubled waters by themselves?' 'But of course one can!' replied Otto irritably. 'I am not such a fool as you imply. Did I not always keep the American heiress up my sleeve? It is true you have done your best to prevent my success. Somehow or other I find her suddenly transferred to Eugénie's flat! Franz Salvator hardly had the wit to put her there, but even he cannot fail to take advantage of her presence. I tell you frankly, when I see Franz and Eugénie interfering—and interfering successfully—with my arrangements, it is not to their account that I shall present my little bill for damages! It is to yours!' Eugen waved a protesting cigarette. 'Surely! surely,' he murmured soothingly, 'a little accident should not be suspected as an intrigue? What has become of your nerves, my dear boy? Not brandy, I know. You were always a moderate drinker—then it must be the Bleileben—it is she who has brought you to doubt your oldest friend in this painful and unnecessary manner! Come, marry the heiress if you will—and can! But, if not, listen to me! Dismiss your present establishment, sell your motor and horses, let this flat to the English as well as the one above it. Live for a time with me. We will get rid of this Jewish lady together; and, as soon as you have cleared the mortgage, make a good marriage—or find a profitable speculation which you and I can undertake by ourselves with our unaided natural resources. They are not despicable.' 'And I should be in a position to make good speculations, should I,' asked Otto scornfully, 'when I had put down my motor and sunk into apparent penury? My dear Eugen, you may have the best legal mind in the world, but you know as much about high finance as your little Lisa! Appearance is everything! You must look as if you were on the top of the wave or you will soon find yourself at the bottom of it. Mandelbaum has four motors!' 'And he has five factories,' replied Eugen. 'One looks from the motors to the factories, and one sees where they come from. Your motor, my dear, runs on air. I look at it, and I look behind it. I don't say, "This man is rich—trust him!" I say, "This man is extravagant—beware of him!"' 'You have the logic of a mouse,' replied Otto; 'in speculations such as mine timidity gains nothing. The public is impressed if you know how to be impressive. I may not have many gifts, but I flatter myself that when I wish to impress—I *am* impressive.' 'I am not sure that in the end,' replied Eugen cautiously, 'one does not find that one has impressed only those whom it would have been wiser to escape impressing.'

Even as he spoke the door opened abruptly, and Conrad announced breathlessly, with less than his usual impressive dignity, '*Ihre Excellenz Frau Bleileben.*' Conrad liked to make his announcements slowly and in due form; Elisabeth had plunged upstairs at a reckless speed and hurried his form. Much had happened to Elisabeth since her first appearance in Otto's library, and she came in now in a very different manner. She was without shyness, and the glance she cast about her was the proprietary glance of someone to whom the room—or the man in it—belongs.

'Ah,' she said, without pleasure, 'Baron Erdödy!' Elisabeth had expected Eugen. Otto had insisted on his presence and she had resented his insistence. Elisabeth knew a little too much about Eugen; he was an influence, and she had never been able to bear influences other than her own. She intended, since the occasion was forced upon her, to find him his place and put him into it. He was either to be their man of business and do what he was told—or she would quarrel with him. If she quarrelled with him, Otto must, out of mere courtesy to her, give him up. Her sharp irritable eyes took in both men at a glance. It would be necessary to go very carefully with Otto, and only to quarrel with Eugen when she had a good enough pretext. Otto looked tired and depressed. Fortunately she had very good news for him; her eyes softened and sparkled. She ignored a little brusquely the chair Eugen had hastened to offer her, and, crossing over to Otto, patted him gently on the arm and sank into the chair nearest him. It was a very deep low chair, and required a graceful figure with long legs. Elisabeth's legs were short, and her fat little feet barely touched the ground in front of her. 'Now,' she said, 'business first, and pleasure after, or, in this case, perhaps both together. I'm sure you're both dying to know what I've got up my sleeve.' Eugen regarded her impassively; anything less like a death from anxiety than the fatigued politeness of his manner could hardly have been imagined. The woman was better dressed, he thought to himself, but even more common than he had remembered her. All her gestures, and she was a woman who made many gestures, were as stiff as if they had been made with drumsticks. 'The beauty of the whole thing,' Elisabeth went on, 'is that it's so simple, so legal! One has only to act with dispatch and one turns over a sum!—I shan't pretend to give it in *Kronen*, but the total amount will be a hundred thousand pounds—for which one puts down only ten thousand pounds! It sounds like a joke—but about money I don't make jokes.' 'You should, Elisabeth,' Otto murmured under his breath, 'you should. Money is a subject that lends itself readily to wit—and is far too serious for most of us to face comfortably without laughter. Your figures are amazing. Where do you put down ten thousand pounds to draw in such a beneficent return?' Elisabeth leaned forward; she forgot that Otto had once warned her not to lean forward in that particular chair. The effect upon a short-legged woman, he had explained, was disastrous. Traces of the disaster were visible upon the faces of both her listeners, but Elisabeth seldom observed the faces of her listeners. 'You know Regenswirt—the transport people?' she demanded. 'They run between Linz and Buda. They have twelve steamboats, and it has always been a good line. Regenswirt, father and son, and the two Pistors owned it. Before the war it was the best river service we had, and in 1914 they put on fresh steamers. Well, one knows what trade is now. Naturally, like all the other firms, they have run down. But, unlike all the other firms, they refused to sell. You know the English are taking all the river traffic? They mean to have the Danube under their pillow. But, if you will believe it, this Regenswirt—the son was killed—and the two Pistors are Pan-German! Pan-German to the ears. Idiotically Pan-German! I ask you—because you have lost a son in the war—do you wish to lose all the rest of your possessions? They hold on—they run at a loss, they say they would rather die than sell to the English. And die they will of course unless they are rescued. Regenswirt came to my husband last night to appeal to him for help, some kind of Government help even. As if any of our Ministers would be such fools! Even my husband, who hasn't a high intelligence, nearly laughed in his face. It was pitiable, Regenswirt's condition. He told us he would sell gladly for twenty million *Kronen* in any solid *Valuta*, lock, stock and barrel—to-morrow—to a fellow countryman—but to the English—not until all three of them were drowned in Danube mud! I said nothing. I signalled to my husband to play with the idea sympathetically; to say that a loan was possible and then to get rid of him—as quickly as one could get rid of his gratitude. Then I said, "Go at once to the English—find out from them what their figure is, tell them you will use Ministerial pressure to induce Regenswirt to sell—if the figure is high enough! Be very careful, say it is for the good of the country, that you can only advise a sale if the price is substantial enough to capitalize a good land scheme. Talk a great deal about land schemes—the English think we should do much with the few hundred miles of stones they have left to us—! Say it must be a figure to cover the boats and the dock rights—the good-will—everything as it stands —but about this do not lie, for the English must have spies on the river and will know the facts! Promise delivery of everything within a fortnight, and come away with a hundred thousand as an offer!'' My husband, when a line is laid down for him, follows it well. He returned this morning with the offer in his pocket. All that remained to do was to meet Regenswirt and tell him of a buyer—an Austrian of course. The poor creature jumped at it. I have the rough draft of the agreement in my pocket. Now what do you say, Otto, to your little Elisabeth?' Otto said nothing to his little Elisabeth. He drew his eyebrows together and looked down at the carpet. The thick soft rug at his feet had no communication to make to him but its accustomed softness; still it was a refuge; Otto did not want either to look at Eugen or to see Elisabeth. Eugen never took his eyes from Elisabeth's excited face. He read in it her happy greed, the complete absence of the faintest scruple, and a naïve and childish pleasure in successful acquisition. She had Otto—she had money with which to keep Otto. Life was for a moment simple to Elisabeth, simple and satisfactory; and such moments are rare. The expression on her face did not make it beautiful, but it made it curiously touching. 'Of course,' said Otto, without raising his eyes from the rug, 'it's a very astonishing offer. What do you think, Eugen?' Eugen settled his eyeglass firmly in his eye; he spoke without a trace of either surprise or annoyance. 'It is indeed,' he assented blandly, 'a very large sum. And you really think the Regenswirt firm would be willing to sell for the equivalent of twenty million *Kronen?*' 'To-night they will be willing. We need only an Austrian signature to the agreement and Otto's five thousand pounds, to which five thousand I add my own. Naturally my name must not appear on account of my husband's position.' Elisabeth spoke triumphantly. 'It is as simple,' she said, 'as holding out one's hand for a cup of tea.' She held out her hand, and both men watched her as if fascinated; while she held it, her thick broad thumb, closed like a vice on her short fingers. 'And Regenswirt,' asked Eugen, after a pause, 'will not limit the sale by a condition that it goes only to fellow countrymen?' 'That will be understood,' said Elisabeth indifferently. 'We will give our word of course, but nothing legal. Here is the agreement; I took advice on it myself from my husband's lawyer. One can go through it as if it were a paper hoop!' Eugen read the document out loud to Otto in a slow expressionless voice without moving a muscle of his face. Then he folded it carefully and returned it to Elisabeth. 'Yes,' he said quietly, 'I agree with your

E   129

lawyer; there is nothing in the document more binding than the fact that you have given your word of honour to a patriot.' Elisabeth bounced round upon him, her eyes sparkling with anger. 'You call yourself a business man,' she said angrily; 'what kind of an objection is this for a business man to make? All you are asked to say is if we are legally safe.' Eugen bowed. 'I should imagine,' he said, 'that you would always be—legally safe.' 'You forget who you are speaking to,' said Elisabeth; 'in fact I don't know why you are speaking at all—this offer has been made to Otto. It is for him to speak!' 'Speak, Otto,' said Eugen gently; 'this—lady—listens!' 'It is an enormous sum of money,' said Otto thickly; 'it is an amazing opportunity, Elisabeth, and your handling of it is of course also amazing. But one hesitates, does one not, to take advantage of men who love their country?' 'But, Otto,' said Elisabeth passionately, her voice softening marvellously at his name, as if it flowed round him, 'they will gain nothing by their obstinacy. What we do now others would do—if we left it—later on! Or, if they did not, our poor friends would ruin themselves. Ten thousand pounds will be a god-send to them. Remember we are not depriving them of the sum the English offer; they would not touch it!' 'Yes—remember, Otto,' Eugen murmured, 'we are only touching—what these Jewish gentlemen—will not touch.' 'Will you hold your tongue!' cried Elisabeth, now thoroughly exasperated. 'It is nothing to do with you, and if you get anything out of it, it will be only a small commission! I suppose it is that knowledge which makes you speak like a fool? The grapes are sour, are they not, for you? But for Otto and myself they are the finest in the world. If you don't wish to help us get them—keep your hands off!' 'Excellenz,' said Eugen, and into his usually quiet voice came the sudden rasp of a Prussian officer, 'you can insult your husband, because he is your husband, and you can insult Graf Wolkenheimb because you are his mistress, but there is no relationship between us of which you may take advantage.' Elisabeth struggled with her breath; she was so angry that she dreaded the sound of her own voice, and yet even while she burned with rage she was afraid of the cold inscrutable eyes fixed on her own. She felt that she was struggling against a power that no matter what she said or did would control itself, and her own powers flinched at her lack of self-restraint. 'Is your paid man of business,' she said at last, turning to Otto, 'to insult me in your presence with impunity?' 'My dear Elisabeth,' replied Otto, with bored displeasure, 'please lower your voice. Both you and Eugen seem to be behaving in a most tiresome way about nothing. I thought I had already told you that if my greatest friend undertakes my business for me, the obligation is mine, not his—and I must say you have added to that obligation considerably in the last five minutes. Eugen, my dear fellow, don't be brutal. It's quite unnecessary, and it sounds rather badly in this room. I don't think the acoustic properties were arranged for plain speaking. I expect I differ from you both about this affair—but under no circumstances do I propose to lose my temper.' 'Excellenz,' said Eugen in smoother tones, 'Otto is of course perfectly right—those who have nothing in common are under no compulsion to express their differences. Let us both overlook this unfortunate interlude and return to our business. The plan you suggest is perfectly practicable no doubt—I daresay such things are done every day in a commercial world by commercial people—but for men like Otto and myself—it is simply impossible—you understand me —impossible.' 'But why impossible?' asked Elisabeth in a lower voice, but with even more incisiveness. 'I don't understand you. Either a thing is legal or it is not legal. This money lies there to be picked up. Nobody is robbed by it, and Otto and I are the better by ninety thousand English pounds. You cannot mean that you will refuse it, Otto? I simply will not accept Baron Erdödy's word for yours. You admit yourself that you differ from him. As I said before he is secondary in this affair—if he doesn't choose to touch it we have my lawyer to fall back on, or you can arrange matters yourself. If you refuse I shall be broken-hearted. Indeed you *cannot* refuse what it has been my greatest joy to procure for you?' 'I am grateful,' said Otto, going to the window, 'and it is hard to refuse it, Elisabeth, since if I refuse you also suffer—but I think that I agree with Eugen—it is a shade harder to accept.' 'I cannot believe,' said Eugen firmly, 'that if you refuse to accept this partnership Excellenz will be obliged to renounce her project?' 'Am I a fool or mad?' demanded Elisabeth hotly. 'Because you both are! On the contrary, since Otto is mad I will be sane for him. I shall take my plan immediately to Mandelbaum; he will fall upon it like a cat on a sardine.' Otto turned round suddenly from the window. 'Mandelbaum?' he asked. 'Why Mandelbaum?' 'Because he has five thousand pounds always handy for a good investment,' said Elisabeth, 'and because, if you wish to know, we see eye to eye on such matters. I shall not need to break my heart to get *him* to accept a fortune which involves my own!' 'There is your husband,' suggested Otto weakly. 'You are right,' said Elisabeth, 'there is my husband, and there he is likely to remain! He is a little man who has not got five thousand pounds in the world. What there is on his plate—I put there!' 'And apparently upon mine also,' said Otto, under his breath. He turned his back on Eugen and looked down at Elisabeth. 'It is a handsome sum, dear Elisabeth,' he said gently. 'I always hoped to sell myself for a good amount. I still hope that Eugen will do the business part of this deal for me, but even if he refuses—I agree.' Eugen said nothing. Elisabeth looked up into Otto's eyes, her face transfigured with emotion. Never in her life had she felt so overwhelmed by relief, and never had any triumph tasted so sweetly on her lips. 'You have done this for me,' she whispered. 'I shall never forget it.' 'And for ninety thousand pounds,' said Eugen in a low voice, but neither of them heard him.

It was all over; Otto would not go back on what he had said. He would have refused the offer if it had not been for the mention of Julius Mandelbaum. Elisabeth had inadvertently, in the very moment of her failure, called up the spirit of Otto's vanity, and it was a spirit which never failed to respond to a call. Eugen took out his eyeglass, wiped it, replaced it and rose slowly to his feet. For a moment, as he stood at the door, his eyes and Otto's met. Otto's eyes were full of a sick distaste; he turned away his head as if he were ashamed for Eugen to see his shame.

XVIII

It was raining, and the natural thing for Eugen to do was to go home to dinner. But he could not go home; he felt as if his heart was homeless.

Behind the Votiv Kirche there is a small café; ivy and pots of pink geranium sheltered its little tables from the dust of the street. Eugen said of it, that the food smelled like the waiters, and the waiters smelled like the food; but he could get cognac there;

and it struck him that that was what he wanted more than he wanted anything else. He longed to have the raw edge of fact blurred to him. Cognac would fortify him in what he had done. After a time his legs would become irresponsible, and his wits would cease to fling their home-thrusts at his heart. There was no one else in the café. After a moment, a very small, very shabby old waiter sidled out of a door behind Eugen and approached the table. He was a forlorn old waiter, his head was bald, his shoes brown, his seams staring. A vague accumulation of grease, the baptism of years, hung drearily about him. 'Cognac, Herr Ober,' said Eugen courteously. The old man, his self-respect faintly stirred by a title he had never deserved, padded swiftly back into the darkness and reappeared with a thick glass on a splashed saucer.

The streets grew emptier; the lights shone mistily in the rain; behind Eugen the Alserstrasse was like a shining black funnel; in front of him, the open avenue and the space around stretched wide and empty into a formless sea. The two spires of the Votiv Kirche thickened in the sky. Each street lamp made a pool of light in which the occasional passers-by shone suddenly and vanished. There was an island of lights in the middle of the avenue where people waited for the trams, and there, late in the evening, Eugen easily distinguished the brisk impatient figure of Elisabeth Bleileben. He watched her clambering fiercely into a crowded tram; she pushed through the passengers as if they were made of cardboard. Ruthless and efficient, giving and receiving the full brunt of contact, she moved as if in her elation nothing could withstand her will. Her elbows were lifted, her head lowered, and her feet thrust pitilessly forward. 'What a moment for an artist,' Eugen murmured to himself; 'it would be profane to make such a figure and call it the "Assumption," but it would reveal something in this essentially modern type which needs revealing! Otto would like the idea.' Then it came over Eugen once more that Otto and he would no longer exchange ideas as they used to exchange them. This separation of values would make all intercourse a difficult thing. The sense of their difference was what Eugen wanted to forget, but the cognac was not acting as he had hoped it would act. It cleared his brain with the same pitiless energy with which Elisabeth had mounted her tram. What would happen if he agreed to undertake the business he had refused? One could at least ask oneself that? Life would go on the same, Otto would be infinitely relieved and protected. Elisabeth Bleileben would lick her lips, and despise him the more; but Eugen cared nothing for the opinion of people who were beneath him; what he cared for was his own opinion of himself. On the other hand if he kept to his decision he would gradually lose Otto. He would lose Otto because Otto would not be able to bear Eugen's knowing what had happened to him unless Eugen participated in it. He would feel that he was no longer superior, and Otto never forgave, and indeed never associated with, those to whom he could not feel superior. There were two dangers that would arise in leaving Otto alone; one was the danger to himself, for Otto was his life; and the other—and Eugen thought of the other with a deeper pang—was the danger to Otto. If he left Otto to Elisabeth, he would be in very great danger. Not at once; Elisabeth had a head on her shoulders, she was less shifty than Mandelbaum, and about her desire to serve Otto there could be no doubt whatever. But this desire to serve him was the product of her ardour. As long as Otto played straight with Elisabeth he was safe. But how long would Otto play straight with Elisabeth? He was not used to disgust, and he never accepted with patience what he disliked. Otto's vanity would blind him to his personal danger; he believed in an Elisabeth whose one desire was to please, but Elisabeth was a single-minded person—suppose that her one desire became—to displease? Eugen had seen the flash of hate in Elisabeth's eyes when he thwarted her will, and he had measured it with some care. He thought it was an active quality. 'In another class of life or perhaps under other circumstances,' Eugen said to himself, 'she would throw vitriol, and what she threw would hit. It is important that the vitriol—and in all business intimacies there is something which takes the place of vitriol—should remain in my hands. Otto will be careless—he will let her lawyer hold proofs against him—he won't know how to protect himself, and Elisabeth, even while she is in love with him, will collect these proofs, and when she ceases to be in love with him or finds that her love is useless, she will fall back on being poisonous. One does not get into trams like that for nothing!' 'Herr Ober! another cognac. You have a clock in there; perhaps it will be simpler if you continue to bring me a fresh cognac every quarter of an hour until I tell you to stop.' 'For myself,' Eugen went on gloomily, sipping at his fourth glass, 'I give up Otto—and I cease to be amused. What would Eugénie say! Eugénie would again urge upon me her idea of a new life. I might have accepted the idea once, but I am too old a man for a new life. New lives, what do they mean in the end? A fresh set of little troubles, more solid perhaps than the old. People who talk of new lives believe there will be no new troubles. They are idealists. Eugénie is one; Franz Salvator, though he flatters himself he is a materialist, is another. They make out of their fancies little playgrounds for their energies. I too should like to make for myself a little playground, but of a different kind. I should have liked a wife, I should have liked children—I flatter myself I could have removed from Youth some of its stumbling blocks—but my playground was inaccessible, and Eugénie's would fatigue me. Poor Eugénie! what will she make of her enlightened lower classes? Austrian *Hausfrauen* playing at Cassandras; Englishwomen, who look as if they had been born in waterproofs, without sufficient attraction to seduce umbrellas. Jews who think philanthropy a good disinfectant for gutters. And in the middle of them—I see her! My Princess with the beauty of the lost centuries upon her, history in her eyes, and romance upon her eyelashes. The last of the Renaissance Madonnas! And it is with this group she suggests to herself the restoration of our Empire! I don't believe in making the world better, I found it quite good enough when I had the means to enjoy it. I don't believe in the recovery of Austria. Austria is dead. We are a little group of parasites playing on a dead body. Some play on it to live, as Otto does, and others because they think to make it alive again, but we are all parasites, and the body is dead, and the dead do not return. Herr Ober! this brandy is made from wood, from very rotten wood; will you do me the favour to drink a glass of it, and after you have drunk it, will you tell me what you do when an action is impossible to you, and to refrain from that action is equally impossible?' The hovering waiter bowed very low, he suppressed a yawn, and his bewildered eyes settled gratefully on Eugen. A glass of brandy would warm him very much. 'In that case, Herr Baron,' he murmured, 'I find often—that such an action is not impossible.' 'Bring me then', said Eugen, 'a pencil and some paper. Here is five hundred *Kronen* for yourself, and when you return I think it will be the moment for the next cognac!' The waiter vanished with a sudden spurt of speed. The gentleman must be a real Baron and mad—but what a pleasant form madness takes in the higher walks of life! But there was a doubt to be laid, before the waiter could drink his share of the stranger's madness in peace. 'It is a great deal of cognac,' he murmured confidentially, returning with the tenth glass, 'already it amounts to two thousand *Kronen*!' 'It repays itself,' answered Eugen, 'but here is the money that you may feel reassured. So far I rob only on a large scale. Now leave me. Before one does what is impossible— one likes to be left alone.' The waiter scurried inside the café, but he kept his eye on Eugen from the doorway. Was this mysterious gentleman about to commit suicide? There had been a great many suicides lately and some of them took place late at night in solitary cafés; and it was often very inconvenient for the waiter who was left in charge of the café. Also they sometimes called first for a pencil and paper, and wrote wills. But this was a very short will. It was written in a moment, and the gentleman did not seem to want to part with it after he had written it. He drew it back hesitatingly into his left hand.

Eugen stopped talking to himself; pictures took the place of words, pictures of his youth, scenes in which he had acted sometimes so capably and well, and sometimes, in spite of all his sense, with so much futility! Here he was at the end of forty years, and he had won none of the things which at twenty he had set out to win; not even (though he had worked harder for these things than for any ambitions of his own) had he done what he had longed to do for his friends. He had wanted to help Otto to be a Prime Minister, and to see Franz Salvator a General; and Eugénie— well—he wanted to see Eugénie a happy woman. Eugen had still believed that if Otto saw Eugénie often enough, any other woman beside her would be eclipsed as easily as the light of a fire is eclipsed by the sun. Even lately, behind his wishes for Franz Salvator, had lurked the hope that when Otto saw the little American under Eugénie's roof, he would be unable to resist the passion of his life. But now he was less sure; even if Otto asked Eugénie, would she want him? Eugénie saw now, with eyes too clear for happiness, what had become of her dreams.

To give her whole-heartedly to Otto, without a sign of his own love, had been the great surrender of his youth; and it had been useless. Otto was not worthy of her; and he had taken no advantage of Eugen's invisible sacrifice. But a man's loyalty to a woman is narrower than his loyalty to a man. Eugen would have died many times over for Eugénie; but he could not help being a little resentful that she had not stooped to Otto. He would have preferred to see Eugénie less perfect than to see Otto sink lower than he need have sunk. 'I am a sentimentalist!' he said to himself. 'No woman ever changed a man's character—and yet I make Eugénie responsible for Otto's! The truth of it is that I wished to replace Destiny, and Destiny decided that I was too small a man for the part. If I could have helped to win them happiness, I would have been content to return to my carpets and my Lisa. Being a man of habit I shall return to those blessings without content, having—after forty years—made nothing, except a pretty interior and a useful cook. One isn't after all middle-aged for nothing, one sees what has taken the place of all one's hopes!'

Eugen slowly unclosed his left hand, the waiter in the doorway trembled. Was this the moment for the revolver? 'Herr Ober!' called Eugen, 'you will infinitely oblige me by carrying this note across the road to number 15 Universitätstrasse, and leaving it with the *Hausmeister*! There is no answer. No-one will be likely to come here in your absence. If they do I will make your excuses.' Once more Eugen read through the few scrawled words. They satisfied him. 'I will obey the orders of the Jewish lady.' Yes, Otto would understand—they were enough. He thought he had made up his mind to leave Otto, but the habit of years was too strong in him, he could not face the emptiness of a future without Otto. 'I am too old a dog,' he said to himself. 'You can take a young dog away from its master, but it is not fair to drag away an old one.' The waiter shot a cautious glance up the Alserstrasse and down towards the Schottenring. If only there was a policeman, but there was no policeman! After all the gentleman looked very quiet; and he had just got a fresh cognac. One would not surely shoot oneself before one had drunk a perfectly good cognac? The waiter clutched the note, and hurried across the road, looking back anxiously now and then over his shoulder. Eugen watched him with a faint smile. 'There goes my honour,' he murmured. 'What a messenger!' Rain pattered heavily down on the awning above his head. All the little green tables in front of him were dripping. The trams had ceased to run—the night and the storm together made their own sounds undisturbed by man.

Eugen gave a sudden start when he heard, 'Shall I bring you

another cognac, Herr Baron?' murmured in his ear. 'Ah, you have returned already?' he asked with horror in his voice. 'What a little time—what a little time it took!' 'But it was only just across the road, sir,' the waiter reminded him; 'one does not take much time to cross a road.' 'No,' said Eugen in a low voice, 'that is true —one does not take much time to cross a road. One more cognac then, to wash the memory of that crossing down.' 'Certainly, Herr Baron,' the waiter replied with relief, 'at the Herr Baron's orders!' To the waiter—this was curious, Eugen thought—he was still a gentleman, but to himself he would never be a gentleman any more. Gentlemen did not deceive patriots; they took no advantage of legal flaws; they did not stick to their friends in their base actions because they thought it was more base to let them do wrong alone. What, Eugen asked himself, did gentlemen do in his circumstances? Probably they killed themselves, but if they did that they were of no more use to their friends. There was the Danube. He could go through Am Hof; down the Judenplatz; stop for a moment at his favourite church Sta. Maria am Gestade. —He would look at the spire of very ancient, very surprising Gothic; grotesque without the clumsiness of the grotesque style, and Gothic without that smack of empty dignity which he was too Eastern to appreciate.—Then in a minute he would reach the bridge over the Canal. But he would not drown himself, since— if he did—the very thing he still believed he might prevent, would happen to Otto, he would be left in Elisabeth Bleileben's unfettered hands. If it had only not been the English to whom he was going to betray Regenswirt! How wonderful it would have been to take Otto's five thousand pounds to Regenswirt and say: 'Take this—run your line longer—and when this is finished I have some little carpets that are worth a thousand or two—I will sell those for you. It may be in a year or two commerce will have improved, and your hard corner be turned, but whatever happens I will help you to the last moment to resist the English!' Not that Eugen liked Germans, they were too efficient, and organized as no Viennese ever dreamed of organizing. He had looked down upon them because they had neither ideas nor manners, and they were too solemn ever to laugh at themselves; but they had made a magnificent fight, their will-power was enormous, and their industry unflagging. They would have success again; they were still a country. 'We shall not,' said Eugen, staring straight before him. 'We shall never have power again. We shall make beautiful music, and people will buy our embroideries and our ladies' little hand-bags. They will visit our palaces as if they were museums, and our Archduke's castles in the mountains will become hotels. Perhaps some day, if our Jews are energetic enough, we shall become a second Switzerland. We shall be liked better than the Swiss, but we shall not be so efficient. People will have forgotten by then that we were once—Austria! God! and I sell my brothers to the English! I who know—and no one better—that if it had not been for their intervention we should have won the war! Russia was top-heavy; she was rotten at the core, France had no tenacity. We shook them loose in 1914, and we would have dragged them down by 1917. Our nerves were stronger than theirs, and in the long run men win on their nerves. But the English! They have no armies—they know no discipline, their education stops before their minds are open; and yet—they win! Their reason is never a scarecrow to act upon their nerves. They come into a war casually as into a game of play, and they never go out until their side has won. We should have so easily conquered without them! America would never have come in—those little spiteful Latins would have been held down under our thumbs. But Fate has turned us back. Germany she has injured—Austria she has chosen to destroy; and since I can do nothing for a country that has ceased to exist, since all that I stand for is dead, why should I not let Otto decide how best we are to face together the years that are left? Something of mine has ceased to exist to-night; one dies little by little all the time! It was not a useful possession—my honour—still I valued it—and it is gone! Herr Ober!—this is the last cognac. I go now, if I can stand upright. Yes! I stand wonderfully. The Votiv Kirche has a cluster of towers, and I perceive that the street rears, an action not habitual to streets. No, do not trouble yourself, good Herr Ober—if you have a bed, go to it. It is a little late, is it not? You think that light is the dawn? You may be right; I should have said it was a lamp reflected in a puddle. You have been very attentive.' The waiter's eyes glistened as Eugen fumbled at his pocketbook; the thousand *Kronen* he found in his hand was like a fortune to him, he hurried off into the darkness lest his magnificent patron might come to his senses and recall it. Eugen lurched heavily against a tree—then he found the back of a bench—he moved forward cautiously until at last all support failed him, and he waded out into a sea of faint and empty light; into this he fell headlong, and found himself in the gutter. A sense of peace stole over him. This was what he had been wanting all night. One did not fall out of a gutter, one did not sink beneath it. One had indeed no feeling left that could be associated with height.

At length the cool dawn wind roused Eugen out of his stupor. It was light now, only without sunshine. The city lay as silent and as lifeless as an empty glove. 'All over,' said Eugen, rising first to his knees, and then, with a great effort, to his feet, 'world's dead. Good thing too—only I've got to bury it. Most unfortunate coming out like this without a spade. Must go home and fetch one.'

XIX

Franz Salvator dressed himself with great care; he first laid his clothes out on the bed and brushed them till not a speck of dust or a deflected hair betrayed the lack of a professional valet. Fortunately his clothes were very good; they had been made in Savile Row before the war, and they resisted the processes of time. Then he stood in front of his small glass and spent several ineffectual minutes trying to take the curl out of his hair; finally he satisfied himself that his tie, his handkerchief and his socks coalesced exactly as they should, without revealing too conscious a partnership. It was a moment when he would have liked to wear his dress uniform and all his medals, but uniforms were now forbidden in the streets so that he had to do the best he could with civilian clothes handled by the smarter type of military mind. It might have been supposed from the extent and intensity of Franz Salvator's preparations that he was going to pay court to a Duchess; but he was not; he was going to make a call upon Dr. Carl Jeiteles. He felt that it was not a step to take lightly; in taking it at all he was breaking the traditions of his class, and even though he must break with these traditions he was unable to imagine a moment when a change of spirit could do away with the scrupulousness of form. Eugénie had not mentioned Carl Jeiteles to him since the night in the Rathaus

Gardens. She had left the initiative to him. Franz felt that she had done right, but that her having done it forced upon him the obligation he most wished to avoid. She was not going to put any pressure upon him because she knew that Franz Salvator would put pressure upon himself. On the way to the hospital he meant to consult Eugen as to the best way of carrying this obligation out. Eugen would naturally disapprove intensely of his visit, but that would not make any difference to his advice. You might do exactly what Eugen most disliked, but if you went to him for advice he would show you how to succeed in doing what he did not like with the same scrupulous skill with which he advised you how to accomplish the plan nearest his heart.

Lisa opened the door to Franz Salvator, with reddened eyelids and eyes that looked half drowned in tears. 'Oh,' she cried, 'I am so glad that you have come, Herr Kapitän! If you had not I should have telephoned to you this afternoon! Things are wrong with my dear Herr Baron—they are *very, very* wrong!' 'What is it? Is he ill?' Franz Salvator asked anxiously, 'I have not seen him since last week, but then he was quite as usual?' Lisa led the way into the Biedermeier room and stood there wringing her hands. There was no dust or damage visible to the naked eye; the furniture still blazed about them, as if the sun had been caught and held captive in the old polished surfaces. Lisa's anxiety was deep, but it had not gone deep enough to betray the exquisiteness of her daily care. 'No, it is not an illness,' she said, in a low shaken voice, 'at least if it is—it is an illness of the heart! Five days ago he went out as well as ever—he was to come back for dinner but he did not return—he came back at dawn—deranged as it were——' 'Drunk?' interrupted Franz Salvator gently, with eyes in which an anxious sympathy prevented the slightest condemnation. Lisa nodded. 'For a few hours', she said, 'one expected he would be—what one is naturally at such times!—but at twelve he got up and went out again. He was very steady and quiet then, but he would take nothing to eat, and when he came back an hour later he went straight to bed, and he has lain there ever since—with his face to the wall. He does not notice what he eats, and he speaks as if there was nothing left to say!' Franz Salvator looked very grave; he paused for a moment while his eyes met Lisa's. 'And all this time he has been drinking?' he murmured. Lisa would not have admitted this fact to anyone in the world except Franz

Salvator, but experience had taught her that he had an unchanging heart, and that her master would be as safe with him as with herself. 'Yes,' she said simply, 'but it is not the drink that I mind—the poor one—it is the unhappiness! I cannot find out what it is. It cannot be money for when I urged him to take less brandy he said, "Ah, Liebling, I can afford it now!" ' 'And the Herr Graf?' asked Franz Salvator, glancing away from her. 'He calls daily,' said Lisa, 'and each day after he has been I think that I find my Herr Baron worse!' Franz Salvator sighed deeply. 'I will see him,' he said, 'and tell you what I find. It may be necessary to ask my sister to come to him, she has great influence over him.' 'I do not think he will see the Princess,' replied Lisa, without enthusiasm. 'He has turned her picture out of his room.' 'What, the miniature of her before her marriage?' asked Frank Salvator incredulously. 'It is no longer there,' said Lisa impassively, 'and in its place—there is nothing!' 'Strange, very strange,' Franz muttered, passing quickly through the vision of carpets extended like fields of mountain flowers upon the shining floors, and through Eugen's sitting-room, in which the skilful comfort, spread out and tenantless, left a curious impression of mockery. Eugen's bedroom was a small room, looking out upon the Hof Bibliothek; a shabby cliff rising up on three sides of a square to the golden brown roof which faced his window. It was his habit to look out at it daily from his bed. It was Eugen's theory that a view should be the furniture of a room in which you wake—and he had very little else—only an old Dutch clothes press, and a Tudor four-post bed with its ancient hangings. On the grey walls hung water-colours of all the horses Franz Salvator had ridden, and the most famous of those Otto had owned. Eugen had moved his bed away from the window with its back to the Hof Bibliothek. He lay with his face turned on a blank space of wall, haggard, unshaved, his eyes sunk into his head, his colour blotched and mottled. As Franz Salvator entered, a smile of affection rose to the surface in his eyes and sank back again, leaving the face more hopeless than before. 'You have come to see how I am?' he asked in a low thick voice. 'Well—you see—I am an Austrian—that is how I am!' 'But, my dear fellow,' protested Franz Salvator, drawing a chair forward close to the bed, 'this won't do at all—we can't let you go to pieces like this. You have your friends and family as well as your country to think of. How do you suppose we are to get on without you? And the little Lisa—half drowned in tears. Tell me what has struck you down like this—some new blow?' 'Was that needed?' asked Eugen. 'I should have thought there was enough. No, my dear—I have been carrying out what I intended—and it has disagreed with me —mortally disagreed with me! You are young, too young to realize that sometimes there comes a moment when the will ceases to act because the human being who possesses it ceases to care. Why do we live? Because on the whole we do not wish to die! Why do we die—only because it is too uncomfortable to go on living. I do not say we die when we wish to die, for it has not been arranged so considerately, but we die when we have no wishes left.' 'But you have not ceased to care for us?' asked Franz Salvator in a deeply moved voice. 'You have lived for us, Eugen—I know it— that is why, whatever you do—whatever you leave undone—we belong to you and shall always need you. Even to-day—I did not come here to find out how you were—I came to ask your help.' 'Ah, if you came for that,' said Eugen, rousing himself suddenly, 'perhaps I have still that much energy. About what is it you want my help? I thought your affairs and Eugénie's were going very nicely?' Franz Salvator was silent for a moment—he was too greatly shocked and moved by Eugen's condition to mention what his errand was. He felt conscious of a deeper need; the thing he had buried—put away from him perhaps forever—came rushing back. If this were a moment for confidence at all, it was the moment for a great confidence. Eugen's eyes rested upon him with a flicker of life in them. They had looked burned-out when Franz Salvator came in; but life still smouldered there, a life that Franz Salvator might call up and hold if he went deep enough into his own heart. 'Eugen,' he said at last, 'something has happened to me since I saw you. I think it happens only once in a man's lifetime. People say that one loves many women—but it is atrocious nonsense to call what one has for women—love! What one has *once* for one woman is love, what one has for the rest—is only a snatching at something pretty which passes and which we want to hold in our hands.' 'Even more—afterwards—one wants to let it go again,' murmured Eugen, 'that something which breaks— and will not go.' Franz Salvator went on after a pause. 'I do not know if it is sorrow or happiness that has happened to me. Sorrow, I think, because she is so strange—of another race. I only know— because I have had fancies before—I have known women before

—that this is quite different. It is something that will stay in my heart always, as long as I live.' 'Ah,' said Eugen softly, 'that is interesting. Yes, it is very interesting, and it is true what you say—one gets over everything else; and probably one gets over that if one marries satisfactorily, but if not—one does not get over it. I am glad you have told me, it alters my plans. Should you say the little one returns your feeling?' Franz Salvator fixed his eyes on Eugen's. 'You will say I am a fool,' he answered, 'or perhaps even a boaster—on very slender grounds. I have not put my feelings to the test; and yet a hundred times a day whenever my eyes meet hers, I know that my eyes speak, and I think that hers answer me!' 'She is in love with you, of course,' said Eugen reflectively, 'there is no reason why she should not be. Women would always fall in love with you—unless they happened to be in love with someone else; and you are constantly together, so there is the last inducement—propinquity. Therefore, my dear—my advice to you is, make love to her a little more. It is difficult to resist love-making when it is continuous, and if the heart is involved, it is impossible. Make fierce love to her then, and after a time it will be convenient for her to contemplate marriage.' Franz Salvator's eyes returned to the floor. 'She is in my care,' he said in a low troubled voice, 'and she is very innocent. That stays in my mind as it would in yours. It is curious, for one would suppose she could not be so innocent. I take her out often in the evenings; to the most unsuitable places, cafés, night clubs, wherever she thinks she will find a "story" for her paper. It is sometimes her idea to write about the night life of Wien. At first it shocked me to think she knew of such a life, but now it only touches me. She does extraordinary things, and she does them—not like a Madonna—but like a shrewd little child that knows how not to get hurt, but has in her none of the things which in themselves are hurtful. How could I make love to her unless she will be my wife? Don't you see—if she should not—I should be taking away from her the armour in which she is safe against the world? I must not touch her hand—I must not call her by her name—unless she will be my wife; and I must not ask her to be my wife until I am quite sure that her feeling for me is as deep as mine for her. It is the accursed money that keeps me silent!' 'You have the military mind,' said Eugen impatiently. 'It goes backwards if it moves at all. My poor child—make love to her—and she will be your wife—

she will be anything that you want!' Franz Salvator shook his head obstinately. 'It may be true what you say,' he replied, 'but with me she shall run no risk. This going about constantly alone with such a girl has been a revelation to me, Eugen. The little one knows how to live. She thinks for herself, she works hard, as hard as a man, and she sees with the eyes of a woman, which see deeper and quicker than ours. I discover new things with her every day which I should not discover if I spent a lifetime alone. I know now that many of our old traditions were wrong. It is necessary for the world to change, even to break up in order to change, and I see that Eugénie is right, we must change with it—we must lift Austria by changing—not by lamenting change! It will not be a great Empire again with the most brilliant Court in Europe, but if it becomes a self-respecting small country like Switzerland which pays its way and keeps its culture, its universities, its sense of beauty and art, it will not lose its soul. And we can contribute to it by our own work and by our steadiness of outlook. It is the integrity of our work that Carol most admires. She says we are a country of artists, that we make hay and pastry with the same perfection with which our musicians make their symphonies and sonatas. Perhaps it is true? And what we have to give to Europe is a higher standard of beauty. You see, I used to know nothing except about horses, and now I am talking to you, who are an expert on art and beauty! That is what comes of falling in love with a girl who is above one's intellect!' Eugen groaned. 'All men', he said wearily, 'discover a new world when a little girl succeeds in attracting their attention! You feel very naturally that she must be a combination of the Madonna and Minerva to have been capable of so affecting you. Believe me, your intellect will climb up to hers in time; and then you will discover that the world has not changed because two young people have been remarkable enough to discover their reflections in each other's eyes. But now, Franz Salvator, let us be practical. I think it is as well you should marry this girl—better even than I thought in the first instance—but there is one very serious obstacle.' 'Her birth?' asked Franz Salvator doubtfully. 'No,' said Eugen, 'her birth, since she is an American, is out of the question; it is not a matter, therefore, that need concern us. She is as you say a good girl; probably not quite as good as you think, but that she should be good at all with this freedom of modernity is remarkable; and no doubt her goodness is warranted by experience to last; but she is not a girl to fall into the mouth like a ripe fig. Somebody else wants to marry her, somebody who generally does what he wants.' 'Otto?' asked Franz Salvator, in surprise. 'But there is Otto's liaison with the Jewess!' 'He has indeed a liaison!' replied Eugen grimly. 'He is like a fish with a hook in his jaws; but the hook is well baited. What do you say to forty-five thousand English pounds falling into his hands? Otto can be as rich as he likes now, only what he gets with it is like poison to him. He sees in your little American a way out. She has a great fortune. I approached the American Minister to make sure; he told me that he knew her father's name well, and that he made at least a million by his paper; and left it to his only child. Presumably the million remains, and Otto feels that with it he could say good-bye to the very disagreeable experience which has put him on his feet. To tell you the truth, if you had not shown me that your heart was in it I should have urged you to stand aside, for I believe that Otto would be a different man if he married successfully and had enough upon which to support life tolerably. But he can gain enough by other methods, and it is obvious that you cannot.' Franz Salvator rose to his feet, and walked slowly towards the window. The roof of the great Bibliothek shone at him, a shabby golden brown; below was the arch which led to the iron gates of the Hofburg. It was the heart of Wien; the shell of the old traditions which had been housed for centuries in its mild secretive serenity. Franz Salvator looked on its emptiness and its dignity with an aching heart. The Bibliothek was as dignified as it used to be—but the people, whose old traditions housed there, were not being quite so dignified. It was not altogether surprising that Eugen had turned his back on the walls of the Hofburg. 'Money,' Franz Salvator murmured in a low voice, 'I don't like that, Eugen—all that money!' 'My dear good child,' said Eugen impatiently, 'what does it matter to you? If you love her you are not marrying her for her money! When one loves, nothing matters! Make love to her then, and make love to her quickly or Otto will get her. He means this business very seriously indeed.' 'If her heart is mine,' said Franz Salvator under his breath, 'he won't get her!' 'You talk the language of a fool or a lover,' said Eugen huskily. 'Otto will get her because he knows how to make women take him whether they love him or not. He'll watch the girl for a weak moment, and snap her up. Don't waste time.' 'It is detestable to me to think she has all that money. I did not know it was so great a fortune!' said Franz Salvator; 'I wish to Heaven you hadn't told me.' 'I see what it is,' said Eugen; 'I shall have to get up. Ask Lisa for some hot water, and tell me while she gets it what made you come to call upon me dressed like a Crown Prince?' 'I am going to make a call upon Dr. Carl Jeiteles,' Franz Salvator explained gravely; 'Eugénie wished it. You have heard of her scheme of intellectuals meeting at our house? He is, I suppose, one.' 'He is not an intellectual,' said Eugen, getting out of bed with surprising agility. 'He is a little Jew doctor. If you go to call upon him like that you will put God knows what ideas into his head. I see I must go with you. We drop in by accident on our way to a wedding. There is a church somewhere in the neighbourhood where such an event could take place. As we pass by the hospital we remember Eugénie is anxious to know about one of her sick little girls. There is a Mitzi I remember, with a bad spine. It is fortunate that all little girls of the lower classes are called Mitzi. In the course of conversation we mention Dr. Simmons, she leads naturally to the thought of relief conferences. We remind him that Miss Hunter will draw to these meetings important American and English visitors, politicians and editors of newspapers; and we suggest that he should come to tell them about his hospital and the needs of his children. He will be quite satisfied with this suggestion—and Eugénie also—and nothing need happen which looks more personal than it should. Ah, Lisa! you will have the kindness to brush my clothes. Try to make them look like the clothes of the Herr Kapitän in whose boots one could see the reflection of a maiden-hair fern. But you will not succeed. No woman—not even you—takes boots to heart as they should be taken.' Franz Salvator followed Lisa out into the kitchen.

When Eugen joined them he still looked ill, and he walked stiffly to conceal his feebleness, but it was impossible to connect him with the broken figure with its face to the wall. His hand shook a little as he lifted his monocle to its usual position; but his ironic, twisted smile was perfectly composed. He looked with friendly approval at Franz Salvator leaning against the immaculately scrubbed table talking to Lisa. When he died, it was to Franz he had left the care of Lisa. Franz knew how to treat her, he was as natural and as kind to her as if she were Eugen's sister. Otto would have been charming too—he always was charming to Lisa—but he always made her feel uncomfortable, as a tribute to his charm. The kitchen was a delightful room; it had a spotless red-brick floor, and on the walls and dresser were the pride of Lisa's life—her copper pans—and the deep-blue and white china which she thought ought to be put in a cupboard, but which Eugen insisted on displaying. Everything was in order and as it should be. Their youth and their friendliness; the sunshine in their faces; the gleam of the copper pans, made a picture of a happy interior. As Eugen stood there looking at them he felt like a visiting ghost. His inner world had gone to pieces; there was no youth left in it—no sunshine—no illusion. He would not have felt regret if a bomb had dropped into the middle of the kitchen floor—and spread ruin to his carpets and his Brueghels. Life was a series on messes, and one spent one's time cleaning them up; if one had any heart at all, one also gave a part of one's time to cleaning up those of other people. Franz Salvator knew nothing about life, he had spent all his maturity in the trenches studying death, how to inflict it and how—for his men at least—to avoid it. He was therefore peculiarly prone to mix his ingredients wrong. Eugen had no feelings at all for a strange American girl; it would have saved him a great deal of trouble if Carol had married Otto; but it was plain that Franz wanted her, and that if he did not get her he would take it hard. The trouble therefore could not be saved, and Eugen, with a last tilt of his hat a fraction of an inch to one side, slipped his hand in Franz Salvator's arm. 'We are going to make a call upon a Jew,' he explained to Lisa. 'It is the modern equivalent for going to Court, so that I am afraid we cannot ask you to accompany us. *Leb wohl, mein Liebling*, and prepare something peculiarly good for me on my return. I find these excursions to the pinnacle of modern society exhausting!'

XX

Franz Salvator closed a book of Heine's poems and looked elaborately away from Carol.

The bitter heart-twisting words he had been reading aloud had gone sharply home to him. This was how he knew life; and yet when veil after veil had been caught away from it, there was always this ache left. Disillusion could not shake that final hunger. It could shake everything else, it could tell you where beauty failed, and what selfishness lay hidden at the bottom of the finest sentiments. But what disillusion failed to solve, was why these things, with nothing in them, haunted you forever.

Carol watched him curiously between her long fair lashes. She too felt the prick of Heine's searching spirit; but the poems took with her a more concrete form than they had taken with Franz Salvator.

She asked herself, if she dined with Otto at Cobenzl, and took whatever he had to offer her, why she should mind doing without what Franz Salvator had never offered her? Austrian men were strange. Carol had been so often warned against their primitive love-making; and yet for a year she had been in daily contact with Franz Salvator and he had not so much as kissed her hand. He sat near her now, so near, that if he had leaned back, his shoulder must have touched hers. She knew in every nerve that he was intensely aware of her proximity; but she knew that he would not lean back. Again and again she had tried to shake his self-control and after each failure she had been more certain of his ardour; and less of her own immunity. His eyes stirred her senses and drew hers, even against her will. His voice when he spoke to her summoned her heart. When they were alone together his silent presence made her feel as if she were near a fire. She knew what his starved heart was trying to hide; she even knew why he was trying to hide it. He was too poor to ask for anything; too poor and much too proud.

If only she could have felt there was nothing else to care about, nothing else but him, it would have been simple to break down his pride at the cost of her own. But how she hated poverty and insignificance!

Carol had been poor enough to know how poverty hampers life, how it strangles youth and joy—and why not love? Why pretend material values were not of vital importance? She supposed she could take life hard if it came hard—but why this unnecessary galling hardness of marrying a man who really need not be poor?

It was a fault in Franz Salvator not a fault in her that kept them apart.

Otto had said that Franz Salvator would be well off to-morrow if he were not so medieval. Medieval of course meant fantastic and old-fashioned. Anger stirred in her as she looked at Franz Salvator's handsome resolute features and the tell-tale hollows in his cheeks.

He turned his head and met Carol's eyes.

'Is it with me or with Heine that you are angry?' he asked smilingly. 'You would like the truth to be prettier perhaps? Well! It isn't! But it's not my fault! If I could make it prettier for you—be very sure I would—and for myself into the bargain!'

'I don't mind truth when it is truth,' said Carol, taking a deep breath. 'If reality comes along and hurts—I can put up with it—but I won't put up with any pain from shams! Give me a light, will you? I think better when I'm smoking. Do you suppose a girl and a man can ever speak the truth to each other?'

'They might,' said Franz Salvator, bending over her to light her cigarette, 'at least the girl might——' He drew back carefully. 'I am not so sure about the man!'

'There you are!' said Carol angrily, 'all you European men at the bottom of your hearts despise women!'

'No, forgive me for contradicting you,' said Franz Salvator, 'it is not because I despise you that I would hesitate perhaps to speak the truth to you, but because I should fear that you might be angry—as you are, I think—a little angry now! The truth is an unpleasant substance and some of the unpleasantness clings always to the man who speaks it—even if he only reads it out loud!'

'And wouldn't you be angry, just as much, if I spoke the truth to you?' Carol asked defiantly.

Franz Salvator's eyes flew to her face, but he took a long time to speak: 'I should have more to lose *if* I were angry with you,' he said at last; 'probably I should prefer to control myself than to lose it. But in speaking the truth would you desire to make me angry? I think if it were not your desire I should not be angry. But if you wish to make me angry, with or without the truth, I am sure you could! It is your intention—not your words—that would influence me.'

'Well,' said Carol after a long pause, 'I'm going to risk it. Are you satisfied with the way you are living now?'

Franz Salvator dropped his eyes from hers, a faint smile touched his firm-set lips. 'No, not very,' he said quietly.

'Then why don't you change it?' Carol demanded, leaning forward till her arm touched his sleeve.

Franz Salvator's eyes followed her arm and rested on it; but he did not move. 'You wish me to tell you,' he said at last, 'what I thought you already knew? I am too poor to change my way of life.'

'You are too proud!' said Carol, indignantly withdrawing her arm and leaning back in the corner of her sofa. 'That's what is the matter with you, Herr Ritter von Hohenberg! You are too damned proud!'

'What a discovery!' laughed Franz Salvator. 'You have known me—how long—over a year? And you have just discovered I am proud! I thought your American methods were quicker!'

Carol bit her lips. Somehow she felt that she could arrive at the truth more easily if she succeeded in making Franz Salvator angry.

'I am going to dine with Otto at Cobenzl to-night,' she said, fixing her eyes on Franz Salvator's face. 'I don't know whether you know it or not, but I have been seeing a lot of your cousin lately.'

'So I should suppose,' said Franz Salvator. He stopped smiling.

'What do you mean by "suppose"?' Carol demanded. 'Do you think I've been trying to hide it?'

'On the contrary,' said Franz Salvator quietly, 'you apparently proclaim it. I said "suppose" because if you had not been seeing a great deal of Otto, I imagine you would not call him by his Christian name—or dine with him alone at Cobenzl.'

Carol coloured hotly. 'Thank God I am an American girl,' she said, 'and can do as I like!'

'I think it is for Otto to thank God,' said Franz Salvator; 'no doubt he does! The use you make of your freedom, however—leaves me no room for gratitude!'

'And yet I would go with you if you asked me,' said Carol. Franz Salvator merely looked at her. 'I would go with you alone —anywhere!' Carol went on, her voice shaking a little, 'and I would rather——' Her breath failed her.

'At least you know,' he said in a low moved voice, 'why I must not ask you, and you know that I would give my life to go with you—always—everywhere!' He got up and stood looking down at her with his hands clenched on the edge of the table.

'If you really wanted to,' said Carol, 'you'd make enough money! Oh! I know all about your refusal to look after Trauenstein! I know you think Otto's all wrong because he does business. And I know you could do the same if you wanted to. And there is

151

Eugénie as white as cotton and thin as charity—and God knows what privations you both have to put up with! And you not able to act the way you want to act—and poor Otto wanting to help you and being despised for it—let alone me sitting here and doing nothing—but read that wormwood of old Heine's, and all because you're proud! You think more of your old mouldy medieval self-respect than of anyone else's life or happiness. There! That's the truth! You can pinch that table into a pudding, it won't make it any different! And you can be just as angry as you like!'

Franz Salvator let the table go. 'You say it is the "truth" you have told me,' he said slowly, 'but I think you must feel it is not *all* the truth. Otto knows why I have refused his offers; and Eugénie, whose judgement I think you value, fully agrees with my refusal. Even Eugen would not expect me to have acted differently. Please don't think I feel in any way angry with you for wanting me to make money. On the contrary, I realize how it must seem to you and your indignation with me is a proof of your friendship for—for us both. Please believe that I take money seriously too, though not as seriously perhaps as Otto does. I think that there are things beside which money is nothing.'

'But you admit you could make it if you did what Otto suggested?' Carol asked, throwing away her cigarette.

'If I could do what Otto suggested—yes——' said Franz Salvator reluctantly. Carol sprang to her feet.

'But you're too noble!' she said contemptuously. 'Is that it? And Otto, the head of your house, a man as well bred as a race-horse, is not noble enough? Why don't you try to convince me—if what you say is true—that Otto is a rogue? You see it's pretty plain to me that either you are a fool or Otto is a rogue; and I think I have a right to know which is which?'

'Not from me,' said Franz Salvator, turning away from her. 'Half of truth is confidence and you have not got that half. I will not try to convince you of anything. It is much better that you should consider me a fool than that I should blacken Otto to you—even if I could!'

'Ah,' said Carol eagerly, 'then I am right—you could not!'

'You are perfectly right,' said Franz Salvator, bowing to her and opening the door. 'Have you not arrived at the conclusion at which you wished to arrive?' And before she could answer him, he was gone.

Carol opened her lips to call him back, but she closed them again without a sound. This sudden desire to have the truth out between them had not ended very successfully; but it had ended: there wasn't any use calling Franz Salvator back. He would come —but he would be just the same. Men were like that. They were not, Carol told herself bitterly, really fair.

Now she had got to make up her mind all over again—without fresh evidence. Unless indeed she could get Eugénie to help her? Eugénie knew all about Franz Salvator and a good deal about Otto.

Franz Salvator was not fair to Otto. Otto lived the right kind of life. He was older and more generous to women. He was more tolerant too of people who did not agree with him. It was not any good expecting Franz Salvator to change his way of life, and if Carol meant to be practical it followed that she could not share it. Eugénie would know if there was any real reason why Carol should not share Otto's. Carol rang the bell for Marie.

'Please ask the Princess', she said, 'to come to tea, and then bring in a good tea with *Schinkenbrot* and little cakes.'

'And the Herr Kapitän?' asked Marie in her wooden voice. 'Does one ask him also?'

'No, one does not!' said Carol shortly. Afterwards—meeting the eyes of Marie, black and still like dead water—she rather wished she had asked Franz Salvator. It would have looked better—and he might have come. But it was too late, Marie had automatically vanished; and when she returned it was only to say that the Princess thanked her and would come immediately and might she bring her embroidery with her? She always asked these perfectly unnecessary questions, and when Carol assured her that she was to use Carol's rooms as her own, she thanked her without retaliating by any corresponding concession or subsequently taking the least advantage of Carol's lavish offers. 'It's lovely having you here,' Carol greeted her. 'This room is too large for any one person, even with a parrot. Don't you think Annabelle looks too cute against all this tapestry? She might have been made for it.' Eugénie agreed as to the appropriateness of Annabelle, and, taking out her embroidery, a very fine white linen tablecloth which she hoped to sell for enough to enable her to buy a pair of shoes, she settled to her work. Carol curled herself into a corner of the high-backed, brocaded sofa. 'I wish you smoked,' she said, lighting a cigarette. 'Somehow talking and smoking seem to go together—and I wish you weren't a princess!' 'One is so little of a princess now,' murmured Eugénie apologetically, 'and there is not the slightest need for you to consider me in that light if it is an obstacle to conversation!' 'May I call you Eugénie then?' demanded Carol. Eugénie's beautiful, pencilled eyebrows rose a fraction, and then subsided. 'But certainly, call me what you choose,' she said tranquilly. 'You know my plan, which you so approve, to have all the intellectuals meet here together for the service of Austria? It will be a good beginning to throw all titles away. But I shall leave you to reconcile Franz Salvator to the idea. Men move slower in these matters than women.' 'Oh, I'll settle with Franz Salvator all right,' said Carol unhesitatingly, 'but what I want to know is why you don't invite your cousin Otto to join your new society? He's lots more modern than Franz Salvator, and no-one can say he isn't intellectual!' Eugénie sewed steadily for a moment without answering, then she said, 'But I do not think that Otto would care to come. It is one thing for him to have the pleasure of your company, and quite another to share it with people he has never shown the slightest inclination to meet. It is true they are intellectual, but there are different kinds of intellect, different kinds of modernity, and I do not think —that this kind— would be Otto's kind.' 'Eugénie,' said Carol, fortified both by the Christian name and the cigarette, 'I wish you'd tell me just what you think of Otto Wolkenheimb, and why you're not so friendly with him as you used to be? He told me you were once great friends, and now you are nearly strangers. Why is it?' Eugénie continued to look at her embroidery, and Carol felt that she needed all her reinforcements. Eugénie's face did not promise any confidence. It looked as shut as the locked doors of an official building. At last she said, 'If Otto told you as much as that, I am surprised he did not also give you the reasons—such as they are—for his statement. Personally I have never quarrelled, and I hope that I never shall quarrel, with Otto. His mother is my nearest relation.' 'He didn't say you had quarrelled with him but he said you disapproved of him,' explained Carol, 'and that Franz Salvator disapproved even more than you did!' 'Ah!' said Eugénie, and that was all she said. 'I can't think', Carol continued, when she had recovered from the finality of Eugénie's gentle mono-syllable, 'why you disapprove of him, Eugénie—if you do—because after all his going into a business world and making a fortune is about the most modern thing he could do, and must be good for Austria, since losing a fortune—which is what most of you do—isn't!' 'I think', said Eugénie reflectively, 'that Franz Salvator thinks Otto's business is not good for Austria. I know very little about business, but just at present I suppose that all sudden fortunes won—perhaps through speculation—are disconcerting to the economic life of a ruined country. I should imagine that to earn enough for one's needs by means which do not fluctuate is more honourable than to make such a fortune. But as I say, I know practically nothing of such questions, and I am so relieved that I have enough money to live on without having to deal with problems which I am quite unfitted either to solve or to judge others for solving.' 'But if you aren't friends with Otto because of what he is doing, you *do* judge him!' persisted Carol. 'You don't know how he spoke of it—of course ironically as he always speaks—but I could see it had cut him to the heart.' 'Poor Otto,' said Eugénie gently, 'it is true I am sorry he is so rich. He had his choice, my dear, and he took it. He knew well enough what we should think of him—and, knowing what we think, it is perhaps natural that it should not give him pleasure to be with us.' 'But why do you think it?' Carol asked impatiently. 'What right have you to condemn him? Making big fortunes doesn't necessarily upset a country—it is how they are made and what a man does with a big position when he holds it that counts. Otto Wolkenheimb is the cleverest man I ever met, and I think he is the most disinterested. What I want to get at is why you think he isn't!' 'I have not said that I believe Otto to be corrupt,' said Eugénie with that sudden plainness of speech which sometimes took the more direct Carol's breath away. 'He is the head of my house.' Eugénie gave a little apologetic laugh. 'There,' she said, 'now you see how democratic I am after all! As if it mattered about one's house! That little difficulty, the difficulty of the blood, how hard it is to blot out! I suppose what I mean is that, if I cannot praise Otto, I would rather not speak of him.' 'But you haven't yet told me why you can't praise him?' urged Carol. 'If you don't understand money, it can't be money. Look here, Eugénie, you owe him a loyalty, but don't you owe me one? I'm not only your friend—but I'm another woman. I don't ask all these questions about Otto simply in the air—or out of interest in Austrian ethics. I don't know if you know it, but Otto likes me. He's made himself pretty clear already, and if I don't hold him off he'll make himself clearer. Now what I want to know is, ought I to hold him off? Is there anything about him I ought to know—and don't? Haven't you a loyalty to me?' Eugénie let her embroidery sink into her lap, and met Carol's eyes unfalteringly. 'I cannot answer any such question,' she said slowly. ' Your own heart must answer you. If you love Otto you must risk your heart, and if you love Otto you *will* risk your heart, whatever I tell you.' 'You don't, then,' Carol persisted, 'know of anything very bad he has done to any particular woman—so bad that it would hurt another woman to marry him. I'm not too particular. One sees his genre. Otto Wolkenheimb doesn't give one the impression of a pure and snowy lamb, but I wouldn't want to have another woman on my conscience as well as what men call their "experiences". ' 'You need not have another woman on your conscience,' said Eugénie gently, 'as far as I know. But you must remember that the Otto I knew has long ago ceased to exist. Of the things which really counted in his past I knew something. Of what counts in his present I know nothing. Men of our country and of Otto's class do not have the same ideas nor the same sense of their duties towards women as Anglo-Saxons have. Sometimes I wish this were not so. I wish that women could be treated as human beings and not as objects to possess or to discard. I wish that men were our companions and not our hunters or our slaves! I think if I were a free girl like you I would marry a man who held me free or else—I would never marry!' Eugénie's eyes sparkled and the colour rushed into her cheeks, she folded and unfolded her work nervously on her lap while she was speaking. Somewhere behind her words was her heart; but Carol did not perceive Eugénie's heart. 'Forgive me,' said Eugénie, rising to her feet, 'I must go and cook our supper—I hope that Marie gives you all that you want?' 'She gives me everything—every damned thing!' said Carol, 'except a little human speech. She seems to think Annabelle one point nearer to humanity than I am. But, Eugénie, before you go—did you mean Otto was like the men of his class—a hunter —or a slave—to women—or did you mean—just Austrian men in the abstract?' Eugénie shook her head and hurried to the door. 'I am an Austrian woman,' she said quickly over her shoulder, 'do not pay too much attention to what I say. For me there are no men in the abstract.'

XXI

Eugénie leaned back and closed her eyes. The concert room was full, but in that mass of intent listening faces she felt safe from discovery. She was afloat like a fragment of sea-weed, long cramped and dried by sterile sands, set free at last by the returning tide. She saw nothing, felt nothing, but release. Otto watched her for a moment before he sank unnoticed into the empty seat beside her. He had not planned his moment but it came to him with wonderful celerity. Would she know that he was there, or, before she had time to put her armour on, give him an unguarded response?

The last movement of the Symphony began slowly and without excitement. There was nothing in the music to lift the long dark lashes from her cheeks—but they lifted suddenly, and for one brief moment she looked into Otto's eyes. Eugénie could deny what she liked afterwards—hide what she could—her eyes had not denied him. They had opened wide, with a swift flash of welcome, and let him in. She closed them again swiftly, and turned away her head. Otto looked discreetly at the conductor. The movement drew to a dramatic end. Under the cover of the applause Otto leaned towards Eugénie. 'Dearest,' he said in English, 'I did not know you would be here. This is not my seat; but if anyone comes to take it he will find that he cannot. I saw your face—and came. One should not hesitate to support one's luck even by robbing one's neighbours.' 'I come to these concerts very seldom,' said Eugénie. 'To-day Carol gave me her ticket. It surprises me a little to find you care so much for music?' Otto smiled. 'It is always rather startling, I know,' he observed, 'to find one's taste shared by the stage villain; but you should leave the poor fellow margin enough for one or two innocent hobbies. Don't murderers keep pet mice?' He took the programme out of Eugénie's hand, and as he did so slipped his fingers over hers. 'Is it necessary that you should sit in the lap of that wide lady, who extends beyond you, simply because you have your wicked cousin on your other side?' he asked. 'What are we to hear now, Schubert's "Unfinished Symphony"? I, for one, should be glad if it had no end.' Eugénie tried to keep the lines of her face stern. She was angry with Otto, very angry with him; and she felt that she needed all her anger to protect herself against him. He did not press his shoulder against hers, but she could not prevent his light touch, and at his touch all the tides of her being set towards him.

She knew what he had seen in her eyes. She tried to stiffen herself against the insidious beauty of Schubert's 'Unfinished Symphony.' It was music they had heard together in their innocent youth; Eugénie could not escape her memories; they played on her like a hand, touching with infinite skill the familiar strings of her heart.

Otto was happier than he had been for years. He leaned back in his chair, his shoulder touching Eugénie's, his heart aware of every beat of her heart. Without looking at her, he saw her; he watched the quick rise and fall of her troubled breasts, the stiffening of her mobile lips, the faint colour that came and went under her delicate skin. Her anger touched him; her strength to resist him deepened his tenderness. She was not an easy quarry, and Otto's affections were always quickened by his hunting instinct. Women who wanted to hold him bored him; the woman he had never held enchanted him; she almost controlled him. How charming that episode of his youth had been! Like the music itself—love had swept into their consciousness; and like the music itself, there had been no completion. Neither had been on guard, each was equally willing, equally surprised and enchanted at the response of the other. Their love had never gone beyond one shy swift kiss. Passion had been there, but a bewildered unself-seeking passion. Eugénie's beauty had possessed the world; Otto had never possessed her beauty. This incomplete and pure emotion had gone further into Otto's being than any subsequent and finished incident of his maturity; and in spite of all the intricate and clouded years which intervened the magic still persisted. The purity and the bewilderment alike had gone; they were both on their guard now, and Eugénie was unwilling. He had abused and neglected her faith in him until her supreme proud confidence had wasted away. He put this thought quickly from him. His senses hungered for her still; and as for his soul—that extravagant sense of wanting to please and serve her was of course merely a boyish ignorance of what the main business of passion is.

She was far too thin now; but she was lovelier and younger looking than when she worked in that accursed Jew's hospital! Her eyes were like the golden waters of a pool, luminous and deep; but they refused his image. He became uneasily aware that Eugénie had withdrawn into herself, and that he had ceased to hold her. He turned a little so that his arm and hand touched her; she did not move away from him; but her senses had stopped fluttering. The secrets of her heart were safe. The music had reached her, and she had passed, as if on its wings, out of his power. The wrongs he had done were like a wall that hid him from her.

The music swelled and deepened around them, pressing back the limits of sense and letting in a rush of life so great that it broke the shell of personality. Ah! if they could only escape as the music escaped, if all their discords could be resolved and they could be melted together, moulded together into a perfect whole! But the music stopped. The symphony was over; and it was not finished; they were still acutely separate.

The audience left their seats and stormed towards the platform. 'Will you come to my rooms for tea?' Otto asked in a low voice. 'No,' said Eugénie. 'Then will you let me come to you?' She shook her head. 'You will have nothing at all to do with me?' Otto persisted. 'I will talk with you—if you wish it,' said Eugénie slowly. 'I will go with you to Demel's. We can take tea there. It is on my way home. Do you wish to stay for the Concerto?' 'No,' murmured Otto. 'I could not bear any other music. You remember it, don't you? It gave you to me once—I felt your heart in mine. Dearest, look at me. Did it not give you to me again?' Eugénie got up quickly, and passed, without answering him, through the crowd to the door.

The gold of the western sky had dropped into the streets. The long hot summer was over, but the spirit of it lingered in the heavy air like a remembered passion. 'What a bore,' said Otto. 'Here is Demel's! They must have moved it nearer the Musikverein since I was here last! What will you take? Coffee that has been promoted to two coffee beans as well as a handful of acorns —chocolate—a medicinal mixture cooked in water—or what they call English tea, a pale bitter fluid rather like Victorian morals, warranted to keep your pulse exactly as it finds it. And do you propose to sit surrounded by European adventurers or Austrian brigands one of whom you will have at any rate to confront? I see that you are in a condemnatory mood?' As he spoke Otto led the way to a small table half screened from the rest of the room. 'And I insist upon taking my punishment as privately as possible. What new crime do you want to scold me for, or is it an old one? I am not particular, I only ask to stay as long as possible with my judge!' 'I wish that I were not a woman,' said Eugénie in a low voice, 'or that you would forget it for half an hour! Then perhaps you could talk to me honestly, and I should know what you really meant, and feel free to tell you what was in my mind without the constant threat of your impertinent love-making!' 'Judges must not be unfair!' said Otto quickly. 'I do not make love to you against your heart! If I did I should be impertinent. But if you—for some abstract reasons of your own—choose to make yourself into a prude and pretend you don't like me, it is you who are dishonest and not I!' 'I never pretend I do not like you!' replied Eugénie, facing him suddenly with steady eyes. 'Although you make it difficult for me to feel anything for you but anger and disgust. You count too much upon a weakness in me which you have yourself destroyed!' 'I do not admit love to be a weakness,' said Otto, smiling, 'and I think you must not say "destroyed". Very truthful people cannot afford sweeping statements.' Eugénie turned her face away from him. 'You have destroyed something in me,' she said a little wearily. 'I do not always know what it is!' 'Well, I can tell you!' said Otto. 'What is destroying—or at least excessively upsetting us both, is your taking the attitude of the Ancient Mariner in the English poem, who obstinately refused to be separated from a dead bird. If you will carry this adamantine sense of virtue round your neck long after any life there was in it is extinct, your habit of mind is bound to be funereal! Do tell me why you should be the only member of our family with these bourgeois notions! As to your husband's people, you know as well as I do that they were not even satisfied with the little irregularities of normal sexuality. I don't ask you to follow the vagaries of the Hungarian temperament, but why be as rigid as a pastor's wife?' 'It is perhaps because I have seen too much of these things, Otto,' replied Eugénie, 'that I cannot look on them as lightly as you do. I have learned to value constancy and truth. To make, out of the deepest thing in one's heart, a vulgar intrigue—— No! It disgusts me! But I have something else of which—since we are together—I want to speak to you! Why are you dragging Eugen into the dust? No! Wait! I know as well as you do Eugen's weakness; and his power to control it. He is not a drunkard! And I know that he is drinking now simply because he has lost something which was worth the effort he used to make to keep sober. This something is his self-respect. What have you done with Eugen's self-respect? Never mind your own! I know that is not available; and you appear to be able to get on quite well without it; but give Eugen back his!' Otto's nostrils quivered, his eyebrows rose, and for a moment he looked as wicked as a vicious horse. The moment passed quickly, but not the emotion which caused it. 'Surely, my dear child,' he said in a voice of dangerous softness, 'Eugen is man enough to look after his own lost virtues? If his self-respect is of so loose a character as to have become detached from him, I fear I cannot be held responsible for handing it back. You say that I do very well without my own? It is flattering of you—but what then leads you to suppose that I should be so ready—even if it was within my power—to restore Eugen's?' 'Because,' said Eugénie, 'you are his greatest friend; I cannot think you wish to see him die!' Otto shrugged his shoulders. 'Drunkards rarely die before old age,' he replied coldly. 'Eugen will get over this unfortunate bout, and soon be restored to us. I only wonder that your influence has not already assisted him to recover. But I have often observed that though women like yourself frequently drive a man to drink, they seem powerless to save him from it!' Eugénie ignored this taunt. She looked at Otto again, and as their eyes met, their hearts softened towards each other. 'If you love me,' said Eugénie, 'you would save him for me! He is the best friend I ever had. In fact, he is the only one.'

Otto put his arm along the back of her chair and leaned towards her. 'But I am not to love you—you forget,' he said, smiling into her eyes. 'I am impertinent if I make love to you and heartless if I don't!' Eugénie's eyes did not smile in response. She was less angry with him, but the lessening of her anger only made her more just. 'You are only impertinent,' she said, after a pause, 'if you make love to me while you are living with another woman.

I think any man can fairly be called impertinent who makes love to two women at the same time—or is it three?' Otto's breath was for the moment taken away by this unexpected thrust, but he recovered it so quickly that no-one who knew him less well would have known that he was hit. 'You should take no notice of such things,' he said quietly. 'People of the type you allude to—are not your rivals; and you know it. Besides, what do I gain by living alone? Am I to exist like a Trappist for the reward of telling you how much I should like—what you decline to give me?' 'I should suppose,' said Eugénie slowly, 'that you gain one of two things, either the freedom to marry Miss Hunter or——' She could not go on. She felt Otto's arm tighten against her shoulders, his eyes burned on her face. Her lips quivered. 'That by itself,' she said at last, 'is enough for an honest man.' 'That is not, I think,' said Otto, 'the way in which you meant to finish your sentence. May I finish it for you? My other alternative—if I were of course the honest man you so generously offer to call me—would be my freedom to make a penniless marriage with the woman I love? You overlook the fact that beggars cannot be choosers.' Eugénie lifted her head proudly. 'Yes,' she said, 'I suppose I do mean that. I know that I bitterly resent your manner to me while you are not free! But I resent, if possible, even more your seeking this child in marriage for anything but her heart. She is a good, charming, clever girl. Why should she be deceived into marrying a man with a Jewish mistress, who pretends to be in love with his cousin?' Otto's arm dropped from the back of her chair. 'Enough!' he said. 'You wish to give me pain! I accept your wish—you have given me pain. This is my answer to your saying I "pretend" to love you. No other woman has ever given me pain.' 'That is not what I wish,' said Eugénie entreatingly, 'and indeed I do not wish to give you pain at all, Otto—unless there is no other way to move you?' 'Ah! you could give me pleasure, too,' said Otto ruefully; 'that's the devil! We come back to where we started from. You are too good to give me pleasure, and I am so bad that I can only give you pain!' 'No! no!' cried Eugénie eagerly, 'that is not true. You can give me great pleasure! And I shall be so pleased that you will have at least the satisfaction of knowing it is in your power to make me happier than any one else can!' 'You make me out more unselfish than I am,' said Otto, 'but that is more inviting than being painted a perpetual black! Well—what

162

am I to say? I will try to pull Eugen up. If I succeed in marrying Carol Hunter, I will follow no more financial adventures. I will certainly abstain from the other occupation you alluded to! What will you do for me in return, Eugénie? Will you give me what I want most in the world?' 'I will thank God,' Eugénie said quietly, 'and believe that I was not foolish to have given up my life to caring for you!' 'Always God,' said Otto softly. 'Am I never to be thanked myself? I feel somehow that I deserve it rather more than He does! Surely Heaven and its representatives here on earth drive rather hard bargains?' 'I have never said I will not be yours,' said Eugénie faintly, 'only that I could not be your mistress. I understand you hate marriage without money, and I forgive it. Will you not forgive me that I cannot be your mistress, since I am willing to be your wife?' Otto was silent for a long time; then he said. 'There are some wrongs for which there is no for-giveness. I think it is your willingness that I cannot forgive! But if I agree to your requests—I suppose you will permit me a few little pleasures in return? Your company sometimes, for instance? And your eyes when they are not angry? And your smiles when I am happy enough to amuse you? And I may be allowed to talk to you as if you were a little kinder than you appear? You will not hinder my obvious arrangement with the little American either?' 'But that I should not do in any case,' said Eugénie. 'I will neither hinder nor help you there, Otto, for I must not think only of you!' 'You mean you must consider the hopes of Franz Salvator?' he asked. Eugénie shook her head. 'I must consider the girl herself,' she said. 'If you are going to do as you say, and be what I know you can be, I shall not in any way influence her heart against you or towards Franz. She must follow her heart, but at least, I must be sure that her heart, with you, will be reasonably safe.' Otto was silent for a moment. He gave Eugénie her tea and poured out his own—then he said, holding her eyes with his in an unmistakable sincerity, 'I am afraid I can only give you a qualified promise. I cannot be as faith-ful to her as I should have been to you—if you had given me a different answer!'

XXII

Carol sat curled up in a nest of bed-clothes; her arms clasped round her knees; her heavily thatched golden head bright against the embroidered pillow case. Marie moved softly about the room. She placed the reading-lamp at the right angle; and wanted to pull down the blinds—but Carol objected to the blinds being down, she liked the noises of the night and the broken darkness. She said 'good night' to Marie with a friendly smile, and received in return the mere resting of Marie's eyes upon her face, expressionless and wary.

After Marie had gone, Carol drew out her writing pad and prepared to make up her 'story'; but, in spite of several sheets of scrawled and underlined information spread in front of her, the story was slow in coming. For the first time in her life Carol did not know what she was going to do—or what was more curious still, even what she wanted to do. If Fanni Wilchek's information was true she ought to go to Budapest; but one had to take into consideration the staggering inaccuracy of Fanni's mind. Fanni belonged to one of the oldest families in Hungary; and was a determined Monarchist with a wildly romantic heart. Her father, a swashbuckling Hungarian bully with the instincts of a bandit, had occassionally some political influence. He had joined the Government and was one of the leaders of the Monarchist wing. A great many interesting things had happened to Fanni, but her habit of exaggeration had taken the vitality out of them. She was very plain and had never been loved, but since the age of eleven she had imagined herself winning and won by every man with whom she came in contact. She always asserted that during the days of the Red Terror, a Jew Bolshevik had made an attempt upon her virtue, although it was usually believed that the object of this assault was her jewels. Apart from her traditions, Fanni was a warm-hearted, generous creature; and although she believed that Carol's position on an American newspaper put her in touch with the world, she was equally certain that her political sagacity built up the reputation of her American friend. Every fortnight she poured out her soul to Carol, and every fortnight

Carol, with knitted brows, tried to edit the account of Fanni's redundant experiences. Fanni was in a position to know facts, and she sometimes did know facts, but unfortunately what interested her most had seldom happened. To-night, for instance, there were thirteen aeroplanes hidden in an orchard. Carol knew those thirteen aeroplanes by heart; they were generally hidden in an orchard, and when she took the trouble to go down and locate the orchard, they turned out to be threshing machines or a new kind of plough. There was a *cache* of revolvers too—within a railway arch —you took out a few bricks and there you were—the hollow arch tottering with revolvers! Carol knew there were any amount of scattered arms in Hungary, but not in railway arches—places much more convenient could be found for them, but less romantic. There remained the fresh rumour of the Kaiser's return. '*This time*,' Fanni wrote, 'I am sure it is perfectly *true!* You asked me in your last letter, dearest, for *proofs*. Well, you know Father! I took my courage in both hands after dinner last night, and told him what I had heard at the Club. He shrugged his shoulders and growled. After a moment he said, "Don't repeat that story!" You know what that *means* from Father. He wouldn't have the slightest objection to my repeating it if it were not true! The poor E. suffers terribly. The English are—as I always thought—at the bottom of it *all*. The French *understand* us, and never insult, even if they can do little to remedy our misfortunes. It is the English who have insisted on tying the whole family up in Switzerland—the dear E. *hates* Switzerland, and I do not think it is very healthy for the *children*, the mountains are so high and *gloomy*, and the cows full of tuberculosis. They say *He* (poor darling) has given his *word* not to come to us, but Amélie, who knows them all *most* intimately, says she does not believe this. Besides, a "Parole" *forced* upon a *bleeding* heart does not count! Amélie is quite wonderful! You know she married O. merely to detach him from the Government, and turn him towards the E.? It was all done so cleverly. He is a *perfect* Brute, and has no birth; once he even broke off the engagement because he suspected her! But she managed to meet him again in a *wood*, and persuade him of her sincerity. She has *such* courage and is lovelier than ever. Once she sat and watched O. hang two men outside her window—he did it to impress her of course, but she never turned a hair, and when she was quite sure the men were dead, she rang the bell for lunch and called out to him to come in and not let it get *cold!* She met me yesterday in the Club for tea. She says she is quite fond of O. *in a way!* Although he always has her shadowed by two detectives! She told me that marriage with him is like taming a lion. If the E. comes he has promised her to remain neutral; she may be able to do *more* by jealousy *later on.* But if O. is neutral and L. is definitely for us, all may go well. H. is the problem. He *acknowledges* his *master,* but says it is not the *time!* He is afraid of course of the horrible Allies! Forgive me, darling. I do not mean America is horrible. On the contrary the American Attaché here has the most heavenly blue eyes, and a *warm Southern* manner. There is something extraordinarily sympathetic about him, but alas! he is married! Why do sympathetic men always *marry so soon*—before they have found their *true* mate? I spend all my time at the Foreign Legations and Missions, trying to find out what they really do think about the E.'s return. Papa says it's the most useful thing I can do, but they are terribly dense, and never talk about anything except hunting and shooting. One of them collects butterflies! Butterflies, darling —when we are all being *broken* on the wheel! I need not say he is English! There is a feeling in the air that great events are about to happen. We will not give up the Burgenland to the *crawling* Austrian Bolsheviks, be quite sure of that. H. is terribly *slack* about Jews! A most unfortunate thing happened a few weeks ago. Trouble was stirred up at the Legations about one of our informal executions. A perfectly simple thing, as dear Papa says, "If a mosquito stings me—where is it?—wiped off!" But H. was quite annoyed, he actually sent for dear A. and N. and said it mustn't happen again! When one thinks of their burning hearts full of outraged patriotism it is very hard. I know you don't quite agree with me, darling, about these little things; but if you had been through *my dreadful experience,* when that Jew Bolshevik attacked me with his diabolical leer, you would understand. Think what would have happened if I had not had the presence of mind to give him my jewels instead! We have had as usual a *very bad time* lately. The result of the elections was fairly good, but the opposition methods were awful! Papa had three forged telegrams sent him to postpone meetings which were *vital* to us, and when he tried to send telegrams *against the other side,* he had to pay the most *enormous* sums and one of them never got through! But Papa keeps perfectly firm and cool, and never gets down-hearted. If only the dear E. had a little of his sangfroid. Now, darling, have I told you *all?* No! I think not—Amélie, who *of course* knows everything (she gets it out of her O. by sacrifices I *shudder* to think of!) said, "If your little newspaper friend wants a sensation, let her come down here this month!" Thank you for asking about Mamma and Carl—they are still *interned* on our own estates, barely twenty-five miles to move about in. Of course, Mamma hates the city and Papa is always far *quieter* when she is away—but still the *injustice* of it all! We could not go abroad even if we wished to; the Government refuses us passports! *I* am especially suspect (you know H.'s old *tendresse* for me—and can guess *why!*). So one bears one's shaken life! Do come, darling—Amélie says O. would like to meet you—he looks terrible, but always behaves properly *while she is there.* If he took a fancy to you he might let you go with him to the Burgenland! Of course dear Papa got in. Only six people were killed during the elections—the calm before the storm! Ever your devoted Fanni.'

Carol drew out another cigarette (she had to hide them as Marie objected to her smoking at night) and grinned. Was the storm coming? She could of course go to Budapest if she had to—but she would like to stay a little longer in Wien to decide a personal question. Perhaps two personal questions? There were her relations with Franz Salvator to define, and the fact that every day at five o'clock Otto Wolkenheimb took her for a drive.

Franz Salvator was always charming; but he did not take her for drives. He worked all day at his wretched language school, and although he devoted himself to her service in his spare time, it was a devotion that stood still. She had told him to call her by her name, and he had only smiled and never called her anything at all; but when he said 'you' it was as if his silence was more significant than a name. She was conscious of him always, conscious of him not only when he was there but in her thoughts. He blocked the path to other things. She could not, for instance, see herself going back triumphantly to America when she thought of Franz Salvator, or plan with the old light-heartedness a dramatic future without his presence. And yet she did not want a future with Franz. It would be like living at concert pitch. He was always thinking of what other people ought to have and denying himself in order to give away what Carol thought he ought to keep. Carol loved Eugénie for precisely the same quality; but it

167

irritated her in Franz. She thought a man ought to make more of a splash for himself; and she hated his poverty.

'Well—I'd marry him,' she said to herself, defensively, 'if we were living before the flood, and he didn't take eternity to ask me in! But I can't go burrowing back to Noah now! I'd rather have Trauenstein than the Ark any day.' She resettled herself against the pillow and flushed uncomfortably. She had told Eugénie lightly enough that Otto liked her—and so he quite obviously did—but supposing that he did not want to marry her—and after all, with his queer European standards, why should he? Was she prepared for the other proposal he was quite as likely to make? Otto was thrillingly interesting to her. He built up out of the confusion of Europe endlessly entertaining histories. His manner with her was so personal and so intimate that she felt as if she had known him all her life. His caressing brown eyes laughed into hers with no shadow of constraint. She felt conscious that there were no barriers between them; she was not on her guard with him, and yet she never felt for a moment the least safe. There was nothing so dull as safety in the intimate sophisticated playfulness of Otto's manner with women. He simply seemed to say, with eyes that ignored her defences, 'Come, it's no use having secrets with me. I know you through and through, and as I'm enchanted with what I know, your transparency hasn't any drawbacks either for you or for me.' Was she in love with Otto? Well—she did not want to go to Budapest. She wanted to please him; she sharpened her wits to meet his; when she knew he was coming, she wore with care the prettiest of her carefully chosen clothes. She was at her best with him—and most people like being at their best; but when he was not there, she did not think of him very much. He was not in the back of her mind, and Franz Salvator was always in the back of her mind. Carol gave a little impatient gesture of her shoulders. It was no use thinking about men, she must write her 'story'. Perhaps after all she could use the thirteen aeroplanes hiding in the orchard, and stay where she was? Rumours about the Emperor Karl were not enough. Amélie, it is true, probably knew something. She saw in her mind's eye the beautiful flowerlike face of the Countess Amélie; the expressionless rosebud mouth; the blue eyes as clear as glass. That provocative exquisite creature, tinted with rose and pearl, had a heart harder far than any coal-heaver's. Idle rumours did not emanate from her. The Countess Amélie spoke very seldom and always to the point. It might be worth her while to go down after———? After to-morrow night, for instance, when Carol was to dine with Otto alone at Cobenzl? She remembered how he had glanced down at her as she stood on the pavement—holding his daring horses with such easy skill. 'I don't know just how far the transatlantic margin extends,' Otto had observed lightly, 'but Cobenzl is out of doors, and I believe married people go there together, and dine in that rather cheerless silence which marriage seems after a while to produce. I can offer you that security, and I can provide you with everything, except perhaps the silence.' And Carol said that the transatlantic margin would take her that far—and that she did not care much for silence anyway; and then she had gone in—and quarrelled with Franz Salvator. She looked wistfully at the blank page on which she meant to write her story. Thirteen aeroplanes buried in an orchard —well—why not—the calm before the storm! And if they turned out to be threshing machines there was still the rumour of Karl!

Carol wrote quite a good 'story'; but when she had thrown the cigarette ashes out of the window so as not to arouse the suspicions of Marie, and put out her light, she had still not decided what was going to happen at Cobenzl. 'I shall do what I like anyhow,' she said to herself reflectively. 'I won't be held back by Franz Salvator, and I won't be pushed forward by Otto Wolkenheimb. I shall just look well all around me, and when I decide to leap—I'll hit it! Thank God, I've handled boys since I was knee high—so I don't get what's coming to me without wanting it!' In spite of all her youthful experiences Carol did not know that if you let matters drift with a person who knows how to steer you are likely to land precisely on the spot where he intends to land you.

XXIII

Otto watched her with appreciation. He approved of the blue taffeta dress, the grey suède shoes and silk stockings, the blue and silver cloak which fell straight from her slender shoulders; and above all he approved of her little, close-fitting, azure-blue toque, with little bunches of forget-menots round the brim, which filled the eyes beneath them with colour. Carol had had the sense to wear a veil, so that he knew she would look as well on their return as at the moment of their departure. She reminded him of a patch of blue scyllas breaking out of the earth into a shock of azure light; and no one could appreciate the shock administered by blue scyllas better than Otto. Her charming, cheeky little face was, for the first time since he had known her, sad. He had had to make her sad because one cannot propose to any woman who is in the best of spirits and meets every attempt at sentiment with raillery. Otto had given her a very dramatic picture of the Breakdown, and the sorrows of his country adhered picturesquely to himself. This was not surprising, as he had chosen his phrases with care while he drove his turbulent horses up the winding slopes of Cobenzl. Unfortunately he had driven them so well that in her ignorance of horses Carol had been unaware of all the dangers they surmounted. It had really been the devil to avoid flaxen-haired, hatless families spreading out like fans under his horses' feet; and to choose his English phrases with bite enough to hold her attention while his wrists were half dragged out of their sockets.

The evening was perfect. The terrace of the famous restaurant was filled with rows of little tables, set among balustrades of flowers as high as the tables. Beneath the terrace green fields sloped into the dark beech woods; and out of the plain beyond them rose the city itself, encircled by the pale thread of the Danube. A mist rested over the distant roofs and filled the streets with blue. The roof of the Stephans Kirche rose up like an ark out of the flood. The squalid fringe of suburbs was swallowed up in an enchanting vagueness of orchard and encroaching shadow. The dark deepened, and one by one the lights sprang out. First the Ring was outlined in a stream of stars, and then little flames broke out hither and thither, solitary or in groups. There was no sound; the City lay like a heap of jewels, dumb and shining on the misty plain. It was incredible to think how close against the beauty of the summer night stood the acuteness of want.

'My city is half dead,' said Otto gently. 'It is beautiful, is it not —that shell down there? Fortunately the outside of things does not always correspond to the hollowness within! When I look down there I think of the ghosts of the two last winters. Every day people streamed along this road to the Wiener Wald for wood.

You could watch them for miles, staggering like ants under the burden of the fir wood they were allowed to cut and carry home. It was like watching the woods themselves moving. Poor frozen ragged creatures—who had been so well off once—dazed under the weight of necessities they had never imagined! Sometimes they staggered to the roadside to rest, and never went on again. The next comer took the wood they had gathered to cook his own last meal. The food is here now. You will, I hope, have a favourable specimen of it to-night, but the people are dead. Don't think as you look round you at these little tables you are seeing many Austrians. I am an exception, and for me this occasion is also a great exception; all the rest are profiteers, the chosen people, and our charming neighbours from the Balkans—who eat with their hands and feet. You will see that I have arranged so that you may sit with your back to them and have nothing to look at but the lovely ghost of what was once a great Capital—and is now—a collection of old curiosity shops, where people sell their treasures to foreigners in exchange for bread—until their treasures cease!' 'Do you— do you hate us?' Carol asked under her breath. 'I often wonder —you have been so charming—you and Eugénie and—and her brother—making me feel as if I were at home, and yet my money must seem dreadful to you! Like a mockery! And it's so awful the crumbling feeling Wien has—Eugénie never complains, but she came in yesterday from market without anything in her hands, and Marie tells me that what paid for a week's meals last week won't buy a potato to-day. Sometimes I feel as if I couldn't bear to stay here a day longer!' 'Don't feel that,' said Otto gently. 'You are like the dawn—to people who have suffered all night. We may laugh at our foreigners sometimes, but we never resent them. Why should we? They bring health and life back to us, and stimulate trade; some of them, like yourself, do more—they see—and try to relieve our sufferings!' Carol looked up at him quickly. There was real feeling in his voice—a feeling that took fresh life from the sympathy in her eyes. 'As for me,' Otto said gravely, 'I am much more in your debt than that! Human beings don't show, any more than cities at dusk, their real necessities! And yet if you looked—past the circle of outside lights, through the street walls still standing—into the want and emptiness within! I don't know whether you even trouble to think of me, but perhaps, if you do, it is to say: "He at least is untouched by the fall of his country!"

Well—I wish people to think this—but I should like you to look further. I will not speak of sorrows and losses. Others have perhaps had as much or more to bear, but I once saw life for myself quite differently. I was trained first as a soldier, then as a diplomat. I rose quickly, perhaps too quickly. I missed many things that come to others, but what I gained seemed solid—and is gone. Ah! here is dinner. I hope that you like this caviar? It is not very good, but caviar is scarce just now. It is to be followed by a Russian soup, chicken cooked with asparagus, and a dish they are rather famous for here—iced peaches with strawberries and cream whipped over them. The peach-cup is good; it is made from a receipt Eugen gave them before the war, at a time when we liked to have our special tastes studied at our favourite restaurants. What was I saying? Well—the individual has been wiped out. That is, I think, the lesson of modernity. One built up a personality, and now one finds oneself rather an unimportant part of an incongruous whole. Suppose, for instance, that one believed oneself a master and trainer of dogs, and suddenly one discovered oneself to be—not even a dog, but a tail that wags when the dog is pleased!' 'I can't somehow see you like that!' Carol said, smiling a little uncertainly. 'I don't think you'd wag if you weren't pleased!' 'On the contrary,' said Otto, 'I should if it was in my power make rather a point of wagging whether I were pleased or not. It is all that has been left to me of my manners. But the point I wished to make is that I had not been pleased for a very long time until you came to Wien. That is my reason for gratitude!' He raised his glass, and—holding her eyes—drank to her. 'You have done more than please me,' he said as he put his glass down. 'You have given me a new standard of womanhood. Perhaps a part of my regret is that in my old life I knew only one type of woman. Our ladies of the Court were charming, very beautiful many of them, and untrained for any other profession than beauty. We appreciated this beauty—and—since there was nothing else they had to offer us—we profited by it. It never occurred to me until I met you that women could have for men—not only beauty to madden them—but wit to keep their madness in check—and, may I add, a heart—to make their madness permanent.' The provoking twinkle came into Carol's eyes again. 'Well—you're wagging all right,' she murmured, 'but Heaven knows if you mean it or not! I'd think more of my compliment if it weren't that it seems to shut out Eugénie—with her all the time to look at I should think you could get mad and keep mad without straining a nerve!' 'My cousin,' said Otto dryly, 'married young and confined her influence to her husband.' He had for the moment completely forgotten Eugénie. Carol's reminder not only put him out because Eugénie was an argument for Carol, but because in his heart he knew how damnably good an argument she was. 'Well—she has rather a keep-off-the-grass look about her,' Carol admitted, 'but I should have thought that made it all the more fun for you!' Otto dropped his eyes. This was the kind of thing one had to expect from Anglo-Saxon girls; they were expert, when all a young girl ought to be was immaculate. You could apparently do what you liked with them, until you came on their hidden armour of chaff which was quite disconcertingly efficient. Otto, however, knew how to meet a check. He raised rather indifferent eyes, as if the subject bored him, and looked away from Carol towards the other diners. His attention became fixed rather more sharply than he had intended. A little to the right of them he saw Julius Mandelbaum; his heavy head and jutting-out chin were bent over a conspicuously dressed young woman, who was certainly not Excellenz Mandelbaum. 'Don't bow to him!' said Otto sharply, as Carol's eyes followed his own. 'Really one had expected to be safe here! I apologize, Carol—it is such a pretty name, may I call you Carol?—these new rich never know where to go or how to behave when they are incognito. This is a place where one brings one's wife—or if one does not—one does not flaunt a conspicuous substitute. But Jews go everywhere; and know nothing. He appears to expect, the good Mandelbaum, that I should recognize him! He is strangely mistaken.' Julius Mandelbaum half rose to bow, sat down again, and decided that he had not been seen. Finally he rose and left his remarkable companion plodding through her second slice of *Torte*, and strolled across towards them. His small blue eyes glittered with amusement, his heavy saw-edged mouth widened hungrily as he looked down at Carol. 'I had no idea', he said, with what he imagined was a pleasant smile, 'that one had a chance of bringing you out here to dinner without a chaperon.' 'And you were right,' Otto replied, before Carol had decided on a reply, '*You* will have no such chance, Excellenz!' Otto's eyes were fixed with a curious intentness upon the big figure above them; but his voice was as soft as silk. Julius Mandelbaum's leer vanished promptly from his face; his heavy head dropped lower, like an exasperated bull's. 'Are you trying to teach me my manners?' he asked Otto with a snarl. 'God forbid!' said Otto gently. 'It is inconceivable that anyone should teach you manners. I am trying to make it easy for you to return to your own table and to the lady you have brought here to entertain!' Carol held her breath. She thought the enormous bulk of Mandelbaum would be precipitated across the table. He seemed to be swaying over it for a dangerous eternity. Otto gazed into space a little to the right of the infuriated face above him, as if no such landmark existed. The curtain of his indifference obliterated the outer form of Julius Mandelbaum— with no more effort than if he had pulled it across to shut out an unpleasant draught. Julius Mandelbaum clenched his fist, and Otto's eyes came back to his face; but though Otto's eyes rested on Mandelbaum's with a curious light in them, they still looked as if Julius's face was not there; and a moment later, to Carol's intense surprise, Julius had gone. He opened his lips, muttered something that sounded like the word 'Bleileben' and moved clumsily off between the flowered tables.

'I think after that one would like a little music,' said Otto with a smile, and he raised his hand in the direction of the head waiter. Instantly the air filled with a quick rush of sound. 'You don't mind Hungarian music?' Otto murmured. Carol shook her head. She began to think she would be willing to take whatever Otto offered her. The clumsy incident of Mandelbaum had played into his hand. A girl respects a man more for presence of mind than for any other quality; and when to presence of mind he adds something formidable to be used in case mere wit fails, she is in danger of complete surrender. The violent gypsy music of a Hungarian band fell upon the air like fiery hail. Otto leaned back so that his face was in shadow and watched the girl curiously. She was nervous, a little fluttered, but was she stirred enough? He felt uncertain about her; an amusing but rather an odd feeling.

On their arrival he had given the reins to the groom behind him, and jumped down in time to catch Carol in his arms. Elisabeth in making similar descents hung on Otto with a weight which he compared to a party of Alpine climbers slipping into a crevasse, upheld by the single efforts of an Alpine guide. Carol was so light and supple that she had slipped through his hands almost without the sense of touch. Otto would have preferred a moment's passivity. A woman should not leave your arms before you have had time to know if she likes being there or not. Still it was a blessing to realize that he was not going to have another eager woman on his hands. Carol was indeed the exact opposite of Elisabeth. Slim, young, delicious, nervous—she asked for the most delicate touch upon the reins—and she would get it. Let her pull as much as she liked, he would hold her; but so gently and so quietly that she should not feel the intention of control. She would simply go, at the pace and in the direction that he wanted. Otto smiled softly to himself. He was far too much of a tyrant to sink to the level of a bully.

The first violin came forward to their table and stood in front of Carol. He flung back a long lock of black hair, fixed her with intent inscrutable eyes, and began a slow languorous waltz tune. All the innocence of the night vanished. The haunting melody of the violin left the quickened senses in no uncertainty; the delicate, unscrupulous, passionate music poured out the history of pleasure. Carol's eyes fell. She knew that Otto was watching her intently; under the cover of the cloth, his hand groped for hers and covered it with a quick fierce pressure. She made a movement as if she would withdraw her hand, and then, biting her lips nervously, left it in his. It did not mean anything, she said to herself; lots of men took hold of a girl's hand. If she wanted she could take it away again. Franz Salvator had never touched her; but then, if Franz Salvator had taken her hand it would have meant something—and she would not have wanted to take it away again.

The gypsy music whirled like madness in her blood. Suddenly it ceased; after the perilous hurricane of sound the silence came upon them with an actual shock. Something had vanished since the music began; life itself had moved at a quicker pace. It did not come to Carol as a surprise when Otto leaned towards her with an unmistakable intention in his eyes. She felt the table was a very narrow space and she could not take her eyes away from his. They fixed her with intentness, but without softness. 'Carol,' he said in a low voice, 'how does one say such things? You please me—you please me very much. It is charming, I find, to be together. Life is not all music, but a little of it is! Give me that little! This is my first proposal of marriage, and I am a little nervous since I intend it to be the last. I have very little to offer you—an old name, an old castle, a man a little old too, perhaps, but one who can I think make you smile, who will never, if he can help it, make you cry—and a man whom you will altogether satisfy.' It had come, and she could not stop it. Did she want to stop it? 'I don't know how to answer you and that's a fact!' she said hesitatingly. 'You're so grown up, and I feel kind of—young! I'm not really so green—I've been about a lot and picked up a thing or two. I can't think why I should satisfy you—and I'm half scared to try—and I'm not very keen on getting married anyway!' 'Your feeling,' said Otto with a faint smile, 'has hitherto been my own. Don't be afraid, Carol, I will learn to please you; and marriage needn't be very difficult with people of tact. I express myself badly, but I know very well what you mean. I want you very much; but I won't tease. My heart is impatient, but it has never yet got the better of my manners. We will go as slowly as you like!'

Carol still hesitated. Otto was the most brilliant man she had ever met and the life he offered her was like a dream come true. She would be the mistress of an ancient castle, the wife of a great nobleman, the companion of a man who had had one—and would, she felt sure, make himself another—great career. Her heart beat quickly; was that not a sign she was a little in love with him? His grasp of her hand had made her a little angry, a little confused, but also a little pleased. Otto waited very patiently for his answer, but his face was grave. Carol remembered with a wave of generous tenderness what a bad time Otto had had. All she felt for the beautiful broken city at her feet, for the long agony of his conquered country, the personal losses of all her Austrian friends, rose together to take her heart by storm. But there was another feeling which pulled her back—a useless and more tender feeling, a compulsion not of the will but of the spirit, a longing that had never left her since she first read the same longing in Franz Salvator's eyes. She believed in Franz Salvator as she could not believe in Otto. Deep in her heart she rested on his chivalry. She had felt his strength, she knew his courage, but it was too proud for her—it would not come out into the open and make a splendid dash in the eyes of the world; it kept itself for little invisible things. To be with Franz Salvator was more than rapture—it was peace; but very young people undervalue peace.

Carol asked herself if her feeling for Franz Salvator was not a demand for something that did not exist? He thrilled her and was as handsome as the hero of a cinema; and he had behaved like one up to a certain point; and there, like most heroes, he had stuck. The interest passed on to the stage villain, or at any rate to a live man who moved things and did not just do his duty at a Berlitz school, eating nothing but dry bread till her imagination faltered. That was just what did not falter with Otto—he used up all the imagination she had and asked for more.

Carol lifted her eyes slowly to his smiling ones; they had begun to smile as if her silence pleased him. 'You remember that motto of yours', she asked, 'you told me about the other day? "What I will—I win——" wasn't it? Well, I don't mind sharing it—if you want me to—I like the sound of it!'

XXIV

The next morning Carol woke with a faint shiver of anxiety to meet as usual Marie's menacing eyes. If Carol was in any doubt of Eugénie's and Franz Salvator's affection, she was kept in no doubt at all about the hostile attitude of Marie. Marie did what she had to do and gave what she had to give, but she filled the margin with hostility. Carol had all her physical wants supplied, and she was astounded at the little she continued to pay and the quantity and the quality which she received for it; but she was under no delusions as to the feelings she inspired. At every turn she was met by a stone-like rigidity which never broke up into a semblance of cordiality. Marie never spoke to her new mistress unless she was directly questioned, and then she replied by a monosyllable of the sternest nature. Everything she did for Carol she did flawlessly and with the same air of unflinching disapproval. Carol tried for months to win Marie's unresponsive heart by every blandishment in her power; but the more she coaxed and blandished the more rigid was Marie's manner, the stonier the glint of hostility in her small black eyes.

'Marie,' she finally demanded, receiving on her lap the beautifully prepared breakfast-tray, 'what is it you dislike so much about me? Is it that I am not a Catholic?' Marie retreated a step or two from the bedside, smoothing out as she did so the blue satin counterpane which it had once been her pride to spread over Eugénie's bed. 'I judge of people's religion,' she replied, 'by their conduct. It is true you are the first heathen I have ever worked for, and that one does not expect one's Gnädige Fräulein to dodge about the streets all day like a dog without a master. Still it would be all the same to me if you only went to Mass accompanied by a nun and spent two hours a day upon the rosary.' 'Then where do I go wrong?' Carol demanded. 'You can talk, for I have heard you often enough talking to the Princess and the Herr Kapitän. I do the best I can to be a good mistress to you. I only go out about my work, which you as a working woman ought to respect, even if it is different from your own; but I can see you'd rather serve a pig in a sty. Is it because of the war you've got such a *"Gott strafe"* attitude towards me?' 'Certainly not,' said Marie. 'The war is over now. It did not concern me. It was a war of great people, and if they have taken their own eye-teeth out and suffer for it—let them suffer. Where I live everything is the same. Snow in winter—sun in summer. Cows, sheep, fields and harvests are what they always were, and what they always will be. We have food, and we make our own clothes, and we work as we are accustomed to work. If you wish to know why I dislike to serve you—and it is true I greatly dislike it—you have only to come with me next door into the Princess's apartment.' 'But that', said Carol hesitatingly, 'is what they have never asked me to do.' Marie shrugged her shoulders and left the room in silence. Carol ate her breakfast slowly and thoughtfully. She wanted to know how her friends lived, because she longed to help them. Perhaps there were things she could do to make their lives easier; and how could she do these things when their lives were as hidden from her as if they inhabited a tract of equatorial Africa instead of the same flat? She was devoured by curiosity about the rooms next door. Bluebeard's wife had not an acuter longing or so much excuse. When she had dressed and opened the door of her own enormous salon, she was again confronted by Marie. 'I have the key,' Marie remarked with significance, 'and the *Herrschaften* are out. The Princess is at High Mass in the Cathedral. The Herr Kapitän has gone, as usual on Sunday morning, to visit the stricken ones of his regiment. Neither will return for an hour.'

Carol still hesitated; it was of course wrong to go into their rooms in their absence, even if she was not found out. But was it not also wrong for them to keep her out of their rooms? Did not she know them well enough to make a joke of her curiosity? She would not examine anything that was private; she would merely take a general impression of how they lived, and come out again. She was going to be their cousin soon. Then she could play the good fairy to their needs—probably this was what Marie meant: they had needs, and it was Carol's duty to find out what they were and supply them. Still she felt uncomfortable as she followed Marie through the door between the two apartments and found herself in a little empty hall. 'This', Marie said, 'that my family now use as a hall once led to the second kitchen and was only used by tradespeople and servants. Now there are no servants and they use it themselves.' Then she threw open the door of Eugénie's salon. Carol saw a great wide empty room, with a little sunshine on the parquet floor. 'This', said Marie, 'was the boudoir of the Gracious Princess—it was once full of fine things— as is the salon of the *gnädigen Fräuleins*—I have seen Archduchesses in it. No-one uses it now, except mice. One I found here yesterday.' 'But why——? What has happened to all their furniture?' demanded Carol. 'Much of it the Princess sold to save her friends from starving,' replied Marie dispassionately, 'and much she put into the rooms of the *gnädigen Fräuleins*. They kept for themselves part of what their servants had used. Even from this they sell bit by bit what they need—for others whose need they think is greater than their own!' Marie turned once more and threw open a door upon the right. 'This is the room of the Herr Kapitän,' she said. 'When one says it is better than the trenches one has said everything.' Franz Salvator's room was scrupulously neat. He had a small iron bed, a wooden table with a cracked jug and a tin basin, a kitchen chair and a shaving-glass. His clothes hung behind a sheet, meticulously placed in cotton sacks. Upon a trunk near the window stood a gold statuette of a man upon horseback, jumping; above it was a large signed photograph of his General, Archduke Eugen, in uniform. Opposite from this hung a photograph of his regiment; and over the bed was a water-colour of a medieval castle on the side of a hill surrounded with pine trees.

Carol stood in front of the statuette. 'But it's solid gold,' she said in amazement. 'That', observed Marie, 'was given to our

Herr Kapitän by the Emperor Franz Joseph. It is not practical —the gifts of Emperors are seldom practical—but the family prize it. Here by the bed is a tin bath, and all winter long, with the water turned to ice, the Herr Kapitän washes in it—washes of course, as all *Herrschaften* do, much too much. The bathroom is in the flat of the *gnädigen Fräuleins*—with hot and cold water— because the *gnädige Fräulein* can afford a good fire in the kitchen.' Marie looked curiously at the strange young lady, who with a dazed look stood fingering the golden image on horseback which was supposed to represent Franz Salvator jumping.

She followed Marie without a word into the passage and through a further door which led to Eugénie's room. Eugénie's room was the counterpart of Franz Salvator's except that she had a prie-dieu, with an ivory crucifix hung above it, and that there were three photographs in the room. One picture by Eugénie's bedside was of a very beautiful little boy five years old; one was of Franz Salvator in uniform with all his medals; and one of a young man whose face Carol felt was vaguely familiar, but for a moment she looked at it without recognition. It was a photograph taken from a portrait, and hung on the wall where the light from the window fell full upon it. There was youth and eagerness in the face, and an unexploited power. 'Is this Graf Wolkenheimb?' Carol asked. Eighteen years had changed him; the power was exploited now, and the youth and eagerness were gone. 'It was the Herr Graf', agreed Marie, 'before he lost himself. If I were the Princess I should destroy that picture. But she has the heart of a Madonna. She would get Judas out of Purgatory by her prayers if the Holy Ones hadn't the sense to keep him there.' 'Why do you say Graf Wolkenheimb is lost?' demanded Carol curiously. 'Has he done anything wrong?' Marie's lips closed firmly. She had thought that everyone knew what the Herr Graf had done—and had not done; but if this strange Fräulein was ignorant—let her remain ignorant. After all the Herr Graf belonged to the family, and his sins, however great, were above the heads of vulgar foreigners. Marie backed out of Eugénie's room without replying and opened the kitchen door. 'Here they live,' she said briefly, 'and this is what they live on!' As she spoke she took two slabs of black bread from a box and a handful of turnips and small black potatoes from a bowl of water. These she flung upon the white wooden table. 'They live on this—my *Herrschaften!*' she exclaimed fiercely, facing Carol across the table. 'This is why my Princess is half a ghost and my Herr Kapitän teaches the accursed English tongue to *Schiebers!* Now perhaps you see why I dislike you! It was because they had not enough food that I left them after twenty years' service. And it is because they have not enough food that, when I come back to them, I find myself serving a foreigner!'

Carol found no words to answer Marie. This was worse than the worst she had feared. It was not going to be a happy fairy tale; it was a nightmare with no awakening. Marie stared at her vindictively, and then turned to replace the slabs of bread.

They heard a door open and shut and a quick firm step across the hall; the kitchen door opened, and Franz Salvator looked at Carol with eyes in which blank amazement turned slowly into stern contempt. 'Go immediately into your own kitchen, Marie,' Franz Salvator said sharply; 'I am astonished to find you here in the Princess's absence, but I will speak to you about your conduct later.' Marie disappeared as if by clockwork. She was not in the least afraid of being spoken to by Franz Salvator. She invariably obeyed the voice of authority when she heard it, and usually circumvented the authority later on when it had ceased to be vocal.

After Marie had gone an interminable silence filled the little kitchen. It seemed suddenly impossible to Carol to explain to Franz Salvator that her visit was half a joke and half an errand of mercy. For weeks she had grown accustomed to Franz Salvator's homage. She knew that he regarded her as often strange, but always immaculate. She had been half amused and half touched by his scrupulous reverence for her, and in a moment it was gone. Carol had violated not a custom which he could excuse, but an instinct of delicacy which lay deeper than any custom. She had a curious moment of vision: behind Franz Salvator she saw centuries of privacy; homes which were castles, and castles which had always been homes. He would not understand that she had not ever had a real home, or even—until now—apart from a hall bedroom in a third-class apartment house, a room to herself. She had not been able to afford privacy. How could she explain this to Franz Salvator, who took privacy as a matter of course? Even her friendly desire to help them became suddenly an insult.

She had no right to help them since they had hidden from her their need of help. The colour burned in her cheeks; had not she her pride too! Could not Franz Salvator realize how his silence struck her—did he expect her to apologize? She was sorry for what she had done; sorrier than she had ever been for any action in her life, but she would rather die than admit her sorrow under those scornful eyes. Franz Salvator waited for Carol to speak; but she was held, in a miserable flushed silence, impossible to break. At last he asked her icily if there was anything he could do for her. 'I —I think you're real mean!' cried Carol defiantly. 'It isn't so very awful what I've done anyhow! You and Eugénie ought to have asked me here before!' 'It remains—that we did *not* ask you,' Franz Salvator reminded her. 'Well—I don't see why we need have the Day of Judgement about it!' Carol protested. 'It seems to me friends have a right to go into each other's homes without the roofs coming off! Marie said if I'd come here she'd show me why she hated me—I hadn't any idea—how could I?—what it was like! And, oh, Franz, why didn't you tell me? Eugénie hasn't got any dressing-table. She has to stand up to do her hair!' Carol collapsed suddenly on to the nearest seat; her legs were shaking under her and she kept swallowing her tears. She did not notice that in her excitement she had called Franz Salvator by his Christian name. She always spoke of him as Franz Salvator to herself, and in her panic his name slipped out with a naturalness that touched his heart. It suddenly occurred to Franz Salvator that perhaps he and Eugénie had made a mistake in not letting Carol into their empty rooms. He moved quickly round the kitchen table, and bent over Carol's chair. She sat hunched up—a disconsolate and shrunken figure—with her head upon the table. He did not touch her; she was only aware that he was very near her and that there was no anger in his nearness. His arm was close to her, and she put her head against it. She felt his other arm move lightly across her shoulders and then enclose her. It was strange how at home and comforted she felt in Franz Salvator's arms. Her heart was without questions. 'You see, if you like people,' she whispered into the friendly darkness, 'you must want to know how they live!' 'If you like them very much,' Franz Salvator whispered back, 'you must want to live with them!' And then Carol remembered Otto Wolkenheimb. 'Otto!' she gasped, springing to her feet and pushing Franz away from her. He instantly released her. 'Why do you speak of my cousin Otto?' he demanded. 'Because I must! Because I'm going to marry him!' Carol exclaimed. 'But, oh, no! no! I can't now! I didn't know! You hadn't said anything, and I didn't know about the furniture or that awful bread or the way you had to live. And you hadn't kissed me!' Franz Salvator grasped her by the wrists. 'What do you mean?' he asked sternly. 'What difference does my life make? How dare you pity me? Never let me hear you speak like that again! It is the last insult that you should pity me! If you have engaged yourself to Otto, you must keep your word; there is no more to be said!' 'I don't pity you the way you mean anyway,' Carol pleaded. 'You've just upset me! And I can't marry a man I don't love—engagement or no engagement. We have more sense than that in my country! Stop holding my wrists as if I needed handcuffs! You can hold my hand if you want to—but that's not the right way to do it. You were gentle enough a minute ago—why can't you go on being gentle?' Franz Salvator dropped her hands. 'I beg your pardon,' he said stiffly. 'I have no right to touch you. You forget that I did not know of your engagement to my cousin just now. You will not have to reproach me again.' 'I will,' said Carol angrily. 'I shall reproach you right along—you ought to be pleased I like you better than I like Otto—instead of standing yards away like an iced coconut on a pole!' 'Why did you engage yourself to Otto?' asked Franz Salvator still more sternly. 'You must have known I loved you! For months you have been under my roof. And because you were under my roof—and rich— I did not ask you to be my wife. I wanted to be sure—as sure of your love as I was of my own; then nothing would have mattered, my poverty or your wealth! I had nothing to offer you but myself; but I have offered myself to you every day. Did you not know I loved you?' 'If you felt that way,' said Carol defensively, 'you shouldn't have been so silent! Otto wasn't! That's all there is to it. He spoke first; it was only yesterday. I felt all mixed up, and you hadn't said anything, and I do like him anyway; but it can't go on now. What are you going to do about it, Franz Salvator?' 'It is perfectly simple,' replied Franz steadily. 'You have given your word to my cousin Otto Wolkenheimb, and you will of course keep it. I shall never see you again. You will stay here, I hope, until your marriage. I shall live altogether on the land settlement where I am already working in my spare time. No-one will ever know what might have happened. You must forget what took place here this morning. I also will try to forget it.'

Carol looked at him in astonishment; that he should dare to speak as if their relationship were under his control took her breath away. Before she had time to disillusionize him, the door opened and Eugénie stood there lifting faintly surprised eyebrows. Franz Salvator turned quickly towards her. 'Eugénie,' he said, 'forgive me, I asked Miss Hunter to come in here. It was a sudden impulse—I should have waited till your return, I know—but she is our friend, and now I fear she is a little distressed to find our rooms so empty. I think perhaps we were to blame not to have explained it all to her before!' Eugénie looked at Carol, and then she opened her arms. Carol flew into them. 'Oh, Eugénie!' Carol sobbed. 'You're both so hateful, and I love you so much!' Franz Salvator dashed out of the room. When the two women were alone together, Eugénie made many promises about the future. They would not be ludicrously proud any more, they would divide the furniture and take their principal meals together, and Marie should wait upon them in common; Eugénie would even spend some of the rent upon themselves as well as upon their starving friends; but in spite of all these concessions Carol wept on. She said, between her sobs, that Austrians were cruel; that Americans had their pride too; and that you could feel just as badly about what you had as some people could feel about what they had not. Eugénie was anguished by Carol's misery; but her apologies seemed unable to lighten it. Finally Carol admitted that it was something unforgivable Franz Salvator had said. She could not repeat it, and she could not get over it; but he was not a bit like his cousin Otto; and after she had said that, Eugénie asked her no more questions.

The only person who was thoroughly satisfied with the morning's events was Marie. She went about her work with a beaming smile. 'Everything', she said to herself, 'will now arrange itself, but one has to start these things. Puddings cook themselves—but not until they have been properly mixed first and the fire prepared for them.'

XXV

Eugen leaned back in the armchair he had taken so much trouble to select; he closed his eyes and outwardly relaxed his entire person to the illusion of comfort.

It was eight months since he had decided to ignore the claims of the Danube, and nothing had happened to re-assure him as to his choice. He went over the objects of his existence one by one; they were all a little worse off than they had been before. Otto indeed had flourished, but his flourishes lacked the bloom of finality. The transfer of the shipping company had long ago been completed; but the sting remained. It had been no worse than Eugen had expected, but it had been as bad. He flinched now at the recollection of the Regenswirts' gratitude; it was worse to remember than their amazed incredulity when subsequently they discovered that they had been tricked, not only out of a fortune, but out of a principle which they believed Eugen shared. When they found they had no legal redress they had not even been violent—they had been broken-hearted. 'You cannot, gentlemen,' Eugen had said at the termination of their long, unpleasant interview, 'have a poorer opinion of me that I have of myself. It would be impossible.' Perhaps they thought he was laughing at them, for they had only looked at him with stunned unquestioning eyes, and gone away. Eugen had kept Otto's name out of the business, it was all he succeeded in keeping. Otto had liked the completion of the affair scarcely better than Eugen. When Eugen informed him that it had succeeded and that forty-five thousand pounds reposed in Eugen's strong room at the bank, with the slur of the infamy upon Eugen's head, Otto looked at him as a man looks at his jockey who has won a fortune for him by pulling his horse. He had even had one of his waves of sentiment on the subject, and against Eugen's judgement refused to pay off the Trauenstein mortgage. 'I must have cleaner money to free myself with,' he had said, looking away from Eugen. 'Then you must make it in a cleaner fashion,' Eugen had retorted grimly. Except for five thousand pounds for his immediate expenses, the sum had lain there, increasing in value as the *Krone* fell, until it was the largest secret hoard in Vienna. Eugen had considered it the moment for opening negotiations with one of the chief banks, and making an arrangement by which, in return for the placing of his great fortune, Otto should become one of the leading directors. Such a position was one of financial security and would release Otto immediately from the shady transactions of a Mandelbaum and from the increasing distastefulness of Elisabeth. Instead of cheating Relief Commissions, Otto would be able to watch the rush down of the *Krone* and gamble with the ruin of his country in a manner that defied criticism and would reap permanent advantages. And now without a word of explanation Otto crashed through his own security. He had rung up from Budapest and demanded his entire fortune to be sent to him within twenty-four hours, and he had said that it was impossible to tell Eugen over the telephone what he intended to do with it.

It was not often that Eugen felt so utterly at sea or so incapable of discovering the handle of a situation which nevertheless, as he told himself, must have a handle. Perhaps Otto's good fortune had turned his head, for he had added a piece of information which might be a key to his recklessness. The engagement with the little American, which had hung fire since the autumn, was to be announced, and the marriage would take place as soon as Carol agreed to a date; and Elisabeth must be duly notified. Eugen was to undertake this duty. Eugen smiled to himself as he visualized the effect of such an announcement upon Elisabeth. It would be like entering the cage of a very hungry lioness in the absence of her keeper, and suggesting the cutting down of the meat supply. Nevertheless Eugen had courage, and his sporting instinct was roused by the contemplation of this scene. Elisabeth had great natural weapons, but she was vulnerable, and Eugen was less vulnerable; he might have been invulnerable if it had not been for the shipping deal. She had him there, and she knew that she had him; but while Elisabeth had been happy (and she had for a time been very happy) the taunts she had addressed to Eugen had been, for Elisabeth, delicate and friendly taunts. He had climbed down, and there is nothing so pleasantly amusing to the unscrupulous as the descents of those whose standards pretend to be higher than their own. But there had been other scenes lately, threatening and ominous, scenes which dealt with the possibility of Otto's treachery. For weeks Elisabeth had not been able to see Otto himself; the massive figure of Conrad filled Otto's doorway. Bribery was nothing to Conrad; insistent women were less than nothing. He was as faithful as a wolf-hound. It was to Eugen Elisabeth had turned her small eyes, slanting and glittering with suspicious rage; it was to Eugen she would return, now that her rage was justified. She would think of course that he had arranged the marriage, instead of disliking it very nearly as much as Elisabeth herself disliked it. The person to be blamed was Franz Salvator, but Eugen was unable to blame him since his fantastic integrity had resulted (as fantastic integrity usually results) in deep personal disappointment. Eugen sighed impatiently; the second object of his existence hung heavily upon his mind. Franz Salvator's folly had been worse than Eugen had expected; it had been more thorough. Once a week with gloomy disgust Eugen plodded through the suburbs of Vienna to a small untidy plot of ground to inspect the amateur building operations of Franz Salvator's land-scheme. Here Franz Salvator lived, dressed like a workman, slept in a carpenter's shop, and pretended that the smartest officer in a crack Hungarian regiment, and one of the best riders of his day, was happy. Eugen would have preferred a weekly pilgrimage to a cemetery to lay a wreath upon his young friend's grave. 'War graves are at least respectable,' he said to himself. 'These burrowings into the lowest reaches of democracy are not!' He could hardly bear to let his mind rest upon the final object of his existence. Eugénie had carried out her intentions. She gave a fortnightly meeting, for foreigners and relief workers, at her house; and Dr. Jeiteles visited her regularly as if he were a friend of the family. Eugénie was probably under the impression that Dr. Jeiteles came to see her to talk over his cases. It was quite probable that their conversation consisted entirely of the needs of the hospital and the methods of supply. 'A man', Eugen said to himself bitterly, 'can make love while he is discussing surgical instruments quite as dangerously as if he were writing poems to his mistress's eyebrows! Franz Salvator has become submerged under the waters of affliction; even one's visits to him should be paid in a diving bell! It is no wonder that he no longer sees what is taking place above his head; and as for Otto, some maggot possesses his intelligence. He searches for money as if he were a dog hunting fleas, and has neither heart nor time to catch happiness. I am useless of course. I keep sober to enable Eugénie to meet Franz under my roof, when I should much prefer their meeting under hers; I do not say I should manage things better if I were drunk, but I should suffer less. I supply Franz Salvator with one meal a day— I suspect it of being his only one—between the hours of his absurd little language lessons. My rooms are no longer worth looking at since I have sold my china and my Cranach. I go in and out, and see nothing but gaps, like the wounds of a friend. And yet although I know no life is in the least worth saving, what can one do? One cannot watch one's friends stagger down the road to a demoralizing death, and keep one's little treasures on one's wall. It is an outrage that the lives of people one knows should be at stake, and it is another outrage that one should be obliged to succour them; and it is the greatest outrage of all that there should be a Reparations Committee dancing its heels off in our midst, while we die of its abortive efforts! There is nothing of the artist about God; he does not know when to stop. My wits are not what they were either, or I should have guessed this little mystery of Otto's. What does he want forty-five thousand pounds for at Budapest? There is no stability there, and no banking future. Besides, if there were such a possibility, there is no hurry. People with forty-five thousand pounds need never be in a hurry over their investments. Usually too Otto does not do these things alone —my mental powers up till now have been serviceable to him.'

Eugen got up suddenly and began walking up and down his room. It was no use pretending any longer that he was being comfortable. There was a possibility as to Otto's fortune which had occurred to Eugen even across the telephone, but he had put it swiftly away from him. He did not want to deceive himself, and the possibility was so splendid a hope that his cautious mind instantly receded from any reliance upon it. It made his blood run fast even to think of it. What if Otto meant to fling his fortune (won from the cursed English) into the restoration of Karl? That was a cause into which Eugen would gladly see any fortune flung, and even more gladly know that the hand which flung it was Otto's. Otto was at Budapest, and it was to Budapest that the Emperor, if he ever returned, would go. Was Otto redeeming that damned unpleasant deal by making Karl's return possible? He would not of course if he had not been sure of the American marriage; but even with this certainty, would Otto give up the whole of his own fortune? It was a magnificent risk, and Otto was fond of making large serious gestures with money. The Emperor had always distrusted him; would it not be rather like Otto to drown this distrust in a flood of generosity? If he could buy Vienna with forty-five thousand pounds, he could certainly buy Budapest. Budapest was richer than Vienna, but it was a great deal more venal. There were things you still could not persuade Austrians to sell, but there were no such restrictions in Hungary. There rich Jews provided the money for officers to persecute poor Jews; and the aristocracy played with the remnants of the feudal system as if they were loaded dice. 'It is possible,' Eugen murmured to himself, 'even good things may come by a kind of accident, and with Otto accidents go far! He reinforces his luck with his wit. It is a good combination. God! I could face daylight again if I could say to the Regenswirts, "You lost your boats, my friends, but you restored the Kaiser!"' A knock at the door stilled his sudden passion. He turned his sunken eyes under their thick suspicious brows upon Lisa. 'The Princess Felsör would like to see you,' said Lisa, without enthusiasm. Lisa guessed what Eugen felt for Eugénie, and she thought that everyone's admiration for the Princess was grossly exaggerated. 'I will see her immediately, of course,' said Eugen; 'ask her to have the kindness to enter.' 'Dear Eugénie,' he exclaimed, bowing low over Eugénie's hand as she stood hesitating a little in the doorway. 'You do me too great an honour. Franz has long ago gone to his little grocers, and you should have sent for me to come to you.' Eugen placed the chair he had been sitting in for Eugénie and sat down opposite her. He looked at her for a moment in silence. How would she take, he was asking himself, this marriage of Otto's? It was an atrocious personal insult, and she would take it probably as if it did not concern her. That was the way for a woman to meet an emotional disaster. Eugénie seemed in no great hurry to tell him the object of her visit; she looked round her appreciatively. She too knew and felt in her heart the gaps in Eugen's treasures, but she would not speak of them, she would only love him the more for his unwilling sacrifices. 'Do you know,' she said, 'of all the beautiful things you possess, I most envy you that little marble hand you have upon your desk. Did you not tell me you found it yourself?' 'I had that happiness,' said Eugen wistfully. 'It was my greatest find—long ago on the beach at Anzio. It was washed up at my feet from Nero's submerged palace. It comes from a good period; if not the work of Praxiteles it was born in his happy hour. It is very young, very touching, and open with the generosity of youth. The little fingers are curved back so that it could keep nothing. It was made only to give. You look at it with so much pleasure that I am amused. Why do you not look into your lap instead? You would find two such hands there. Nature broke her mould I think after she had made them!' 'Oh, my dear! My old thin hands!' laughed Eugénie. 'What beautiful things you say to me!' 'Vein for vein, and curve for curve,' said Eugen gravely, 'that hand is yours: even the length of the fingers is the same, and when your hand lies in your lap, it lies always like that—open. Now tell me, Eugénie, what is troubling you?' 'I do not know that I am troubled,' said Eugénie thoughtfully. 'It is true that a few days ago I was not sure that the marriage between Otto and Carol would take place, and now I am sure. It is a great grief for Franz Salvator—and yet it may be that for Otto it will be salvation. For Carol herself I hardly know. Girls' hearts are not easy even for another woman to read; they are not easy for the girl herself to read! She thinks that she knows her way because she is modern and life is an open book to her. But life is not a book; one has to live first, and know what one's life has meant afterwards. Meanwhile there is something I can do for her, and something I should be glad if you would do with me. Tante Augusta has been a little difficult. She has so disliked these six months that have been neither the one thing nor the other—and Carol does not know how much it matters to please Otto's mother! I have arranged with Tante, that their first meeting is to take place at Sacher's. There is to be an opera party, and then supper. General Swalkin will be there, and I count upon your arranging such a supper that the dear Tante will be at her best. Then she will invite Carol to Trauenstein, and I hope that you will come too. I also have promised to go there; and if there is anything that does not go well, I shall think it strange if together we cannot make it smooth again. The wedding will probably take place from my flat at the end of the month.' 'And Otto knows that you will do all this?' Eugen asked gently. Eugénie nodded. 'I will not make it hard for him,' she said beneath her breath. Eugen said nothing. He was used to his astonishment over what Otto took from women. All that Otto valued in life had come to him from women; and he despised them. Eugen had received nothing from women, and given much, and he thought more of them than he did of men. 'Then we will, as usual,' he said after a pause, 'act together? It is to be hoped that since there must be this marriage it will turn out happily. Is it your impression that it will?' Eugénie gave a little sigh. 'Until last night', she said, 'I was convinced it would. That is to say, I thought Otto would have from the marriage what he looked for in it; and I believed that if this happened, he would make Carol happy. He knows how to please women. But last night I discovered something that has made me a little anxious. I had understood that she was to bring Otto a great fortune, he had frankly spoken to me of it as his reason for the marriage—although I hope it is not his only reason. Last night Carol told me that she possessed nothing beyond what she earned.' Eugen sat bolt upright—his eyeglass swung out upon the air. 'The devil she did!' he exclaimed incredulously. 'No fortune! but the girl's mad! Her Ambassador answered for her fortune!' 'It was a mistake,' Eugénie explained tranquilly; 'she says that there was a relation of the same name as herself, but quite distant; he made a fortune out of a newspaper, and left it not long ago to his only daughter. Carol writes for the same paper—and her father died recently. One sees that the confusion was possible. Tante Augusta spoke as if she believed in the fortune, but I had not myself thought about it again although Franz Salvator mentioned to me that you too thought she was very rich—and that he was troubled by it. What frightened me yesterday was wondering if Otto knew the truth. Of course I could not ask her if he knew.' 'Ah!' said Eugen slowly, 'it is not necessary to ask her. I happen to know that Otto's affairs depend entirely upon his belief in her fortune.' 'Then,' said Eugénie hesitatingly, 'ought he not to be told immediately? If Otto is to be at all influenced by the fact that she has no money, I think we should act before the girl is any further involved?' Eugen closed his eyes. 'One moment, Eugénie,' he said; 'more depends upon this revelation than you know. I think I must tell you what is in my mind, though in a sense it is a breach of confidence—a breach of confidence to Otto.' Eugénie raised her head proudly. 'I think,' she said, 'you may tell me what you like—about Otto.' 'I think so too,' said Eugen, 'but he must not know that I have told you. I would like your promise not to let him know.' 'You have my promise,' said Eugénie steadily. 'Otto,' Eugen went on after a pause, 'won a fortune some time ago from one of his speculations. I was just placing it for him to very great advantage, and in perfect security. To-day he telephones from Budapest and tells me to send it to him immediately. It is in English bank-notes and is reposing at this moment in that box of Coronas at your elbow. The bottom layer is composed of something even richer than tobacco. I have been employing my time since lunch in steaming off and then replacing those very cleverly arranged seals. I think the result is satisfactory. The English courier is a charming fellow with a great sympathy for Austrians. The box will accompany him to Budapest to-night. It will be quite safe. The English have one great quality—their honesty—one may I think rely upon it. The box will reach Otto to-morrow. Otto informs me that the American marriage will take place in a few weeks. I know that he expects to receive from it a greater fortune. You understand, I am morally sure that he would not touch this money unless he was sure that Miss Hunter brings him more than its equivalent. If we wait twenty-four hours before telling him that she has no fortune, this money will be gone perhaps beyond his reach, and he will have precisely nothing.' 'But why should we wait?' Eugénie demanded. 'Think for a moment, Eugénie,' said Eugen, dropping his voice lower. 'For what purpose can Otto wish this money? Not for any business advantage. All such advantages I have obtained for him here. I think—I am not sure—but I think—there can be only one purpose for which Otto needs this money in Budapest. Can you not guess the cause?' Eugénie leaned forward. 'Oh,' she whispered, 'Eugen! You mean the Emperor? The return of the Emperor?' Eugen looked up and met her eyes. Youth had rushed back into her face. It filled the hollows of her cheeks, and invaded her whole being with colour and life. 'Oh,' she said under her breath, 'Otto is going to do this great thing—to give his fortune—his whole fortune for the Emperor!' All her faith in Otto rose to Eugénie's eyes—her broken, damaged, faltering faith—restored suddenly by a miracle into a triumphant certainty; and following her faith down the path of least resistance, poured her heart. Eugen, looking at her intently, caught some of her exultant confidence. It was possible, he thought to himself; it was even probable. For such a sum one could almost insure Karl's restoration, and Otto would regain by it all his lost influence! The world—the old world

—might come creeping back, as waters find an old accustomed channel, and return. 'I cannot say,' Eugen murmured, 'I do not like to say too much. But it is more than possible, Eugénie; only remember, we throw away that possibility if we tell him now. He will not strip himself of *everything*—even for the Emperor.' Eugénie sprang to her feet. 'Can we not believe,' she cried, 'that he would give all he has, everything! everything! to bring back Karl! Otto is *generous*, Eugen!' Eugen took her reproach in silence. He rose slowly, and stood with his back to her triumphant figure. It was hard for him to have to undermine that triumph, to see that flush die out. 'Not everything,' he said at last. 'We should be wiser not to expect too much. There are complications which you do not know. Otto cannot at a moment swing clear of them. I may say that I know the American fortune is vital to him. We are taking an enormous responsibility on ourselves if we let him sacrifice his capital without the knowledge that he is left penniless by such a sacrifice. As an Austrian I am prepared to take the responsibility in order to restore our Emperor. For good or ill—let Otto give all he has—not knowing that it is all he has! I know our Emperor, Otto will be repaid for what he gives. But, Eugénie, for God's sake let him give it!' Eugen faced round upon her—and he saw that he had been right. Her colour had faded, and half the light had gone out of her eyes. 'I am sorry that you doubt him, Eugen,' she said slowly, 'but I am glad—oh, yes—I am very glad—that he gives *much!*' They looked at each other as if some great and unexpected treasure had been pressed into their hands, and yet they had only been given back a little faith in the man they loved. Eugen took both Eugénie's hands in his, and held them for a moment. 'We have done what we can to help him,' he said gravely. 'But the result may not be favourable. It may be that the marriage will not take place, because Otto refuses to go on with it; or it may be that not even his fortune can replace the Emperor. If he fails to restore Karl, he will have neither the fortune he expected with his marriage nor the recompense the Emperor would have made him. He will have exactly—nothing.' Eugenie drew a long breath of anxiety, but the light lingered in her eyes. 'I know! I know!' she murmured, 'but we must not measure this action by results. He will have done at last something worthy of him! I think he only needed to win back his honour. This will give him courage to go on doing right! He must marry the girl of course, he has given his word; and she will help him face any future, she is made of audacity and has the vigour of her new race. Whatever happens, nothing is hard for me now! Oh, Eugen, you don't know—not even you—how happy I am! I ought to be heartbroken for Franz, I should be anxious for Carol, and more than anxious for you, upon whom all that goes wrong— if anything goes wrong—must fall. But I will tell you the truth. I cannot feel as if anything else matters now! Think that Otto has redeemed himself at last! Perhaps he meant that all along? He knew better than we how to serve Austria, and all that we hated was perhaps necessary and even right in such a cause!' She caught her hands away from his and covered her face with them. 'I cannot bear even you to see how happy I am!' she whispered. Eugen turned quickly away from her; as he did so his eye caught the receiver of the telephone, and he found himself wondering if that small, firm voice at the other end of it had been meaning to do anything so very noble after all.

XXVI

Like an island rising out of a flood, the opera house, with its classic pillars and its fountains, rose above the miseries of Vienna. It was to the life of the city what the Bank of England is to London, what Wall Street is to New York, what St. Peter's is to Rome. It might freeze in the winter; it might stagnate in the summer; it might give performances to empty houses; its singers might be half starved and its scenery a dilapidated farce, but as long as the orchestra trooped to its place (thin and yellow like last year's leaves, but with their subtle élan and rhythmic responsiveness undimmed) the city could still breathe. Mozart, their patron saint, was safe in his shrine; and they could still offer up before the impassive Heavens the incense of his music. One day the Heavens might hear; and the thin stream of ebbing life pour back into its ancient channels.

It was the first time that Otto and Eugen had stood together in the great gilded vestibule since the days when the Court filled the opera house and used it as if it had been a private drawing-room.

Now the 'new public' moved across the hall in congested packs, as if at a railway station fighting for a train. Most of them were in morning dress; very few of them were Austrian. Their earlier existence (if indeed they had existed before the war) had been conducted discreetly in some underworld, but now the whole surface of the city was theirs, and they poured through the shrines of privilege like a barbaric horde which has overrun an older civilization and neither knows nor cares how to handle the exposed and ancient deities. Otto and Eugen, waiting on the steps for the arrival of Eugénie and Carol, exchanged glances full of memory and disgust. 'Ah, there is Eugénie!' Otto observed. 'The Balkans appear to flow between us—if you go to the right of the pillar and I go to the left we may be able to rescue her!' Otto hardly knew if it was purpose or accident which brought him first to Eugénie's side. She looked at him as if she were possessed by some strange gladness; there was colour in her cheeks, and she held her head as if she were crowned. 'The announcement of my engagement has made you so happy that you look ten years younger,' observed Otto, with a lift of his eyebrows. 'I had not counted upon that particular effect! No! It is no use trying to run away from me. You cannot get through six fat men and a woman with shoulders like the roof of the Stephans Kirche—lean against this pillar, and if you can, explain to me why you have such a light in your eyes and such a colour in your cheeks—and forgive me for touching your hands because I cannot possibly help it!' 'Don't spoil what I feel,' murmured Eugénie; 'it's because I've heard you have done an action which I think is great. Not your marriage—that too pleases me if it makes you happy—it was time you should settle down, and the little girl you have chosen I love very much—but the other thing that you have done pleases me more.' Otto felt frankly puzzled. What the deuce had he done to win Eugénie's praise? He put his arm around her to keep the indiscriminate pressure of the crowd away, and drew her a moment against his heart. 'Dearest,' he murmured, 'dearest, what an opportunity these Balkan pigs present! Don't draw yourself away from me! I assure you I'm behaving with the strictest austerity compared to what I feel; and if you are pleased when I do what is right it is nothing at all compared to the pleasure I should feel if you would consent sometimes just for a moment to do what you think is wrong. I wanted to say—though it sounds rather brutal—that I'm marrying your little friend because I have to—not because I want to—but I'll try and make her a tolerable husband.' As he finished speaking the crowd freed them and they found themselves at the foot of the stairs, at the spot where Eugen had already succeeded in piloting Carol. Otto transferred himself to Carol's side without a perceptible pause. 'It's been such a stupid forty-eight hours,' he murmured as he moved away with her. 'I hope you haven't enjoyed it. My mother is full of apologies, but nothing will induce her to re-enter the opera until the return of the Emperor. She will await us at Sacher's.' Carol had felt faintly apprehensive of this first meeting with Otto since the finality of their announcement; the excitement and the pleasure of his company had been shaken out of her mind by deeper feelings. She had been everywhere; she had done nearly everything; but she was only twenty-three; and this marriage to a man nearly twice her age and of a foreign race weighed on her like a responsibility which she had not the power to meet. But the friendly reassuring irony of Otto's presence put all her fears to flight. His eyes fixed upon hers, half in ardour and half in mockery of his ardour, challenged her spirit of attraction. 'Is your mother like you?' she asked, smiling. 'If I please you— will I please her? Or must I begin all over again and try something else—more European in style?' 'Be just what you are,' said Otto, laughing, 'you will then be sure of pleasing every man— and any woman over sixty. I find the little white dress delightful. It makes you look like a fairy on a Christmas tree, and I see the orchids go very well with it. It is the right contrast, perfect simplicity and a little touch of sophistication to make it go down. We are to hear Jeritza in "Salome" to-night. Eugen has just informed me that it is very improper, and that I ought not to have taken you until we are married. At my age one forgets these little distinctions; whether, that is, we should be improper first or improper afterwards! It is so much simpler to be improper all the time!' Carol laughed. 'You forget,' she said, 'as he does, what a lot I've been about the world—why, I've heard "Salome" twice already, but not with Jeritza, and I guess I'm improper enough to be able to hear even her interpretation!' 'And you look as if you were only fifteen and had seen nothing but the cloak behind the Madonna's shoulders,' said Otto admiringly. 'Still, at fourteen if I remember right, Juliet had an extraordinarily intelligent knowledge of rope ladders and the uses to which they might be put. But the Jeritza is very fine in her interpretation; if you have anything left of the Puritan spirit she'll let it down very easily.'

The conductor took his place. Otto was glad of the music. He wanted a few minutes to think. What had he done to please Eugénie? Could she have heard, could Eugen have told her, of the withdrawal of his money; and had they together, taking into account his unexplained visit to Budapest, pitched upon the possible return of the Emperor? He was supposed then to be financing the return of Karl? He would not scold Eugen for betraying his affairs to Eugénie, since the betrayal had had such a satisfactory result. The idea itself could do no harm shared by these two, whose devotion to the Emperor was only less than their devotion to Otto. Eugen had asked him no questions, and Otto had not yet felt called upon to yield his confidence; nor would he yield it. Let them think what they liked. He must not go on looking at Eugénie. There she sat with her dark head outlined against the dull red of the curtains, her neck and arms as white and firm as the petals of a magnolia. She wore an old-fashioned black velvet dress; yet what woman in the house compared with her—those long shadowy eyelashes covering beauty that stirred deeper than the senses; her blessed stillness, as if she had grown in some occult and sacred place without noise or hurry! When she moved, how subtly she did it, like a seagull's effortless poise of wing! He drank in the happy line of her features—at once vivid and austere. 'Not Venus—Psyche!' he murmured under his breath.

He dragged his eyes back to Carol. The pretty bobbed-haired girl in front of him, alert, and with certain rather good points, was not finished; she would not last! Nature had hurried over her. She had not paused and let the secret of old selected beauty pass into her blood. And yet nothing in his new life was as good as this girl, who was not fine enough to please him! It was atrocious that he could not reconcile himself to the life he had chosen. He had had to choose it; but it was full of vulgar things. He had had to accept stupid, ugly relations which made his finer instincts smart and feel cheated. The harsh, restless music with its undertone of menace stirred him unpleasantly. Life was devilish. Beauty caught at your senses like a snare, and when the trap closed on them you found Beauty had remained outside. Take his own life, for instance. If he could be put back ten years ago into the old world

197

with its old prizes, how differently he would choose! He would not flounder about like an overburdened bee, drugged with honey, from flower to flower. He would choose Eugénie, and be more or less true to her. He would not throw himself into half a dozen lives —be half jockey—half politician—a hunter of women—an intellectual—a firebrand of the aristocracy, and a student of finance; he would select a line and force his wits into one deep successful channel. It had all been so exciting, and he had been too young to know the worth of what he had sacrificed. Now he knew its worth, he was tired of riding a dozen horses at once, and making love to women who only repeated in half a dozen keys the same brief refrain. Life itself had begun to bore him. He had all his powers intact, but the incentives had become dim. His wits were —thank God!—sharper than ever, but his will flagged. He could be ruthless with others, but he had ceased to be able to deny himself anything that he wanted, and in another ten years what would become of him! The music shot up suddenly into flaming discords, and trailed off in smoke. 'You look so cross,' the child in front of him whispered. 'What has happened to you?' 'The first scene of an opera always makes me cross,' murmured Otto. 'Ah! here is the Jeritza, now I shall be less cross—she is something that happens!' In the bar of light across the palace stairs stood Jeritza; she was looking down upon the well of the dungeon in which St. John was imprisoned. Carol became suddenly aware that she was not going simply to listen to a voice, she was going to receive the impact of a great personality. The Salome, when she moved, slid down the stairs like a lizard. In a moment there seemed to be no such thing as safety; all the world was balanced on a razor edge of danger, ready to kill or to die. Jeritza's voice, when it came, cut the air; at first it sounded hoarse and rough. It won its way slowly into beauty, as if what it must prove, before anything else came from it, was its power. In the scene that followed with St. John the Baptist, it was terrible to feel the tension of Salome's instinct, held back like a weapon tearing at the thin sheath of her control. Salome was astounded at the strength of a spiritual repulse; all her nature was in revolt against it. Again and again she flung at the saint the force of her beauty, overwhelmingly sure of herself, overwhelmingly powerful, incredulously checked. 'I suppose I am like that to Eugénie,' Otto thought bitterly, 'a kind of inverted Salome, keeping her in prison, or walking about with her head on a charger! I can't help it. I don't see the sense of this resistance to pleasure! Why can't that livid snail of a saint respond to a beautiful woman? Why can't Eugénie let herself go with me? She loves me. When I touched her to-night I knew she was pulling herself away not because her instinct refused me, but because of some silly scruple in her mind. People don't light up as if someone had set a flame in a dull lantern because they think you've done something rather fine—unless all their feeling is involved in what you do. I can't marry her because I must have money, but what on earth has money or marriage got to do with love? It's beastly materialistic when you come to think of it, all this ice and iron about a ceremony! . . . Jeritza hasn't gone off. Gad! if one could have the distinction of Eugénie and the kick of a woman like the Jeritza, what an emotion for any man! The devil—there's Elisabeth!' Otto's eyes hardened to a cool deadly stare, as he met the eyes of Elisabeth Bleileben across the stalls. Her face was white and ravaged; it looked like a strip of country across which armies had fought; but her eyes were alive—slanting, sparkling, livid with rage, they met his, and forced their way through the hard armour of his indifference. Otto turned his head and murmured, 'Eugen!' Eugen Erdödy gave him a curt nod, and a moment later disappeared unnoticed from the box.

Eugen slipped out into the corridor, and met Elisabeth face to face. She had cleared her way rapidly through the flesh and blood which stood in her path, and for a moment Eugen wondered if she did not mean to force herself past him into the box. 'I must see Otto!' she said in a low voice. Her lips moved upward like a snarling dog's; she did not tremble as a weaker woman would have done, she was stiff with rage. Eugen stood in front of her, impassive and formidable. 'Don't make yourself conspicuous,' he said quietly; 'take my arm. Women should always appear to be enjoying themselves in public, it is unbecoming to them to do otherwise. I am not Otto, but for the moment please accept me as his substitute. It is quite impossible that you should speak to him now. He is entertaining a party for the evening.' 'It has been impossible for him to speak to me for weeks,' said Elisabeth vehemently, 'impossible for him to write—impossible for him to telephone. I can no longer accept all these impossibilities!' She spoke in a hurried guttural voice, as if she were swallowing her words to prevent herself from shouting, but she took the arm Eugen offered her and walked towards the foyer. Choked as she felt with bitterness, there was something like exultation in appearing even in the empty foyer on Eugen Erdödy's arm. 'I tell you,' she went on, her vivid slanting eyes moving swiftly from side to side of her, 'I cannot bear it, and what I cannot bear—does not get borne! It explodes!' 'But one does not explode in an opera house,' replied Eugen imperturbably. 'One leaves these great moments of sudden expansion to prima donnas who are trained for them, or else, Excellenz, one gets turned out.' 'This marriage,' she went on without heeding him, 'this marriage must stop! I have come to say this to Otto and I mean to say it, either here or elsewhere. Nothing, no one, shall prevent me!' Eugen was silent for a moment. No one could possibly have disliked his companion more than Eugen Erdödy disliked Elisabeth, but his dislike was not uppermost in him at the moment. He found it quite compatible to sympathize with a being he hated—as compatible as he found it to judge with disgust the actions of someone whom he loved. 'Excellenz,' he said at last, 'you may not think of me in the light of a friend, but I give you the advice of one. Do not attempt to force anything upon Otto. You will not succeed, and you will be made to suffer more than you are doing now.' 'I must see Otto,' Elisabeth repeated. 'You do not know! Something has happened. My life is breaking up around me. I am a proud woman. I should like to hurt him, it is true, but if I could get on without him I would have left him alone.' Eugen looked down at her. He saw that she spoke the truth, something had broken in her. Her eyes had the startled anguish of a drowning creature, it was as if she suddenly felt the cold weight of waters covering her head, and knew that she could not surmount them. 'If it is possible I will arrange a meeting with Otto for you,' Eugen replied gently. 'But I fear I must ask you to give me the grounds for such an interview first. In what way is Otto responsible for your fresh unhappiness?' Elisabeth turned slowly with him at the end of the long foyer, and paused. 'This is what has happened,' she said rapidly under her breath. 'Yesterday I told my husband everything! I think I went mad when I received your message. I threw it at him. He was all I had to hurt! Should he stand there fat with his happiness and I torn to pieces by treachery? No! I wiped off that smile. He will never look so satisfied again. He ran away out of the house like a whipped dog. After he had gone I repented, and when he returned late last night I told him it was all a lie and that I had only said it to pay him out for his own unfaithfulness. He licked his lips —for he is always afraid of me—and said he had found out that what I had told him was not a lie, but the truth. He had got proofs! I thought he had run away because he was afraid of me— the cur—but he had run away only to find evidence. Now he has found it he will divorce me. He is no longer afraid of me. To-night he turned me out of his house!' Eugen walked on slowly without speaking. Each word she said increased his loathing of her; he was as conscious as she was of the surprised glances of the people he passed. Everyone connected however remotely with Viennese life knew Eugen Erdödy, and knew that he had for the first time in his life a Jewess on his arm. Nevertheless this was a woman who had not received common justice. She had made Otto's fortune, and he was getting rid of her as if she were the end of a cigarette. Eugen could not do very much for her perhaps, but he could walk beside her as if she were a queen. 'This is very serious,' he said at last. 'I quite agree with you that this is serious, though I must point out to you that your confession brought it upon yourself. Women should never confess anything—nothing at any rate that they have really done. To-morrow I will call upon your husband, and see if it cannot be cleared off. A divorce is the most culpable of human failures, because it is quite unnecessary. It relieves no-body, and involves every one in scandal. As a Minister your hus-band will be making a great blunder. I think this may be brought home to him. Candidly, Excellenz, I do not believe that any one can prevent Otto's marriage, but as a man of honour he will doubtless help you to the utmost of his power to avoid the conse-quences of your culpable impetuosity. Rest assured it is to the interest of neither of us to let this divorce take place. Therefore I think it will not take place. Where do you propose to go on leaving here?' 'I have not made any plans,' said Elisabeth, biting her dry lips. 'I mean to see Otto—it is for him to make my plans.' 'Forgive me,' said Eugen, 'but I do not think Otto will see the matter in such a light. It is best that we should consult together to do what is safest for you. I will give you a card to my secretary, and she will look after you in my rooms until Otto is free. You can have an interview with him then—and afterwards I will take you to any friend of yours who will receive you for the rest of the night. If you will wait here for a moment I will tell Otto what we have arranged, and let you know at what hour to expect us.' Elisabeth gave him a long searching look. It was incredible to her that this man, whom she had triumphed over and insulted, should speak to her with such grave deference now that she was at his mercy. She wondered if he was playing a part, and meant to trick her— as she would have tricked him if she had been in his place. But she had no one else to trust—the horror of her doom was upon her, and she grasped at the only help in sight. A divorced woman in her class loses everything, and Elisabeth had much to lose. If Otto listened to her—married her—she had everything to gain, and between her and that possibility of safety was Eugen's enigmatic face and this strange sense that, without having anything to bribe him with, she had yet somehow or other obtained Eugen's protection. She was not attracting him, she had too much sense to believe in her own charms for a man like Eugen—but he pitied her, and since this was all she had to use, she must use it right. 'Do what you can for me,' she said simply. She watched him disappear down the long corridor, his tall, upright figure nonchalant and unhurried. Then she shut her eyes and waited.

Salome was dancing. Herod and his Court watched her strip off her veils one by one and haunt them with her loveliness. An instinct moved Otto to turn his eyes from the stage to the back of the box. He rose noiselessly and joined Eugen, who stood silently close by the door. 'You must see her,' Eugen murmured. 'It is essential. Her husband threatens a divorce.' 'Nonsense,' Otto whispered back sharply, 'it is out of the question. The divorce must be stopped of course. There can be no evidence. My servants are safe. You will arrange all that. What should I see her for? To tell her that I have finished with her? She knows that I have finished! It is enough.' 'Nevertheless you must see her,' repeated Eugen gravely; 'you owe her at least that, and I have promised it for you. Do not forget what she has done to serve you! She goes immediately to my rooms and will await us there. The woman is desperate, Otto. She has neither the self-respect nor the strong nerve of a young girl. She was middle-aged and innocent when you took her—you should have left her what she was, or be prepared to protect her!' 'My dear boy, you're mad,' replied Otto impatiently. 'I was not responsible either for her middle age or her innocence. I am sick of the sight of her, and it will not make her any less desperate to be told so.' 'I shall refuse to assist you about

the divorce unless you agree to see her,' said Eugen slowly after a
long pause, in which their eyes met and sounded each other. 'I
regret to say so, but I shall refuse.' Otto shrugged his shoulders.
'God! what an idiot you are!' he murmured. 'Well! have it your
own way then—the way of a sentimentalist, who thinks to make
facts less unpleasant by dragging them through scenes. What does
she want me to do? Marry her I suppose? And do you think I
should marry her whatever unpleasant excuses I am forced to
make? I tell you, my dear child, I had rather jump off a cliff than
touch her again! I am also middle-aged, and if I am not innocent
—I have nerves!' The music ran higher and higher, they could
no longer hear each other's whispers, the stage darkened. Jeritza
lying on the ground sang her broken, bitter, puzzled exultation
over the severed head. Her voice filled the house and challenged
Heaven with the shock of her defeated will. Otto crept back to his
seat behind Carol. She put her hand on his knee—it was the first
time she had voluntarily touched him. 'I'm frightened,' she whispered. 'Oh, Otto, it sounds as if—as if she didn't know what she'd
got.'

XXVII

Carol did not find eating a dinner in a starving city a satisfactory form of amusement. She could not shut her mind
to the sharpness of the contrast. She found herself imagin-
ing that even the head waiter was watching the bread by
her plate, praying that she might leave it; and she thought that a
mob and a lamp-post should have been added to the last course.
How could Eugénie stand the taste and feel of the luxury surrounding them? For the last two years Eugénie and Franz Salvator had stripped life bare to the bone. Carol had never understood before why they shrank from Otto's prosperity; but she
understood now; great contrasts are always cruel. The thought
had a curiously disturbing effect upon her. She began to criticize
Otto. Why had he spent all this money on unnecessary splendours?
The lights on the round table shone as if they were imprisoned
gold; beneath them was a floating sea of niphitos roses. The heavy
frost-like silver, the delicate cobweb damask cloth—the food a

series of unprocurable delicacies, handled by extravagant skill—what was it done for? Why could not she just have met his mother over a cup of tea? She thanked God Jane was not there to see the kind of dinner given in her honour. Carol had never been able to forget Jane's first criticism of Otto, 'An uninteresting little man with predatory instincts!' Her eyes sought Otto's face. It was quite expressionless, and when it was expressionless, was it not a little hard? This was not the background she had intended for herself when she came to Wien; but it was, she saw with a sudden intensity, what she must be prepared to accept now. This would be her new life—luxury—fastidiousness—exclusion. Otto and Eugen knew nothing else; they had preserved through the cataclysm of their fallen empire, through the drifting away into death and destitution of all their friends, a fortune which they could expend upon the tastes they had once cultivated. They could not use their talents upon anything else because they had no other values. Perhaps this was what Eugénie had meant when she had pointed out to Carol that the life Otto had chosen was too different for real friendship to be possible? Eugénie was here to-night, and she was looking as if she enjoyed herself, but she was not here for Otto, and she had made it clear to Carol that she would never come again. She had come to help Carol meet the Gräfin because it was supposed to be a formidable event to meet the funny, stumpy little old lady with a crooked chestnut wig and flat active eyes, who looked as if she was paid to prevent the waiters from carrying off the spoons. The Gräfin herself considered the occasion extravagant, but she liked food, and her eyes rested caressingly upon the oysters and brown bread and butter. On her right sat her greatest friend. He was an old man with white hair, bushy eyebrows and gentle tired eyes. He looked as if he was made of very thin brown paper, and as if all the solidarity left him had gone into keeping his shoulders erect. General Swalkin had been the Emperor Franz Joseph's oldest comrade, the only personal friend —apart from reasons of State—Franz Joseph was known to possess. He had been quietly starving for months, and he had only come out of his obscurity to do honour to the son of one of his oldest friends. No astonishment at mere circumstance had ever shaken his self-control, so that he hid his bewilderment at the meal before him as if he had not been used to dining daily off black bread and vegetables and wondering if the *Kronen* sufficient for his next meal would be forthcoming. When the *Krone* fell further he would not have any more meals. None of his friends knew exactly what his circumstances were, so that he would not be interfered with. The old world had ceased to exist, and he was perfectly content to follow its example. He had been at Sacher's constantly in his former life, and his eyes lingered on the familiar tapestries with pleased recognition. He ate very sparingly, with a good deal of consultation with the Gräfin and Eugénie as to what his *Magen* could be induced to stand, and sometimes he looked across and smiled at the young American who, his friend the Gräfin had explained to him, stood solidly entrenched in dollars behind this and any other entertainment Otto might choose to indulge in for the rest of his life. General Swalkin was glad she was pretty as well as rich, because he was a gallant old man and believed that Otto would give to beauty the tribute it deserved. Otto had to marry money of course, but it would have been very unpleasant if the little girl had not managed to be pretty as well. The Gräfin ate systematically and with critical appreciation; probably she would not get such food again in a lifetime, and even if the whole affair went smoothly and Otto allowed her enough to indulge all her tastes, the money would then be her own and she would not have the same lawless feeling about it that she had now in passing from Otto's oysters to plovers' eggs, keeping well in view the tournedos with mushrooms, the Styrian chickens cooked with pâté de foie gras à la Lyonnaise, and the ineffable *Torte* at the end! But why should such splendours have an end? There, above the flood of niphitos roses, were grapes and nectarines to follow. But the Gräfin knew her capacity—not raw fruit at the end of such a dinner! 'My only criticism,' she murmured to the General, 'is whether Eugen would not have been wiser with pork cutlets instead of beefsteaks? One has one's passion. Nothing in life has ever seemed to me quite like a pork cutlet!' 'It is true,' said the General gravely; 'taken by themselves—perfect—but, dear Gräfin—would they not be, with all these other delicacies—oppressive to the *Magen*? I feel myself that in beef—if it is not overcooked—and here one is safe from such savagery—Eugen has found a happy inspiration; beef accompanies better than pork.' 'True,' murmured the Gräfin, 'and fresh mushrooms! But where *can* Anna Sacher get mushrooms? These taste upon the palate as young as morning dew.' The General shook his head, and the Gräfin turned suddenly upon Carol. 'I wonder if you can cook,' she asked briskly. 'In your wonderful country I am told there are excellent dishes and some attention paid to domesticity, but the Anglo-Saxons as a rule are deficient in homemaking.' 'I can', said Carol, 'do anything about a house if I've got to.' 'Ah! in that case you are more practical than the English,' replied the Gräfin with a flicker of cordiality. 'Englishwomen are the most helpless in the world. They should be kept behind purdahs as they are in the East, to produce babies and eat nougat. They may have learned better since the war, but in former days my hostesses in England knew literally nothing about their kitchens—and the result! Terrible! Terrible! Terrible! I said, "Have you no sauces?" They said, "Yes, we have sauces." One of them was mint sauce. Would you believe—it was nothing but vinegar and water! A few green herbs, chopped raw, floated in this sea of bitterness! And then they had another—made of bread and milk. When I tasted it I could have wept. "In our country", I said, "the poor give this to young babies." I was not surprised when our good German submarines failed to starve the English, since after centuries of malnutrition they had failed to starve themselves!' Otto took the conversation gently into his hands; it passed away from the good German submarines, and Carol, who knew conversational causes, was a little pained to notice that Otto's—sparkling and vivid as champagne—was nevertheless founded entirely upon his own self-esteem. It was strange that she had not noticed, until now, the hard core of egoism in Otto's delicate wit. Everything that Otto talked about, and he talked this evening a great deal, re-dounded—subtly and without emphasis—but still redounded—to his own credit. He talked away from himself, but the point of the talk came back. He listened—he was an extraordinarily good lis-tener for so good a talker—but his listening magnetized the con-versation either upon his personality or his experiences. Once only did he forget himself, and the occasion was so curious that, though it was over as quickly as the flight of a bird, the impression of it remained with Carol. They were talking together about American politics. It was a subject very familiar to Carol and very interest-ing to Otto. Carol was aware that she was handling it well and that all the table, except Eugénie and the old General, were lis-tening to her. Eugénie was giving the old General rather a point-less little reminiscence of a ride she had taken with Otto in the

Imperial woods. Otto's eyes grew fixed, his attention wandered, he even forgot himself so far as to turn his head. Immediately his attention was called back by Eugen's asking him a direct question, but by then Carol's eyes too had wandered; they had rested on Eugénie's face and seen a deep rose colour rise from her neck to her forehead. Eugénie got to the end of her little story without faltering, but she had blushed beyond the possibility of doubt when Otto had turned and looked at her. Why had she blushed, and why had Otto given up his researches into American politics to look at Eugénie? It was peculiarly noticeable because, even apart from the interest of a topic, men seldom give up listening to the woman they adore in order to look at a woman they do not. Otto's attention never swerved from Carol again, not even when she dropped rather skilfully out of his restored self-impressionism and asked General Swalkin to tell her something about the old Emperor? The General roused himself from his startled interest in a plover's egg with an attention he had for no other subject. 'His Imperial Majesty Franz Joseph!' he murmured. 'My dear young lady, he was my master! What can I tell you of him except that he was a very good one? And that I think—I still think—in spite of this world that is now around us and which despises masters—that obedience to a good master is the best life for any man who is not born a king. I am an old man, and I would not choose another life. Those old dogs who die on the graves of their masters are the happiest. I saw very little of His Majesty after war was declared. I think about the last, certainly the most noticeable of my audiences, was on the occasion of the Archduke's murder. I was allowed the privilege of entering unannounced into His Majesty's presence, if he was at liberty. I do not think anyone else about him, except of course the Empress, knew him better than I—but it will be no wrong to His Majesty's confidence in me if I repeat what occurred on this sad occasion. It bears out a point that has often occurred to me, how little one knows the heart of anyone else—even of his greatest friend! Not even the man one has watched all one's life, as, for instance, I may say, Eugen has watched Otto, or Otto Eugen—for I know that they are true friends, as it was my great privilege to be my master's friend. One day—it is like yesterday, for six years are nothing to an old man, the young possess the hours and leave to us the minutes, an official brought me a telegram—and asked me to break the news of the assassination of the Archduke Ferdinand and his wife to the Emperor. She was, you may remember, his wife, but not the Archduchess. By courtesy of the Emperor she had become Countess of Hohenburg. Still she had died with him, and if what they say is true she died trying to defend him. I took the telegram, and I said to myself, "This is the end. He has had everything taken away from him. All the past is in ruins, and now the future. Also it will mean war." He was in the room where he worked daily, seated at his desk. I thought he looked very old and tired, as if all the years and all his sorrows had got upon his back at once. I stood by his side and waited; and I would have liked to give the rest of my life to wipe out that telegram. At last he looked up, and said, "Well, my boy, what have you come to tell me?" "Bad news, your Majesty," I said, "bad news." He looked up at me; there was no fear in his eyes, and now that he was old there was no curiosity either. I thought it best to put the telegram into his hand. He read it through carefully, and then laid it down by the letter he was writing. "Very interesting," he said, "very interesting indeed. So Providence has carried out what I myself was powerless to perform." And he sat up quite straight as if some of his old sorrows had fallen off his back. It was, as I say, a surprise to me. I knew that he had no great love for the Archduke; their natures were dissimilar, and the Emperor had bitterly opposed the marriage, but after all the Archduke was his heir apparent, and the Emperor had never let his hatred show. Perhaps there was no hatred, only His Majesty's sense of order, which was very great. At any rate it was a great relief that what I may call the last of his personal tragedies failed to touch him.' 'I did not know that——' Eugen murmured, with a look in his eyes which Carol had never seen there before. 'I also am glad! But you say one does not know one's friends? It is true you were surprised, but it is true also that His Majesty had not done anything against his nature; he had merely had a deeper feeling for precedent and breeding than even you had imagined, a deeper feeling than he had happened to have for the Archduke Ferdinand.' 'Yes, but yes!' said the old General almost irritably, 'that is what I mean—which is the deepest feeling in any of us—who can say for another? One is lucky if one knows what it is for oneself, and one is luckiest of all if one is allowed to act upon it!' Eugen rose slowly to his feet, he had tried to meet Otto's eyes, but Otto's eyes this time were bent, where they ought to have been bent earlier, upon the face of his future bride. Eugénie was looking at her plate, and the Gräfin pushed away from herself, with a wistful sigh, a little dish of salted almonds. Nobody noticed Eugen until he had left the room and returned with a bottle reclining at a careful angle in a basket. 'This', he said with great gravity, 'is a wine of which I have very little left. It is suitable, I think, for the occasion. Three bottles of superlative Tokay remain to me; one I keep for the restoration of the Monarchy, one is to be opened after my death at the discretion of my executors, and one I am about to open in order that we may drink to the health, the prosperity and to the success of all the purposes of my old friend, Otto Wolkenheimb, and of my young friend, his bride!' With cautious deliberation Eugen took a silver corkscrew in his hand, and, wrapping a small embroidered napkin round the neck of the bottle, drew the cork with infinite dexterity. It was a liquid that ran like a sunbeam into their glasses and tasted like fire and honey. After drinking it, the honey lingered on the palate; the fire stirred in the blood. Eugen lifted his glass, slowly touched each of their glasses in turn, and Otto's last of all. This time the eyes of the two men met and lingered in each other's. 'And to all his purposes!' Eugen repeated. After he had drunk, he threw the glass over his shoulder. The surprise of the little crash remained in Carol's memory. Everyone had started, except the old General, who followed Eugen's example, murmuring, 'Such a wine is history. It would be a pity to pour a meaner wine into the same glass'. 'It would be for me—impossible,' said Eugen solemnly. 'When the best of anything goes one does not keep what held it.' The occasion melted away rather quickly after the little ceremony. The General made a kind little speech, Otto replied with exquisite neatness. The Gräfin embraced Eugénie with some warmth and held out her small, rather fat hand cordially to Carol. 'I shall have the pleasure of receiving you at Trauenstein in a few days, shall I not?' she asked. 'It is a poor crumbling old place, but you will do it a great deal of good; you belong to a new country and have plenty of vitality. Otto will need it all.' The Gräfin did not resemble her son in any point except perhaps the expression of her eyes. These organs were as remarkable as Otto's. They seemed capable of taking everything in without falling into the weakness of ever letting anything out. They rested upon Carol for quite a long time as if enjoying this process to the full, and then they turned in the direction of Eugen. 'This has been a very successful occasion,' the Gräfin observed, giving him her hand to kiss. 'The extravagance is doubtless Otto's and the intelligence as usual—yours. Pray divide my thanks. Everything was perfect. You may tell Anna from me that I was satisfied. Perhaps another time, if there should be another time, you will reflect carefully before choosing beef? A very young pig has no dangers and a peculiar delicacy of its own. That, my dear General, was a point we overlooked in our little argument! If taken young enough—even pork is not oppressive.'

XXVIII

As soon as they were alone in the car, Eugen faced Otto. 'It is then for our Emperor', he asked in a low guarded voice, 'that you withdrew your fortune?' Otto hesitated for a moment. 'You have guessed it,' he answered, 'but do not ask me any more questions. One is afraid of the very paving stones, and I promised to give no details to anyone till it is over.' Eugen gave a quick deep sigh, the sigh of a man who has seen a danger escaped, a danger so great that some of his being had passed into his fear. 'I am satisfied,' he murmured; 'I ask no details. You did well. Has the whole sum gone?' 'Every penny,' replied Otto with a nervous frown. He moved uneasily in his seat. 'I wish my bride had worn jewels to-night,' he said; 'I thought American girls dressed in diamonds when they had them! One hears of her wealth, but so far one has seen no tangible sign. She keeps no maid, no car, no establishment. I cannot easily bring myself to believe in money which is so much in the air.' 'It is true she has no background,' Eugen admitted, 'but she has good taste. To appear hung with jewels when Eugénie had none would have been execrable taste. I thought it one more point in her favour.' 'Perhaps,' said Otto doubtfully. 'Certainly she is intelligent; but she talks too much, and she listens as if she were criticizing one's self—not only what one says. I dislike critical women. It is one of Eugénie's charms that she takes what one says as if she were receiving a benefit—and so she is; the best of a man's experience is a benefit for any woman to receive! These countries where the experiences of men and women approximate must be extraordinarily dull. Damn Elisabeth! Fancy having to finish one's evening off with her! It takes the taste of your excellent Tokay out of one's mouth! It is strange the tricks one's nerves play one; whenever I looked at my little bride at Sacher's I seemed to see Elisabeth's face! This divorce might be a nuisance, if she has not invented it to catch me out?' 'I do not think she has invented anything,' said Eugen thoughtfully. 'But be careful that she does not. If you show her no consideration she may make herself extremely dangerous. It would be wise to let her think she still had something to lose.' 'So she has,' said Otto with a little laugh; 'she has forty-five thousand pounds, but trust Elisabeth—she won't lose it. What consideration do you expect me to show her? If she gets divorced I shan't marry her, and if she escapes the divorce she needs no consideration from me.' 'She has given you a little present of a very great fortune,' said Eugen dryly. 'It seems to me that it would be well not to forget it; also to an Austrian gentleman it used to be considered something, that—a woman granted him her favours!' Otto swore bitterly. 'You are throwing up at me the life I told you I should forget,' he said angrily. 'Don't remind me that I used not to do things like this—for interest. Remember only that I used to have no need of anyone's interest in order to live as I pleased! I hate all these women and their money.' Eugen made no further comment. As the car drew up before his door he said briefly, 'When you have finished with the Jewish lady, I shall be prepared to escort her to her friends, and if you will await my return here I will take the car'. Otto nodded and walked into the *Biedermeier* room alone. Elisabeth had not, however, remained where she was shown. She had ranged all over Eugen's flat. Lisa provided her with food and drink, and Elisabeth ate ravenously, for she had taken nothing for twenty-four hours. She penetrated into the room of Eugen's carpets, and, seeing immediately that they were of great value, she proceeded to put Lisa to the question. The unequal contest lasted for a long time. Elisabeth had at her disposal all the chief methods of successful curiosity; she hit wildly in the dark to see what sprang up under her blows; she worked underground; she used conciliation, flattery and fear. She appeared to know everything already, or she pounced with incredible ferocity and swiftness upon a lurking

211

possibility; but she had never before come into contact with the mind of a mountain peasant. Lisa had sound nerves in a sound body; she wanted nothing that she had not got, and she had no fears, except one she knew silence would never expose, that of vexing Eugen. Elisabeth never once got past the guard of Lisa's intensive stupidity. 'I do not know.' 'The Herr Baron has not told me.' 'Perhaps it is so, perhaps it is not.' As far as this Lisa went; her eyes were mild and her ignorance as impenetrable as the armour of the most finished Jesuit. Elisabeth gave her up at last, and returned to Eugen's pictures. Lisa took a seat in the hall behind the hat-rack, to see that Elisabeth did not walk off with any of her master's treasures. 'Only dishonest people', Lisa said to herself, 'wish to know the business of others.' Elisabeth examined everything within her reach, and then sat down heavily. 'I must not speak to him of the money,' she said over and over to herself. 'Oh, God help me to hold my tongue! If I remind him that he owes me anything he will hate me—but that he should forget!' This fact really astonished Elisabeth. She had no very high moral standard, but she had the integrity of the orthodox Jew and his gratitude. She kept all her bargains, and if anyone had given her money she would never have forgotten it, and when occasion offered she would have given a practical proof of her remembrance. It did not astonish her that love should be repudiated nor shock her that Otto should have broken down her virtue only to betray her. But that he had repudiated money—that he had betrayed a gift of forty-five thousand pounds—this seemed to her abominable. It was incredible as well, for it was not all she would have done for him—it was the beginning, and Otto had deliberately turned back from this path of gold.

When Otto entered at last she remembered with a literal pang of agony how she had first come to his rooms. Otto had the same dreadful ease. He met her as if nothing had happened, only his eyes were changed. Then they had been kind and full of laughter; now they were very grave, but the gravity was for himself; and of his kindness nothing whatever remained. 'You wish to see me?' Otto asked. He stood with the breadth of the room between them —the clear, soft, shining room. Eugen's most beautiful rug lay like a fallen rose at Elisabeth's feet. She leaned forward and spoke hoarsely as if a hand was pressed against her throat. 'I am to be divorced', she said, 'for you! It comes to this then, what you told me was so simple to carry out, so easy to conceal, such an advantage for a woman!' 'I thought you were a woman of the world,' replied Otto coldly. 'Women of the world do not confess their intrigues to their husbands, nor above all do they choose the moment when the intrigue is over! I am amazed that you could have made so criminal a blunder. It is of course excessively awkward for us both. Still I can hardly conceive that your husband will proceed to extremes. Eugen will do what he can, and I think you will find the result satisfactory.' 'You think', said Elisabeth, 'that because it is inconvenient to you this will not happen? That is where you aristocrats always make the same mistake. You will find it *will* happen! My husband is a good bourgeois, he is also a weak man. Where he is good is as inconvenient for us as where he is bad! He will never take me back. He will on the contrary jump at his release and remarry immediately. I have no proofs that his faithlessness preceded mine. Such an error on his part did not seem important to me until you took away from me the position which was my safeguard. The divorce will take place. You will be inconvenienced and I shall be ruined. You know our Wien. There is no circle in it where I shall be allowed to move. I am too old for the one alternative with which you have presented me. I cannot take up a life of sin. You should have begun and finished with me ten years sooner!' Otto stood still with his hands behind him. Only his eyes moved; they flickered impatiently over Eugen's treasures. 'You speak bitterly,' he said, when Elisabeth had finished, 'and it does you no good. A woman should appear to believe in her own charms even when it has become difficult for others to do so. I can only repeat that I shall do everything in my power to stop this divorce and to free your name from scandal. The Chancellor is as you know a man of the very greatest moral integrity; such men do not like colleagues who divorce their wives in order to remarry; nor do they care for colleagues whose commercial morality is frail. It is in my power to expose your husband's frailty. Eugen will warn him of these facts. I will, I repeat, do my best for you and for myself.' 'Unfortunately for me,' said Elisabeth, with her anger rising, 'the best that you can do for me no longer occurs to you as the best you can do for yourself. You are not yet married. If this divorce takes place, you can save me by the one act of an honest man. You can make me your wife.' 'My word is already given elsewhere,' said Otto coldly. 'It is a pity that one can seldom appear honest in every direction simultaneously, but so far as I remember I never suggested wishing to marry you, nor did I say I would refrain from marrying any one else. I am of a marriageable age. It is very necessary for me to possess a fortune, so I therefore marry a fortune, and you as my very good friend might, I think, be prepared to congratulate me!' Elisabeth trembled. The worst had come now; the demon of her anger broke across her self-control as if her will were tissue paper trying to dam a flood. 'I have already congratulated you', she said, 'upon another fortune. A fortune without encumbrances, and if you wished to add to it, that also I could have procured for you. I only asked in return a little of your fine gentleman's honour! You are too proud to keep faith with a Jewess, though you may put your hand in my pocket and live off my wits! God, you stand there grinning at me with your shining clothes and your scented face—till I could spit in it!' 'May I remind you', said Otto with extreme gentleness, 'that my whole capital—five thousand pounds—enabled you to take up the successful deal to which I suppose you refer? I excessively dislike mixing these questions up, but if one must do so, let us at least—without informing the whole of Wien—get our facts straight. Of this fortune, which we earned together, I have already given up my share. I am quite penniless, and I consider myself free to make any fresh arrangements which occur to me. I was interested in you when our affair began. I find—I am sorry to say so—but you force me to speak clearly—that this interest has wholly ceased.' Elisabeth stared at him; even her anger sank beneath the weight of her incredulity. 'What!' she cried, 'you have parted already with forty-five thousand English pounds? You are mad! What have you to show for it?' 'Precisely nothing,' replied Otto carelessly. 'I do not take so great an interest in money, you perceive, as you imagined. I admit that it is necessary, but one does not live by money alone, any more than by the spiritual graces which pretend to exist without it. You have, my dear Elisabeth, misunderstood my nature, and I must confess that I had not taken in the consequences of your own! This is not surprising, for men and women live by misunderstanding each other. It is what brings them together, and, when understanding arrives, it is what drives them apart. I find it a great lack of culture to suppose that any one is to blame for this rather entertaining state of things.' 'But what have you done with the money?' insisted Elisabeth. 'Is it too late to get it back? Cannot Baron Erdödy help you? You stand there looking at me like a silly child who thinks it can walk on water. I tell you one drowns without money! One drowns!' 'Possibly,' said Otto, looking at his polished nails, 'but one does not make too much fuss about it, and if one has the wits one uses them to prevent such a dénouement. It is three o'clock in the morning, and the poor Eugen waits to take you to your friends. May I not call him in?' Elisabeth stared at Otto for a long moment without speaking. She believed this time what he said, but her brain refused to take it in. What had he done with forty-five thousand pounds? This fearful problem took the place of what he had done with his more frail affections. If a man could get rid of solids at such a pace, no wonder that more intangible substances evaded his safe-keeping. But as Elisabeth looked at Otto, the knowledge that she would never see him again swept over her with a dreadful certainty. She rose slowly to her feet, with her eyes fixed on him. She took him in—every inch of his hard polished fineness; his high domed forehead; his quizzical chestnut eyebrows, arched over his bright inscrutable eyes; his clothes that seemed as much a part of him as a shell; the diamond and onyx links, little points of light above his long slender hands, which hurt her like his eyes. All his image sank into her being. She had known him only two years, but she had known him as one knows the air one breathes. She had drunk him in like life. Everything else went out of her mind; the money, her ruin, and his perfidy. This was death, this last look at him. She felt the sensations of death, the dimming of the eyes and the slipping forth into an unknown night. She held her breath; and, fumbling with her hands, as if she were already in the dark, she moved awkwardly and slowly towards the door. Otto sprang forward to open it, but he kept his eyes away from her. She said once, 'Otto!' and again, 'Otto!' as if her whole being summoned him, and when the summons failed she walked quietly out into the hall and took Eugen's arm. Elisabeth did not speak during the long drive out to Schönbrunn through the early dawn. They passed the palace and the gardens, still and empty in the pale hard light. Nothing stirred in the streets. Eugen got out at the door of her old governess's rooms and lifted Elisabeth on to the pavement. She looked up at him and saw that his eyes were full of kindness and a respect which she had never seen there before. In a curious shadowy way his look helped Elisabeth. 'It is all over,' she

215

said in a low voice, 'no one can do anything for me now.' 'Nevertheless I hope to be able to do something for you,' Eugen assured her gravely. 'Excellenz, one goes on living! One marks time—until time itself becomes obedient to life, and in the end—the taste of things comes back!' Elisabeth shook her head and shivered. She felt as if she did not want it to come back. She was afraid of the taste of life, for it was Otto who had taught her what life tasted like.

XXIX

Dr. Simmons, through the smoke of her cigarette, observed Dr. Jeiteles with a cool, faintly weary expression. She saw that she was going to receive a confidence; and she hated self-exposure, feeling that all emotion should be as perfectly concealed as the action of the lungs. Breathe you must; but, unless diseased, you should not pant. Dr. Jeiteles had come into her room as if he had been blown there. He shot up and down the narrow space between her desk and the window like a man just stung by a wasp.

'It is a most painful—a most delicate matter!' he said with an anxious roll of his eyes in her direction, 'and it is bewildering—it flings itself into one's work like a bomb! I don't know how to begin. Nor how to explain myself. You may say, why should I disturb you—my esteemed colleague—because I have been disturbed myself? To that I can only answer, that you are a woman, and it is by a woman that my feelings have been outraged. It is possible, therefore, that you should advise me what I should do. If it were for myself alone it would not matter, in a time like this one should have no feelings that are for oneself alone. What I fear is that she will extend her violence to others!'

Dr. Simmons leaned back in her chair, it was a hard one, but by leaning back she seemed to be able to get further away from Dr. Jeiteles' emotion. 'Perhaps you do not know', Dr. Jeiteles continued rapidly, 'that outrageous—that devastating—woman, Frau Bleileben? Her title is purely complimentary in a democratic Government and I shall therefore not use it! It is from her I had this most painful, most surprising, visit this morning!' 'Ah,' said

Dr. Simmons vaguely, 'I do not know her very well!' 'She told me—I assure you it was quite uncalled for——' Dr. Jeiteles continued, 'that Graf Wolkenheimb was a scoundrel and—I hardly like to mention the fact in your presence—he had just discarded her after a two years' intrigue!' 'Two years is a long time,' said Dr. Simmons reflectively. Dr. Jeiteles stared at her. 'That aspect of the affair', Dr. Jeiteles replied after a short pause, 'had not occurred to me. But, yes! Now that you mention it I see what you mean. It seems incredibly long! And why any man unless he were obliged to——! I told her that I had operation cases waiting, but she literally barred the door. If there had been severed arteries from my consulting room to the gate, I doubt if I could have reached them. And the terrible details she poured into my ears!' 'But what, I wonder,' asked Dr. Simmons in her precise and careful German, 'was the point of her making these disclosures to you?' 'Why to me? Why to me?' repeated Dr. Jeiteles, drawing his hand through his hair with a gesture of desperation. 'She was once rude to me at the Hospital Supplies Committee! On the strength of this she expects me to interfere between Graf Wolkenheimb and his betrothed. I am to tell that innocent, respected young girl that her fiancé lives a life of depravity, that he is a well-known swindler, and has even cheated the Relief Societies over the milk supply! And if I refuse to tell Miss Hunter these things this She Devil threatens to go to the Princess Felsör, expose her own cousin and head of the family, and force the Princess to break off the match. I would rather die than allow the Princess to suffer such an indignity! And I could weep when I think that by my foolish suggestion to Miss Hunter I have been instrumental in throwing her into the hands of a reptile like the Graf! She might never have become engaged to him if she had not gone to his cousin's flat!' 'Pray do not weep,' said Dr. Simmons with some asperity. 'Miss Hunter met Wolkenheimb some time before she went to the Princess's flat. What is it that you propose to do?' Dr. Jeiteles flung out both his hands. 'Do!' he exclaimed. 'What can I do? Have I not come to you—this young girl's friend and sponsor? Dr. Simmons, I implore you to relieve me from this office, for which I am not fitted! I know no English; Miss Hunter's German makes me dizzy; and I cannot under any circumstances go to the Princess and attack her cousin!' 'Do smoke, won't you?' suggested Dr. Simmons in her carefully expressionless tone. 'You take it the Graf *is* a scoundrel, I suppose? Under the circumstances you mention, can we consider Frau Bleileben a reliable witness?' 'She gave me a string of facts and dates,' replied Dr. Jeiteles with an effort at composure, 'and I went to my brother-in-law on my way here. He is a clerk in the Wiener Bank. He tells me that the Graf is looked on with suspicion, he is supposed to be associated with Mandelbaum and his set. What more does one want? He is also hand in glove with that fellow Erdödy, who made that infamous shipping deal. Even if nothing can be proved against Wolkenheimb, look how he lives! Where does his money come from? His land is a burden round his neck, his fortune was in *Kronen*, his hand must go into somebody's pocket! There is no doubt either about the Bleileben intrigue— her husband is divorcing her for it. It is this that has sent her mad! I implore you to tell me quickly that you will consent to act for me, and stop this marriage!' 'I'm afraid I can't do that!' said Dr. Simmons, lighting a fresh cigarette. 'I never under any circumstances interfere with people's love affairs. Miss Hunter already knows my opinion of Graf Wolkenheimb; he always struck me as a light-fingered gentleman. But there is no need for the Princess Felsör to be distressed. Will you excuse me one moment while I speak to my secretary?' Dr. Simmons drifted out of the room, leaving Dr. Jeiteles to a fresh tussle with his agitation. When she drifted back a few moments later, there was the suspicion of a smile upon her lips. 'We may expect,' she said, 'Frau Bleileben to join us in a few minutes. I am afraid I must ask you to remain, in case I need to ask you to verify anything that passed between you this morning. Before she comes would you mind repeating to me whatever you remember of her accusations against Graf Wolkenheimb? Not of course the personal ones!' Dr. Jeiteles groaned aloud. 'You ask me to remain?' he expostulated. 'Do you know what took place between us? It was terrible—terrible! Before she left I had called her a bad woman to her face!' 'Dear me!' said Dr. Simmons with unbroken calm. 'And that is not the worst of it,' Dr. Jeiteles went on in a low shocked voice, with his eyes fixed intently on the floor. 'It was frightful what she said to me! She fixed upon me an insult I can never forget! She told me that all I said was like an air bubble, because everyone knew I was in love with the Princess Felsör.' 'Very rude indeed,' agreed Dr. Simmons serenely, 'about the air bubble, but why do you feel it was an insult to be supposed to admire the Princess?' 'Any man might well be proud to love her,' said Dr. Jeiteles bitterly, 'except a Jew!' 'Ah!' said Dr. Simmons. For the first time during their interview she leaned forward as if the subject interested her. 'You make a mistake, Dr. Jeiteles, if you suppose the Princess has retained any such childish prejudice. I think her work in the hospital has taught her more than you know.' 'But you do not know how heavily custom binds Austria!' said Dr. Jeiteles sadly. 'It is like a frost which turns the living earth to iron!' 'We live in a broken world,' said Dr. Simmons thoughtfully, 'but misery has this advantage, Dr. Jeiteles, the line between those who desire to heal it and those who desire to profit by it becomes unusually distinct. You and the Princess both belong to the side that heals. No other difference counts in the same scale.' 'No! no! You are not right!' said Dr. Jeiteles. 'It is too deep, this caste system. Even if the Princess had freed herself, how could I bring myself to believe that she had? Also, her family would bind her down to their observances. The soul can be free, but one's acts—never!' 'And yet supposing that I should be right?' said Dr. Simmons gently. 'My God! if——' murmured Dr. Jeiteles, turning away his eyes from her face. 'And now do you mind telling me what you remember of the milk deal?' she asked dryly. Dr. Jeiteles became himself again; for ten minutes he spoke succinctly and efficiently, while Dr. Simmons with her head bent over her desk took careful notes.

At the end of this time Frau Bleileben broke into the room like a storm troop. She moved forward with a fierce rapidity, and without an attempt at greeting seized a chair that stood between them, and sat down heavily, her feet planted firmly at some little distance apart. She held her black suède bag with a diamond clasp as if she were trying to strangle it. The suffering of the last few days had coarsened and distorted her; but her vitality had come back. She was no longer the crushed and broken woman who had clung to Erdödy's arm at dawn; she was an avenging Fury. She could not prevent Otto's leaving her, but she could prevent his receiving any benefits from having left her. With the same direct unflinching spirit with which Elisabeth had entered the supreme adventure of her life she faced its end. Only now, instead of altering her stubborn will to meet Otto's wishes, she was about to tear his wishes to shreds to meet her need for revenge. She glanced from one to the other of her adversaries with snapping eyes. What did it mean that they had put their heads together? Had she gone too far in her wild outpouring to Jeiteles that morning? She had had no fear of the little monomaniac tied up in his hospital, but could this woman of a larger world have put two and two together in any inconvenient manner? Was Elisabeth in this bare stupid room —stark with discomfort—to get what she wanted or to receive another set-down? Let them try, that was all! She had had to behave properly before, but, thank God, she had not got to behave properly now! 'Ah!' she said in a low guttural voice, 'so Dr. Jeiteles is here, is he? I thought I had finished with him!' 'Won't you have a cigarette?' Dr. Simmons asked politely. 'Yes, I asked Dr. Jeiteles to remain. I understood that you had taken him into your confidence?' 'And you,' Elisabeth demanded, whirling around upon Dr. Simmons, 'so you no longer knit? You do not need then, I suppose, any help as to what to say to me—you find it easy? Good! I also shall not stop to measure my words. If this Jeiteles had been a man he would have acted as I told him to act —and not come whining here to you. I don't care who breaks the engagement! But it shall be broken! and quickly! I don't depend on slugs to set the pace for me! If it is not publicly broken in three days, I act as I choose; and I shall take my gloves off when I act!' 'I understand', said Dr. Simmons gently, 'that you think Graf Wolkenheimb an unsuitable husband for Miss Hunter and that you are kind enough to wish her friends to warn her of this fact before it is too late?' 'You may put it like that if you like,' said Elisabeth, moistening her lips. 'She shall never marry him! If you ask me why I do not go to her myself, I will tell you frankly I do not know where she is! The Princess Felsör and the Baron Erdödy —whose finger is in every pie, though he pretends that nothing sticks to it!—keep servants who are mentally deficient. I say nothing as to their morals though everyone knows that Erdödy lives with his cook! The Princess—who has also vanished—returns in three days' time—that I know! She has one of her insensate social gatherings with her pet Jews and goggle-eyed foreigners—they go there because of her title; and she thinks they go there to uplift the Universe! That is what it is to be intelligent in the higher classes—but no matter! If the marriage has not been publicly given up by then, I will be in myself a social gathering! I shall tell her all I know—and it is not a little—about her noble cousin!' 'What is it that you expect to gain by this interview with Princess Felsör?' Dr. Simmons asked, her eyes narrowing a little as they fixed themselves upon the glittering organs of Elisabeth. 'May one not suppose that she knows at least as much about Graf Wolkenheimb as you can tell her?' 'Ah, you ask what I gain?' asked Elisabeth, leaning forward with a triumphant smile. 'Well! I tell her, her old lover is mine—that is always something to tell another woman! And I warn her that unless she stops this marriage I ruin him! I can have his precious Trauenstein in the market in a year —and in the papers such a story of his dealings that even our mild Viennese will discover what his neck was made for!' 'You lie!' cried Dr. Jeiteles, who had started to his feet at the beginning of Elisabeth's speech, 'and it is your own neck that should be wrung! The Princess has never had a lover!' 'Except a Jew!' said Elisabeth with a derisive grin. 'That too can go into the papers!' 'One moment,' said Dr. Simmons. Something in her voice made Dr. Jeiteles suddenly reseat himself, and Elisabeth's grin vanish from her expressive features. 'Publicity is a two-edged weapon, Frau Bleileben,' Dr. Simmons observed. 'Do you really wish to provoke it? I have kept an account of our last interview together, which, when it is joined with your confidence to Dr. Jeiteles this morning, produces a curious impression. A publicly discredited Relief worker has no ground to stand upon; and although I quite think you might escape any legal penalty, I am convinced that you could not avoid being publicly discredited through the evidence which I possess.' Elisabeth's eyes dulled as if she had drawn a sheath over them. A long silence followed. Dr. Jeiteles wiped his brow. Dr. Simmons, shrouded by a mist of smoke, grew more and more shadowy; and Elisabeth—crouched, intent, shaking with hidden force—made the small room feel as if it held a dynamo. There was something terrible in the silent conflict of the two women. Finally a slow smile spread over Elisabeth's face; she hitched her chair closer to the shadowy figure and tapped her bag emphatically with her closed fist. 'Why do we beat about the bush?' she asked insinuatingly. 'I am not empty-handed, my dear friends. No! no! I have here something that speaks! Now, what is your figure? For is there not, sitting in your minds, a little figure ready to pounce? I don't say that I will meet it—but I shall not be disposed to haggle about the price of this tittle-tattle you have pieced together against me. Out with it! We will settle this affair first, and then go back to mine!' 'Miserable woman!' thundered Dr. Jeiteles. 'If you feel no shame at trying to bribe a fellow

Austrian, at least respect this noble foreign lady who has come here to help us!' 'Nonsense!' said Elisabeth sharply. 'I could be foreign myself if I chose to travel to other countries, picking up there what I had not the wits to find for myself at home! One knows the English do not come to Wien for their health! Even this good lady——' 'Please let us be practical,' interrupted Dr. Simmons brusquely. 'Frau Bleileben, you may take my word for it that we have no information which we intend either to sell or to buy.' Elisabeth dragged at her suède bag with such violence that the clasp snapped, and the diamond fell to the floor. Dr. Simmons picked it up, and laid it on her desk. 'If the Princess Felsör is left undisturbed,' she went on dispassionately, 'it is quite improbable that it will be necessary to rake up any unpleasant scandal against any one.' 'Ah!' said Elisabeth, drawing a deep breath, 'but what do I gain? Who'll stop the marriage? If Jeiteles is too much of a coward, why don't you tell Miss Hunter yourself? It is after all to your interest as well as mine, for if she is a friend of yours you cannot wish her to marry a man who has escaped the gallows by an accident!' 'I do not care to repeat second-hand evidence against anyone's character,' said Dr. Simmons calmly, 'but you are at liberty, as far as I am concerned, to tell Miss Hunter what you choose!' 'Ah!' said Elisabeth with a long hissing breath. The sparkle came back into her eyes, and her lips tightened. 'But if I do not know where she is until after the marriage, how can I tell her anything? No! no! I must have her under my thumb first!' and Elisabeth pressed her thumb upon the black suède of the bag: the mark remained visible for a long time after she had removed her thumb. 'There will be no harm', said Dr. Simmons thoughtfully, 'in letting you have her address in a few days' time. The date of the marriage is not yet settled.' Elisabeth rose to her feet. 'I assure you', she said with renewed confidence, 'I shall be doing the girl a service; and you, too, perhaps. I see well enough that your disinterested heart is after all a woman's! It is not too set on a pretty young girl making a good match.' 'No,' said Dr. Simmons without acrimony, 'I don't suppose that it is, if you mean by a good match a marriage with that very unattractive little man!' 'Very what?' asked Elisabeth incredulously. The light faded suddenly out of her face, her lips closed. Was there anyone on earth so blind, so lucky, that they could despise Otto Wolkenheimb? Dr. Simmons rose a little awkwardly to her feet; and while she held out to Elisabeth the snapped-off diamond, she hesitated over what she was about to say as if she were ashamed. 'Please forgive my saying', she murmured uncertainly, 'that for the future you should be careful not to mix your charitable activities with your business arrangements. Austria needs all her workers; it would be a pity for your services to have to stop!' Dr. Jeiteles sprang quickly forward; for one awful instant he imagined that Elisabeth was about to strike the head of the Relief Mission. It is possible that Elisabeth thought so too. She drew herself up, bared all her teeth, and dislodged the one word '*Fisch!*' full in the face of the passive Dr. Simmons. 'I forbid you to speak further!' cried Dr. Jeiteles, swinging open the door. 'Go out, or I shall put you out!' Elisabeth jerked her thumb over her shoulder in the direction of Dr. Simmons. 'Ah, ha! you show some spirit at last!' she cried, as she passed the enraged Dr. Jeiteles. 'It seems I underestimated your performances! You have *two* mistresses! God! what a thing to love!' and she banged the door exultantly after her. 'A thousand, thousand pardons!' cried Dr. Jeiteles helplessly as he turned to confront the insulted English lady. 'I really could not stop her, because how can one stop what one cannot conceive!' The words died on his lips; that inestimable but curious Englishwoman had at last melted—into inextinguishable laughter!

XXX

Otto set out from Wien to Trauenstein with a light heart. He had got rid of Elisabeth, he had got rid of a fortune for a purpose that was the equivalent of a greater fortune. He had his future bride beside him, and Eugénie sat in the back of the car with Eugen. A man likes to do what he knows he can do well, and Otto knew that he could make love to two women at the same time better than any man in Vienna.

His six months' engagement had lain lightly upon Otto's shoulders. He had been in no hurry for the marriage, and it was better not to announce his engagement until various little deals between himself and Elisabeth had run their natural course. He had told Carol that he was not at all platonic and that if she wanted a long engagement, they must meet in public places and seldom if ever alone. He had taken the wind out of her sails; she also it appeared wished for secrecy—for postponement—for an absence of demonstration; but she was at first surprised, and eventually a little piqued that Otto had the same inclinations.

But Otto knew better than to begin his engagement as an unwelcome lover. He saw that as long as Carol was free from love-making she would enjoy his presence. Her heart lay in her breast a stupid unused thing, leaving her wits free to play with Otto. Otto played very tenderly with her wits, but under the play he saw what had happened to her heart. It belonged to somebody else; this was the last touch needed to charm him. No really distinguished cracksman would care to be presented with a pearl necklace, but if he knows that it is another's, every nerve in him responds to the challenge. Otto watched Carol with ceaseless vigilance. He saw that she believed Franz Salvator would come back to her, he saw her hopes fade one by one as the time passed, he sustained her forced spirit with admirable adroitness; and when they became a mere cynical outpost to hide her heart, he took advantage of her new-born recklessness. That was the moment to make love; and he made it with a fierce ardour which was the more overwhelming from his long restraint. Carol's pride was in the dust; her starved senses responded to his sudden passion. She no longer cared what happened to her, provided that she was saved from thinking or carrying on her life alone. 'I'll have Otto, I'll have Trauenstein, I'll be a Countess!' she said to herself defiantly. She would not look beyond these things. She had Otto's kisses on her lips, his ring on her finger, and a curious hunted sense of not being alone any more in her heart.

'She will feel better', Otto said to himself on their way to Trauenstein, 'if she has laughed at Franz Salvator! At present she doesn't dare think about him, and that prevents her thinking suitably about me. But when she finds him a little ridiculous, she will return to me with relief.' He glanced sympathetically at the face beside him; he felt like a good physician who—without underestimating the pain he inflicts sees beyond it—to his patient's ultimate relief.

Carol looked extremely charming with a blue felt cowboy hat crushed down over her eyes and a long blue scarf floating around her. She was, however, thinking her own thoughts; and they skirted Otto as if he had been a precipice.

He was silent, but from time to time he made Carol meet his eyes, and every time she caught his look it was as if he had laid his hand suddenly upon her heart. 'It is strange', he said to her at last, 'that I take you to my house for the first time, and that I have never been to yours! We have never discussed your affairs or mine, and yet within two weeks they are to be the same! I hope it seems as amusing to you as it seems to me. We shall come fresh to our marriage—we have worn out nothing in these six months—except my patience!' 'Yes, you've been very good—till now,' Carol answered, looking away from him. 'As for myself and my affairs, that's the least part of the business to me. I'll tell you anything you like to ask.' Otto hesitated, he looked at her carefully, and then away at the white interminable road, which had already begun to zigzag upwards towards the foothills. There was a good deal he would have liked to ask. 'To me also,' he said slowly, 'money is not interesting. I leave all my affairs in the hands of my cousin Eugen, he will talk to you about them to-morrow. As to asking you questions, does one find out things from being told? That seems to me a clumsy way of managing. I would rather go by something in the air—by your smile—by your charming eyes which you keep so resolutely away from me at this moment! You are young, and you have no family with you, I should like to re-assure you a little, though I know you are brave and face life for yourself! I can think of no better way of doing it than by letting you share my family, and by being received by them as if they were your own. Our dinner the other night was incomplete without my cousin Franz—my cousin who is also, as I suppose you know, in certain contingencies—which we will not contemplate—my heir? We pass by his land settlement in a few minutes. It looks like a railway accident after the bodies have been removed, but I believe that it already calls itself a Garden City. I propose to stop there. Since Franz Salvator has not come to us—we will go to him. It does not do to stand upon ceremony in these matters.' 'Ah, but is it necessary?' asked Carol in sudden panic. 'You know, I know your cousin anyway——! I don't think——?' She bit her lips and faltered. Otto's eyes rested keenly on hers. Dared she say she would not meet Franz Salvator? What reason could she give for such a refusal? But dared she meet him under those dancing ruthless eyes? She flung her head up in defiance. No two men in the world should ever make a coward of her. Let them do what they liked, she would outface them both. She was a free woman out of a new world—they were the slaves of an old one. She gazed sternly at the littered field. 'They don't seem to me such bad-looking little houses,' she said defensively. 'Simply charming for rabbits,' agreed Otto, smiling, 'idyllic little hutches, a few scraggy lettuces, a goat and a tomato can—what a spot for a determined hermit! And not one determined hermit—but dozens are to inhabit it. And I am told they combine together to produce these architectural masterpieces, and intend to share the disgusting habits of each other's chickens. I never can understand the spirit of co-operation; even the air one breathes is so much better if one can persuade one's brother man to breathe it somewhere else!' 'Those people', said Carol sternly, 'haven't anywhere to live except half of somebody else's cellar or a railway car. Jane thinks this land scheme the best kind of relief there is. Everybody gets what they put into it. The little houses they build will be like a paradise to the men who build them!' 'And Franz Salvator', said Otto reflectively, 'will of course appear in the character of an angel. Wasn't there one in Jacob's dream—ascending and descending a celestial ladder, no doubt with the last type of concrete brick under his arm? What distresses me is that Franz Salvator was once a human being like ourselves. One did not have to go to sleep with a stone for a pillow in order to be able to think of him appropriately. Look! there he is, lightly decorated with cement, wheeling a barrow full of some loathsome substance across a plank! How the mud-pie instinct clings to a certain type of character!' Otto stopped the car at the verge of a sand pit and helped Carol more elaborately than he need have done to descend. 'Franz!' he called genially to his astonished cousin, checked in the middle of his plank by the sight of the car. 'Mahomet has come to the mountain! Pray be as genial as the occasion demands. We have come for your congratulations—which are a little overdue!' Franz Salvator left his wheelbarrow and advanced to meet them. 'I cannot shake hands,' he explained, trying to smile, 'since mine are dirty. You have taken me very much by surprise. Of course I congratulate you both. Eugénie, you should have told me you were coming!' 'Eugénie', said Eugen, glancing coldly at Otto, 'knew no more than you did what was in store for us; this is one of those surprises of Otto's called "happy", because they are sudden. I do not know if he has any more of them up his sleeve.' Otto laid his hand upon Franz Salvator's shoulder. 'Eugen's manners deteriorate daily,' he explained. 'It is the spread of democracy caused by Eugénie's tea parties—he doesn't go to them—I don't think we've either of us been invited!—but the spirit has passed into the family and the infection spreads. It is always a pleasure to see you, my dear boy, even surrounded by these very raw materials of your new vocation! I suppose you feel like Michael Angelo? Do you go to bed like the historic sculptor with sixteen apprentices and never wash? Please show us everything. My bride has the curiosity of a Continent to satisfy; but as for me I shall be content with the ground floor and my imagination.'

Otto let his fancy ride roughshod over the half-made settlement; he was sometimes very funny, and Carol laughed and laughed. The look in Franz Salvator's eyes hurt her so that she could not stop laughing. This was how she meant to show them all how little she cared. She was the youngest of them and the most afraid of ridicule. Eugénie never spoke at all and seldom smiled. Eugen stalked beside her, saturnine and grim, his heavy eyebrows dragged low over his sombre eyes. From time to time he tried to break up Otto's flood of banter, but Otto turned his remarks with fiendish agility into fresh occasions for mockery. He was making his bride see what she had escaped and punishing Franz Salvator at the same time for the image he had found in her eyes.

Franz Salvator took his punishment like a man. He parried Otto's jokes and joined in Carol's laughter. As long as he was not alone with her he knew that he could manage. But Otto knew this too; and he proposed to leave them alone together. Eugénie went over several of the houses in their different stages and then said she had had enough. Eugen turned back to put her into the car. Otto insisted upon showing Carol Franz Salvator's own house before joining them, but when he had reached it he begged them to take his inspection for granted. 'I shall leave you in the kitchen,' he said, 'and watch them making bricks. I do not know why, but the earlier stages of this affair seem to me the more enchanting. Pray don't imagine I am not an admirer of your work, my dear boy, but the artist in me makes me prefer the "Victory of Samothrace"—headless. Take Carol all over everything, and explain the kitchen taps. I will come back for you shortly.' 'I cannot,' began Franz Salvator stiffly. 'But I don't want to see the kitchen taps!' cried Carol. Then they found that they were alone.

They were in a little empty room splashed with whitewash and full of the western sun. Carol stood by the mantelpiece and looked helplessly across at Franz Salvator. He stood rigidly with his back against the wall as if he were facing a firing party. Only his eyes moved, they seemed to be trying to get away. 'You're so thin,' Carol said in a queer choked voice. 'Why are you so thin?' 'I am very well,' stammered Franz Salvator; 'I did not expect—this room we are in is meant for the kitchen!' His eyes stilled at last on her face and found that they could not leave it. 'It is six months!' said Franz Salvator helplessly. 'Well! why didn't you come to me!' cried Carol. The words rushed out of her lips in spite of herself, her dignity collapsed as completely as Franz Salvator's indifference. 'It is incredible you should ask me such a question,' Franz Salvator answered violently. 'You were not free!' 'Free!' cried Carol angrily. 'What do you mean by not free? I'm a woman and not a stock or a stone—I can move as quick as most things! It's you who tied me up—I *was* free!' 'I cannot stay here with you—I must go!' said Franz Salvator hoarsely. 'Go then!' replied Carol angrily; but neither of them stirred. They could not take their eyes away from each other. Otto came back and found them with the breadth of the room between them; and they looked as if his coming were a relief. 'No doubt,' said Otto, 'you have seen everything—and Franz Salvator has explained where he intends to keep his pigs and where he will wash his potential family? I suppose even in the most communistic homes some little divisions are desirable? I would ask you to come with us to tea at Waldberg, my dear boy, if you looked a trifle more presentable! As it is we must say good-bye. You know Trauenstein is always your home— I invite you—may I not, Carol?—in my bride's name as well as in my own.' Carol said suddenly, 'For God's sake let's clear.' She thought for an awful moment that somebody, she was not sure whether it was Franz or herself, was going to break down. But nobody did. They sauntered out, in an interminable manner, towards the car. Otto expected Carol to take her former seat, but she refused bluntly. She said something to Eugénie in an undertone, and Eugénie with obvious reluctance took her place. Franz Salvator stood bareheaded on a pile of planks and waved to them. Otto had forgotten how well a handsome man can look when he is untidy. He had not intended to present Carol with a picture of Franz Salvator like a Greek figure on a broken frieze; and he had meant on their way to Trauenstein to drive the moral of the land scheme home—but not home to Eugénie. He opened the throttle with a petulant jerk, and did not dare to look at Eugénie until her silence became more oppressive than speech. Her chin was lifted and her eyes looked colder than he had ever seen them. It was unfortunate that his lesson to his bride had reacted so sharply upon Eugénie. 'I suppose you think I am a brute?' he said at last. 'A little of a brute,' said Eugénie, without turning her head, 'and more of a fool.' 'And may I ask why I am a fool!' Otto demanded as they shot back dangerously into the main road. 'Certainly,' said Eugénie, 'because a malicious man is invariably his own antidote. You wished to give a bad impression of Franz Salvator, and you have given a singularly poor exhibition of yourself.' 'And that is why you are so angry with me,' said Otto, laughing under his breath. 'Your indirect compliments are not without a certain charm, even when they take the form of insults. But I owe you an apology. I had to teach my little bride a lesson. She does not like cottages—especially not half-made ones—but she took an inconvenient interest in the person who is making them. Our visit to Franz Salvator this afternoon was a first lesson in arithmetic. I wanted Carol to see that two and two make four. That I had to hurt you while I was doing it distresses me; but that I had to hurt Franz Salvator leaves me a little cold. It is not more than he deserves. Why does he let you be talked about all over Wien? His place is beside you, and his duty is to kick Jeiteles out of your house. Do you suppose I don't know that you receive that Jew Doctor once a fortnight or oftener?' 'I shall receive him as often as I choose,' said Eugénie quietly. 'And it matters very little to me whether you know it or not.' 'Do you mean to marry him,' asked Otto, lifting his eyebrows, 'or merely to throw away your reputation? As your nearest male relative next to Franz I think that I have a right to ask.' 'Hitherto I have not considered marriage,' replied Eugénie carefully; 'I have not felt I needed its protection; but I see that I may be driven to it. I shall certainly not give up the friendship of the most disinterested man I know because of a little gossip.' 'All I ask is that he should confine his great gifts to the hospital,' said Otto suavely, 'and not display them to you in your drawing-room. You turned me out of it once, do you not remember, when I was showing you mine?' 'Ah!' said Eugénie, 'but there is this difference between you and Dr. Jeiteles. You wished to break down my defences, and Dr. Jeiteles is in himself a defence. You do not know how a woman loves to be respected!' 'It is true,' agreed Otto, 'that the women I have known have generally liked other things better. But I will respect you to your heart's content if you will give up Jeiteles! Or at any rate give me your word not to marry him? I am at your feet with contrition for suggesting anything else; but I am jealous; and a lover who has no rights has no confidence.' Eugénie's lips softened, her face ceased to look as if it were chiselled out of marble. 'What can I say?' she answered. 'I do not want marriage. Rudolf has been dead five years, and I have never spoken to anyone of my life with him. But it was horrible—so horrible that the first bearable day of it—was when he had proved himself so base that even the Church told me not to live longer with him!' 'You bore all that,' said Otto under his breath, 'knowing that I could have saved you from it—and yet you told me that day at Demel's that if I were free you would still marry me.' 'I suppose I would then,' agreed Eugénie hesitatingly. 'At least, if you could have changed! But it is well we have not tried—we think and feel too differently! And now you are not free even to talk of such things to me! You have chosen a girl of wit and beauty, whom it is easy to love. If you want my respect and my affection you must leave me alone and play no more tricks on her like to-day. If you do not, I shall have to give up, not only my friendship with you, but the friendship of Carol herself. Then I shall be left to Eugen and to Dr. Jeiteles—to Eugen, who does not share any of my new ideas or occupations; and to Dr. Jeiteles, who does not share any of my old ones! The answer to your question lies in your own hand, Otto! I will only marry Dr. Jeiteles if you rob me of all my peace!' 'I am a beast,' said Otto with a flicker of real contrition, 'a shabby beast to torment you. But I am a man haunted by a passion he can never satisfy and frustrated by an ambition which he must sacrifice love itself to gain. I want power—I am capable of using it. I need money to obtain this power, and I have had to stoop so low to gain it that I have lost my self-respect. At least let me gain that for which I have made such hideous sacrifices. If I don't marry a fortune, I go to the devil. But believe this of me, that I know what I am losing. I was happy once at Trauenstein in our youth, when I held you in my arms. I shall never be happy again. Don't marry Jeiteles! After my marriage I will leave you alone. As it is now—God! how hard it is to see your lips! I should like to put on a little more speed and drop over the edge of one of these corners and end it all! You would let me touch you then perhaps—not otherwise?' 'Not otherwise,' said Eugénie, scarcely moving her lips. Neither of them spoke again. The pines began—a black shadow above the white road—as clear as the cut of a knife; between the shadow and the road the sun filtered softly on the bare pink stems. The pungent odour of the pines came to them in long fragrant puffs as if the sunshine itself had turned into a scent. Otto stopped the car before the door of a brown chalet. Fixed in a tree above their heads was a large painted wooden eye, a reminder of the watch-fulness of an unsophisticated God. Tables with red and white checkered cloths were laid out under chestnut trees. The girl who brought them their coffee was pretty. They looked over an expanse of Alpine meadow brimming over with the first Spring flowers. The March sun was hot as May. Far away in the fragrant pine woods they heard the tinkle and check of wandering cow bells. There was no other sound, only the continuous splash and hurry of a mountain stream, clear as gold, tumbling and dashing over great stones, leaping tiny precipices and subsiding into deep brown pools. A sense of happiness, of fugitive but real companion-ship, stole over them all. Even Eugen relaxed his rigidity. Otto was a little grave; but he looked at his bride and smiled, and for the first time Carol saw in his eyes a kindly gleam that had noth-ing to do with laughter or love-making. Her taut nerves sank to rest. 'Well,' she said appreciatively, 'I don't know, but if I'd got to choose, I'd rather be a cow on a mountain pasture than anything else—to roam about and make music with a little bell, to eat the loveliest flowers and get half a sunset on your back—like that one over there—and to know that you're the only thing anyone in your world thinks about except God—that's some kind of a life!' 'Ah!' said Otto. 'How delicious are the illusions of others about oneself! Of oneself too, no doubt, about others! Shall I tell you of what the life of a cow on an Alpine pasture really consists? To begin with, do you see those very stout fences which surround the meadow opposite to us? The cows, you will observe, are not in that field, their bells come from the distant woods. That com-panionable creature under the trees has been allowed to return simply in order to be milked. Remarkably dry unnutritious pine needles cover the floor of the woods. The meadows full of sweet rich flowers and grass are certainly destined for the cows, my dear Carol; but not until the grass has lost all its succulence and become hay. The fences are to keep out the cows; their tinkling bells are not the pleasure to them that they are to us; without them the cows might perhaps find or make a weak place in the fence and enter their paradise unseen and unobstructed; but the bells upon their necks betray them. Small boys with sticks take the place of angels with flaming swords, and are quite as efficient. The woods are full of flies. A benevolent Deity provided the cows with a tail, but flies have wings; and a tail is unfortunately fixed to one spot. They live, these poor creatures, the restricted lives of nuns! Heaven, as we know, is to be the reward of earthly dedication. I wonder if the analogy is complete, and if those who have refrained from the bloom and freshness of the pastures of life, will find preserved for them, in Eternity—in a state of desiccated nourishment—the delicious little flowers of Time.' Otto's eyes wandered from the amused ones of his bride and rested upon those of Eugénie. Eugénie's eyes were amused too, but they were turned away from him. 'Whenever', Otto went on reflectively, 'I wish to find a moral reassurance for a peccadillo of my own, I shall not go to that officious pedant, the bee, still less shall I seek the bourgeois activities of the ant. I shall resort to the memory of a cow on an Alpine pasture, and say to myself, "After all, my dear Otto, you won't very much care for that dry hay later on! Perhaps your little excursions into the blossoms while they are fresh and fragrant is really a more profitable method of existence!" and I shall feel greatly reassured. My thoughts do not often take these grateful turns, but I find myself thanking whatever gods there be that mankind has not been provided with those little tinkling bells!' 'Ah!' said Eugen, 'do not be too sure, the paths of mankind may be wider, and the little fences not so stout, but that fatal instrument, the tongue, draws a good deal of attention to our movements!' 'It is time that we go,' said Eugénie softly, 'the hour of our freedom is over.'

Once more Carol found herself beside Otto, but it was a different Otto; she found him an altogether more friendly and approachable person. She thought to herself that it was because they were nearing Trauenstein, and Trauenstein was his home. The sun was sinking, far below them the blue plain lay like a distant jewel. The mountains stood in front of them clear and cold in the last light. The moon, a tiny hoop of silver, floated above a sea of pines. They passed a small white church above a water-fall—a little thinned-out mountain village—and then suddenly Trauenstein rose over them, a massive shadow. They crossed a drawbridge, and the great gates rolled back. In a moment they were in a wide dark courtyard full of figures with lanterns, dogs barked in a fury of welcome, and the Gräfin herself stood under the arch of the doorway to greet her son's future bride. Otto sprang out, his face in the flickering light was strangely expressionless, but he moved quickly forward and gave Carol his arm. 'They have a saying in the East,' he murmured, 'my house is your home. I hope that you will make it true.'

XXXI

Carol felt that she had known Trauenstein always in her dreams, and then she remembered that she had actually seen it in one of those unforgettable moments in life when something structural takes place in the heart. It was Trauenstein she had looked at on the walls of Franz Salvator's room. He loved it too then, this vast Schloss, this home like a city; and he belonged to it, even as Otto belonged; that backward stretch of years was part of the fabric of both their lives. They spoke of their heritage very seldom, but they never forgot it; Trauenstein was as necessary to them as the air they breathed. The Schloss was very old, and broken by many wars; it had a look as if the outdoor world had been driven into it; the pines that hung in a black fringe around the massive walls sent their shadows and the echo of their perpetual reverberation through the dim empty rooms. On the walls were antlers, big and little; spiral horns like twisted sea-monsters, stuffed heads of wistful stags, with great Auerhähne and golden eagles balanced on imitation branches— all melting off into shadows; but there was very little furniture, and that was either old and worn or made from the larch and pine at the castle doors. A great fire burned in the hall in a fireplace as large as a room; whole roots of trees fed it, and bay leaves, flung on it, filled the air with scent. After dinner they all sat there

while Otto sang to them. He had a light baritone voice, flexible
and dramatic, through which emotion ran delicately like a secret
flame. Eugénie played for him. Their music joined the shadows
in the room until it became a part of them. The Gräfin sat bolt
upright in a high carved chair knitting a pair of very thick
woollen socks. From time to time she looked at Carol, and Carol
felt a chill run down her spine. It was an inscrutable, quite imper-
sonal vivisection. Carol wondered if, before the evening ended,
the Gräfin had left a shred of her being—mind or body—unex-
plored. For the first time in her life she felt that to be young was a
disadvantage. But the Gräfin could do nothing more than look at
her. Otto was the person that she feared. To-night for the first time
Carol knew that she feared Otto. She felt that if he kissed her she
could not bear it; but Otto did not kiss her. He barely let his lips
touch her hand when he gave her her candle and left her with
laughing wishes at the foot of the shadowy staircase. It was as if he
had known whose presence stood between them. This presence
was only a shadow, Carol told herself impatiently. She would get
rid of it now that she was alone with the quiet night. She would
stop those deep blue eyes fixing her so piteously and so indomitably
and making her heart cry out. Franz had done worse than wrong
her by his absurd pretentious code, he had wronged himself. All
his life he would be starved for love of her, and all her life the sense
of his hunger would move in her like a living thing. It was this she
could not forgive him—not that she suffered—but that she could
not staunch his wounds. She leaned from her window over the
wall, which sprang downwards like a precipice into a glade of
pines. The wind in the trees was the only sound she heard. Far off
and tremulous it stirred in distant branches; mysteriously gathering force upon its way, it broke in a series of crashes under her
window, withdrawing itself as waves withdraw themselves, a
melancholy, reverberating sound without the weight of water. Life
flickered in her like a candle in a draught; in spite of her youth
she felt suddenly its deep impermanence. All her activities and
emotions, her stalwart sense of equipment for the battle of time—
left her. She felt herself as easy to break as the wing of an insect.
The lives of a thousand years had crushed into the darkness
around her, an accumulation of vitality—yet the lives themselves
had gone; only walls and whispers and this strange feeling of in-
vasion remained. This feeling of gathered invisible vitality had

something menacing in it, something expressionless but powerful like the small lidless eyes of the Gräfin pressing in upon her mind; or like Otto's eyes, when they caught at her heart as a hawk's eyes fix a bird. It was as if his very ardour was an indifferent feeling, a mere instinct to strike and glance aside without respect for personality. She belonged to herself, she said passionately into the night. She was not a possession, a mere thread for these Wolkenheimbs to grasp and weave into the web of their history. The pines mocked her with a long procession of sound, without beginning or end. 'What is a self?' they murmured continuously. 'Wind in the trees—wind in the trees! There is no self!' All night long she fought with shadows and with silence; but when she woke into brilliant March sunshine, clear and shining, full of the songs of innumerable birds, she felt her buoyancy return. Yesterday— Franz Salvator—the night and the pines— were quickly buried out of sight. This was a new day, and she was going to be glad in it. The sunshine moved in her blood. The old centuries were like dead cobwebs high up, out of sight; and Otto was only a man to be kept and held in his place.

After breakfast Otto took her for hours wandering over the Schloss. They stood in the sunny courtyard looking up at the famous terra-cotta reliefs while Otto told her the humorous and tragic stories of his line. He explained the fables pictured above their heads. The solid sword of Damocles hanging over the round pink crown of a serenely unconscious monarch, while Hercules just below him brandished terra-cotta clubs to break the backs of rose-coloured dragons. They finished at last by lingering in a small roof garden under the soaring Hunger tower. From the little garden, ruinous and grass grown, Carol could see the whole of Trauenstein. The land dropped gently into the Danube plain; far away the broad silvery river stretched under the yellow walls of Melk. The mountains rose behind them, a deep delphinium blue. Between the long undulating ranges were gaps of meadowland and shining air. Down in the garden below the tower lay a thirteenth-century jousting court with the ruins of a banqueting hall, and over the hillside, breaking in and out of the pines, was a Roman wall, with bricks as old as time and as thin as biscuits. From the centre of a second courtyard rose a tall Italian campanile. 'The dungeons are down there,' said Otto, pointing beneath the tower, 'oubliettes and little hints to undesirable enemies or troublesome friends! They say that one of my ancestors led his wife there with the utmost courtesy, after a pleasant dinner, and walled her up alive. She had looked a little too long and a little too pleasantly at a visiting Knight. We have never taken the walls down; and I suppose she stands there to this day, regretting that her glances went astray.' 'I think you ought to take all those bricks down and get her comfortably buried,' said Carol seriously. 'I hate to think of her standing up there like that, hundreds of years!' 'She must be used to it by now,' said Otto, smiling, 'but I'm not vindictive; she can be buried whenever you like!' Otto stood with his hand laid lightly on Carol's shoulder. She looked like the Spring itself, as she sat on the low wall, her head flung back and the sun shining on her maize-coloured hair. He felt as if some spirit from the distant years had drawn near and touched him. Otto loved the bloom of youth. This child—so like a fairy, dainty and delicious in the light Spring sunshine—gave him a moment of pure gratitude; and he used it to draw her to him with a tenderness he had never yet displayed. He felt her draw back from his caress with a quick pained movement of her whole body, and in an instant his tenderness died. He pulled her roughly into his arms, holding her closely against him, and covered her face and neck with kisses. She struggled fiercely, and then held herself rigid and cold under his passionate pressure. Her eyes closed, and her face whitened; she had not yet learned her lesson. He released her at last with a half-apologetic laugh. 'I'm sorry!' he said. 'I love the Spring. You look too like it! Have I hurt you?' 'You've made me very angry,' Carol said in a low choked voice. 'You knew I did not want you to do that!' 'But how am I to make you want me,' Otto protested ruefully, 'if you won't let me try? Making love is half the business!' 'But force isn't!' said Carol quietly. 'I'll never forgive you if you touch me again against my will!' 'That is a terrible punishment,' said Otto, 'and how am I to know what I may do? Shall I be told?' 'You don't need telling!' said Carol. 'You knew before! You know now, only you don't care!' 'Ah! but I care too much! You're so sweet!' protested Otto, slipping his hand over hers. 'Tell me I am forgiven?' Carol nodded; a curious languor spread over her, she wondered at the fierce hate she had felt in Otto's arms a moment before. His voice, low and close to her, was like a spell; she felt a vague pleasure at the touch of his fine strong fingers. It was foolish to be so angry with him. She lifted her eyes to meet his, smiling down at her, and when he leaned forward and touched her cheek with his lips she did not draw away from him. 'You make me nervous!' Otto said laughingly. 'A timid lover always bungles his job! I shall feel as if I were kissing with a sword hanging over my head, like my terra-cotta friend in the courtyard! When do you intend to fix our marriage day? I suppose the sword will be dropped then? I wish you would cable for your solicitor at once. Eugen can't draw up settlements with you alone! The legal mind never talks in words under four syllables and has to be matched with champions of its own calibre.' 'But I haven't got a solicitor,' said Carol in surprise. 'What would I want a solicitor for?' Otto stared down at her. 'But, my child,' he exclaimed, 'your fortune? Somebody presumably cares for it. You have a man of business?' Carol laughed. 'Give me another cigarette,' she said. 'How beautifully you light them! and I love your motto on the case, "What I will I win!" Well! I daresay I'd have a man of business if I'd got any business! As to my fortune—I have enough to buy a trousseau with, and I can earn more. It isn't every girl that gets fifty dollars a week out of her wits and the back chat of Europe!' For a moment the eyes so close to her own flickered and went black; they looked as wicked as murder; then they became inscrutable again. 'What do you mean,' Otto asked imperturbably, 'that you have no fortune? Is it a joke? You know I have not yet been broken in to all the forms of American humour.' 'Why, do you mean to say you've heard it too?' Carol asked incredulously. 'Eugénie has got hold of a story that I had flocks of almighty dollars at my heels! I suppose it's because I've got a millionaire cousin's name; but the name's all. They don't give me anything to keep it up with.' 'Then you have no money at all except what you earn?' Otto asked carefully. 'Nothing,' said Carol, looking straight at him. 'Does it matter awfully? If it does, we'll call this engagement business off. I wouldn't have you tied to me against your will for worlds!' Something vivid and happy shot into her heart. She turned her eyes away from Otto lest he should see the sudden joy that had invaded her; and yet it was not only joy. She felt pleased and humiliated, freed and disappointed. Was she in love with both men at once? She was in love with Franz Salvator clumsily and irretrievably, she had no doubt of that; but she was half in love with the man beside her too, and with what he stood for— those queer roots hidden in the ages! He had made her laugh so often. Would he never make her laugh again? Those smiling shining eyes had taught her so many things. She had believed in his love; it was true she had seen that some tie, deeper perhaps than his feeling for herself, bound him to Eugénie; but she had trusted him because she thought he was disinterested. He could not have Eugénie, so he wanted Carol. Well! she could not blame him for that. She too could not have Franz Salvator, so she wanted Otto. But what if he had never wanted her at all except to use her money—and worse, if he had only felt for her that light desire without respect, as momentary as the instinct of an animal? The hand that held her cigarette shook a little. Well! she would let him go—but something went with him—something that she was ashamed to have given him; and he should not get clear away, a piece of her very lucid mind should accompany him. 'How goes it, Otto?' she asked, lifting her chin a little higher and looking at him steadily through half-closed eyes. 'I'm waiting to be told whether I'm the future Gräfin Wolkenheimb or the future Carol Hunter. I'm willing to back either, but I can't back both, can I? The position is a little undignified for each of us—suppose you just for once light out with the truth?' 'My dear child,' Otto said quickly, 'this is a shocking business, and I'm more sorry—more sorry for it than I can say! Will you believe me, I wonder, that although money is a sheer necessity to me—I had a large fortune and I am capable perhaps of making another, but for the moment I have nothing at all, except these quite impracticable ruins—I wasn't marrying you for it. I have *le bon motif*—any man who knows you would have! I should have been tempted to make love to you if I'd always known that you had nothing at all. You say that you will set me free, but with us a broken engagement is as serious as death, and I am a little anxious as to how we can either keep it on or break it off without difficulties it would be foolish not to foresee.' 'Fortunately,' said Carol lightly, turning her head away from him and back towards the shining fields which were no longer to be her own, 'you're saved by my being an American. With us an engagement is only final when we've left the altar steps; up till then it's a mere legitimate practice. I don't shut a door till I'm through it—and I never have felt on the other side of this one. Just publish that the marriage won't take place. I'll never let anyone know the reason why we've given it up. All the same, Otto, I am going to speak plain to you before we part. You

deceived me. You never told me you were in love with Eugénie!'
'What the deuce do you mean?' Otto asked her angrily, dropping
his hand from her shoulder as if it had been stung. 'Who told you
any such tale?' 'You,' said Carol. 'You're very clever, Otto, and I
suppose you think I'm a good deal more ignorant of life than a
European. But I know a lover when I see one, and I know when
a man's another woman's lover, even if he's paying the prettiest
kind of court to me at the same time; and that cow in the Alpine
pasture business didn't get past me! I've done you a wrong—I
didn't mean to, but you've done me one, and I think you meant
it all along!' Otto hesitated, then he said, 'In a sense what you
say is true. I have always loved my cousin Eugénie, but all idea
of a marriage between us was over many years ago. As you know
Eugénie, you will readily understand that any other idea on my
part was destined to be useless. Therefore I was free. Eugénie
herself would tell you I was free if you asked her.' 'She did tell
me so,' said Carol composedly, lighting a fresh cigarette and fixing
Otto with her clear young candour, 'and your eyes, and your
voice, and the way you hit out at her told me exactly the opposite.
I don't say I wouldn't have forgiven you for loving Eugénie the
best. I think I would. She's the only woman I know I should
never feel ashamed to be beaten by; and she would have played
fair, and be damned to you—whether you made love to her or
not! But I'm pretty glad you found out I was penniless, for on the
whole, Otto Wolkenheimb, I consider you rather a poor piece of
goods!' Otto flushed; but he was not angry with Carol's descrip-
tion of himself. He knew that he had moved her, and could move
her again; he knew it better than she did for all her shrewdness.
He did not want to give her up; and it shot through his mind that
there was a way to escape this disagreeable necessity. He would
have to marry Elisabeth because he was in instant need of a sum
of money he could not otherwise procure, but after this extraordinarily painful step had been taken, might he not return to his
original idea, and with Elisabeth for a wife make this charming
child his mistress? Life forced one to do prosaic things, but if one
was clever with it and yielded at the right moments, one could
generally go about with a little romance up one's sleeve. And then
something spoke to Otto; it was not any kind of compunction or
remorse; it was his sense of beauty to which he had always paid a
tribute of respect. He decided, against the pull of a strong desire,

that he would not—even if he could—do any such thing; and he decided it while he still looked down at Carol and felt to the full her delicate charm. He would not use his deadly skill on her half-roused senses. She was straight, straighter than he had supposed women ever were, and he would be straight with her. She had let him go without a stain upon his honour, and in this way, clean and free, he would let her leave him—as you let a bird which has flown into the dark interior of a mysterious human room fly back through an open window into the light. 'I do not wonder', he said gently, 'that you think little of me. I assure you I think very little of myself. But men are queer mixtures. I do love you. I do—what is from me rather more of a compliment—respect you. Try to see things from my point of view. King Cophetua was very well off when he indulged his fancy by making a beggar maid his queen. If he had had the misfortune to lose his wealth and, instead of a beggar maid, to have fancied a successful and brilliant, but still not opulent, American journalist, I think he would have had to kiss her hand regretfully as I do now, and do the best he could for his ruined kingdom without her! I am afraid that I must go off immediately to Wien. My affairs are in a bad way, and I must try to get them out of it. Please stay here as long as you like. I will not inform my mother of what has taken place until you have left. And now we must say good-bye I suppose? Not that I have any grudge against you, chère amie, but because I like you a great deal too much to wish to meet you again.' 'You're a sport, Otto,' said Carol cordially; 'I've lost you a fortune and cut you out of a wife; but I haven't done it purposely or without getting rather hit myself. I'd kind of figured out that I was to have a medieval Schloss and one of those husbands who always keep a woman guessing! And I suppose if I'd been the heiress I should have liked them both!' Otto looked at her and bit his lips. 'It's a damned bore—money,' he said in a low voice. 'My only excuse is that I've got to keep this place. My life is horribly complicated, and it isn't all my fault, as most women would suppose, that I can't follow my heart or keep my word or behave like the very fine fellow I'd like you to believe I am! I was going to ask you for that kiss you didn't give me, but I won't now; you seem to me rather too good for it! Let's shake hands and part friends. Good-bye, young America!'

It is improbable that Otto ever paid a woman a finer compliment by making love to her than he paid Carol by refraining from it; and Carol realized the compliment. She gave him a quick firm pressure of the hand, and watched him go, with a curious, half-regretful smile. It was characteristic of Otto that he had not told her she had not only cost him the fortune she did not possess, but the fortune she had innocently caused him to lose. Nor had he, when she accused him of his divided allegiance, as much as hinted to her of his knowledge of her own divided heart. Otto had sacrificed most of his virtues, but he still kept an uneasy hold upon his courage and his good taste. As he hurried down the long stone staircase which led to the terrace below, no one could have told by looking at him that he had just lost a wife and a fortune; nor that he was about to undertake the most unpleasant piece of business he had ever had to perform, without even the certainty of its being a success.

XXXII

They had moved about the Castle all the morning like conspirators who knew that an infernal machine is timed to explode, but are uncertain of the actual moment, until Eugénie felt that even her unmitigated fears would be easier to bear than Eugen's elaborate reassurances. 'I will go to the lake,' she said at last; 'it will be easier to wait there, I think, and when you know what has happened to Otto you will come quickly and tell me?' Eugen agreed; but he could have told her then. He knew what would happen to Otto. 'My dear Eugénie,' he said, 'try to remember what I have been telling you, that if you let Otto know you had a hand, however light, however innocent, in depriving him of a fortune, he will not only punish you, he will punish himself for the rest of his life. You will deprive him of an ideal, and it is important for Otto to retain the only ideal he has. I claim your word in this matter! You will not, however tempted by the irritant of a most unreasonable remorse, violate a confidence?' Eugénie did not think her remorse unreasonable, but she agreed that she would at least not tell Otto that she had consciously withheld her knowledge from him. It seemed to her as she walked slowly through the scented pines and breathed the sweet clearness of the mountain air as if she had betrayed the beauty of the world. Why had she not let Otto judge for himself what it was right for him to do? She who believed so passionately in human liberty had deprived Otto of it at the crisis of his career. She had not let him choose, and she was to blame if the choice made for him had injured him. It was all very well for Eugen to say that one man's ruin (even Otto's ruin) was as nothing compared to the salvation of their country by the restoration of Karl. Eugen believed that Austria could only be saved by the return of the Emperor; Eugénie had come to believe that Austria could save herself. She still had her loyalty to her Kaiser, but was it anything like so deep as her loyalty to Otto? Had not she sacrificed that loyalty out of a craven maternal fear that Otto would sink beneath his chance? If she had not interfered he might have triumphantly proved that he was equal to his hour, instead of being hustled into sacrifice, like a child over-persuaded to part with a toy by a couple of sentimental nurses. It was not only ruin into which her moral intensity had plunged him (the lack of money never could seem to Eugénie of primary importance), she associated the fear she felt with the angry, unhappy eyes of Elisabeth Bleileben. When Otto had said to her the night before that he would go to the devil if he failed to obtain a fortune the devil his words evoked for her had been the woman at the Opera.

The lake of Trauenstein was a green, deep pool; it lay under a circle of pines, holding them tree by tree, stem by stem in a solid, unshaken mirror. Eugénie sat down at its edge. The day was still and hot; every now and then—into the silence—a pine cone fell on the russet floor with a mild crash. The sun flickered through the dark boughs and set small golden patterns on the fallen needles. Eugénie felt as if the sunshine had cut off time. She was held in a suspended element, that had neither an end nor a beginning; only her heart, beating heavily with fear, told her that she was still alive. At last she heard quick footsteps coming through the wood; the path filled suddenly, and her eyes met Otto's. It was an unfortunate moment for Otto to find Eugénie, because he was suffering very sharply from reaction, and upon no one could he vent it with such thoroughness as upon the woman who loved him. 'Oh!' cried Eugénie, pressing her hands against her heart. 'I thought— I thought Eugen was coming!' 'I am sorry to disappoint you,' said Otto, with a smile which moved his lips but seemed to increase the dangerous light in his hard eyes. 'I preferred to tell you my news myself, I was so grateful to you for being so charming as to wish to hear it. I am ruined. May I ask how long you were aware that this interesting surprise was in store for me?' 'Not very long, Otto,' Eugénie faltered. 'It was to me too a surprise.' 'It seems that Franz Salvator was more fortunate,' said Otto, sitting down at the other end of the bench and fixing his mocking eyes on Eugénie. 'He was warned in time that the train would not carry him to his station; so he very wisely got off. I do not blame him —but our old fraternal feeling for each other, backed by what the English so happily call "fair play", was, alas! not sufficient for either of you to warn me to do the same.' 'Oh, Otto,' Eugénie murmured, 'you know—you know Franz did not seek Carol's fortune! He left us thinking her rich—I myself knew nothing till just before you went to Budapest.' 'Ah,' said Otto, 'you ask a good deal of my credulity, and you present me with an interesting fact. If you had told me, dearest friend, before I made that journey, I should not have gone to Budapest—nor should I now be contemplating that other little excursion to the devil which comes next on my programme. I do not blame your pretty little friend for having nothing but her very charming self; if she deceived me it was at any rate unconsciously; but that *you* should have known what would have altered my whole future, and not told me——! Dear Eugénie, pray explain what part of your moral code this particular reticence supported?' 'Surely,' said Eugénie, raising her beautiful sad eyes to his, 'it was not for me to tell you? It was for her! Otto, when she told me that she was not rich I did not even know that you were ignorant of what she told me! Forgive me. Tell me, what do you mean to do? I am grieved beyond words that you are disappointed, but I do not understand why such a terrible fate awaits you?' 'Women seldom retain each other's confidences,' said Otto bitterly, 'and when they do, blunders of some kind are the result. No, of course you did not know the purpose of my going to Budapest! If you wish to be forgiven, pray accept my forgiveness; the facts remain precisely the same. I let a fortune go in Budapest—a very large secure fortune—because I believed that what your little friend had would amply compensate me for the sacrifice. If I had known she was penniless, I should have retained this fortune; I should still be safe, and, free from this entanglement—I found your little friend quite eager to release me!—I should have been at liberty for the first time in my life to marry the woman I love! Now I am penniless, bound hand and foot by various little arrangements which deal with money, and flung to the mercy of my enemies. There is no escape possible. On the one hand I lose Trauenstein; Wien is closed to me; my life is over; I doubt if I should have enough to buy bread. On the other, I am under the thumb of a rascal I detest, and I marry a woman whom it very nearly makes me sick to think of. Put a trifle more succinctly—I marry Elisabeth Bleileben or I shoot myself. Forgiveness may be personally gratifying to you, but it will not do away with either of these facts.' Otto ceased speaking. His arm lay along the bench on which they were both sitting, but he was so far from wishing to touch Eugénie that she felt as if he would rather have drowned her. His hostility wrapped itself about them both like ice. Eugénie's love and pity were powerless against it; they only made her feel bewildered and dumb. 'Otto,' she said at last after a long silence, 'I am so stupid. What can I say? I have done you a great wrong by remaining silent, and it seems that I cannot put it right! You speak as if money mattered more than anything else; but need it matter quite so much? I have a little; it is not much, but I can live on it. I should not be an expense. It is true what I said yesterday, we think so differently that we might give each other pain, but at least we like to be together. If you married me and we had children, could we not live very simply in the country? Even if Trauenstein goes you could keep a farm. It is not so dreadful to be poor, and I have learned to be practical—I can cook and I make all my own clothes. I know how hard it is for you to give up your ambitions, but you are so clever that wherever you were, or whatever you did, something would come of it!' Otto laughed. It was not a pleasant laugh, and it made Eugénie flinch as if he had struck her. 'My dear Eugénie,' he said mockingly, 'do you really imagine me as a country farmer? In leather breeches and a green plush hat, with a tuft of chamois' beard at the side? And you think that I should enjoy watching you lose your figure and spoiling your complexion over a kitchen stove? Domesticity has never made a striking appeal to me. On very short commons in the depths of the country, what appeal it has is considerably lessened. I am afraid your little picture must fade into the region of dreams. My grateful thanks, nevertheless! I recommend you to reconstruct it for Dr. Jeiteles!

It would be more suitable!' 'Ah, Otto! Otto!' murmured Eugénie. 'Refuse me if you will, but never say what I offered you was not the deepest thing I have!' His eyes flickered with an angry light. 'You don't know perhaps how you torture me,' he exclaimed fiercely. 'Why do you thrust at me my heart's desire in the one form in which I cannot take it? No—take back your hand. If I made love to you now it would not be pretty love! Listen a moment. You love me enough to be my wife—to give me children. But I cannot afford these luxuries, nor, to tell you the truth, do I greatly desire so much felicity. I should, even under easier circumstances, be afraid of marrying you; I should be afraid of being unfaithful to you. Does it sound amusing to speak as if up till now I had kept an inviolable constancy? After all these years in which you know I have had so many experiences with other women? Nevertheless, Eugénie, it is true. I *have* been faithful to you. No other woman has ever touched my heart. I have seemed cruel, base, neglectful, but only because you would not let me be your lover. I have no genius for platonics. I had to avoid you or possess you. Even now, with this disgusting future, you could change all my anger, all my bitterness, into joy. You little know what you could produce in me, what you could set free in me! I should care for nothing in all the world but you! If you would yield me your love, you could do what you liked with me, except make me a model husband! That, unfortunately, is beyond the limit of your power. I shouldn't mind being a bad husband to any other woman. But to you—when I want to be—what I know that I could be—an ideal lover——! As for money, I should only care to have enough to spread flowers under your feet. Dearest, Eugénie, my beloved, will you not come into my arms, into my heart forever? This time I shall not fail you. I love you as men love air when they are held down under a weight of water!' 'Ah, Otto, how can I answer you!' Eugénie whispered. 'It is too late! I no longer love like that. I have for you all the tenderness of my heart. I would be your companion, your wife, I would give you children, and all day long would be full of thoughts of you; but I am no longer a passionate woman. Long ago desire faded out of me— what passion I had was beaten down by life. To be a man's mistress—even yours—is a horrible thought to me. I could not bear the intrigues, the concealments, I could not love behind closed doors, nor make a secret life seem honourable. I have no word now to break or keep to my husband—I have no loyalty which is outraged by what you suggest—but such a life does not appeal to me; it does not please me, and yet, oh, my dearest—I love you! I cannot bear your pain—the thought of your degradation is darkening my life!' Otto caught her to him passionately; his hands trembled, as they had not trembled when he touched Carol, but he used no force against Eugénie's will; his eyes sought first the consent of her eyes. They met his, tragic in their intensity, but empty of all desire. She made no attempt to escape him; she yielded herself to his arms; but the spirit, which could never yield to him, controlled him. He held her as tenderly as if she was a child. It was too late, and Otto knew it was too late. Once she could have given him all he longed for. Her heart was his, and what she had had for him had never been given to anyone else. It had only been wasted. He kissed her lips very gently before he released her. 'There, my darling,' he said, 'that is my forgiveness. Take it—it seems the best thing I have to offer you. I wonder which of us has done the other the most mortal hurt? Think of me at any rate as dead now— and remember that dying I loved you, and took the thought of you away with me into a world of shadows.' Eugénie could not speak; her eyes closed, she felt his arm slacken about her and knew that he was leaving her forever; with him went the last of her youth and the last of her resistance to life. She was free now, free to live and love again— if she had the will to love again—free as the dead are free.

XXXIII

The sunshine sparkled like wine upon the yellow walls of Schloss Trauenstein. Pigeons in the courtyard, poising self-consciously upon rose-coloured claws, carried on their ancient ceremonies, breaking every now and then through the depths of their etiquette to take short sudden flights into the blue air. Twelve struck from the chapel bell, a deep-toned tranquil sound, telling of the ordered centuries stored in the bronze clapper, and hour by hour setting loose its unregarded hint of Time.

Eugen walked up and down, below the terra-cotta heads of a procession of Wolkenheimbs in great uneasiness of mind. It might be that nothing had happened; but it might be that everything had. Otto had hurried through the courtyard more than an hour ago, with curious uneasy eyes; he had asked Eugen abruptly where Eugénie was, and, as soon as he had received his answer, he had disappeared without a word of explanation. A little later Carol Hunter had leaned over the balcony, and with an air of cheerful serenity demanded to be put in touch with the telephone. Eugen had conducted her to it, secretly hoping that her ready speech might throw some light upon the situation; but she contented herself with exclamations on the beauties of Trauenstein, and refused to allow him even the faintest indication of what number she wanted by explaining that he need not help her because she knew how to telephone in any language. Eugen recognized his defeat with a faint amusement. This very young person was capable of retaining a secret with greater ease than the more mature; her transatlantic candour was more difficult to plumb than oceans of experience. Something had happened to her and to Otto Wolkenheimb, but Carol Hunter showed no trace of the storm that must have passed over them both.

The last note of the chapel bell held the air with a tighter grip, squeezing out of it the very core of the great noon silence. Otto's Mercédès passed with a shriek of warning over the drawbridge and drew up in the courtyard; a moment later Otto himself appeared.

Otto was no longer in a hurry; he put his hand on Eugen's shoulder with an unfamiliar gesture as if he needed something to lean on. 'I have been saying good-bye', he said in a low flat voice, 'to Eugénie—good-bye—forever!' Eugen started. 'But, my dear old fellow,' he exclaimed, 'why was that necessary? Why cannot we keep our best, our oldest possessions, whatever happens? This friendship with Eugénie and Franz is an affair of a lifetime, and one has only one lifetime!' 'Between a man and woman', replied Otto gravely, 'there come these moments—when it must be everything—or nothing. No loyalty survives the acuteness of passion! You are right—it was the best thing in our life—but for me it is over! Let us have half an hour's talk together before I seek my too brilliant future in Wien. I feel like an old man.'

Eugen said nothing, but it must be confessed that his heart, hot with sympathy for the two beings he loved best in the world, was critical of Eugénie. He said to himself, 'Was this the moment for her to let him go?' Aloud he said, 'Is this parting a preface, my dear Otto, to your marriage with Miss Hunter?' 'That too is finished,' said Otto more lightly. 'I have gone rather more quickly than usual. In less than an hour I have put an end to both these relationships. The little one has no money. It was an unfortunate misunderstanding. I blame no one; and she has behaved very well. The child must have good blood—she let me go very prettily. There was regret without reproachfulness, a very rare trait in women. I shared her regret; apart from the fact that since she has no fortune I am ruined.' 'But, Otto—why ruined?' Eugen asked slowly. 'You have lost the chance of a great fortune—yes—but surely you have enough to live on and the wits to find other methods of procuring money? Naturally all that I have is at your service, and it is enough to tide you over a crisis. You know my little carpets? We can sell them for the present, and for the future——' 'I tell you there is no future!' said Otto harshly. 'Either I marry Elisabeth—we must work now to secure the divorce—or she and Mandelbaum break me! They have it in their power, and their inclination is as great as their opportunity. I was so sure, so idiotically sure of this child's fortune! It was spoken of at the Club, it was vouched for by her Minister, Mandelbaum and his set joked over it! My mother always said, "Where are her maid, her motor and her diamonds?" but I believed her a dear little sentimentalist, stripping herself of luxury out of regard for our feelings—there have been many such picturesque war workers! And she has good taste—but nothing else, Eugen!' Eugen nodded sympathetically. 'We have lost all our landmarks,' he said gently. 'Is it any wonder that we have lost our way? I regret your disappointment deeply.' 'Disappointment!' exclaimed Otto bitterly. 'You use very insufficient language! Say my destruction! Have you forgotten who holds the second mortgage on Trauenstein, and this Steinz, who holds the first? What do I know of him —except that he is a Jew? Before the break with Elisabeth I was safe—but without the child's fortune—not an hour afterwards! That was why I hurried her a little! You thought me a cad, I know, for that scene with Franz Salvator! But what could I do? It made her fix the date of the marriage. She was ashamed to hold back after that—as I knew she would be! Where, in all my calculations, have I been wrong—answer me that? And yet the Bleileben and Mandelbaum are at my heels—and my only chance is to marry Elisabeth and live on what she retains of the shipping deal. I am being broken like a nut caught in a pair of crackers! If I had been outwitted I could bear it, but I find myself at the mercy of a stupid lie—not even an intentional lie! Do you see no way out for me, Eugen—nothing that I have by any chance overlooked?' 'But surely,' objected Eugen, 'we can immediately let the Kaiser know, and he will return you enough—from the great sum you put at his disposal—to keep Trauenstein? Then when the Austrian Restoration comes your return to fortune is assured!' Otto leaned his hand more heavily upon Eugen's shoulder. 'The Restoration, my dear boy, doesn't come! Perhaps I misled you a little; there was no time for an explanation on my return from Budapest, and my mind was on hot bricks. In a sense what I told you was true, I used this money for Karl—for his best interests—but not as you supposed. I used it to keep him back.' Eugen withdrew himself from the pressure of Otto's hand, but it was so slight a movement, and Otto was so absorbed in his explanation, that he overlooked its significance. 'One moment,' said Eugen resolutely; 'conceal nothing more, Otto! Why did you go to Budapest, and how did you use this money?' 'I went to Budapest on information,' Otto continued hurriedly, 'to find out for myself what were the chances of the Restoration. The Monarchists were boiling over with zeal. Not one of them had the brains to keep still. I went to the Club for lunch. All were talking of the Return. They were discussing their new places in Court; the women what clothes they should wear; Fanni, as usual, what husband lurked in her imagination! If a British officer in uniform smiled at them they considered it a final proof that England and her Navy would act for the Emperor. Both the Allies and the Government were represented at lunch; there was no need for spies—the only finesse required to learn all their plans was to possess a title or to be ready for a love affair. I went immediately to Horthy and after him to three of the Ministers. I learned that the Little Entente was actually fully prepared and ready on its frontiers; at the first word from Budapest of Karl's return they would march in. The peasants are ninety per cent against the Restoration, the intelligentsia—Jews of course—silent and persecuted, are no better off with than without a King. The Army is divided. Of the Allies, the French Mission are willing, even anxious, for Karl, but they dare not say so nor lend themselves visibly to his cause, for if they consented even semi-officially, the Little Entente would promptly accuse them of breaking the Peace Treaty, and that might shake their stranglehold upon Germany. The English are as usual on the fence, whatever happens they will do nothing—but profit by it. Horthy feels very well where he is, and his efforts are concentrated upon keeping his hares at a safe distance from his hounds. I saw at a glance that the Return was impossible. It was worse than impossible, for it might be seriously attempted; and if seriously attempted it would end in tragedy. Money was wanted to hold back the half of the Army which would otherwise have supported Karl, and to assist in keeping everything still. I gave that money. The future belongs for the moment to those who will maintain the present Government. You may ask what I gained by it,' Otto continued, after a pause in which Eugen made no attempt at comment. 'Not anything very tangible perhaps. But I prevented a danger, and I left behind me—in Budapest—substantial friends. Any scheme—and I have an admirable one in mind—is sure now of receiving backing in the most influential quarters, and the Little Entente will look upon me as an ally. It seems that Karl has been gravely prejudiced against me by his new advisers, and that I had nothing to expect in that quarter; I have now at any rate nothing to fear. But I maintain nevertheless that I have served the Kaiser by my action. I may even, in a sense, be said to have saved him!' Eugen's silence broke as if a stone had shattered it. 'You have betrayed him,' he said hoarsely; 'make no mistake, Otto. You have betrayed him! I, like Eugénie, must now say good-bye to you forever!' Otto stared at him for a moment without speaking; he literally did not believe his ears. To lose Eugen was incredible. All their lives Otto had been worshipped by Eugen; his will was Eugen's law; his profit Eugen's pleasure. Panic seized him. 'I don't understand you,' he said passionately, 'forever? Forever? That is a word one uses only to women! It is impossible for us to separate. What have I done that you should leave me? In this affair I have acted with wisdom, with discretion. You yourself would never have joined such a group as the Budapest Monarchists! That tango set, making love out of conspiracies, and conspiracies out of their love affairs! Bah! my good Eugen, they talk of restoring the Kaiser as if he were a chocolate to pop back into their mouths!' 'I do not say they are wise,' replied Eugen, without taking his eyes from Otto's face. 'I say only that you are base! You wrecked a hope—even if it was a forlorn hope. You did not do this thing to save the Kaiser, but because it suited your own purposes. You found he had accepted younger men as his guides, and that his chances were poor, so you threw in your lot with those in power and made his chances poorer. This is the parting of our ways, Otto. We have gone far together, and I had believed we would go further. Nothing but this betrayal could have put an end to our companionship. All that I had was yours, all that I am was at your disposal, but not for this! I believed that you, like myself, put our cause first. Our cause was our Kaiser. I do not wish to reproach you. I say now simply—go! Go to Excellenz Bleileben, to Mandelbaum, to those who believe only in personal success, to those who have no scruples and whose vulgarity is pure. In this good company I do not belong; permit me to withdraw.' 'But, Eugen,' cried Otto, plunging suddenly out of the irony which was second nature to him into the reality of his helpless need, 'you do not understand! I—I—you are all I have! Franz Salvator has gone out of my life—Eugénie has gone—and you?' Otto felt horribly afraid. The future was like an unknown desert in which he might find himself trapped by savage tribes; his wit useless; his courage overwhelmed; his needs disregarded. He looked at Eugen with piteous anxiety, but Eugen was unshakable; he stood in front of Otto, hard as the rocks upon which Trauenstein was built. It was this sense of a fortress behind him which had always given to Otto the freedom of his audacity; and now that the fortress was in front of him, his audacity suddenly wavered and fell flat. You leave me', he said falteringly, 'to live my life alone?' 'You have chosen', said Eugen inexorably, 'a life I cannot lead with you.' 'But you, what will you do with yourself?' demanded Otto with renewed hope. 'You have no life but mine!' 'I will make my own little arrangements,' said Eugen indifferently; 'pray do not concern yourself with them.' 'I don't know what to say,' exclaimed Otto helplessly; 'how am I to account for what has come between us to my mother? To everybody we know? This separation is without precedent, it requires an explanation!' 'Leave the explanation to me,' said Eugen impassively; 'I will do you no discredit. Your honour is safe in my hands.' Otto flinched; from now on there would be no hands in which his honour was safe, least of all perhaps in his own. He made one more appeal. 'Eugen,' he said hurriedly, 'one does not speak of these things! But you are—you have always been my nearest friend. I have had for you an affection which it seemed to me unnecessary to express, and I believed that this deep affection was mutual.' Still Eugen's eyes looked back at him without faltering, as if they had gazed on the head of the Medusa, and, gazing, turned to stone. 'It is finished,'' said Eugen softly, almost under his breath. 'That which was between us exists no more.' Otto drew a long breath. 'Good,' he said, trying to smile with shaking lips; 'now at last I know illusion for what it is! A woman's love—a man's friendship —they depend, do they not, entirely upon interest? The interest is withdrawn, the affection is over, or it is ready to transplant itself elsewhere. I congratulate myself that the day on which I find myself ruined I am deserted by my best friend and the woman whom I have always respected——' 'Enough, Otto,' said Eugen firmly. 'Even to me, do not disgrace yourself by abuse of Eugénie!' Otto turned quickly away. The Mercédès was drawn up, ready, at the courtyard gate; he jumped into it, started the engine with a jerk, and drove recklessly down the road to Vienna. Otto asked for death a hundred times upon that desperate drive; but death was on the side of Otto's friends—it had decided to leave him alone.

XXXIV

Eugen paced up and down the cell of his thoughts hour after hour. The solitary compulsion of his will held him fast; no stone walls, no locks or bars could have confined him more inexorably. He was without hurry or anxiety, but he knew that from his self-imprisonment there would be no release.

It had been a difficult day; the Gräfin was uneasy and had probed Eugen with the deadly persistency of a tireless insect. Eugénie was invisible. She had assured both the Gräfin and Carol through a locked door that she had a sun headache too bad for speech, and not sufficiently serious for attention. Eugen had been unable to supply himself with so convenient an evasion; and he had had to give his company and guidance to Carol, who continued to explore the Schloss with an avidity undiminished by her knowledge that she would never possess it. She referred frequently to Otto with affection but without precision; and what she seemed most to wish, as she leaned from tower windows and bent low to enter the nearly submerged entrances to dungeons, was information from Eugen for a series of articles on Viennese Court life. These efforts of the day were over now; even the Gräfin had gone to bed at last, defrauded of grounds for her uneasiness.

Eugen was alone in the library of the Schloss, a bare bleak room given up to dusty memories and unopened books. No one ever came there except himself, or pored over the old manuscripts, or cared for the century-old secrets of the Wolkenheimbs. A fire burned dimly on the hearth. Eugen flung himself down beside it and buried his face in his hands. There was no sound at all except the sifting of the soft wood ash, and from an open window the stealthy whispering of a little wind in the pines, moving furtively to and fro as if it knew it was a trespasser. Suddenly the door opened, and he heard Eugénie's voice breathe his name. They were neither of them people who violated social customs without a cause, but now it seemed natural to Eugen that Eugénie should come down at midnight to sit with him till dawn. When a man's mind is fixed beyond hope, he no longer observes the artificial barriers of life. Her voice sounded as if it came from within him and was a summons from his own soul. Eugénie moved swiftly to his side, and sat down by the dying fire within reach of his hand. Neither of them could see each other's face. 'I thought that I should find you here,' said Eugénie; 'I could not sleep. I had wanted to be alone all day, but the night seemed so long I felt as if I must come down and share my loneliness with you.' 'Surely,' said Eugen very gently, 'for me too it is better. I stayed on in fact with the hope of seeing you. Otherwise I should have followed Otto to Wien.' 'You would not have gone with him?' Eugénie asked timidly. 'No,' replied Eugen, 'I do not think that I should have gone with him.' 'I have been so unhappy,' whispered Eugénie, 'because I have done him so great a wrong! Oh, Eugen, how did I dare to interfere with his will? To force him into a position where he could not escape from ruin? Ruin would have been bearable if I had let him choose it. But I didn't let him choose; I wilfully kept him in ignorance so that I could pride myself on his "beau geste". I didn't have the sense to see that it wasn't a "beau geste", unless he did it himself!' 'You speak always of Otto,' replied Eugen wearily; 'that was not our point; we acted to save the Kaiser, nor did we expect of Otto what we should not have done, as a matter of course, ourselves.' 'But have we saved him?' Eugénie demanded. 'If we had—if all that dreadful money had secured Karl's return, would Otto be ruined? Surely in that case something could have been done to help Otto? The Kaiser himself would have done it.' 'His Majesty is powerless to act until his return,' said Eugen after a pause, 'and money cannot do everything. It may very well be that in spite of Otto's action, Karl will not return.' It seemed to Eugen that he heard a slight movement from his companion as if he were rousing an anxiety she would not willingly admit. He waited for her to speak, but Eugénie said nothing; she only listened as if her whole being had passed into the intensity of her silence. 'I even think', Eugen continued steadily, 'that the lack of money cannot ruin a man, unless he has attached to this lack a false value—something stronger than money—his honour, for instance, or his wits.' 'Ah, you are hard on him!' exclaimed Eugénie impetuously. 'I was afraid of that! Afraid I mean that, just when I had failed him, you who have been his perfect friend all his life might—for some foolish reason—cease to stand by him now! But you will not, you must not, whatever happens you must remain the same!' Eugen appeared to accept Eugénie's reproach; he asked more gently still, 'And for what reason, my dear, did you fail him?' Eugénie was silent. She couldn't quite tell Eugen everything; she couldn't, for instance, tell him what Otto had offered her—that would make him angry. What she had offered Otto was another matter, only *her* pride was concerned in that. Eugénie wanted the reassurance of anger, but what she wanted most was for Eugen to be angry with *her*. It would have been a wonderful consolation to Eugénie to feel that she was at the root of all Otto's lapses. 'I failed him', she said after a pause, 'because I was selfish, because I was stupid and dishonest and mean—that's how I suppose most people fail each other!' Eugen remained motionless beside her in the dark. She could not tell whether her passionate self-accusations had impressed him or not, but she felt the tension of his being.

He wanted to take the most out of what she said to him, and in order to receive it he had emptied himself of everything else. 'Do people fail each other for so many reasons?' he said at last. 'I could understand better what precisely happened if you accused yourself of one act. We confuse ourselves with our feelings, but an action is a clarifying event. Can you not tell me what you did to fail Otto?' 'I tricked him,' said Eugénie swiftly. 'I can only call it a trick, that secrecy about Carol's fortune, and having done it —although I had promised you I would not reveal to him that I had purposely concealed my knowledge—I was too weak, too stupid to help him! If my conscience had been clear my wits would have acted better—I could have found a way to help him. Instead, I could only think of one thing to do and it wasn't— the thing I thought of—what he really wanted most!' 'And may I ask what it was, this thing you thought of doing to help Otto?' Eugen said after a pause. 'It was just', said Eugénie tentatively, 'that if he had got to be poor, and since his engagement with Carol was broken, he might—I thought—have liked to marry me. Otto has always cared for me!' 'That I have understood,' replied Eugen in a controlled impassive voice, 'and this offer that you, a proud woman, made is what you call failing Otto? Oh, Eugénie!' 'Please, please don't excuse me,' cried Eugénie. 'I did it so badly! If I had done it better, he might have liked it more. But it wasn't, you see, what he wanted, and I can understand that; Otto is very ambitious, and, like you, he is a true Viennese. Life is not life for him without the race-course and the opera. Men of thirty-nine cannot become boys again and make fresh pleasures for them-selves. My offer was a mistake, and, since Otto cares for me, it was a cruel mistake. Worse still, it makes it impossible for us to meet again. I wanted to give him a life in return for what I had tricked him out of; but all I succeeded in doing was in taking away from him a friendship which he had prized. So you see why I want you more than ever to be good to him.' 'Eugénie,' asked Eugen abruptly, 'do you trust me?' 'With all my heart,' said Eugénie instantly; 'my dear, the earth under my feet is not so solid as my trust in you!' 'Then if I tell you', said Eugen quietly, 'that I too have a reason, not a foolish reason, for letting Otto go his way —the way he has chosen, knowing well that I could not go with him if he so chose it—will you forgive me—as I forgive you—for leaving him alone?' 'Oh, must you! must you!' cried Eugénie imploringly. 'Don't you see it's only because I'm a woman that I let him go! I couldn't have deserted him now in his great trouble if I hadn't known that it would only hurt him more to see me again.' 'I think that it would also hurt him more to see me again,' said Eugen gravely. 'One can patch an ordinary friendship, but if the friendship of a lifetime breaks, the rent is too large, no patch will hold. A man puts too much of his own weight upon a great friendship.' Eugénie sat quite still, turning Eugen's words over in her mind. 'Eugen,' she said at last, 'if you cannot tell me what it is that has made this dreadful break between you and Otto, can you tell me what it is not? When I said just now that you might have quarrelled for a foolish reason, I meant a reason that concerned me. That, you know, would be foolish, for Otto has never done me any grave wrong.' 'No grave wrong, Eugénie?' Eugen asked under his breath. 'To rob you of all the joys of life—is not that a wrong!' 'No, no!' cried Eugénie, 'no one can take away from anyone all joy who does not take away the power of loving. I have had from Otto both sorrow and joy; but I have had something deeper than either! And, Eugen, all the pain has gone now. I am like a ghost, but like a ghost that knows he is cured of the disease of life. There is no pain in me, no feeling even, but the one pain that Otto has to go unhelped, alone, into this ruin! If you will swear to me that you have not left him for any reason that concerns me, I will accept your leaving him—I will not ask you why. But if it is for my sake I will never accept it!' 'Rest assured then,' replied Eugen gently, 'my separation from Otto is a different count. It has nothing to do with you. Nor need it surprise you that no matter what he has done to you, or how utterly he has robbed you, I have not made it a cause for quarrelling with him. I happen to know that Otto loves you profoundly, and that the very springs of his being are darkened by the pain he has caused you. If he has not loved you as well as he has loved himself, he has at least loved you better than anything else.' 'Then don't judge him hardly,' said Eugénie in a low moved voice, 'don't judge him hardly for my sake, Eugen, for what you judge would be a part of me!' 'Men are not judged by other men, I think,' replied Eugen; 'they are judged by their own acts. What others say of us influences our feelings and sometimes we think that we are judged by it, because the opinion of others changes our thoughts of ourselves; but what we do is our real judgement and in that judgement there is no mercy to be found.' Eugénie sank once more into silence. An infinite fatigue stole over her spirit. She hesitated to speak again; there was still no light in the sky, but the darkness had become thinner, she could see the outline of Eugen's head bent low. 'Tell me,' she said, leaning forward, 'this lady—Elisabeth Bleileben—will she make life very horrible for Otto?' 'You wish to know about her?' Eugen asked, rousing himself from his own thoughts. 'Well, she is like the rest of us—this Jewish lady—a mixture of bad motives, strong emotions, and a certain confused sense of justice and duty. I know her better than I did and I dislike her less. Otto, on the other hand, knows her better than he did and dislikes her more. She also knows Otto. I should think that his life with her would present many interesting problems. You know that game children play—see-saw, is it not?—when they try which has most weight to make a board move up or down? They cannot change their weight of course, but they vary it as much as possible by brisk and stealthy movements, and the shifting of the board under them gives them a certain pleasure. Otto and Elisabeth Bleileben will not bore each other, I think; on the other hand they will not put much strain upon the affections since the affections will not be there.' 'Why does she marry him if she doesn't like him?' objected Eugénie. 'Did I say she didn't like him?' asked Eugen dryly. 'You do not know much about passion, Eugénie. The lady of whom we speak has passions—not affections—also she is to be divorced, and her position requires Otto as a husband as much as his pecuniary difficulty requires her as a wife. Their interest in the marriage is therefore mutual. I think that they will marry, and that Otto will not get as much money as he wishes, nor will Excellenz Bleileben get quite so much of the commodity she prefers, but each of them will have to yield a little to the other in order to get anything at all. One might call the situation ideal—for the game we have just mentioned—and I should hesitate to say which on the whole will succeed in tipping the other up.' Eugénie sighed deeply. Eugen put out his hand and laid it over hers. 'You would have given him too much,' he said softly, 'and she will give him perhaps too little! But Otto will take what is necessary for his comfort and his ambition. Let this pain go also. Turn your eyes back to life without tears in them, for you are still young and life has many surprises.' Eugénie returned the pressure of his hand;

they sat for a long while in silence, listening to the fugitive tune of the dawn wind in the trees, and watching the shadows of the night darken and give to each object they were going to leave a sharper outline. At last Eugénie said in a low voice, 'Eugen, have you ever wanted children? Wanted them so that your life without them was like an empty shell? You see that is what I must give up now—Otto's children. I have had them always in my heart, only they have never been safe, as my Rudi is safe—who came to me in life; and is dead. I shall never lose him. But these children who have never been born must leave me now; and it is very hard to let them go. I thought they had gone when Otto was to marry Carol, but they had only hidden. Now I know that I see their faces for the last time.' 'You will be free when they have gone,' said Eugen under his breath, 'free perhaps to think of other children who may still be yours. Do you not think that you may marry again? Forgive me if I hurt you, but would it not be possible? Not now, but when the weight of this parting is over—you know, don't you, that no matter how heavy a parting is, time robs it of its weight? If I may do so, I should urge you when your vitality returns, to give yourself afresh to life.' 'Yes,' said Eugénie slowly, 'it might be possible I suppose for me to marry again. If I met someone who had nothing to do with my past life, who would never remind me by a word or thought of Otto. It is conceivable, although I am too tired to think of it now. I want to feel safe from the return of feelings. I shall ask Dr. Jeiteles to let me go back immediately to the hospital. But you have not answered my question, Eugen, about yourself?' Eugen withdrew his hand, and rather elaborately relit a cigar, which he had—perhaps for the first time in his life—allowed to go out. 'The idea of continuing the race', he said without replacing his hand, 'appeals to all men I believe. One wishes the life that one has—to go on. I do not know why, since one does not particularly value it! You have shivered twice in the last five minutes, Eugénie, and there is enough light to show us just how dark the dawn can be. Will you not go upstairs now and try to sleep?' Eugénie rose to her feet. 'I can't see you yet,' she said; 'I suppose it's why I have been able to talk to you like this, and yet I have a curious feeling that I wish I could see you, now we have finished talking.' Eugen rose also, but he stood with his back to her, as if he was afraid in spite of the darkness that she should see his face. 'To-morrow will be time enough,' he replied. 'To-morrow,' said Eugénie resolutely, 'I go back to Wien, and you stay here, Eugen—and I am afraid of your staying here alone! There is something in your voice that makes me afraid. For me to give up Otto is only to continue what has been my life for the last ten years—but for you to give him up is to give up all you have had since you were children together. Have you thought well what you sacrifice?' 'It has occurred to me —before now,' said Eugen after a pause. 'You remember when I got drunk and stayed drunk some time ago? I was facing the possibility of this separation then; but I postponed it. You are naturally afraid that I shall get drunk again? Very possibly I might, if I had not thought of something to do which requires sobriety. No! do not be afraid to leave me. I am not a man to make rash promises, but I have given up that particular sedative; it was insufficient. I shall try something else another time.' 'Perhaps', said Eugénie wistfully, 'there is something left for you to do to help the Emperor's return? I will of course ask no questions. But we need not give up that hope. After all Otto did something for Austria. You were right and I was wrong. He would not have done it willingly; but it is done—and the consequences may be the return of our old life; and then if we are not comforted we shall at least feel justified! We shall not have sacrificed Otto for nothing!' 'I do not see that you need make yourself too uneasy about this great sacrifice of Otto!' replied Eugen with sudden bitterness. 'Otto is safe enough! He will always get something out of life—it is we, who set our hopes higher, who will find ourselves left with empty hands!' 'But there is not a single thing that Otto has which we either of us envy him!' Eugénie protested, with her hand upon the door. 'No,' said Eugen, 'you are right; there is only something that Otto has thrown away—for that I envy him! No man knows better than I how uselessly!' Eugénie moved towards him. 'Can I not help you to gain it?' she asked urgently. 'Will nothing make up for what you have lost?' 'No,' said Eugen harshly; 'if there is one thing upon which I congratulate myself, Eugénie, it is that I am not a man for whom sacrifices need be made!' Eugénie drew back. 'You are too proud,' she murmured; 'you will not even say what it is for which you envy Otto?' 'Forgive me,' said Eugen with renewed gentleness. 'If you could give it to me I would ask for it. But it is not in your power to give it. The dawn is breaking, Eugénie—good-bye!' 'But I shall see you to-morrow,' Eugénie said, 'it is only good night!' 'True,' agreed Eugen, ' and since it is day already, there is no need even for that, but I will keep your good wish—for the night!'

After Eugénie had left him, Eugen knew that the cell of his thoughts had become perceptibly smaller; he no longer walked up and down in it. He stood quite still.

XXXV

Frau Mandelbaum sat in her husband's library pouring out coffee. It was called a library because there were books behind glass doors, gorgeously bound and never read. She looked and felt disapproving. She thought it improper for ladies to have coffee in a room where men habitually talked business and smoked. Downstairs in one of the reception rooms was the place for coffee—downstairs was the place for ladies; and, if in all the universe there was a place for Elisabeth Bleileben, downstairs—as near as possible to the front door—was that place. Elisabeth Bleileben was staying at the Mandelbaums' indefinitely. Elisabeth was not an easy visitor; and the fact that her heart was broken and her fortune at its lowest ebb did not make her any easier. Frau Mandelbaum had always disliked Elisabeth in a passive, lukewarm, feminine way, even when Elisabeth had been a faithful wife; but now that she was under the shadow of a divorce she felt for her all the fierce hatred and scorn of an unhappy woman who knows that however unhappy she is, she will never get rid of her own husband. So intense had been Frau Mandelbaum's emotion that she openly rebelled against Julius' commands. She had used the time-honoured threat of all outraged wives, 'If this woman enters my house I go!' And Julius had grinned and replied, 'Very well then, go!' And as she had not really known where to go, and did not want to leave her home, Frau Mandelbaum had remained; but she had stiffened. She might be forced to receive Elisabeth, but at least she would show her that an outcast woman *is* an outcast woman; and every time that Elisabeth had a lump of sugar in her coffee, it was as an outcast woman that she had it. No smile ever touched Frau Mandelbaum's heavy features when she looked at Elisabeth, nor did she ever say anything to her except '*Doch!*' '*Nein!*' '*Ich danke*' and an icy '*Allerdings*'. Unfortunately Elisabeth barely noticed these massive hints. She felt like stone; and stones do not observe the finer shades of other heavy objects. She knew that Frau Mandelbaum took up so much cubic space in a room, and that when she left the room that cubic space was vacant; there consciousness of her hostess ended. Elisabeth liked being with Julius because Julius neither knew nor cared what she suffered. Sometimes she could talk to him as if she did not suffer at all; and sometimes she talked to him as if she could make Otto suffer. This made her feel a little more alive.

Julius clasped two sandwiches together and swallowed them in one brief spasm. It was his leisure hour, and he liked to spend it eating, smoking, and gently chewing the cud of one or other of his little affairs. 'That mortgage on Trauenstein, now!' he said contentedly. 'I shall form a company with American capital and run the place as a hotel. Would you believe it, our friend the Graf thinks he is safe because I hold only a second mortgage? In matters of business he is like a baby—a greedy baby that thinks the world was made to please it! Steinz holds the first mortgage. I need not tell you that I hold Steinz. When I lift my finger—out goes your little manikin—naked into the world as when his mother bore him!' 'Wait a little,' said Elisabeth with a gleam in her sunken eyes. 'To-morrow that dried tobacco plant of the Relief Mission is to give me the girl's address! Let him lose the heiress first— then Trauenstein, then the coat off his back! Before I have done with him he shall stand in the rain at a street corner selling matches!' Julius chuckled and closed two more sandwiches together. 'What a woman you are, Elisabeth!' he said appreciatively. 'And what a fool he is to think we'd let him off between us! I would have wiped my doorsteps with him long ago if it hadn't been for you and that stuffed doll of his with the eyeglass! Fortunately Erdödy can't protect him from the mortgage. But do you think you can make the girl let go? If he's got her fortune he's safe. I can't foreclose before the legal period.' 'After I have told the girl what I know she would rather marry you!' said Elisabeth with unintentional irony.

Frau Mandelbaum cleared her throat. It was all disgustingly wicked, but it was very interesting, and what made it more interesting still was that she could see from where she was sitting the figure of Otto Wolkenheimb himself strolling up the drive. He did not look like a beggar at a street corner, he was dressed in the newest shape of morning coat and the most impeccable trousers. Frau Mandelbaum did not warn her companions of his approach. From the moment she saw Otto she was on his side. She had that instinct common to many respectable ladies, whose temptations have been limited, of promptly forgiving any man who has wronged another woman; and she remembered the marmalade.

She waited, fingering a large slab of chocolate *Torte*, with her eyes fixed upon Elisabeth, until the servant announced Otto. '*Mein Gott!*' gasped Elisabeth. If Otto had been a supernatural visitant she could not have been more horrified to see him; in fact she would have been less horrified, because the other world was unsubstantial to her. 'Give him a cup of coffee and then go away!' said Julius in a loud whisper to his wife. 'Don't weaken!' he added in a slightly hoarser whisper to Elisabeth. Elisabeth made no direct answer, her lips moved back and bared her teeth. It was the look a cat gives a bird under its claws. It seemed to reassure Julius. 'Well! Graf!' he said, rising very slowly from his chair, 'it is a long time since you gave us the pleasure of your company!' Otto bent low over Frau Mandelbaum's hand and pressed it gently. He turned to Elisabeth, and bowed gravely in her direction. Elisabeth's hands were fastened in her lap; she neither moved nor spoke; only her eyes travelled over him with a curious hard glitter as if she was looking for a place to strike. 'The pleasure is of course mine,' Otto murmured, 'and as for the infrequency—these miserable times deprive us of all our greatest pleasures. I assure you I have no social life left; that odious little creature the busy bee has become my daily example!' 'And business I suppose brings you here now!' Julius replied, sitting down again. 'Well, I like business. I don't pretend to like anything else much, and I am always ready for it—my own, or another man's.' 'I fear', said Otto, accepting his coffee from Frau Mandelbaum's hand with graceful agility, 'that I haven't any business to discuss; I simply came to call on my old friends. How enchantingly you have arranged this room; one sees traces of your intellectual activity, my dear Mandelbaum, softened by feminine presences! Does he read aloud to you while you knit?' Otto asked sympathetically, meeting the fascinated eyes of his hostess. Julius interrupted his wife's response. 'I hear you are going to have a domestic idyll of your own,' he mumbled with a leer. 'That pretty little piece you didn't want me to chip in with, at Cobenzl? You've put it off a long time, Graf, I'd have got to the point sooner with that little girl if I'd been you!' A faint shadow of a frown passed over Otto's brows. 'No,' he said quietly, 'I am not about to be married to Miss Hunter. It is true I believe that an announcement to that effect took place a week ago, but I understand that it is to be contradicted to-morrow.' 'Dear me!' said Frau Mandelbaum, divided between sympathy and excitement. 'Well, you know best, I'm sure! And I must say once and for all—that to sit on a sofa uninvited—and showing so much stocking—is enough to break any engagement! These foreigners think they can do anything with us now the *Krone* has fallen!' Julius made an expressive movement of his thumb in the direction of the door. Frau Mandelbaum rose hurriedly. 'If you will excuse me,' she said to Otto, 'I must go and give an order in the kitchen.' Otto sprang to his feet, and while he was opening the door for her, Elisabeth leaned forward and said to Julius, 'Go also—I will deal with him!' Julius nodded, and a moment later departed.

When they were alone Elisabeth raised her eyes slowly to Otto's face. He was astonished and even a little appalled by the change in her. Her cheeks were sunken and drawn, her clothes hung on her, as if she had been melted in a fire, thick lines ran from her nose to her lips, her eyes looked swollen and set further back in her head. 'What are you doing here,' she asked hoarsely, 'dressed like a bridegroom and without a bride? Do you like the feeling of being jilted? *I* did that, my friend! I did it that we might compare notes—alone or apart. What she knows of you—came from me!' 'But she knows nothing, my dear Elisabeth,' said Otto, leaning back in his chair and crossing his legs. 'You tell me more than you need. There have been no disclosures. Don't be so truculent, it doesn't suit you. You must have caught it from the good Julius. It is true my engagement is broken off. It was, as I told you, to be a marriage of reason, and the reasons were found to be insufficient. You are quite guiltless of any hand in it, my dear Elisabeth, as I am sure you must be relieved to feel!' Elisabeth bared her teeth again. 'And you are ruined,' she said, 'if the marriage does not take place?' 'I am inconvenienced by the insufficiency of the

263

reasons for the marriage taking place,' agreed Otto gently. 'That is very true.' 'So you come to me,' said Elisabeth, 'to me—and to Mandelbaum, whom you have insulted as deeply as a man can insult a man—less deeply than he can insult a woman!—it is to us you come when you are ruined to seek for a way of escape? My God, I thought you had a finer wit!' 'Incidentally, of course, I wish both mortgages cleared off,' said Otto pleasantly, 'but that is not my full purpose in coming here. Elisabeth, when you made your appeal to me the other night, I was not free—I am free now.' 'Free for what?' asked Elisabeth, drawing back, although Otto had not moved towards her. 'Free for more philandering? You have come to the wrong place, my good friend! I don't philander any more; I do business.' 'All the better for me then,' said Otto cheerfully. 'You have an interesting mind, Elisabeth; use it a little to overcome your natural annoyance with me. Let us put it like this. If I do not marry a rich woman I am ruined financially; if you do not marry me you are ruined socially. Your reputation and my stability stand or fall together. Life is not pleasant when one is ruined. Personally, I shall not in that event continue it; but life—the life of reasonable and successful people spent under the same roof, each free to lead their own lives in their own way— is not unpleasant. This is what I have come here to-day to offer you.' 'Ah!' said Elisabeth in a deep voice. For a time she said nothing further; she seemed to have sunk into a world of her own. Otto was not certain if he had any business there. She was calculating, but he had no key to her calculations, for she neither looked at him nor showed any awareness of his presence. At last she said indifferently, 'And you mean to die if I refuse? It is not merely an appeal to my pity? If it is, it is amusing—for I have none. I should prefer you to live—because the living suffer; but dead or alive you are the same to me now, you are nothing!' Otto blinked; no woman had ever told him before that he was nothing; at least if she had she had not meant it, but Elisabeth meant it. It was grossly humiliating to have to hear in one day, from the little American that he was a poor piece of goods, and from this middle-aged Jewess that he was nothing at all; fortunately Eugénie—who had more cause than either of them for a poor opinion of him—was not given to definitions. But he must not think of Eugénie now or he could not carry this intensely disagreeable business through. 'But you are not nothing to yourself, my dear Elisabeth,' he pointed out blandly; 'certainly I shall kill myself if you refuse to marry me. What a réclame for you! But not, I think, sufficient to restore your reputation.' 'That is true,' agreed Elisabeth tauntingly, 'and if I marry you—mark that "*if*" —I am to be received by all your friends? I shall go when I like to Trauenstein? Your mother will accept me as a daughter-in-law? Your cousin Eugénie will be like a sister to me!—I have heard so often that you have been a brother to her that I look forward to that relationship! And you yourself will be—what to me, Otto Wolkenheimb? You, who ask to be my husband, to save yourself from ruin?' 'I have said', replied Otto incisively, 'that of course we will lead our own lives. You will naturally be received at Trauenstein where my mother resides for her life-time. You will bear my name, and what friends I have left will call on you. My cousin, the Princess Felsör, does not receive me, and therefore she will not receive my wife.' 'Yet she stays with you?' said Elisabeth, with a sharp glance. 'She visits my mother occasionally,' said Otto quietly. 'I think, Elisabeth, you have reached the limits of my offer.' 'And you ask in return', Elisabeth demanded scornfully, 'only another fortune to squander, God knows how! You are very modest! and you think a woman you have sucked dry like an orange more modest still! You misunderstand me, Otto. I gave you my reputation, not my brains! Such as they are I keep them to crush you with!' 'Perhaps you would like to know what I spent that fortune on?' asked Otto after a reflective pause. Elisabeth leaned forward; curiosity sparkled in her hard, narrowed eyes. 'You can tell me,' she said. 'It commits me to nothing to know your secrets; and I know enough already to get you hanged!' 'I think that you exaggerate,' said Otto, smiling, 'but since I believe our interests are to be the same, in spite of the thorns you rather unwisely strew upon the path, I will tell you how I spent it. The Kaiser will shortly make an attempt to return to Budapest; and I have stopped any possibility of his remaining there. I did this for two reasons; I found that I was out of favour with the old régime. I should have no career even if I helped the Kaiser to return, and my help would not make his return secure; whereas I could make his failure certain; and if I did this I had at least the new régime open to me. If Karl's return were per-manent, we should make no more money, Elisabeth.' 'You really did this?' Elisabeth asked with animation. 'Then it was not for nothing the money went? You did well. To tell you the truth I thought I had wasted myself on a sieve. A creature that could hold nothing, except a looking-glass!' Otto looked at the toes of his patent-leather shoes; his nostrils dilated a little. He had a curious sensation as if something inside him were going to take out a pistol, shoot Elisabeth, and then shoot himself, but the sensation passed. Violence would be final, but it would not be so interesting as a victory over Elisabeth. 'I keep what I earn,' Otto said at last. 'My conditions for such a marriage would be very simple. I should ask the entire control of your share in the shipping deal; this I should place as my own share was to be placed in a leading bank. I should become its chief director on a sufficient salary. You would keep the rest of your fortune intact. I should run my household as I am accustomed to run it. Your rooms would be in the upper flat. As my household is accustomed to a bachelor superintendence, I should suggest that you either had your own servants for your apartments or permitted me to manage mine. Your very interesting philanthropic career would be open to you more satisfactorily by our marriage, and if you cared to carry on any commercial affairs with Mandelbaum I should have no objections. I should, of course, free Trauenstein with part of the fortune you made over to me. On my part I have nothing further to suggest.' 'Nothing?' said Elisabeth, under her breath. 'Nothing further to suggest to me, Otto?' Otto rose to his feet; he had a moment's amused reflection. Was this—he asked himself—what women felt like when pressed for an affection they had not got? For a woman to express repugnance is not undignified, but a man who expresses it to a woman looks a fool. Otto disliked this appearance, and he thought that he could escape it. 'We seem at one upon a good many points,' he said, looking down at Elisabeth. 'Your indifference is matched by my indifference— your convenience by my convenience. The absence of emotion seems to me rather an advantage for experienced people like ourselves. Come—we are both ambitious creatures, let us cultivate our ambitions together! You shall never ask me in vain for a helping hand in that direction; and I shall count upon your help in mine; and as for love, all I ask of you is a little discretion—you have learned how to play the game—stick to the rules and play it with whom you like—and in return, I fear I can only offer you—a little discretion of my own! I also know how to play the game, and I have never yet broken any of its rules!'

Elisabeth got up too, but she moved away from Otto and stood with her back to him. 'If you had squandered that money', she said, 'I should have laughed in your face. I do not laugh now; but I hesitate. You have cost me more than you have to offer me.' 'You too have cost me something, Elisabeth,' said Otto softly. 'You—and my attempt to stop the Kaiser. None of my dearest friends will have anything more to do with me. My return to you is the final cleavage. You know that Eugen has been more to me than a brother. I shall not see him again.' 'Erdödy, too?' cried Elisabeth, turning round and facing him. 'Then I will certainly marry you. What fools! what fools the old lot are! They deserved to lose an Empire!'

This was Otto's worst moment; he had won and because he had won he had to take Elisabeth's outstretched hands. This was to be his new Empire.

XXXVI

Eugen leaned over the balustrade and gazed down at the terra-cottas beneath. They shone out with a singular clearness in the last light of the March sun. His heavy eyebrows were drawn together, his eyes rested on the delicate work with the deliberate attention of a connoisseur. He looked as if nothing more important than their execution had happened, or could conceivably take place. Carol appeared like a whirlwind from her room, which opened upon the outside corridor, and flung her news at him in a sentence. Eugen neither moved nor changed his brooding saturnine expression. 'Doesn't it get you, to hear your Kaiser is in Hungary?' Carol demanded. 'I thought you were all to pieces because you couldn't have a Kaiser, and now he's on the spot you act like a log of wood! I should have thought you'd have beat it to Budapest before the words were out of my mouth! I never shall understand you, Eugen Erdödy; you must have seen those terra-cottas any time these thirty years—but countries don't turn upside down under your feet more than once or twice in a lifetime!' 'Let us trust not,' replied Eugen, without turning his head, 'but do you not confuse the importance of what is taking place with the unimportance of my being there? No! I shall not go to Budapest. History will, I imagine, construct itself without my assistance nor do I find any immediate occasion for rejoicing. That the Emperor should at this moment be in Hungary strikes me rather as an anxiety than as a pleasure. One sees there is an opportunity, but one does not see what is to become of the opportunity.' 'Well, I hope Franz won't feel the way you do,' said Carol with pronounced disapproval in her voice. 'I've succeeded in digging him up on the telephone, though I might have got him quicker if I'd walked. He's agreed to come here anyhow. The frontiers are closed, but I have a Red Cross pass for the two of us, and Eugénie's a Hungarian subject and can get through on her own. We must catch the boat at Melk. I suppose we can use Otto's horses?' 'Everything in the castle is at your disposal,' replied Eugen courteously. 'The horses can drive you to Melk in two hours. The weather is good, and the road no worse than anything else in Austria. Budapest is a delightful town. One eats well at the Ritz, and there are one or two cafés where the music is still tolerable. I hope that you will enjoy your little visit.' Carol looked at him curiously. 'They say you know everything,' she said abruptly. 'Did Otto tell you, before he beat it, that he had called our engagement off?' 'I have been led to understand that the marriage will not take place,' agreed Eugen, after a pause. 'Forgive me for saying that I find it rather a matter for congratulation than for regret. You are too young and attractive to let any man marry you for your money. Now that you are free, you will, I hope, make a better marriage!' 'I wouldn't have married Otto for worlds!' said Carol hastily. 'I surely don't know what got me to say I would. But there are some people that make you fall for them when you don't really want to. I don't know why I'm letting out to you like this, but I don't want to hurt Eugénie's feelings, and I've got to get some of it off my chest. What I mind about the whole thing is that I feel as if I hadn't had a square deal. I don't mean from Otto—Otto acted according to his make-up! But you and Eugénie and Franz Salvator aren't like Otto! Couldn't one of you have told me, before I'd got in so deep, what Otto stood for?' Eugen considered this question carefully before he answered it. 'I think we were under no such obligation,' he said at last. 'We owed Otto a loyalty which forbade us interfering with his plans, however little we approved of them. It is true that I did try to interfere with them up to a certain point because of a conflicting loyalty; but I failed. Obviously Franz Salvator and Eugénie could say nothing to warn you since they were interested parties. When Otto was young, he shared all that he possessed with us. This castle has been our home; we have played here as children together, and as young people we dreamed together our gay and idle dreams. Otto was not the same man that he is now. He was our leader, and had, as well as his great talents, an open and a generous heart. Defeat changed and hardened him; our world broke. You love your country, do you not, Miss Hunter? And you know perhaps how secure and permanent its civilization and comfort seem? But it is a mistake; they are no more secure than ice over a frozen sea; and when they melt, morality melts with them. No one is safe who goes too near a drowning man. Do not judge Otto harshly, and do not blame us for not intervening to save your pride. We had to think of our own. You do not know how these old walls speak to those whose blood is part of them! It is impossible that you should understand us, but you are of a generous nature, so that I ask you to judge us generously.' Carol hung her head like an embarrassed schoolboy. 'Give me a cigarette,' she said quickly. 'I'm not out to judge any of you! Only if I don't understand you —I'd like to! I'd like to understand pretty quick too—before Franz Salvator blows in! Look here, Eugen Erdödy—I've always felt you were a kind man, if one could get past your manner; and I know you're burglar proof as to secrets, so I'll tell you all there is to this business. Franz liked me a good deal better than Otto did—and I liked Franz! I don't say I was downright foolish about him—but I was well on the road that leads there. But Franz held back; he was too damned slow in the up-take. If there is any light to be got on why he held back, I'd like to have it before he comes!' 'Franz Salvator has not the reputation', said Eugen reflectively, 'of being slow either in his affections or in his actions. He was perhaps one of the most dashing cavalry officers we possessed. The delay you speak of was probably caused by this mistake as to your fortune. He will, I think, act quickly enough when he knows that you have no money. He does not own a limousine so that he cannot drive towards you as quickly as Otto could drive away. But he will not lose time.' Carol gave a little sigh, and flung the end of her cigarette into the courtyard beneath them with an impatient movement. 'Well,' she said, 'I suppose I'll risk it! But Franz doesn't carry much along with him, does he? I feel as if I could forgive Otto for being mercenary; I like the world myself, and you can't have it without paying for it, can you? I'm pretty keen on old castles too, and I stand for a good time as much as any Wolkenheimb!' Eugen was silent for a moment, then he said slowly, 'While I was walking on the terrace early this morning I had a vision. I saw Trauenstein in young hands. I heard the voices of children—not Otto's children. I thought that the instincts which form old races and linger in them yet were once more freed from the lust of money and the break-down of honour. I recall that on the occasion when we drank to your happiness and Otto's—you remember perhaps our drinking to it in my not wholly negligible Tokay?—before I broke my glass I said to myself, "To the health of the race!" If you marry Franz Salvator the race will be the same. I am not a man given to visions, and the modesty of my imagination is so great that I am prepared to believe what occasionally takes place there as if it had the solidity of fact.'

Carol was silent for a moment, then she laid her hand on Eugen's arm. 'Do you remember', she asked him in a low voice, 'the first time I met you? I asked you what Otto was like, but you wouldn't tell me. Will you tell me now?' The arm under her hand stiffened suddenly and then relaxed. Eugen bent his round head lower. 'In my rooms', he said gravely, 'I have a little bowl. It is of a good period, made out of one very fine crystal resting on claws of gold. It has been admired by many—connoisseurs have praised it—I myself prize it; but I do not show it very often. It is one of my few mistakes, for there is a flaw in it. The bowl was not worth what I paid for it. I am not a moralist, but when you said just now, with a regret I can well share, that Franz Salvator carried nothing with him, I thought of my little bowl. I can at least assure you that Franz Salvator has a value of his own and that he is a piece without a flaw.' Carol withdrew her hand from Eugen's arm; she hesitated a moment before she left him, then she said, 'Well—I've made up my mind about you anyway! I don't think you're unkind any more!' Eugen took her to the door of her room, and kissed her hand before he left her; then he returned to his former post.

He continued his prolonged and indolent scrutiny of the court-yard until the last light faded and the pines drew in towards the castle. Darkness covered Trauenstein; and for some time longer Eugen remained, looking into the darkness.

XXXVII

Night was falling; the Danube, spectral and vague, rolled silently beneath them; the banks were lost in a white river mist. It was the first moment in the day that Franz Salvator and Carol found themselves alone. The walls of the fog shut them in upon each other as if they were the only inhabitants of a dead world. All day long Carol had watched Franz Salvator plan and execute their expedition with a swift authority and skill which made her wonder what had happened to the laughing, easy-natured young man of Eugénie's flat and the tortured mechanic of the land-scheme. The Franz Salvator she had known was swallowed up in the grim and vigilant young soldier who stood like a stranger by her side. Franz Salvator was intent upon carrying their purpose through; but he was not excited. Whatever happened he would give all he had towards it, but he had lived too long with defeat and despair to count on any reward from the thoroughness of sacrifice. The Kaiser's return was the crisis of Carol's career; but it was more than this to Franz Salvator; it was the purpose, brought back into possibility, of the four years of danger and the dull misery of war. To give the Kaiser his throne would not be victory, but it would take the bitterness out of their defeat. It would be their old life restored. 'I have taken Eugénie downstairs,' Franz said, at last. 'She is tired, and there may be work before her. I thought perhaps you would like to stay on deck a little, so I have brought your cloak up. It is cold.' Carol submitted to be wrapped in fur and made comfortable on a deck chair; but there her spirit of submission ended. The more formidable this stranger was, the more determined she felt to resist any claim he might make upon her. She could have granted Franz Salvator a favour, but nothing in the world would induce her to admit that he had a right. 'It was kind of you to send me that telephone message,' Franz Salvator observed in a tone of courteous formality. 'I have not yet thanked you for it. This is the chance of a lifetime.' 'It is the chance of my lifetime,' Carol admitted; 'whether it comes off or not, if I see Karl, I get my scoop. You only get yours if he can stay on top.' 'If one has had no hope for a long time,' replied Franz Salvator steadily, 'even a forlorn hope feels like something solid. The Hungarian Army fights well when it wants to fight. I think we are a match for the Czechs in spite of their fine new guns, if the Entente lets us—and the people are agreed.' 'You've got a good many "ifs" against you!' said Carol. 'Yes,' said Franz Salvator, 'but in war and love, uncertainty is an incentive to action.' Carol was silent. Franz Salvator bent nearer to her so that he could see her eyes; he measured her powers, and held his own in reserve. 'Before I received your telephone message,' he said, after a pause, 'Otto had called upon me on his way to Wien. He gave me rather an astonishing piece of news.' Carol bit her lips nervously. One thing was very sure, Otto would not have gone to see Franz Salvator to display his own defeat. Had he gone to exhibit hers? 'He told me', Franz Salvator continued, 'that your engagement was broken off on what appeared to be a very insufficient—and on Otto's part a dishonourable—ground. I took the pleasure of telling him so in such a manner that I hoped he would require satisfaction from me. My cousin Otto has faults, but want of physical courage is not one of them. The reason he gave me for refusing my suggestion was that you had no complaint to make. He told me that you were much more pleased than he at the termination of your engagement?' 'Did he?' said Carol dryly. 'Well, the men of your country seem very ready to give women away behind their backs. I suppose since he no longer wanted me himself he handed me over to you? I am much obliged to him; but as I never belonged to him I don't find myself as disposed of as you seem to think. I told you the other day that I was a free agent; and I am no less so now that my engagement is broken off than I was before.' 'I had not thought of you as disposed of,' said Franz Salvator softly, 'and I knew that you considered yourself free. Please do not be angry with Otto, for I think, when he told me you were not distressed, he meant kindly by us. It is contrary to a woman's pride, is it not, to be considered in need of consolation? And it is certainly an incentive to a man who wishes to win her to know that she is not inconsolable.' 'I can look after my own pride, thanks!' said Carol coldly, 'and when I want men to have incentives to win me, I hope to be able to raise them!' Franz Salvator was silent for a moment, then he said in a voice which had lost its softness, 'I was not afraid you could not protect your own pride; but I have sometimes wondered if you gave much consideration to the pride of others. There are certain situations in which a man's pride is more defenceless than a girl's. Some women have the generosity to spare men when they see this; but others take an advantage of it which it is not easy to forgive.' Carol was silent for a moment; she felt bitterly the justice of what Franz Salvator had implied, but she would have accepted his reproof more readily if he had spoken with less justice and more anger. 'It is not very easy', she said, at last, 'to be generous to anyone who won't share things with you!—either their emotions or their handsome moral code; and who leave you, though they say they love you, to fight your battles by yourself.' 'What would I not share with you,' asked Franz Salvator, moving closer to her, 'if I had it? Did I seem stupid—backward—cold? You might have guessed why, I think! Even if you had not been, as I believed, burdened with a fortune which must have made any man seem base who pursued you, how dared I ask you to share my penury? A man gets used to many things, Carol, to danger, to cold, and last of all to hunger, but when a man longs to give all the treasures in the world to the woman he loves, he does not get used to giving her nothing!' 'A man has always himself to give,' said Carol shakily. 'I think', said Franz Salvator scornfully, 'that he must think very well of himself to offer the woman he adores—so little! He must be a clever man like Otto perhaps—a man who can make a woman laugh!' 'Isn't it enough', Carol said, bending her head low down over the rail, 'if he can make her cry?' Franz Salvator bent quickly towards her in the sheltering fog, and drew her into his arms. 'Never! never!' he whispered, passionately kissing her eyes, and her hair, 'that never! Don't you know I would die for you gladly, a hundred times a day? I love you! I love you! I would not touch your hand without your leave! I care for nothing but your wishes. You speak of your freedom! Will you be less free that I shall be near you always to do what you want? You have only to tell me what it is! Now that you are in my arms, close to my heart, do you not feel sure you are safe? Tell me to go, and I go forever; tell

273

me to stay, and I serve you forever! I can do anything in the world for you except change! I loved you from the first moment you stood with your little hands in your pockets and cursed like a man because our babies suffered! You see you were not so very like a man in spite of your fine curses! And I shall love you when I crumble into dust, and have no other memory but that I once held you in my arms!' 'Well! let me breathe a moment!' whispered Carol. 'I can't think properly like this! And though it's foggy, there might be a lookout that could get through to us! You needn't take your hand away too! I've got something to say now, and I want you to believe it. I like Otto; but I never, never for one moment wanted to marry him! And what made me so mad was your letting me! I would have broken off my engagement the day after Cobenzl if you hadn't gone on about people keeping their words—a pack of nonsense if the words have been silly ones—anyway! Between your cast-iron principles and Otto's under-cut in morals, you as near as possible had me married to the wrong man; and then I suppose you'd have been too strait-laced to run away with me?' 'I am glad that you did not put me to the proof,' said Franz Salvator, laughing. 'It is much simpler to run away with you now! But even this I cannot do immediately! Try to believe that I am not a poor lover, because I am first a soldier! I must serve my Kaiser before I can serve you but with how different a heart! If we fail now—I have still this great joy that changes all the world to me; and if we succeed I add to my joy because I can once more offer to you a life that is not bare or ugly! But I have more to ask you! You will not make this a long engagement, and before we get to Budapest you will tell me that you love me? So far you have only said that you do not love Otto!' 'Well,' said Carol, 'I don't know what more you want! You know Otto? Wouldn't I have loved him if I didn't love you? As to getting married I suppose we can get married in Budapest as well as anywhere else. I can't stay there long anyway. Once I've fixed up the Kaiser, I've got to go back and sit on Wien. This is going to be the time of my life, Franz Salvator—as a journalist, I mean!' 'No! it is not!' said Franz Salvator, drawing her back into his arms. 'I'm damned if I don't make you forget that you were ever a journalist!' They were too engrossed in each other to notice a shadowy figure which came towards them—and then drew back suddenly into the mist. Eugénie could not rest. She had come up on deck to see the approach to Vienna, but Vienna was as hidden from her as the uncertain future. In her heart there lingered the dreadful image of Otto and Elisabeth Bleileben balancing against each other upon their precarious see-saw. If Karl succeeded would not Otto be released from this approaching nightmare? 'Bad actions bear fruit,' she said to herself. 'Cannot good actions?' Then she saw the lovers. She turned from them; but their happiness lingered triumphantly with her. There was faith which was worth faith, love that was worth love, after all! Eugénie felt no longer like a ghost in a world of ghosts—but like the moon uninhabited and lonely, suddenly flooded with the warm light of a reflected sun.

XXXVIII

It was dawn before they reached Budapest. The river lay a pink path under a golden cliff. Pest, blue and shadowy, a mere smudge of night, slept on the left side of the stream; upon the right Buda flashed out at them under a mantle of gold. The terraced gardens swept up the hill to the long line of the Palace. The spire of the Stephans Kirche shone like the sacred crown which marks forever the rights of the Hapsburg race. In spite of the earliness of the hour, the little quay was crowded. Soldiers were everywhere; patrols were trotting briskly up and down the broad thoroughfare beside the river; troops were crossing the Gelert bridge, their short, grey cloaks tossing in the wind. Fanni Wilchek was there upon the landing stage and splashed her welcome at them like a breaking wave. 'Thank God, you've come!' she exclaimed, kissing first Eugénie and then Carol, and gazing at Franz Salvator, who barely knew her, as if there had long been between them an intimacy too deep for words. 'Hush! we must not speak here! Later!' and with a confusion of bustle and menace she delayed the simple process of their passports until they were the last to leave the quay. 'It's all too terrible,' she assured them breathlessly, as they turned towards the Ritz. 'He's been! He's gone! It's all over! I suppose you heard nothing in Wien? Nobody ever does, that's why I came—so that you should hear everything!

everything from the fountain head at once! Oh, Carol, why didn't you come sooner? and you, Herr Kapitän, without a uniform! But it is better—far better as it is. Of course if you had worn a uniform you wouldn't have been allowed to land! The brutes! Even our swords are denied us! I expect to be arrested immediately. God knows where Father is—everybody else is in prison—but perhaps we can have breakfast first over here under the trees—I have reserved a table. Dear Eugénie, it's a thousand years since you have been here—not since—no—we won't uncover the old wounds, the old tragedies! The new ones are too many for that. It is of them we must speak—but not before the waiters, of course —all of them are spies! There! one has one's coffee as usual—mine is probably poisoned—but I am used to that. They are not likely to have tampered with yours as they don't know who you are. Well then—our Emperor is here! No! no! I don't mean at the Ritz—how could I? He arrived yesterday in an Englishman's car. You ask me who the Englishman is? A long while ago he meant more to me than he does now—but we needn't go into that! He is over six foot tall, fair hair, blue eyes, a remarkable manner! I have never heard him speak—he is not the Prince of Wales—that was a rumour yesterday, but I myself can prove it false—for I have never met Wales. What was I saying? Yes! at 6 o'clock—famished —he arrived—driving through his own city while it slept. He went immediately to Horthy. Can you imagine it?—such a scene! The car at the Palace—my Englishman impassive, grave, capable at such a moment of sitting perfectly still without moving a muscle of his face. Karl entered—they say he announced himself—he fell on Horthy's neck. Then the awful thing happened. Horthy received him with courtesy of course, but with nothing else. All that he had been promised had collapsed. Some say that Horthy is a traitor—others that he was powerless! The Army had melted away from under our fingers. They say our beloved Emperor fainted dead away on the sofa in Horthy's room. Who can wonder? He had been so sure—so happy. He had felt the whole City turn in the beauty of Spring to greet him, and in a moment it was over—his hope was over—his crown vanished—his faith in us all shaken to the core!' 'But, for God's sake, tell us what happened!' cried Carol impatiently. 'Who shook his faith—who took his crown—where in Hades is he?' 'Shuffled', said Fanni dramatically, 'into the car of my Englishman—more dead than alive—he was carried from the city! He is now of course with friends. No names can be mentioned. Everybody knows where he is; but if it is published they will all be cast into prison. They are full of confusion and rage—waiting on him hand and foot; and telephoning to us every few minutes. I must go back immediately to the house as at any moment I may be needed, and, as I say, I have no idea whether Father is dead or alive.' 'He's almost certainly alive,' Carol said decisively. 'What's dead anywhere in the vicinity of your father, Fanni, isn't himself. Don't you worry, but before you go—here's Franz Salvator bursting to get in a question—now, Franz—take your time—I'll hold her down while you speak!' 'What has taken place with the Army?' demanded Franz, freed from his courteous refusal to interrupt. 'If, as you state, it was all prepared for the Emperor's return, why on earth didn't it, when the time came, fight?' Fanni, with her elbows on the table, her fair hair waving wildly in the breeze, bounded in her chair with excitement. 'Because we were betrayed,' she said, her voice rising to a piercing whisper; 'that's why—at the last moment we were betrayed! God punish the miscreant! Everything was prepared; we knew each one of us what we were to do. The Army was solidly with us, the Allies—inert and as usual suspicious of each other—were on the whole not unfavourable to our plans. The Czechs were out upon the border, but who cares for the Czechs? A turn of our cavalry would have whipped them across the Carpathians! And then—we failed! At the last moment, a week ago, half the Army on which our plan rested were bought over!' 'But who—apart from the Allies—has money enough for such a deed?' Franz Salvator cried. 'To buy over an Army devoted to Monarchy, whose officers have shown and would always show loyalty to the last drop of their blood? Who has the money or the wit to reach the soldiers?' 'You are right to say wit!' said Fanni slowly, enjoying the significance of each word she used. 'It was not an enemy who did this thing. It was one of ourselves. He brought a fortune —a colossal fortune—but he knew us. He knew us, as people say, by heart. He alone could have picked out waverers—have missed the loyal—have corrupted the unsound. He came from Wien, this friend, with his money in his pocket, his lies on his lips, perfidy in his heart!' Fanni paused dramatically; never had she had such an audience or such a tale to tell. They had long ago stopped eating, and their eyes were fixed upon her in a terror as great as she had

hoped to inspire. It might even have struck her, if she had paused
to think, that their terror was greater than the occasion warranted.
It was the terror of those who wait to hear a personal doom. 'His
name?' asked Franz Salvator in a dry voice. 'No! no! not his
name!' cried Carol urgently, as if she were pleading with herself.
Eugénie said nothing at all. It did not seem to her that she listened—she felt as if words fell upon her like the blows of some
heavy instrument. 'Otto Wolkenheimb!' cried Fanni at last, with
infinite relish. It was the most satisfactory moment of her life.
Carol said again, 'No! no!' and covered her face with her hands.
Franz Salvator swore as if no women were sitting there at all; but
as if he were alone with a man who was his enemy. Eugénie looked
for a time straight down at her plate. The terrace of the Ritz was
empty except for themselves. They sat among a waste of white
prepared tables. The waiters yawned and looked into the road-
way. A handful of soldiers clattered by. Eugénie gave a little sigh,
and slipped quietly from her chair to the ground. She was conscious (while the world turned black and faded rapidly away from
her) that Eugen had known the truth—known it and sheltered her
from it. Her last thought was that for Eugen, as well as for her, the
solid earth had opened. 'How the dear thing feels it!' exclaimed
Fanni, with satisfaction. 'She also—like the Emperor himself—has
fainted dead away!' Carol was on her knees beside Eugénie, but
she looked up fiercely to say, 'Fanni, I guess you forget, among
other little things, that Otto Wolkenheimb is their cousin! I wish
to God they'd had you arrested before breakfast!'

XXXIX

Eugénie was glad to be alone at last, even though Franz
Salvator and Carol took with them all that was left of
youth and security. Whatever had been saved from the
wreck of their old lives was in Franz Salvator's unbowed
spirit. His dreams were gone, but his courage was alive. He went
to see the last of the defeated Emperor; but he did not take defeat
with him. Eugénie, sitting alone in the crowded, brilliant hotel
overlooking the river, smelling the piercing sweetness of the flow-

ering acacias, drenched with the light of Spring, kept this defeat. At first she was stunned and incredulous with horror. She knew what Fanni Wilchek had told them was true, but all her senses rebelled against it. Over and over again she heard Eugen say, 'Men are judged by their acts', and yet she would not judge Otto by this act. The ugliness of his treachery invaded her slowly, driving away one by one the safeguards of her confidence. Her own sorrow, her own defeat, receded from her, and she saw instead the more final loneliness of Eugen.

The spirit has its mortal wounds as well as the flesh, and men sicken and die of them. The thought of Eugen took entire possession of Eugénie, and drove a new fear into her heart. What would Eugen do? What could he do with the rest of his life? Was it even sure that he would keep it? If she started at once, she could catch the express to Wien. She could not reach Trauenstein that night, but she could see Otto. She could make him tell her the truth. It could not fail to be bad, but there might be extenuations, reasons which would make it possible for Eugen to bear it, or at least to bear his life.

Men never told each other everything, even in their moments of deepest confidence with each other; they wore armour. If she took Otto in her arms and said, 'Tell me, Otto—tell me everything!' he would be suddenly very simple, like a child, and lay bare his heart to her.

For the first time Eugénie wished that she had yielded to Otto. 'I could have saved the worst from happening,' she said to herself bitterly. 'If I had given up this little thing—this stupid little thing I thought was chastity! What is the use of my body to me now? It will go on living when Eugen will die—when Otto gives himself to a Jewess for gold! If I had been less proud, I could have given Otto something to lose. Then he would not have done these great wrongs. And yet I could not give myself! My chastity was all I had. It was part of my faith. Ah! but I made my offers in the wrong place! It was to Eugen I should have said, "Marry me then —since everything else is gone!" There is nothing clear in me any more. I am fighting in the dark; and though I fight against something, I cannot tell how big it is, nor even against what I am fighting! Ah, Otto! Otto! you who loved our old order best of all, is it you who have destroyed it? But what can be destroyed by mere men has no virtue in itself! Dr. Jeiteles is right. The feudal system has not been torn down alive! It died first, and its ruins fall on us! The new generation will clear them away. I would like to be alive. I would like to belong to what is new, to the Austria that cannot die, but too much of me will be buried in the ruins!'

Eugénie rose slowly and looked out at the river. The brilliant March sunshine flashed on the water and broke over the newborn leaves. Her eyes rested on the Palace and the great church of the Kings, poised like a lifted sword upon its terrace against the blue of the sky. She saw the Margaretten Island at rest upon the wide river like the leaves of a water-lily. Her eyes fastened upon a heavy group of buildings by the riverside which were vaguely familiar to her. She realized suddenly that it was the prison where Bauer the Jew had been beaten into a pool of blood.

The sunshine turned to darkness around her. She groped her way blindly out of the room, down the broad staircase, through a hall peopled with shadows.

Eugénie was not conscious of herself again until she found herself being roughly jolted towards Vienna in a third-class railway carriage. Her mind fixed itself on the coming interview with Otto. Words maddened her by their senseless reiteration, they moved in her thoughts with the deadly regularity of a piston rod in an engine: 'Otto, is it true? is it true? Otto, is it true what they told me in Budapest?'

When Eugénie reached Wien she was penniless and it was evening.

She walked for dusty, chilly miles through narrow, interminable streets. The grey-green houses rose up around her like rocks covered with dead seaweed. She felt as if she moved under the weight of water.

She passed the square of the Hof Bibliothek, but she dared not go in to find if Eugen was there; she must not come to him empty-handed, without a word in defence of Otto.

Conrad opened the big gate of the Palace to her. Eugénie was too tired to notice the change in him; his splendid six foot of manhood was bowed, his old face had lost its weathered calm, his eyes were like the eyes of a lost dog.

'Princess—you!' he exclaimed in amazement; 'and so late! But I fear it is useless. The Herr Graf will see no one.'

'He must see me,' said Eugénie steadily.

'But you do not know, Gracious One, what has happened!'

Conrad explained with trembling, outstretched hands. 'It is indeed impossible! All is impossible! To-day the Frau Bleileben came here. She came here to live. They had lawyers all the morning, and papers everywhere. My Herr Graf was terribly angry, he was white and his nostrils shook; but he signed the papers. The Herr Baron was not here—that will show you how terrible it is. The Frau Bleileben gives orders. I beg you not to ask me, Gracious One, to let you in!'

'Conrad,' said Eugénie, laying her hand on the old man's arm, 'all this does not matter now. Do only as I tell you. Go to the Herr Graf and say, "The Princess is here, she is in great trouble, she asks you as the Head of her House to receive her." The Herr Graf will not refuse. I will see him anywhere—in your lodge here or on the stairs if he wishes.'

'No! no! Princess, it has not yet come to that,' said the old man brokenly. 'The Jewish lady is in the flat above. I will leave you in the library. The Herr Graf has gone to his room alone. He gave orders that he was not to be disturbed. But it shall be as you say. Only the responsibility I cannot take. I am glad that you are here. I am an old man—I understand nothing, but I obey my orders.'

'It is I who make you disobey,' said Eugénie tenderly. 'The Herr Graf shall understand it is my fault, and he will not be angry.' She felt the old man's tears fall on her hand as he kissed it; but his sorrow seemed a long way off, as if it were part of a day that was already over.

She followed Conrad up the familiar broad stone steps above the courtyard, from which the faint smell of horses rose in the air, as it had done long ago in her childhood. The heavy door above swung open and they were in the warm, noiseless hall, their feet sinking deep into the thick carpet. The great reception rooms stretched before them, solemn and empty. They felt like a heart that has ceased to beat.

Eugénie sank into an armchair by the library window. The twin towers of the Votiv Kirche leaned out of the gloom, as if they might at any moment crash down upon the house of Wolkenheimb and scatter it to atoms.

Conrad turned on a shaded lamp behind her, and left her to the pitiless silence of her memories. A door opened and closed in the distance.

Eugénie did not turn her head to meet Otto, so that she failed at first to see the Power—stronger than the Votiv Kirche and far more destructive—which had fallen upon the House of Wolkenheimb.

Elisabeth had hoped to take Otto by surprise in the library. These large, silent rooms, which she had so longed to make part of her life, had a quality that she found baffling. No one was ever in the place where you last saw them. Space lessened the impact of personality, it even diluted the strength of passion. But if Elisabeth had not found Otto, she had at last come on one of his secrets.

She stood and looked down at her beaten enemy.

This, then, was the Princess Felsör: this shabby, tired woman, half ghost, half tramp, with huge eyes and pale lips, who crouched in Otto's big chair like a brittle leaf blown into a corner by the wind.

Elisabeth's sensitiveness to moral beauty was slight, though it had existed. It was bound up with her love for Otto, and with the loss of her confidence in him, she had lost also this sense of higher things.

The beauty of the material life remained, but it had no spiritual counterpart. Otto's semblance of passion had given way under Elisabeth's heavy tread. Elisabeth herself had survived the accident; but all light from another world had gone forever.

She looked down at Eugénie with untroubled contempt. 'You are the Princess Felsör?' she said in her deep guttural voice. 'I am Elisabeth—Wolkenheimb. Allow me to remind you the Graf Wolkenheimb does not *now* receive his cast-off mistresses under his roof!'

Eugénie's beautiful curved eyebrows rose slowly, her eyes fixed themselves with incredulity upon Elisabeth's face. She spoke involuntarily, half under her breath:

'My God, what a punishment!' she murmured.

Elisabeth heard what Eugénie said; but she was too secure for anger. She merely shrugged her massive shoulders and continued to look at Eugénie derisively. It was not true that she was yet the Countess Wolkenheimb, but the contract which bound Otto to her was signed; and Elisabeth believed in contracts.

'You speak of Otto,' she said, 'or of yourself? It is true that you deserve punishment; and you look as if you had got it. You must excuse my saying that if you could afford no better appearance than you present this evening, it would have been wiser to stay away. You are perhaps hungry? Unfortunately we have already dined. But if you wish a cup of coffee, I will order it for you.'

'I require nothing,' said Eugénie simply. She turned her eyes away from Elisabeth as if she had spoken to a servant.

Elisabeth drew a step nearer to her.

'You are foolish', she said, 'not to try to make friends with me. I might do you a good turn. You know who I am, do you not? I am very rich. I spoke sharply to you just now, when I first saw you. I was taken by surprise I confess. Conrad should have announced you; but we are after all relatives. I might do something for you and your brother if I were so disposed! I suppose Otto keeps you? It depends on me, you know, if that is to go on. Come: speak? Let us be frank with one another!'

Eugénie lifted her head when Elisabeth's voice sharpened into finality. She looked at her vaguely, as if she were unable to respond either to Elisabeth's insults or to her good nature.

'I don't know what you mean,' she said after a pause— 'but I thank you—I want nothing.' Her eyes wandered past Elisabeth, and all their vagueness was suddenly driven out of them.

The door of the *salon* which led to Otto's apartments was flung open, and Otto came quickly into the room

'Eugénie,' he said bitterly, 'you do us too much honour!'

Elisabeth moved forward and stood between them.

'You have not yet introduced me to your cousin,' she said, eyeing him intently. 'It is so kind of her to pay us this informal call so early. I feel indeed that I am taken into the bosom of your family; but it would be perhaps as well for you to present me to its members, lest I make some mistake. This person, for instance, has hardly the air of a Wolkenheimb.'

'The Princess has not suggested an introduction yet,' said Otto gravely; 'and I fear I must remind you, Elisabeth, that it is for her to suggest it.'

Eugénie stood up; she laid her hands on the table to support herself, and fixed her eyes on Otto's face.

'Is it true,' she asked faintly, 'what they told me in Budapest?'

'Yes,' said Otto, 'it is true.'

'And you have no excuse?' Eugénie persisted. 'I mean no excuse but—but this——?' She turned blind eyes towards Elisabeth and her diamonds.

'I need not trouble you with my reasons,' said Otto stiffly; 'they would appear insufficient to you. For me they were—just sufficient.'

Eugénie leaned more heavily against the table. 'It meant nothing to you, then,' she said, with a pause between each word, 'the old order—what you stood for—it was not worth suffering for? I am free to think it does not matter any more? Nothing but your personal comfort counted?—neither love, nor honour, nor your loyalty to a cause? You preferred to triumph with what you hated than to lose with what you loved?'

'You are free to think what you choose,' said Otto curtly. 'The worst of me—of course—as usual.'

'I do not think of you any more,' said Eugénie, between her white, shaking lips. 'I think of the Head of my House—and my House has fallen!'

Otto flinched. He had stood quite still at first, with his back to the door he had come in by, facing the two women, his head erect, his eyes hard and dull as stones. But now he turned impatiently away; his hands trembled, something in him which kept him together, his untamed insolence, was for a moment broken. Elisabeth with amazement saw it break; and for the first time she recognized a power in the woman she had derided.

Was there then a power to wound which she had not got? The power to please, even the desire to please, had left Elisabeth; but her revenge was her life. Was it possible that the power to please and the power to wound were the same thing? And that this defenceless broken woman was hurting Otto by some hidden charm which had nothing to do with force? Otto was under Elisabeth's thumb, this woman was in the dust at her feet; yet something in them both had after all escaped her?

'You speak of your house!' she said fiercely to Eugénie. 'This is not your house! Your husband, if he could afford it, should have left you one! Go to that if it exists! And if it exists no longer—go into the streets—where you belong!'

'Pray be silent, Elisabeth,' said Otto, between his teeth. He wondered for an idle moment which was worse, to be attacked by Eugénie or to be defended by Elisabeth.

The door opened again and Conrad came in slowly. He ignored the sharp reproof on Otto's lips. 'The Fräulein Lisa is here,' he said very solemnly. 'She brings bad news. Fräulein Lisa, it is permitted for you to enter!'

The old man stood to one side; but he did not leave the room. At moments of crisis he belonged to his family. Their sorrows were his sorrows, and their shame bowed his proud old head.

Lisa moved quietly into the centre of the library. She walked up to the big table against which Eugénie still leaned. She looked from Eugénie's stern, drawn face to Otto, who stood, once more composed and indifferent, between the two women.

Neither Lisa nor Conrad took any notice of the presence of Elisabeth.

'My Herr Baron is dead,' said Lisa in a hard, toneless voice. 'He has shot himself in a wood at Trauenstein. The Frau Gräfin thought first of me. She sent me this telegram; in it she says, "Tell my son".'

Eugénie moved swiftly towards her, but Lisa backed away from her outstretched arms.

'No, Princess!' she said firmly. 'No! You killed him between you! you and the Herr Graf! The Herr Graf took his honour. And you—you were too proud, too grand to touch him! You are a fine lady, and fine ladies do not feel like us. They do nothing for the men who love them. I cooked for him, I mended his clothes, I lay in his bed. All I had was his. Do I not know, then, what was in his heart? I came to tell you both, before I go back to my mountains.'

Otto's eyes turned to Lisa with entreaty, but against her implacable slow judgement entreaty was as futile as the struggle of water against ice.

'Herr Graf,' she went on steadily, 'one night I found my Herr Baron crying. It was very late, he was in the room of the carpets, where the great china bowls are, and I said, "Tell me, then, what is it?" and he said, "Little one, I have lost something." I said, "Tell me what you have lost, that I may look for it." I thought it was one of his treasures: and he said, "No *Liebling*, you cannot find it, for it is my honour that I have lost, and it can never be found again." Princess, I thought, "Peasant girls do not understand about honour, but great ladies must: she will surely comfort

285

him!'' And you did not! You found nothing to help him. You left him alone with his grief. So between you you have killed him, my Herr Baron!'

'Lisa! Lisa! forgive us!' Eugénie cried, stretching out her hands. 'I know we did not love him enough. It was he who loved us! But I *was* afraid! I came here to find out if we could not save him! It was too late: but, ah, Lisa, I tried—forgive me, for I tried!'

Lisa hesitated: something in Eugénie's voice pierced her heart; she knew it for what it was, a real sorrow: not as great as her own, perhaps, but deep. The ice of her grief melted, she shook suddenly and with a helpless murmur stumbled towards Eugénie's arms.

Otto turned savagely towards Conrad. 'Take these ladies downstairs!' he said. 'Neither they nor you have any further business here. Is there anything I can do for you, Eugénie? I may no longer be the Head of your House, but I am still presumably one of your family. Shall I notify Franz Salvator to return from chasing retiring Kings, or shall I drive you and this poor child myself to Trauenstein to-morrow? I cannot leave my mother alone in these exceedingly trying circumstances.'

'Lisa,' said Eugénie, bending over the sobbing girl, 'you would like to go to him? to see Eugen once more? Yes, and I also. He has left you money, and you can buy many candles and have masses said for his soul!'

'Every day,' sobbed Lisa; 'every day a mass, and candles burning always, so that he may not be alone in the dark? And I may do it all myself? And in the end, if the masses are all mine, and the candles, he will be mine also?'

'Yes, yes,' said Eugénie. 'He is already yours; and he will be yours always. We have no right in him, Otto and I.' Eugénie, with her arm round Lisa, moved towards the door. Otto, without looking at her, opened and closed it after them. Elisabeth cleared her throat. 'I too am sorry,——' she began, but her voice checked itself against the mournful silence of the room. Otto stood with his back to her, staring at the closed door as if his life had passed out of it. Elisabeth's sharp restless eyes lit on Conrad. He too seemed not to have heard her speak nor to be aware of her emphatic presence. He moved slowly forward and groped for his master's hand. Otto patted him gently on the shoulder and, passing Elisabeth with unseeing eyes, sank into a chair by the window and covered his face with his hands.

Elisabeth had longed to see Otto broken; but as she stood and looked at him she was conscious of a vague discomfort, as if a power, that was her enemy as well as his, had accomplished her purpose for her and lowered her triumph.

'Gnädige,' said the old servant quietly. 'It will be well to leave the Herr Graf now. He has had enough.'

A stifled sound that was half laugh and half sob escaped from Otto.

Conrad's immense form towered over Elisabeth. He stood between her and Otto. He was immovable as stone, yet Elisabeth was conscious of a silent pressure which drove her towards the door. The room was full of shadows; they seemed vaguely inimical to Elisabeth. Nothing stirred; there came no faintest murmur from the street below.

Elisabeth tried once more to speak; once more her voice fell flat against the silence. The door opened in front of her; she found herself outside upon the marble stairs.

Otto knew when Elisabeth had gone. His head sank lower into his hands. He was alone at last—with his defeated ghosts.

THE END